TIME IN A BOTTLE

Denise Deegan is a writer and freelance journalist living in Monkstown, Co. Dublin. *Time in a Bottle* follows her bestselling first novel, *Turning Turtle*.

TIME IN A BOTTLE

DENISE DEEGAN

TiVOLi

Tivoli
an imprint of Gill & Macmillan Ltd
Hume Avenue
Park West
Dublin 12
with associated companies throughout the world

www.gillmacmillan.ie

© Denise Deegan 2004
0 7171 3604 3

Print origination by Carole Lynch
Printed and bound by Nørhaven Paperback A/S, Denmark

*The paper used in this book is made from the wood pulp of
managed forests. For every tree felled, at least one tree is
planted, thereby renewing natural resources.*

A catalogue record is available for this book
from the British Library.

1 3 5 4 2

This book is a work of fiction. Names, characters, places and
incidents are either the product of the author's imagination or
are used fictitiously. Any resemblance to actual events or locales
or persons, living or dead, is entirely coincidental.

For Aimée
(luv u)

Acknowledgments

To the Man Who Doesn't Want To Be Thanked – thank you, *Joseph*, for being one of the good guys. Thanks each to Alex and Aimée, though not necessarily in that order, for being quirky, great, cuddly and able to spot *Turning Turtle* from shop entrances. Thank you, Mom, for continuing to be an all-round champ, and the rest of the family for trying to keep up with her.

For reading my manuscript and being brutally honest, many, many thanks: Sarah Ballagh, Amanda Byrne, Fiona Concannon, Laura Concannon, Mary Deegan, Laura Egar, Dee Flynn, Mary Hogan and Patricia Kieran. Your advice is twenty-four carat.

Thank you, Dr Fin Breatnach, for a whole afternoon of your time, (I know how precious it is), for invaluable medical input, for scouring my manuscript for medical and other faux pas, and for your enthusiasm. Roisin Molloy, Niamh Creaby, Nancy Kelly and Eleanor Coughlan, thank you for all your help with other issues medical. Thanks to Frank Coughlan for casting editorial eyes over my fictional world of journalism (I'll send Jack to you for fashion and general deportment tips) and to Liz McCormick for checking out my American dialogue.

Many thanks to Faith O'Grady, my agent, for keeping an eagle eye on business, and to my editor, Alison Walsh, for doing the same with words. Thanks also to Anita Ruane, Nicki Howard, Lynn Crampton, Pamela Coyle, Cliona Lewis, Paul Neilan, Davy Adamson, Chris Carroll, Paula Elmore and all at Gill & Macmillan.

A Great Big Thank You to everyone who helped make *Turning Turtle* a success, especially Sara Corcoran, Bryan Deegan, Frank Kelly, David Cassidy, Jane Alger, Mary Kerr, Austin Vaughan, Catherine Brennan, and, of course, to everyone who recommended, sold and, especially, bought a copy.

If there is anyone I have forgotten, I'm already on my knees. . .

1

'Come on, Mum,' Charlie shouts, tearing up the path ahead of me, red lights flashing on the soles of his runners. He makes it to the door. Jumps to reach the bell. Misses. Tries again. And again. I lift him up to it. Bingo.

'Charlie, *enough*, you'll deafen them,' I say, landing him back down.

'Where is she?' he whines. 'She's taking *aaa*ges. Ring again, Mum.' He starts to hop. I'm tempted to buzz a second time or at least peer through the stained-glass panel surrounding the door. I control myself.

At last, it opens.

Everything stops. Even noise. I hold my breath. Inside, organs hammer into each other. *It's him.* It has been five years. But it *is* him. *What's he doing here? Have I the wrong house? No, I checked the gate. Right house. And he looks at home. Debbie Grace. My God — his daughter!*

'Hello?' he says.

That voice.

He has no idea who I am. *Something at least.*

'Hello,' I say, matching his I-don't-know-you-but-I'm-being-polite tone. 'I'm calling for Debbie? I'm Jenny. And this is Charlie . . .'

His eyes relax. He smiles, small creases forming on his face. 'Oh, hello. Yes, yes, of course. I'm sorry.' He scratches behind his ear. 'I'd forgotten about the baby-sitting. I hope you weren't waiting there too long. I thought you must have been one of Debra's friends. The door's usually for her.' He holds out his hand. And I have to do it — shake it, touch him.

I survive and die at the same time.

'I'm Simon Grace. Simon. Come in, come in.'

Charlie bursts past him. The smell of steak wafts through the warm September air.

'Actually, no. I can see you're eating. I'm sorry for getting you up. We'll wait in the car. Come on, Charlie. *Charlie!*'

'I wouldn't dream of having you wait in the car. Come in. Please. I was just finishing up.'

'Honestly, we're fine, thank you all the same.' I hear myself match his formality and almost laugh. 'It would be handy to have the car turned, ready to go. Honestly.'

He looks as if he's trying to work out whether I'm being polite or honest. In the end, he seems to give up. 'Just hold on a minute then.' And he is gone, pounding up the stairs, calling, 'Debra! Jenny and Charlie are here. Come on.' He disappears.

Charlie heads for the stairs.

'Charlie, *come here*,' I half whisper. 'You can't just barge into other people's houses, especially if you don't know them.'

He stops, turns, still holding the bottom rung of the banisters. 'I know Debbie,' he says simply.

'Yes, but this is her *father's* house. And you don't know him.'

'I do. His name is Simon.'

I sigh, check that no one's coming, march over, pick him up and head back to the porch. 'We will wait here,' I say firmly. He knows I mean business.

We wait in silence. And I think about how little he has changed. Simon Grace. Still that preoccupied look, as if you're disturbing him but he'd hate you to know it. He is taller, leaner than I remember. A bit neglected? Although, stubble at this time of day is probably standard in one so dark. I remember his face with a tenderness that is alarming and I tell myself to cop on. So what if his eyes are sad? So what if he looks strong and vulnerable at the same time?

There is a lighter thunder on the stairs. Debbie.

'I'm *really* sorry, Jenny,' she rushes. 'I was just drying my hair. I didn't hear the door. Hi, Charlie,' she says, her voice higher when talking to him.

'Hiya, Deb!' He wriggles out of my arms and runs to her. 'Is it OK if I go in your house?'

She smiles. 'Of course.'

He turns to me. 'Told ya,' he says.

I laugh as if to say '*kids*'. I'll kill him.

Debbie scoops him up and swings him round. Charlie squeals in delight. She laughs, her sleek black hair lifting from her shoulders and moving through the air as though in slow motion. *She has inherited his colouring — dark hair, pale skin. Her eyes are blue though.* Debbie is the type of girl you'd see coming through the gates of a private girl's school on Dublin's southside, with a group of friends, all sporting hockey sticks. Her look says confident, healthy, well-adjusted. Everything you'd want in a baby-sitter. She settles Charlie on her hip, kisses his cheek and heads for the door. Reaching it, she turns, for the first time, to acknowledge her father, who is hovering politely, waiting for us to leave.

'Why didn't you call me?' she whispers. It's an accusation.

'I did, Debra.'

'Not loud enough, *obviously*. Anyway, I'm off.' She turns to go.

'What time will you be back?' he calls after her.

She doesn't answer, so I say, 'About eleven. I hope that's not too late?'

'No. That would be fine, thank you,' he says. Then adds uncertainly 'Seeing as it's a weekend night.'

'We won't be late.'

'Good, good,' he says. 'Do you have your key, Debra?'

'*Yes.*' The tone is *the-things-I-have-to-put-up-with*. She marches out without looking back.

'Goodnight then. Enjoy yourself,' he tries.

No answer.

I smile goodnight, without meeting his eyes, then turn to go. *Must be tough living with a teenager. If she's anything like I was, his life is hell. Mind you, her mother probably gets the brunt. Mine certainly did. You can tell he cares, though. More than my 'mother', who thought I just got in the way.*

I hear the door close gently and suspect that Dr Simon Grace, paediatric oncologist, is relieved to be left in peace. I *am* glad he didn't recognise me, but also taken aback, and — OK — miffed. But then, it was five years ago. And I *was* different. Little Miss Newshound, wunderjournalist, on her way up and nothing to stop her. Contact lenses, cropped and highlighted hair, fitted trouser suits, heels, always heels. Uptight. Aggressive. Soulless. Not at all like her replacement, the single mum who does a bit of freelancing to pay the bills and keep her hand in. Whose neglected-since-becoming-a-parent hair has grown to her shoulders and regained its waves and colour (auburn). Who'd like to have time for

4

contacts but doesn't, so it's small, rim-free rectangular lenses. This person's clothes are casual and often fun. Though five years older, she dresses five years younger. Hipsters, polos, tatty runners. Relaxed clothes for a person who has calmed, who has nothing to prove, not any more . . . *And anyway*, the thought strikes me, *he'd have known me as Jennifer Grey, the name I write under, not as Jenny Dempsey, my real name, by which everybody, including his daughter, knows me.*

'Sorry about that,' Debbie says.

'About what?'

'My dad.'

'What about him?'

'Dunno.' She shrugs. 'He's a bit stiff?'

'I don't know. He seems nice enough,' I say in his defence.

She looks at me as if my judgement is seriously impaired. I laugh, then open the back door of my clapped-out mini, which I love dearly. Charlie climbs into his car seat and I set about strapping him in.

'Sit here, Deb. Sit here,' he shouts in my ear.

'Sure, Charlie,' she says, giving me an isn't-he-cute smile, and sliding in beside him. 'Who's this?' she asks, picking up a purple soft toy with a green tummy.

'Barney,' he says proudly. 'He's fromourimagination.'

'Oh, I know Barney. I love you, you love me . . . ' she starts to sing. *If only her father could see her . . .*

I hop into the front. We're off.

I slot the key into the door of our apartment. On the other side, I hear the dog snuffling and barking, his nails tapping on the wooden floor, then door. I imagine the scratch marks he's leaving and try to hurry. He rushes out and springs up on Charlie.

'Down, Sausage, down,' Charlie says, with authority.

'Go on in, Debbie. The dog'll move out of the way,' I say.

We all troop in. I turn off the alarm.

'He's lovely,' she says, a little unsure, bending down to pat his head. You can tell she's not used to dogs — too gentle. Sausage isn't fussy, though; he'll take all the attention he can get. He jumps to lick her face. She laughs but stands, wiping her cheek with the back of her hand. 'He's very friendly. What is he — some kind of beagle?'

'He's a mongrel,' announces Charlie proudly.

Debbie throws me another ah-God-isn't-he-*adorable* look.

I give her one back. *Try living with him.*

'Do you want to show Debbie around, Charlie?'

'Yeah, good idea, Mum,' he says, grabbing her hand and tugging her into the sitting room. 'Come on, Deb. We've a great telly.'

I follow them in.

Debbie looks around, then turns to me. 'It's *great*. Must be cool owning your own apartment.'

'Yes, I suppose it is. My gran left it to me. Otherwise I wouldn't be able to afford it.'

We live on the first floor of a three-storey Georgian red-brick, on a wide, sleepy, tree-lined road. Its Glenageary location is upmarket. Or so I'm reminded daily by my editor who holds it against me personally — or at least pretends to. But whatever Jack might say, I'm not complaining. It's a great place to bring up a child. Safe, leafy and near the sea.

The light is wonderful on the first floor, filtering in through ceiling-to-floor bay windows. A crystal hangs in each one, breaking the sun's rays into little rainbows here and there on the walls and furniture. The floors are wooden, hidden in places by brightly coloured rugs. There are so many plants and grasses, it's like

6

having our very own botanical gardens.

I've lived here since I became pregnant. My gran insisted I move in with her. 'You need a home, Jen — not just somewhere to stay,' she said, following it up with a sigh and a faraway look. 'Imagine, Jen — me, a great-grandmother.' And I felt a little less lonely, a little more wanted, maybe even useful, to a degree. I knew she'd make a great great-grandmother. So that's what I started to call her: 'Great'. She didn't object.

No, objections are the speciality of my mother. When *she* heard I was pregnant, there was no talk of homes. There was no talk at all. Not as in a conversation, at least. Just a monologue. As if I didn't already know that a) I was single; b) the 'child' was fatherless; and c) my career would 'suffer'. She didn't say it but I knew that her biggest 'concern' was how all of this would affect *her* image, she being a politician. And Ireland being a small country. How many times have I heard those five words strung together like that? How many times in twenty-seven years? Enough to make me hate them, especially when coming from her tight lips.

But moving in with Great *was* great. She may have been my mother's mother but they were as far apart as A and Z. I've often wondered (understatement) how Great managed to create such a cold, power-hungry . . . enough of the adjectives . . . cow. I never asked if she regretted not being close to her daughter — as soon as I became a mum, I knew.

My mother's view of Great was one-dimensional. She was a potential source of embarrassment, a political time bomb. Great said what she wanted, when she wanted. If people didn't like it, especially politicians, 'tough'. Which made her very popular with me. I loved her honesty, her bluntness. She wasn't trying to ingratiate herself with strangers, wangle a vote out of them. She was also fun. And warm. Interested in and enthusiastic about everything. She was my mother's mother. In all but birth, she was mine. She should have lived forever.

When I moved in, she humoured my nesting instinct. Not once objecting to having her wallpaper stripped or her walls painted white, her carpets ripped up or her floors sanded and varnished. She loved the transformation, whipped out her sewing machine and made bright covers for the sofas. Together, we went out and bought our equivalent of an indoor rainforest. Our new life was beginning. But all this industriousness was a ploy on my part, a distraction from the fact that I was going through pregnancy on my own. If I kept busy, I wouldn't miss having a male hand rest on my stomach, sharing the movement. I wouldn't long for someone to say, 'That's not a man's name'. I wouldn't wish to hear, 'Yes, love. The will is sorted, the pension's organised' when I suddenly decided that everything needed to be *safe*, fastened down as though a storm was coming. I wouldn't look longingly at pregnant couples, holding hands, heads together, planning. It was hormones that had me thinking like that, I know (I'm normally a very independent person), but something had to be done to stop it — and that was work.

I tried resenting my son when they landed him gently on my stomach that ice-cold January day. But it was no use. I caved in almost immediately. How could I close my heart to this little man with the glassy blue eyes that bore into mine as though searching for something? This kind of love was something entirely new. It hit me with force, knocked me over and changed my life absolutely.

Maybe if he had behaved badly, been 'a little tyrant', I could have learnt to hate him. But crying just wasn't his thing. He *never* screamed, was perfectly happy to loll around in a pooey nappy. He smiled early. Slept through the night from eight weeks. It was like he was trying to get me to love him.

So I decided, 'That's it, I'm doing this right.' I listened to the experts. Breast-fed, cuddled, snuggled, tickled, laughed and chatted with the new man in my life. When my maternity leave was up, I couldn't go back. I met with my then editor, fortunately a fellow mother, explained my position and waited for her to come up with a solution. Or fire me. It took her two weeks and some negotiation but her offer was like Baby Bear's porridge. Just right. Move from health correspondent to contributor, writing a weekly health page, from home. I took a salary cut which turned out not to be too extreme when tax liabilities were worked out. I was lucky. The timing was perfect. The 'editorial execs' at the paper had been contemplating a health page — they couldn't remain the last of the nationals, albeit a tabloid, without one. Tough market. She dived straight for their Achilles heel, then topped off their insecurities with an assurance that I'd 'developed a name' for myself in health. It worked. And I owe her.

I was excited. Moving from news to features suited the new me. It matched my shift in interest, from breaking news to breaking wind (my baby's, not mine, or anyone else's). In-depth interviews. Real people with real stories. What happened, how it affected them, how they got through it — these meant a lot more to me than brief reports that focused on action rather than reaction, and changed every day, becoming history. With the change from news to features came a change in editor. I wasn't too thrilled about that at first because I liked working for a woman. I knew Jack well through my ex-fiancé, who used to write for the paper, but I didn't know what he'd be like to work for. He turned out to be great. Easygoing and encouraging. I was very polite and formal at first but, in time, we resumed our relaxed, comfortable relationship. He was even open to a little slagging, which is just as well because he gave enough.

Mostly, I worked in the evenings. It suited the people I had to interview, because I wasn't interrupting them at work. And it suited me, with Charlie in bed and Great engrossed in her crosswords, glancing up occasionally with a contented smile. Not exactly what you'd call an earth-shatteringly exciting life but I'd had enough excitement.

People say that kids are tough work. I haven't found it. It may sound corny, but I don't mind saying that Charlie has given my life meaning. Sometimes I think it only really started when Charlie entered it. Great died last year and I was gutted, devastated, so incredibly empty. But I had Charlie. And he kept me looking forward, focused. I still had my boy. I had to be there for him.

'D'you want to see my room?' Charlie's bubbly enthusiasm breaks through my thoughts.

'Sure,' says Debbie.

'Come on!' He grabs her hand and drags her off. Sausage doesn't want to be left out and follows, barking, jumping and wagging his tail furiously.

'Guys, I gotta go,' I call.

'OK, Mum. Bye.'

'No hug?'

He looks at Debbie than back at me. 'Busy, Mum.'

'OK, well, I'll just have to give you one then, won't I?'

''K.'

'Will you show Debbie where everything is?' I say, squeezing him tightly.

'Yep.'

'Good boy. See you later.' I kiss him just above his forehead.

'Debbie, I've written down my mobile number and where I'll be, in case you've any problems.' I tear out a page from my jotter and hand it to her. 'Charlie can stay up for another half-hour. Then it's bedtime. OK, mister?'

'OK, Mum. You can go now.'

'See you later.' I laugh to hide my hurt.

I walk to the car, jiggling my keys nervously, thinking about how quickly he is growing up. He has just started school and already he's changing. No longer my baby. Becoming his own man. It's good for him, I know. I should stop worrying. Everyone has to grow, build a life for themselves. Charlie needs friends. Independence is good for him. I am too attached. Need to loosen up. It's good that I'm going out, even if I don't feel like it. I haven't met up with the guys from the paper in years. I've missed every Christmas party — I've wanted to. But I need to get on with my life now. Charlie's getting on with his. I'm uncomfortable, though, in the dressy-up clothes, and already regret the perfume — it's conspicuous, not me and, I suspect, with a sniff, that it has gone off.

2

It's a scruffy pub in city-centre Dublin. Dark and authentic, traditional. Themed, without effort. The almost-black mahogany countertop and stools, the mirrors stained yellow from years of smoke, and the 1950s public-house memorabilia are all genuine. There isn't sawdust on the floor — but there could be. Same old barmen serving up the same old drinks. *None of this Bacardi Breezer lark here*, I read their thoughts. *It's Guinness, Guinness and sure, why not, have another Guinness, why don't you?*

We spent so much time in here, it was almost like a second office. And you'd think I'd feel at home, now, for that reason. But I don't. For the first time, I walk in and hesitate. For the first time, I wonder what I have to say to 'these people'. For the first time, I'm aware of how I look, conscious of the sharp drop in my marketability. I could happily turn around and go home.

I spot Jack, about the same time he spots me. Hasn't changed much. A slight bit tubbier, a little less hair. Suited as ever, but not sharply. Relaxed now that the shift's over. His familiar, uncomplicated smile reassures me. But then I wonder if he is doing a similar physical take on me and noticing how less sexy I look — not that I want to look particularly sexy for Jack, just that, well, maybe, in general, I want to look *at least* appealing. I might have a child, but that doesn't mean it's all over, does it?

He stands and waits for me to reach the table. 'How're you doin', Jen?' He pats my upper arm. It's as close to a hug as I, or anyone, will get from Jack. The entire table looks up. They smile, nod, or greet me with a 'Hi, Jenny'. Some do all three. *What was I worried about? I know these people. Well, most of them. The new faces seem very young.*

'Good to see you,' Jack continues. 'How've you been? Here — have a seat.' He grabs a stool and lands it down beside his. People shuffle up to make space.

'Thanks, Jack.' I take off my jacket and sit, leaning my satchel against the legs of the stool. 'I'm grand. And you?'

'Same as ever. Here, what are you having? The usual?'

'No, thanks. I'm driving. A Coke'd be great, though.'

'Oh, right,' he says, a bit deflated. Likes to be joined in alcohol, Jack.

'It's *great* to see you, Jack,' I enthuse, hinting that it doesn't matter, I'm a fun type of gal no matter what I'm drinking. Not sure that I pull it off, though. He pats my arm again, stands, mumbles something I don't hear and is off to the bar, muscling his way through the mob.

Ted, an ex-colleague who was, in all honesty, more a competitor, is sitting on the other side of me. We started out around the same time and constantly kept an eye on each other, both with the same idea — keeping ahead. I guessed he must have been secretly thrilled when I got out of the action. Especially as he got my position.

'Hi, Ted.'

'Jenny, how's it going?'

'Not bad, and you?'

'Good.'

'That was a great piece you did on the tribunal yesterday.' (It wasn't that great.)

'Still reading us, then?'

'Still *writing* for the paper, Ted.'

'Yeah,' he says in a tone that implies freelancing isn't writing. I turn away.

Brenda who writes movie reviews smiles across at me. 'Hello, stranger,' she says.

We discuss *About Schmidt*, which she is just about to write up. Well, she discusses it. I haven't seen it. I used to be a regular movie-goer. Great used to mind Charlie. *Must start again, now that we've Debbie. But, no, I need a new baby-sitter . . . can't risk bumping into Simon Grace again . . . typical, just when I had got it sorted. It took ages to find Debbie. If it weren't for Charlie's school principal, I'd still be looking. Well, maybe I'll have to start again. I can't believe how unlucky I am. Bumping into him again, after five years and . . . .*

'God, it's bedlam up there,' says Jack. 'If we weren't regulars, I'd still be there. There you go, Jen.'

'Thanks, Jack. Cheers.'

'Sláinte.' He clinks my glass, holds his in the air for a sec, then gulps a great big mouthful of Guinness. 'Any news?' he asks, wiping foam from his upper lip.

'I don't think so. No, not really. Let's see . . . ' And then I think of it — the one bit of exciting news I have. 'Charlie's started school.'

'Oh, that's good. School, yeah, great. He grew up fast, didn't he?'

You can tell this isn't his type of conversation. His is the smile of a tolerant priest listening to the sins of his flock — the small, uninteresting ones like lying and cursing.

14

I laugh. 'Jack, you're nodding off.'

'I am not.' He is indignant.

'*Jack.*'

'All right, you've got me. I'm not great on kids . . . The page is great, though,' he tries.

Now, you see, that, to me, is boring. I don't want to discuss work. I'll do it, fine, enjoy it even, but do I really have to discuss it? I used not to be like that. I long for my apartment, the silence of it, with Charlie asleep, the peace. My coffee-maker. My snuggly quilt. The novel I've just bought, still in its paper bag. My CD player, poised and ready for *A Rush of Blood to the Head*. Like Dorothy in the *Wizard of Oz*, I want to click my heels and be back home. But my shoes aren't red and I don't live in Kansas.

A hat, zigzagging above the crowds, catches my attention. It is like something out of a Dr Seuss book, an oversized top hat that's been hammered on one side, giving it a wonky concertina look. Worse, it's spotted, black on white, like a Friesian cow. And it's made from some sort of fluffy fabric (think Cookie Monster). The human sea parts and I realise with shock that I know Hat Wearer. I consider ducking. But she spots me. Just when I thought the evening couldn't get any worse. It's Jane. How did she ever get the job of fashion correspondent? And what's she doing here? She must be 'like, so stressed out' to be away from her usual haunt, Ice. Her eyes widen from squint to saucer — suddenly it seems she has a destination, a purpose. Me. *So that's it! She knew I'd be here and is after a gossip update.* She produces a royal wave, of sorts, then totters in my direction.

'Hi, Jenny,' she squeaks. '*Sooo* good to see you. Excuse me, Jack,' she purrs. 'Can I just squ*eeeze* in here? Have to catch up with *Jen*-ny. You kn*ooow* how it is?' Cue eyelash batting and pout. It's lost on him. He grunts something and shifts his stool up a bit. I frown at him — he knows how I hate her. He shrugs as if to say, 'What could I do?' then turns to the picture editor on his other side, no doubt relieved it's a fellow man.

'Jen-ny, how *are* you?' Long lost buddies reunited following a tragic forced separation.

'Fine, Jane. And you?'

'Oh, *suuuper*.' She frowns. 'You look pale, sweetie. Up all night with your son? What's his name, little . . . ?'

'His name is Charlie, and he sleeps at night like most four-year-olds.'

'Sw*eeet* . . . You sure you're not anaemic?'

I could kill her. And take pleasure in it.

'And how's D*aaave*?'

Dave, as in my ex-fiancé. As in the man she fancies. I wondered how long it'd take for her to get to Dave.

'He's really made a name for himself since 9/11, hasn't he?' she gushes.

'I don't think he'd see it like that,' I snap. Dave had to cover the events of September 11th. He won awards for his work. He obviously didn't set out to. 'It wasn't a career move, Jane.'

I picture the head-and-shoulders shot of him that went with the coverage. How American he had looked in it. How different from the Dave I knew. Weird how you can plan to spend the rest of your life with someone but for things to work out in such a way that they no longer figure in your future. Or present. Apart from routine birthday and Christmas cards, which don't count. One thing. That's all it took to blow our plans apart — plans that were so certain, solid; plans I never doubted. I hope he is happy now. He deserves to be. Maybe he has found someone else. Someone who won't go and mess things up.

I stick it out till half-ten then give the new-baby-sitter excuse. Knew this was a bad idea. I'll have to think up another form of entertainment. Even if it means taking up my old pastime of movies on my own.

3

We're dawdling up the lane to the school, as I used to do when I was a kid. Charlie's taking the puddle route; I'm admiring the patchwork display of yellow, orange, rust and wine-coloured leaves. The rain has stopped and the sun is peeping out from behind a large white, typically Irish, cloud. *Will I come out, or won't I?* it seems to be thinking. I love September, with its crisp air, ethereal light and happy colours. Charlie breaks into a run, his *Monsters Inc.* school bag banging up and down on his back.

'Dara, Dara, wait up,' he calls and I wonder when he started talking like an American. His navy uniform and the starting-school haircut I mistakenly subjected him to have conspired to remove the last remnants of baby. Gone are the innocent blond curls, snipped off in their prime, leaving darker, smoother hair. Grown-up hair. A mistake, I know. I don't need to be asked, 'What happened his hair?' But I am, repeatedly. By people in shops, neighbours, people we don't even know. It's as if I've defaced an angel.

I catch up with him at the classroom door and help him off with his bag and coat. The orange lining is still warm from

18

his body. I'm left holding it as he dashes over to hug his new buddy.

'Urgh. Go away,' says Dara. Big guy, *must be five*, razor-tight haircut.

The protective mum in me feels like telling *him* to go away.

'I just want a hug,' says Charlie, confused.

'No way. Hugs are for sissies.'

'Oh.' The corners of Charlie's mouth turn down and I'm afraid he's going to cry. But no, he fights it off. *That's my boy.* I consider asking the teacher to separate them but tell myself not to interfere. *Maybe I could take him home, though. Just for today. We could go to the beach. Stop it, Jenny.*

Charlie tries to hug another boy and gets the same reaction. *I should have sent him to playschool first. Toughen him up. But I don't want him tough.*

'Don't worry,' his teacher says quietly, leaning towards me as though letting me in on a secret, 'He'll be fine. We'll see you later.'

That wouldn't be a hint?

'Bye, Charlie,' I call over to him, waving. He looks like a little lone buoy, bobbing around in a sea of new faces. I go over to him and whisper, 'Sweetie, if you ever feel like a hug, I'm your woman.'

''s OK, Mum,' he says in a trying-to-be-brave voice.

I leave, trying to be equally brave, but failing. I walk back up the corridor in tears. I've always been able to protect him. At school, he's on his own.

'Don't worry. He'll be fine in a few weeks,' says a more seasoned mum, arriving with a brood.

'Thanks,' I mumble through a forced smile.

I think of Great — will her to look after him, from wherever she is.

I was never religious. You can't be a self-respecting rebel (more, later) and believe in traditional Catholicism. But . . . something happened when Great died. Something that made me believe that maybe there is more, that maybe it doesn't just stop when our hearts do. Great died in hospital. I was with her. I know what happened. It was this. Her room filled with an almost suffocating smell of roses, though there were none. The chaplain noticed it too. He asked me, simply, if she was a 'devotee of the Little Flower'. Saint Thérèse, he explained unnecessarily.

'Yes, yes, she loved her,' I rushed. I should have known — I slagged her about it often enough.

He nodded as if that explained everything.

'What?' I asked, forgetting the usual 'Father'.

'This often happens when devotees of the Little Flower pass away.'

'The smell of roses?'

He nodded as if it were no big deal.

To me it was. To me it was a sign, a message. She was telling me she'd still be around. Still looking out for us, Charlie and me.

But there's more. It took months for the solicitors to sort out her affairs. They called me in one morning to sign some documents. I was putting in the date beside my signature when I realised that it was Great's birthday. It struck with force. *Could she have controlled the timing of her legacy for it to be a birthday present?*

And now, every morning when I'm bringing Charlie to school, I feel her walking beside us. 'Don't worry. He'll be fine. I'm keeping an eye on him now,' she says.

I take a breath and hand him over to her.

I spend the morning interviewing people about sexually transmitted diseases, and reassuring them that we won't be using their real names.

I have to stop myself from running up the lane when it's time for Charlie to be let out.

And what's the first thing he says?

'Can I go to Dara's house?'

Good to see you too, honey.

'I don't know, Charlie. We'd have to talk to his mum.' *Who could be an axe murderer*. I congratulate myself for coming up with such a good fob off — we'll probably never meet her, at least not for a few weeks, and they'll probably have fallen out by then.

'Hi, you must be Charlie's mum? I'm Mary . . .' says an attractive brunette, probably in her mid-thirties, standing next to us, still waiting for her child to come out. '. . . Dara's mum.'

She has a nice smile.

'Oh, hi. How are you? I'm Jenny.'

'Dara never stops nagging me for Charlie to come over.'

'Oh, right.'

With that, Dara comes bolting out the door. 'Hi, Mum,' he shouts. 'Did you talk to Sharlie's mum?'

Ah, God, Sharlie. Maybe he's not so bad after all.

'I was just going to.' She looks at me meaningfully, eyebrows raised. 'He's got three big brothers who do nothing but give him a hard time. He'd love to have a friend of his own over.'

'Ah, well, ah . . .'

'Don't worry if you've something on . . .'

'Please, Mum, *please*. I'll be your bestest friend,' whines Sharlie.

'I thought you were my best friend.'

'Please . . .'

21

Why didn't he pick that quiet kid with the glasses? I don't know. Mary seems nice. The big brothers might explain his 'maturity' and, probably, haircut . . .

'Please . . . '

'OK.'

'Today?'

Argh.

'If it doesn't suit . . . ' Mary starts to say.

'No, no, it's fine. If you're sure it's all right with you.'

'Absolutely. We'd love to have him over. Phil, my husband, is off today so he'll be around to play with them a bit.'

My stomach doesn't like the idea. *I really don't know these people at all.* She gives me her address, phone number, mobile number. I give her mine and Charlie's car seat. *Is she a safe driver? That's my boy she's taking off with.*

'I'll pick him up in an hour,' I say.

'Sure they'll only be getting going at that stage.'

'Right then, two hours — that should be plenty. It's his first time, you know. He might get tired.'

I watch them walk off, chatting animatedly, Charlie jumping every now and again, which he does when he gets excited.

I turn up early to collect him. Mary asks me in.

In the sitting room, a grown man rolls around the floor with two boys, one of them mine. Yelps of laughter from all three.

'We're not ready, Mum,' shouts Charlie, jumping up on Dara's father's back, roaring, 'I'm taking you out, sucker.' I'm surprised he's even noticed I'm here. I can't help but laugh.

'This is Phil,' says Mary.

Her husband waves from the floor just before a cushion hits the side of his head.

'Go, commando,' shouts, *my son?*

Dara spots me hovering. 'Have a cup of tea,' he suggests with alien charm. An obvious delaying tactic.

I smile and look at Mary. 'Where did he learn that trick?'

'Where he learns everything — his brothers. Come on into the kitchen. We'll have a few minutes' peace,' she says, laughing.

'You're sure you're not making dinner or anything?'

'I'll throw a pizza in the oven in a minute, and that, I'm afraid, will be it. It's what they like and I'm tired of arguing.'

'You seem so calm.' The place is bedlam.

She laughs. 'It's a practised art form. With four boys, I've had to give up getting into flaps.'

'Dara's starting school must be a doddle for you.'

'I suppose it's a bit easier when you've been through it before. And sure he's been dying to start. He hates being the baby. Couldn't wait to get going. Charlie seems to be settling in well, too?'

'He seems to love it, all right.' I sigh. 'It's me I'm worried about,' I half-joke.

'It's not easy letting go, is it? God. With James, my eldest, I think I spent the first week in floods.'

'You did?' *Phew!*

'Oh, yeah, I was a complete eejit. Phil had a great laugh.'

We've reached it — that point in the conversation when I should automatically talk about Charlie's dad. In this case, how he feels about Charlie starting school. Happens all the time, this. It's when I offer that silent smile of mine, which I have perfected so well. I do it now.

She doesn't ask. And for that I'm grateful. 'You can't stop progress, can you, though?' she adds instead. 'All you can do is make the most of your free time, I suppose.' She shrugs.

23

'Yeah.' I sigh. 'I suppose.'

'You'll get used to it,' she smiles. 'I promise.'

We spend a leisurely half-hour hidden away in the kitchen, chatting, while the men continue to kill each other.

Teeth washed, face and hands scrubbed, Charlie lets me carry him to his room, though there's nothing wrong with his legs. His Winnie the Poo décor suddenly seems too young for a boy who solemnly transferred his lifelong companion, Barney, from his home on the bed to the cold, lonely, toy box, as soon as he learnt (from Dara) that the dinosaur was 'babyish'. *How tricky would it be to peel off the Winnie the Pooh stickers and replace them with whatever's the latest cool thing for four-year-olds? No doubt I'll be told what that is soon enough.*

'Did you have a nice time at Dara's?' I ask, after our story but before our goodnight kiss.

'The *best*.'

'What did you do?'

'Played the best games in the *whole world*.'

Ah, there's my old Charlie back.

'Did you play with Dara's brothers?'

'No. Mostly his dad . . . He's *mad*.'

'Yeah?'

'Yeah, he played lots of crazy games.'

'It's good you had fun.'

'Mum?'

'Yes, Charlie?'

'Why don't I have a dad?'

I've had years to prepare for this and I'm still not ready. Try honesty, Jenny. I take a breath.

'You do have a dad, Charlie.'

'Well, where is he?'

'I'm not sure, *exactly*.'

'Why? . . . Why doesn't he live here, with us?'

'He's got another life, sweetheart.'

'But I want a dad.' It's a whine.

'I know, Charlie.'

'Can't we ring him and ask him to come for a little while?'

'It's not that easy, sweetie.'

'Why not?'

'Well, he's busy with other things.'

'Doesn't he want to play with me?'

'It's not that.'

'Well, what is it?'

'He's a very busy man.'

'Doesn't he have *any* time to play?'

God.

'Sweetie, he mightn't even be in Ireland. I don't know exactly where he is at the moment. I'm sorry. But, you know what? Maybe we can ask Dara round next week. How does that sound?'

'OK, I suppose.' His head is down and he's picking at a scab on his knee.

'Come here.' I sit him up on my lap. 'I think I feel a hug coming on.'

'Don't like hugs,' he says.

4

I am immersed in warm bubbly water, relaxing back against the white enamel of the bath, eyes closed, miles away. The phone rings. I sit up, spring into action. *Must be that woman I have to interview about ectopic pregnancies!* I grab a towel and race to the hall, wrapping it round me as I go. *Four more rings before the answering machine clicks on!*

I have to take these calls. Always. It's hard to find people willing to be interviewed about their health *and* be photographed. Expecting them to leave a message would be risky — they might get away. So, rather some minor inconvenience like freezing to death than losing an interview. It's not my first time asking the questions that matter, naked, apart from a towel, cold water dripping down my nose from wet strands of hair. I've interviewed naked, semi-naked, in pyjamas, dressed for Halloween. You name it, I've done it. Apart from sex — I haven't had sex while conducting an interview. Might be a bit awkward. Especially since I haven't had sex in five years. *God. Five years. That is so sad . . . .*

I digress. My column. A weekly health page means that there is always a deadline looming. Deadlines! They are relentless. But somehow I haven't missed one. Yet. If Jack knew how close it gets . . . Thank God for the Internet, though. I've been saved by it more than once . . . .

It's not her.

It's Mary.

'. . . I'm dying to see *About Schmidt* but Phil *hates* Jack Nicholson. I've already missed that one with Mel Gibson in it — what's it called? I can't remember — the one with the aliens. Phil hates Mel Gibson too. What do you think? You could drop Charlie over to us, if you haven't got a baby-sitter. Phil wouldn't mind . . . '

'I'd love to go. And it's OK, I have a baby-sitter.' I get a niggle — *do I have a baby-sitter? I thought I was supposed to be changing her . . . .*

'Great. Well, whatever night suits?'

'I don't know — I've such a hectic social life.' I laugh quickly, remembering that we don't know each other — she might take me seriously. 'I'm easy. I'll just check with the baby-sitter — maybe Friday. Her dad doesn't like her out too late during the week. And maybe we might go for a drink afterwards?'

'That'd be great. OK, sure I'll see you at the school anyway.'

'Yep, OK, gotta go.' *Before pneumonia sets in.*

I drop the towel to the ground and drag it along the floor with my foot, drying up the pools of water I've left behind on my way to the phone. When I get back to the bathroom, I drop the towel into the wash basket, slide back into the water and quickly submerge. I stick my foot out to turn on the hot tap and keep the water flowing until I almost can't bear the heat. I start to hum. *I'm going out. I want the world to know . . . .*

My mother is on *The News*. I *almost* switch over. But, much as I want to, something stops me. This happens all the time. What is it? Idle curiosity? A need to keep tabs on her? I don't know. And today's news: When she was on her way to one of her clinics (from the security-driven car to the door), a poster was blown down by strong winds and struck Minister Dempsey 'hard' on the head. It wasn't just any poster. It was of an opposition candidate, in the latest by-election. Unfortunately, we don't get to see live shots of the 'incident'. Instead we are subjected to some recent footage of 'Mother' canvassing, door to door, for her colleague. We also get a brief interview with Minister Dempsey from St Mary's Hospital — *for God's sake, how melodramatic* — where she jokes that the opposition is involved in dirty tricks again. The interviewer laughs. Ha, ha, ha. *The consummate TV performer strikes again.* The 'minor concussion' is an obvious publicity stunt. She is, no doubt, thrilled with the fuss, attention and, let's not forget, sympathy votes that can be stored away and used at the next available opportunity. *And* she gets the added bonus of letting us all know, by default, that the other side wasn't exactly in a rush to take down its election posters. One more day and they'd have faced prosecution. A pretty relevant point coming from the Minister for the Environment, don't you think? I wouldn't be surprised if she rigged the whole thing. If I wasn't her daughter, I might admire her ingenuity.

But I am her daughter. The daughter she never believed in. The daughter who was never good enough. The daughter who became a journalist and not a lawyer, doctor, or other professional, like Mummy wanted. The daughter she didn't trust to find a job – she had to dabble behind the scenes to make sure that said job was good enough. I mean, has she *any idea* what that can do to a person? To find out that the one thing you thought you'd achieved by yourself, without interference, was a sham. You didn't achieve it. You weren't allowed to. And you didn't find out till years later, when someone decided to rub your nose in it, someone who would have liked that job, someone whose mummy didn't have strings, someone who, rightly, resented me and what I stood for. That someone was Ted. And he was right. I was a person who didn't have to work hard for what I got, didn't have to hustle. Though I wanted to be, I couldn't be independent. Not as long as my mother was around. Maybe I should have thanked Ted for making me aware of that. But Ted doesn't deserve thanks — all he wanted was an excuse for his own lack of talent.

I am her only daughter, her only child. She had me and that was enough. Oh, it had its benefits, being the only child of a politician. It meant I was suffocated by the nuns. Watched like a hawk. Fussed over so much that I deserved a good teasing from the girls in my class. A good bullying from the select few.

My mother had no time for me, yet she mopped the floor of every room that could be mopped, at night, despite having cleaners. My mother had no time for me, but the shower tiles got a good old going over with a toothbrush every evening. My mother had no time for me, but she washed our clothes herself and showered before taking them out of the washing machine to put them in the dryer. My mother was obsessive compulsive — I know that now — but she was still a mother. Surely, she could have squeezed me in some-where? Taken me shopping like the mothers of the girls in my class. Taken me swimming. To the movies. A walk. Even a conversation would have been good. I'd have toothbrushed the shower. Doesn't matter. It's over now. The relationship that never was.

My night out approaches and I check out baby-sitting alternatives. I consider Louis, my neighbour on the ground floor. An aspiring keyboard player, in an equally aspiring band called Damage, Louis is a dote who wouldn't damage a fly. Unfortunately, he is also a bit dopey. It may have something to do with the smell of grass that regularly wafts up the stairs. If I were looking for someone to burn the house down, lock himself out, or teach Charlie to curse, Louis would be the man. I picture myself arriving home to find Charlie nursing the zapper, gaping at half-naked women gyrating on MTV, while knocking back a can of Bud, with Louis tucked up fast asleep in bed, sucking his thumb.

The first time I saw Louis was from a first-floor window. I couldn't decide whether he was male or female. He seemed very short, looked about fourteen, with hair so black it had to be dyed, pale make-up and purple/black lips. He was carrying a pair of very large speakers. Louis tells people he meets, in a suspiciously deep voice, that he's twenty-five. Somewhere between eighteen and twenty would be more accurate.

Great loved the idea of sharing the house with struggling artists. I didn't know it then, but she was the landlord and could decide on the neighbours. I didn't find out until she left the house to me. The rents she charged were so small, you could say that she was a patron of the arts. She wouldn't be too impressed with the pair in the basement now. Too normal. Madeleine, Swedish, works in a call centre. Her boyfriend, Tadhg, is from Ballydehob — an accountant, working for the same company. They have plans. They are saving. They are sensible. I feel guilty having broken the unwritten code. It was not deliberate. I am not landlord material — I can't double as a neighbour and some kind of rent collector, so I hired an agency to handle it, forgetting that the agency would control who gets selected to live here. It was they who picked Madeleine and Tadhg, calling them 'low-risk tenants'. I felt terrible but went along with it, seeing as how I'd hired them to do a job and that's what they'd done.

Madeleine crosses my mind now as a potential baby-sitter but I couldn't do it to Charlie. If I'm going to deprive him of Debbie, I should, at least, provide a fun alternative. Nobody comes close to the doctor's daughter. I like her. Charlie likes her. And she seems to like us. It's not her fault her father is her father. And anyway, it's almost Friday.

'Where's your dad?' Charlie asks Debbie. We have just called for her and are walking away from the house.

'He's inside,' she says, picking Charlie up and carrying him to the car.

After a minute's silent driving, Charlie says to Debbie, 'I don't have a dad.'

My eyes dart to the rear-view mirror. Debbie is looking at him, stroking his cheek with her finger. 'Poor you,' she says, then kisses the top of his head.

'He's busy,' Charlie explains.

She catches my eye in the mirror, questioningly. I zip mine back to the road.

'I don't have a mum,' I hear her say to Charlie.

I grip the wheel, sit up straighter. *She died?*

'Don't you?' asks Charlie, fascinated.

'No.'

'Why not?'

'She died, Charlie.'

Oh, God. Oh, no. She did? I hoped she'd get better, make it. Poor thing. Poor Simon. Poor Debbie. I feel so guilty. I mean, I already did. But I had got over it, moved on. I had my punishment — well, not punishment; repercussion maybe — to deal with, to keep me busy. But still, I really didn't think she'd die. Suddenly her name comes to me without trying. Alison.

31

'Great died,' continues Charlie.

Debbie looks baffled. 'What did you say, Charlie?' She looks at me in the mirror again.

'Great is what we called my gran,' I clarify.

'She died,' he repeats.

'Oh,' says Debbie. 'You poor thing.' She holds his hand.

'She's in heaven now. She minds me.'

'Same with my mum.'

'What was she like?' Charlie asks.

I wonder should I stop this now, before someone gets upset.

'She was pretty.'

'Was she great fun?'

'Yeah,' Debbie sighs. 'She used to read me stories and plait my hair.'

'Like my mum. Except she doesn't plait my hair.'

'She used to read *Rapunzel* and *Rumplestiltskin* and *Beauty and the Beast*. But my favourite was *Rapunzel*. Because Rapunzel had long hair, and every time Mum read *Rapunzel* she'd plait my hair. And then the bit when the witch says, "Rapunzel, Rapunzel, let down your long hair", I'd lean over the side of the bed and my plaits would fall down and she'd pretend to climb up.' Debbie has lost her big-brave-fifteen-year-old voice.

'Do you *really* miss her?'

'All the time.'

'Why did she die?'

'She got sick.' Her voice begins to falter.

'Like Great . . . My dad isn't sick. He's just busy.'

Debbie squeezes him to her. 'It's lucky we have each other, isn't it?' she says. Whatever new baby-sitter plans I had have just crumbled.

I'm ready to go. I look over at Charlie, about to say goodbye. He looks so cute, sitting there in his pyjamas, on Debbie's lap, pointing at pictures in his book about whales. He's squeaky clean after his bath, the hairless skin on his arms soft and spongy, little dimples at his elbows. His feet jut out past Debbie's knees. The soles look round and squishy, not hard and flattened like adult feet.

But his hair gives the game away. Gelled, the way he likes it now. My son is growing up. Fast. A few weeks at school and he is officially 'a man'. No more trooping into the Ladies with his mum, not without argument, at least — 'but I'm a *man*,' he says, indignant. No more hand-holding — 'no *way*,' he says. No more blind acceptance of whatever clothes I buy — anything featuring Bob the Builder is a no-no. Action Man, however, is 'the business'. Rude words are suddenly cool. Bottom, butt and boobies are *almost* as funny as willy. And let's not forget poo, the main attraction. They love burps in Asia, apparently. Guess where he wants to go?

To slow down this boy-to-man transformation, I do what little I can. Let his hair grow back to that too-long stage that's so cute, so adorable. Short brown spikes are reverting to long, honey-blond strands with strips of white. In the past fortnight, he's had three proposals of marriage and five invitations to become a boyfriend — all from women in their thirties who *always* want to know if he 'takes after his father'. 'What an unusual mix — dark eyes and fair hair.' I don't tell them to mind their own business, though I'd like to.

'Where's my hug?' I say to him now.

He looks up, makes a face. 'Don't like hugs.'

'Oh, yeah. I'd forgotten.'

'Hugs are for sissies.'

'Right.'

'I'm not a sissy, Mum.'

'I know. But I am. So, can I have one?'

He's sitting there, a finger in his mouth, trying to decide.

'Please. Just one.'

'OOOOK. But just for three seconds.'

He hops down and runs lightly over to me.

'Thanks,' I say hugging him a little closer than usual, breathing in the smell of lemon shampoo.

'Oooone, twoooo, threeeee. Three, Mum. Three. Time's up.'

'Oh, right,' I say, finally letting go.

He takes a quick peep at Debbie, making sure she doesn't think he's a sissy. She has whipped out her mobile phone and is punching buttons on the keypad.

'Hey, Charlie,' she says. 'There's some games on this — want me to show you?'

'*Cool*,' he says, zipping over. He stops short. 'Urgh, it's a *Tigger* phone,' he says, screwing up his nose. 'Tigger's babyish.'

'No, Charlie,' Debbie corrects. 'Tigger's cool.'

'No. Dara said.'

'Well, you tell Dara that teenagers think Tigger's cool.'

Now he looks confused. 'OK,' he says finally.

'Looks like Tigger's making a comeback,' I say to Debbie.

'You'll have to get a T-shirt,' she says.

'I just might do that.' I smile. 'Bye, guys.'

We've lost Charlie.

'Bye, Charlie,' I say.

'Bye, Mum.'

'Finally, a movie that slags off pyramid selling,' is Mary's first comment on *About Schmidt*. I have some idea of what pyramid selling is but ask her to explain. The journalist in me. She does, quite humorously, and that's how I learn that she was in marketing before quitting to become a full-time mum. Overall, *About Schmidt* gets the thumbs up, but neither of us thinks that it quite lived up to the hype. We are comfortably installed in a new trendy bar in the cinema complex. It's a bit hip for us, but, hey, we're out. We could have all sorts of goodies — alcopops, cocktails — you name it, they've got it — but opt instead for a bottle of Miller (me) and a gin and tonic (well, it's obvious isn't it?) We are having a 'proper night out', taxi-ing home. Debbie is staying over, much to Charlie's delight, so at least our time won't be spent downing Cokes and clock-watching. We won't be late, just want to relax, be free agents for one night. Doesn't happen too often. *Look at me, over-explaining a simple night out.*

We chat casually about nothing in particular. Actually, that's the way it feels, but we are covering some ground because I know a lot about Mary. She is the eldest of five, from Cork originally but living in Dublin so long that there is no trace of an accent. 'It comes out when I get excited or cross, boy,' she sings. Phil was her first real boyfriend. They have been married twelve years and planned every child they have. 'It would be nice to have a girl, though,' she says, with a twinkle in her eye. Then talks herself out of it — they'd need a bigger house which won't happen with the property market the way it is.

Eventually we reach that point in the conversation, again. The Charlie's dad point. I take a sip of my drink, put it down. 'I'm on my own. It's just Charlie and me.'

She is silent for a moment, choosing her words. 'Is that OK?'

'Yeah.' I do a half-nod, half-head-shake thingy. 'It's fine. It's the way I wanted it.'

'OK,' she says, nodding, as though understanding. I can tell she doesn't.

But she doesn't ask any more, maybe waiting for me to volunteer it.

I don't. It's not that I don't trust Mary; it's just that this is something I don't talk about with anyone. I don't like to think about it, I don't like to talk about it. And one leads to the other. We move the conversation on without too much difficulty. She makes me laugh. Even her laugh makes me laugh. She is just one of those upbeat people who are good to be around. She'd win an award for her smile — a wide, enthusiastic, toothy grin. She even has dimples. It's a while since I've met someone so easy to like.

We get back later than we had planned, with a definite intention to do this again.

5

I am taking up yoga. Again. This time I might stick it out, though — Mary seems to have enough motivation for at least two.

Charlie and I collect Debbie after my now-standard call to her mobile. She's out the door as we walk through the gate. *What a system!* She looks every inch the cool teenager, wearing a black crop top and pale blue baggy trousers that scrape the ground. A discman is clipped to her low waistband. Inside is probably a CD of Avril Lavigne. Or possibly Pink. She has a folder tucked under her arm. Homework, I guess.

'Hiya, Debbie,' shouts Charlie, racing up to her.

'Hello, Squirt.' She squats, puts the folder carefully down on the grass and holds her arms out for him. He throws himself at her so fast that he knocks her back. They both go over. We laugh and I help them up.

He sees her picking up the folder.

'What's that?' he asks.

'A photo album,' she says. 'I thought you'd like to see pictures of my mum.'

'*Yeah*, I do,' he says, reaching for it. 'Where is she. Can I see?'

'Wait till we get into the car, Charlie, OK?' she says. 'Come on. I'll carry you . . . How's Dara?'

'Fine.'

Charlie jumps into his car seat quicker than I've seen. Debbie straps him in, props the album on his lap and opens it. I start the car, turn off the radio, and keep such a regular check on the rear-view mirror a driving instructor would be impressed.

'Is that her?' Charlie asks, pointing.

'Yes,' she says and I hear the pride in her voice. 'Isn't she pretty?'

'Who's that?'

'That's me.'

He laughs. 'No it isn't. That's a kid.'

'Me when I *was* a kid.'

'You look funny. Where are your teeth?'

'They fell out.'

'Really?'

'Yeah, but I got more. See?' She bares her teeth and pretends to try and bite him.

'Aaargh,' he says.

She turns the page.

'Did someone make you laugh in that one?' he asks.

'My mum. She was always making me laugh.'

He just looks up at her.

'That's my dad, there, with my mum. I took that picture even though I was only seven.'

'Their heads are chopped off.'

'Only the top. That's my favourite picture in the whole world.' Her voice is suddenly childlike.

My four-year-old pats the back of her hand philosophically. She smiles down at him and says, 'Cutie.'

We arrive home. Debbie closes the album.

'Aw,' says Charlie.

'Jenny, can I leave this in the car, so I don't forget it?'

'Sure, Deb.'

The local community hall is not what you'd call a temple of peace and tranquillity. Darkish, kind of chilly, with a faint whiff of socks. The woman at the top of the room has an air of the hippie about her — dangly amber earrings and short spiky hair, oriental designs on her top. She lights a stick and the smell of incense starts to waft its way around the room. *Good idea*. She moves fluidly now to unroll a turquoise mat in front of her. She glances around at us with a relaxed smile — if I worked in narcotics, I'd be suspicious. When she introduces herself (Yvonne), her voice is like honey. *She'll do.*

The class is mixed, but only just. We have a token man. *God love him!* He looks so scared, I can't imagine it's going to be a relaxing experience for him. The rest of us come in a variety of shapes, sizes and styles. Too many toned and tanned torsos for my liking, though. I hope nobody notices I'm wearing pyjama bottoms. I thought they'd look like the real thing — grey and plain and made of tracksuity material. I was wrong.

I wonder if the toned brigade are on some kind of team outing because they're all dressed the same, wearing what must be proper yoga gear because it looks cool and supermodelish. I see that grey isn't 'in'. Just black. Black. And black. Their mats provide the only splash of colour. If you can get designer ones, these are they. Purple. And green. *This is supposed to be a beginners' class*. Mary makes a funny face. She has obviously picked up on my misery vibe.

Things improve. We spend an hour and a half learning to relax, breathe, stretch and mould ourselves into positions named after animals. Dog, Cat, Cobra. If I'd ever wanted an excuse to stick my bum in the air, I've got it now. We learn a whole new language — solar plexus, chakras, auras. Reassuringly, we're told to listen to our bodies not our egos. The Torsos, now known, to me at least, as The Girl Band, won't last then. Not enough pain.

Mary turns out to be a giggler. Any excuse will do — tummy rumbles, pelvic tilts, the token man's attempts at contortion and, unfortunately, some poor woman breaking wind. I hold my composure until the last incident, which causes me to convulse a bit. I manage to stay silent though, but only by turning away, holding my nose for thirty seconds and avoiding eye contact with Mary for the rest of the class. Suddenly I'm back in school on a Friday afternoon.

'That was great,' says Mary, walking down the steps of the community hall.

'What? The yoga or the giggling?' I ask, sarcastically. 'You're *terrible*.' I hit her on the arm.

'I don't know what got into me.' She puts her hand to her chest in mock horror. 'Must have been "the tension leaving my body",' she says, adopting the teacher's voice. And doing a good job.

I laugh.

'No, I mean the peace,' she says, more seriously. 'Wasn't the silence great? What a change from home! There wasn't a *sound* in the place.'

'Apart from that one time,' I say, smiling.

We start laughing again.

'It was good, though,' I say. 'It takes your mind off everything, doesn't it?'

'Except for the pelvic tilts. They tend to put my mind *onto* something.' She raises her eyebrows.

'It's been a while since my poor old pelvis got any tilting action.'

'Is that right?' Eyebrows up again. She really is trouble.

'I don't know,' I say. 'I'll have to stop hanging around with you. You might corrupt me.' I smile.

'Sure, isn't that what you want, a little corruption? Think of the excitement! The living on the edge! Hey. What do you say we hijack that little old dear's car?' She nods to a red Nissan Micra.

'You really are mad.'

'You have to be,' she says, philosophically, grabbing my arm and breaking into a run, taking me with her.

I'm strapping Charlie in his car seat to head to school when I catch sight of Debbie's photo album. It has slipped onto the floor in the back.

'Oh, no.'

'What is it, Mum?'

'Deb left her pictures in the car.'

'Oh, God.'

'Don't say "Oh God", Charlie.'

'You do.'

'I know. I shouldn't. If I say it again, tell me and I'll say sorry. OK?'

'OK but we better give Debbie her book.'

'We'll drop it in when she's back from school.'

We pull up at a red light. I glance at the album on the empty passenger seat beside me. It's *begging* to be opened. *I shouldn't. Why not? She wanted us to see it. She wanted* Charlie *to see it. She wouldn't mind, though. Just one look, one quick peek and I'd know what she was like.*

A horn blows.

'OK, OK, keep your hair on,' Charlie says.

'*Charlie!*'

41

We drive in silence, then pull up outside the school. Charlie undoes his strap, hops out and squeezes in between the front seats. All done in three seconds.

'Can we look at the photos, Mum?'

'No, sweetheart, we're late. I'm sure Debbie will show you them again. Come on.'

'Aw.'

'Look. There's Dara — let's race him.'

We do. And win. When I get back to the car, I regret not having put the album on the back seat. The temptation! I pick it up to put on the floor behind me but find myself opening it. I turn the pages. My heart pounds, feeling like I'm doing something I shouldn't and will be caught any minute. There it is — the happy scene. Simon could be a different man. No sadness, just laughter in his eyes. She is beautiful, Alison — delicate with blue eyes and long, dark hair. The kind of woman who makes you feel big, clumpy, awkward. It could be an ad for multivitamins, they look so healthy, if it wasn't for her making bunny ears behind his head. So much love in one shot. Pity it wasn't shoved under my nose five years ago, in a hotel room in Brussels.

'I'm afraid Debra is not home yet,' he apologises. 'She plays hockey on Wednesdays.' We stand there awkwardly for a few seconds — me hiding behind my hair, my glasses, my clothes; him shifting from one foot to another. Then he clicks into gentleman mode. 'But if you would like to come in, she should be back . . .' he checks his watch, 'in, say, half an hour.'

'No, thanks, it's fine. I just wanted to return this.' I hold out the album. 'She left it behind last night. You might give it to her for me? If you don't mind.' I manage to avoid eye contact by focusing on the album.

'Not at all,' he says. 'She really is enjoying the baby-sitting.'

I wasn't expecting that. I look up.

He squints. 'Have we met before, Jenny? Your face is very familiar.'

'No. No, I don't think so. No. Maybe you're mixing me up with someone else.'

'That must be it. I'm sorry. I see so many people in my line of work.'

I produce an understanding smile. 'Happens all the time. I've just one of those faces. Anyway, we'd better be off. Nice meeting you, again, ah . . . '

'Simon.'

'Simon.' I nod. 'Come on, Charlie, let's go.'

My son gives me a what's-in-it-for-me look.

'I'll give you a treat,' I whisper. 'Come on.'

'OK.'

'Thank you for returning the album. It's very special to Debra.'

'No problem. Bye.'

6

I wake. It's dark. Charlie is calling out in his sleep. I throw back the quilt and drag myself out of bed into chilly late-autumn air. I find him crying, quilt half down on the bed where he has kicked it off. He is still asleep. I sit at the side of his bed and brush his hair back again and again. 'It's OK, it's OK,' I whisper. 'Shhh.'

He opens his eyes.

I smile. 'Hi,' I say quietly.

He looks at me with teary eyes.

'You were having a bad dream, sweetie. But it's over now.'

'Mama?'

He hasn't called me that in years.

'Yes, sweetie. It's Mama. We're home. In your room. You were just having a silly old dream. But you're awake now.'

He sits up, rubs his eyes with two little fists and snuggles into me. I put my arm around him.

'Don't like hugs,' he says but it's a whisper and I know not to let go.

'You were gone,' he says. 'I couldn't find you.'

'I'm here now.' I lift him onto my lap and wrap him in my arms. I rock gently and sing the one lullaby that always comforts him: 'Hush little baby'. I change the words, like I always do. 'Mama's' going to buy him a mocking bird, not 'Papa'. With his finger, he twirls the hair at the side of his head, round and round and round. He gets heavy in my arms, so I rest him back down onto the pillow and lie facing him. He doesn't take his sleepy eyes off me. With each blink, his lids become heavier. But he fights it, forcing them to stay open. His breathing becomes even and deep. His eyes finally close and I'm just beginning to think he has drifted off when he pats the bed with the flat of his hand, feeling around for me, making sure I'm still there. He sleeps. And I stay with him.

'I don't want you to go,' he says, looking at the ground.

We are standing just inside the door of Charlie's classroom. We've hung up his coat, left his schoolbag at its dedicated spot, said our goodbyes.

'But you love school.'

'Don't leave me.'

'Charlie, we're blocking the doorway. And I *have* to go.' I start to walk out. He grabs my leg and clings to it.

'I want to stay with you,' he pleads.

'But what about Dara? He'll be lonely.'

'Don't go, Mama, don't go. I want to come with you.'

This is killing me.

'Charlie,' I say, trying to be firm. 'Even if you come home, it'll just be boring. All I'll be doing is talking on the phone and writing on the computer. We won't be able to play. It'd be so *boring*.'

'Don't care. Want to be with you.' He has his obstinate face on now.

'Come on, Charlie. You love school. It's PE today. *And* treat day.'

Mary arrives with Dara. She grasps the situation immediately. 'Charlie, just the man I need,' she says. 'Dara's in trouble. Can you help?'

Charlie looks at her, then at Dara. She's got his attention. Now what?

'Come here. I want to show you something.'

He doesn't budge.

'Look.' She opens Dara's lunch box. 'I packed too much lunch today. Silly me — Dara won't be able to eat it all. Maybe you could help him with his treats. What do you think?' She smiles.

'No, thank you.'

Dara looks relieved.

'Nice try,' I whisper to her. 'I don't know what's wrong with him today.'

'Ah, they all have their off days. Just go. He'll calm down as soon as you're gone.'

'You think?'

'Yeah. Here, I'll get Ms Ford — see if she'll come and hold him while you head off.'

I walk out on my crying son, his wet face pleading with me, his arms outstretched. *The guilt.*

I get straight to work. It's the only answer. I ring Jack with details of the people I'm due to interview for my next column so he can arrange photos.

'Are they happy to be photographed?' asks the man whose biggest concern in life is that I find someone, every week, who is willing to be photographed for the column. The piece itself could be rubbish. OK, I'm exaggerating. But, to an extent, as long as Jack has a pic of real people with real problems, he's happy.

'Yes, boss, they're happy to be photographed.'

'What's the address? No. Wait. Let me guess. Glenageary.' It's his usual gripe.

'Can't help it if that's where my contacts live.' *Can't help it if my life is a little insular.*

'Don't you know *anyone* who lives outside South County Dublin?'

'Hang on a minute. Wasn't last week's person from Phibsboro?'

'Doesn't count. She'd a double-barrel name.'

'You're a reverse snob, Jack. You know that? Wait, how about someone from Lucan? Will that do you?'

'Great. Lucan. Now we're talking.'

'How're you fixed? Can we do it now?'

'Do what now?'

'The interview. You'd be perfect. Nice ordinary Lucan man like yourself. Talking about a nice ordinary topic like piles. You've had them, haven't you, Jack? You needn't worry. I'd treat the interview sensitively; we could photograph you in darkness . . .'

'Piles? You're not doing *piles*?'

'Why not? They're *really* interesting.' Just as well he can't see my face. I'm enjoying this.

'Yeah, right.'

'No, seriously, everyone gets them. No one talks about them. They could be a sign of something more serious . . . And we can't always be doing heavy depressing stuff.'

'You'll never find anyone to talk about piles.'

'Already have.'

'From the southside, right?'

'Yes, from the southside and happy to be photographed. You know, Jack, you're your own worst enemy. I don't know *what* you'd do if you won the lotto — you wouldn't be able to *live* with yourself. Just think. It would be *terrible*.'

Charlie wants to stay home rather than go to Dara's house as planned. This is despite the fact that it contains one father, three Gameboys and one Playstation. So, Dara comes to ours. I can't resist eavesdropping on their little chats, as they sit huddled together over a great scattering of Lego. They're building aliens. I'm making spaghetti. They're on the subject of babies — stimulated by the fact that Dara is about to have a new cousin. Babies and how they're made have become his favourite topics of conversation. He is driving Mary mad.

'So, where does the seed come from?' Charlie asks the expert.

'It's in the body,' Dara says matter-of-factly, not looking up from his Lego.

'But where does it come from in the first place?' asks Charlie, chewing on a wheel.

'It's in the body but it takes years to turn into a baby.'

'A hundred years?' Charlie asks, getting back to his alien.

'Not that long because it'd be a granny.'

'Only if it was a girl.'

'If it was a boy, it'd be a grandad.'

'Bloody, bloody.' Charlie's alien's head has just broken off.

Dara gobbles up all his spaghetti. Charlie takes about three mouthfuls and decides he's full.

'No ice cream until you finish.' It's my usual trick and works every time.

'I'm full, Mama.'

'But you didn't finish your sandwiches at school. You must be hungry.'

'Do you call your mum, *Mama*?' asks Dara, apparently horrified.

Charlie looks down, doesn't answer.

'Sometimes he does,' I explain. 'What do you call your mum?'

'Mum.'

'That makes sense. Well, different people call their mums different things — mammy, mam, mama, *mother*.'

They laugh at the posh accent I've put on for 'mother'. Tension broken. Plan executed.

'So what do you want to do now?' I ask.

'Football,' says Dara.

'Nothing,' says Charlie.

Dara looks at him. 'How could you want to do nothing?'

Charlie shrugs.

'Come on.' Dara pleads. 'You can be Roy Keane.'

'I'm tired.'

Must be very tired not to want to be his hero.

'But football will wake you up,' says Dara.

'Don't want to. My leg's sore.'

'Is it?' I ask.

He nods.

'Where?'

'Here.' He feels the upper part of his right leg.

'Did you fall today?' I ask.

'No.'

'Did you bump into anything?'

'No.'

'Anyone kick you?'

'No.'

'I don't know. Pull down your trousers for a sec and let me have a look.'

He looks at Dara.

'It's OK, Charlie — Dara doesn't mind.'

'Nah, I see my brudders' butts all the time.'

'I have my undies on. You won't see my butt,' says Charlie.

49

(I'd give out about the language, but butt just happens to be my favourite word.)

'They're just white,' says fashion correspondent Dara. '*I've* got Buzz Lightyear ones.'

No bruising. 'It looks OK, Charlie,' I say, pulling back up his trousers.

'But it's sore.'

'Maybe it's a growing pain.'

'Yeah, I get them all the time,' says Dara. 'That's why I'm so big.'

'Would you like some Calpol?' I ask Charlie, sitting him up on the worktop and reaching up to the press overhead for the bottle.

'Can I open it?' he asks.

'You can try,' I say, handing it to him.

He does. And fails.

'It's broken,' he says.

'Here give it to me.' I press it down to disengage the child lock and pour the pink, sticky, globby liquid onto a medicine spoon. 'Open Sesame.'

He opens Sesame.

'Why didn't it work for me?'

'The bottle's designed so that kids can't open it.'

'How does it know if a kid is trying to open it?' he asks, having another bash himself.

'It just does. Now, do you want to watch a video till Dara's mum comes?'

'*Lion King*,' says Charlie.

'*Spy Kids*,' says Dara.

'Tell you what, why don't we toss for it?'

Twenty minutes later, Charlie is asleep on the couch, Sausage snuggled up beside him. Dara is oblivious, hypnotised by the flickering lights of the television.

My column on piles appears. I am horrified. The headline reads PILES OF PAIN. The sub head, NO END IN SIGHT. The caption under the picture of the man who agreed to be interviewed and photographed, BUTT DOCTOR! I ring Jack who is unrepentant.

'I don't see what you're getting upset about. It's just a play on words. Nobody takes piles seriously.'

'I bet if you had them you would. Look, this man agreed to be interviewed. He was doing me a favour. And now it just looks as if we're taking the piss out of him.'

'The copy shows we aren't.'

'Yeah, but what do people read first? What if they don't read the article at all, just look at his picture and the headlines? Imagine his boss flicking through the paper.'

He starts to laugh.

'It's not funny. This is a person's reputation.'

'If he wants to be in the paper, he should be prepared for . . .'

The hardened hack. I was like that once. I can see it coming a mile off and I'm not letting him away with it.

'Jack, don't give me that. You have to respect the people I interview. I can't have them compromised. It's not easy finding someone every week to agree to be open, be photographed and not get paid. How am I going to find people to interview if they feel they can't trust me?'

'What did the guy think of the article?'

'I'm afraid to ring him.'

'Maybe he doesn't have a problem with it.'

'Or maybe he's outside my house with a sawn-off shotgun right now, waiting for me to come out.'

'OK, OK, I thought it was a bit dodgy when I was doing it up. But you try coming up with a headline for piles.'

'I did.'

'We're trying to get people to read the paper, Jenny, not providing a public service — a headline is meant to attract attention not bore people to death.'

'Look, Jack, will you do me a favour? The next time you come up against one you think is "a bit dodgy", will you run it by me and we can work something out together?'

'I'll be more sensitive. But you have to admit it was funny.'

'*No!*' But I'm not cross with him any more.

I find the courage to ring the man with the piles. He's delighted with the article, doesn't mention the headline or caption, instead focuses on the fact that it should help increase awareness of the need to get haemorrhoids checked out. He had piles, but ignored them because he was too embarrassed to go to his GP. In the end, his wife forced him. He had bowel cancer. Luckily they caught it early. He recovered, following surgery. With this article, he is hoping to help prevent the same thing from happening to other people.

I sometimes moan about having to do the column — the relentlessness of it, week after week, having to find people to talk to within a deadline. But it keeps me company, keeps me sane, reminds me how other people live, how diverse a world it is, how difficult it can be for some and how they cope, often heroically. I would miss it if I stopped.

7

'There's no such thing as daddies,' declares Charlie, climbing into bed.

'Of course there is, Charlie,' I say, closing the curtains.

'No, Mum, there isn't. Only mummies. Not daddies.' He's sitting up, looking over at me, one hundred per cent sure.

I psyche myself up for another you-have-a-dad-but-he's-not-here conversation. I smile at him and try to work out what I'm going to say. I sit on the bed beside him. *Where to start?*

'. . . A mummy's different from a zombie. They both are dead and come out of graves but they're different. Scooby and Shaggy are afraid of them, but I'm not.'

OOOOK, now I get it.

'Lie down, Charlie. It's time to sleep.'

'I want to be a mummy for Halloween,' he says, flopping back onto the pillow, eyes still wide open.

'I thought you wanted to be a skeleton.' *I've got the suit.*

'No, a mummy.'

'Why?'

'Just do.'

'But skeletons are better.'

'Dara's going to be a mummy.'

'Oh.' *Halloween is tomorrow. There's no way I'm rushing around looking for a mummy outfit.*

'Can I, Mum?'

'We'll see. Now go to sleep. Do you want the globe on?'

He nods tiredly.

I switch on Charlie's globe — a warm, cosy football of turquoise and sand-coloured light, bought to help with his nightmares. It keeps the room from darkness and, if he wakes, it's familiar and he knows where he is.

'Lie down with me,' he says.

Another bad habit that's creeping in. 'Only if you go to sleep straightaway.'

'OK.'

'OK.'

He sleeps almost instantly. School seems to be draining him of energy. He is constantly tired. *Must start a course of vitamins.* I sneak out, by moving to the edge of the bed, still lying, slipping one leg onto the floor, waiting, then the other, then sitting up quickly and standing. *Phew!* I ring Mary.

'How d'you make a mummy?'

'You too?' she laughs.

''fraid so.'

Silence for a moment, then, 'Why don't you come over tomorrow? We'll work something out. Hospital bandages, maybe? You could come Trick or Treating with us? There are loads of houses in our estate and everyone's into Halloween. It'll be fun.'

'Are you sure?'

'Yeah. It'll be great.'

'Any of yours want to be a skeleton? I've a spare costume.'

'It'd probably be too small, would it?'

'Age 6 to 7 — their last one.'

'Sure, bring it along. Someone might change their mind at the last minute.'

'*Never!*'

The excitement starts as soon as Charlie wakes. And it builds. Debbie gets involved. She paints their faces white, lips black and around the eyes red. Then we wrap them head to toe in bandages, giving them an instant excuse to ignore us — 'Can't hear you with my bandages.' We start early, before dusk. Our reason: to get it over before they tire. Their reason: to get all the treats before the other kids come. The older boys keep one house ahead of us, not wanting to 'hang out with the babies', but still close enough for us to keep an eye on them. Debbie goes up to the doors with Charlie and Dara — two mummies and a giant skeleton.

'No one's in,' says Deb, when she sees that an outside light is off.

'How do you know?' they ask, amazed at her psychic powers.

'I can feel it in my bones,' the skeleton says in a spooky voice.

It must be a relief for her to be away from the pressure of being a teenager for one night, just to have some innocent fun.

We drive to Killiney Hill to witness the illegal but brilliant fire-work display that happens there every Halloween. We are not disappointed. Rockets whizz, sizzle and pop to the sounds of oooh, wow and yahoo. Kids jump, hop, clap. Mary's second oldest, Alfie, the comedian, announces, 'zank you, zank you', and bows flamboyantly. Luminous blue and white sparks light up the sky. We learn to judge how big an explosion will be by the noise the rocket makes on its way up. They keep the best till last — Catherine wheels and Chinese firecrackers impress so much we are silent. One firework escapes, shooting along the ground, away from the crowd, then fizzling out. The kids munch on their goodies to the sound of U2's 'A Beautiful Day' on the car radio.

We go for chips to the proper chip shop in Dalkey. Charlie wants a whole packet but eats only four. He is too tired to walk so I piggyback him to the car. Less than a minute into the drive, he is asleep.

'He's such a sweetie,' says Debbie from the back.

'Yeah,' I say.

'He's so cute. Especially his little clothes.'

'Really?' That surprises me.

'The little shirts and chinos. He's such a dude.'

'He's going off them now, though. It's all Action Man stuff.'

'I must tell him how cool he looks in the shirts. Like a little man.'

'That might work,' I say. 'If you drop the "little".'

She laughs. 'Where does he get all this "man" stuff from?'

'I don't know. It started with school, I think. And Dara, I suppose.' A thought occurs. *He wouldn't be trying to be the man of the house, would he, seeing as how there is no other man around?* I dismiss this instantly. *He's only four.*

'Jenny, thanks *a mill* for tonight,' Debbie says. 'I'd a great time. I *totally* love Halloween.'

'I'm glad you came. You were brilliant with the costumes and it was great to have an extra pair of hands. And Charlie's mad about you.'

'I *so* love him. You know, I was just thinking. Oh my God, what if the principal hadn't thought of me, when you asked them to recommend a baby-sitter? I'd never have met you guys.'

'I know.'

'The other day, my dad, like, offered to up my pocket money so I wouldn't have to baby-sit? But I said, "*No way*". I've had *so* much fun with Charlie, there's *no way* I'd stop. And it's good to be, like, independent, earn your own money. That's what I said to him.'

'You're right. It is good to be independent.'

We get to her house and she hops out. I wait until she is safely inside before driving off. *Why would he do that? What's his problem? Me being a single mum, a bad influence? Or does he know I'm Jennifer Grey? Has he finally recognised me? Does he think that me being around will bring it all back — his big mistake? Don't tell me he thinks I'd tell Debbie. For God's sake! He's not the only one who's suffered. I lost everything and had to start again . . . Asshole.*

I head home, carry Charlie upstairs and stand outside the apartment, rummaging in my pockets for the keys. All I find is his toothbrush, where it's been since this morning, when I had to do a last-minute job at the school gates. It's one big rush in the mornings now. Charlie is so slow to get started. He seems drained most of the time, so I let him sleep for as long as I can. But it doesn't seem to make a difference to his energy levels and only makes us late. Maybe I should have waited till he was five to start school.

I settle him in, cover him up, switch on his globe and leave the door open. I wander back to the sitting room. Poor Sausage is hiding under the table. He hates Halloween. All those bangs and loud noises. I light the candle in our pumpkin and admire the Muppet-like face we've sculpted — long, narrow nose, eyes too close together. He's lovely. I make a cup of tea, stirring the teabag with the toothbrush handle, too tired to look for a spoon, then slump onto the couch and slip off my shoes. *That's better.* I pat the cushion beside me and call Sausage. He looks unsure as to whether he should stay cowering or take advantage of a rare offer. Doesn't take him long to decide. We sit together looking at the flickering light, as the noise dies down outside, me rubbing his tummy absently. I'm thinking. About Charlie. And the battle I have with him every morning. The battle to get him out of bed. The battle to get him to eat his porridge. The battle to get him to stay at school. He really needs a break. *I* really need a break. Maybe we should take tomorrow off. Relax. Rebuild his energy reserves.

I wake at eleven to find him asleep in the bed beside me. It's such a treat to do nothing, so that's exactly what I do until he wakes. Instead of eating our usual breakfast, in our usual kitchen, I take him to the local coffee shop for croissants. I'm certain he'll eat all round him, considering the change of environment and the fact that I'm not rushing him. But no. Half a croissant and not even a full glass of OJ. Not like him.

We finish up. Charlie wants to pay. He climbs down from his stool and walks ahead of me. I frown. *Is he limping? Ever so slightly?* You'd hardly notice, but he seems not to be pressing down fully on his right leg. *Is that the one he's been complaining about?* A feeling of unease creeps up on me. A sore leg is one thing, a limp another. I watch Charlie interact with the woman at the till and see how charmed she is. I do a quick mental calculation. *It's not just the limp — it's the lack of energy, the loss of appetite, the fact that he has been really clingy. And worried. Almost as if he knows something is wrong. But maybe it's just the nightmares. He is pale, though. I don't know. They're all pretty general and non-specific and probably just him adjusting to school or having a growth spurt or worrying about not having a father — something easily explained. Still, I've got a niggling feeling. The limp. I'm bringing him for a checkup.*

Panicky single mother overreacts again. That's what she's thinking — Dr Finnegan. She has examined him. Found nothing.

It doesn't help that the limp miraculously disappeared as soon as we walked through the door of her surgery. She's 'not worried about' the other symptoms but tells me to come back in a week if Charlie is still getting pains in his leg.

One week later, exactly, we are back. There has to be something wrong with his leg. He won't do PE and has asked for a teacher's note excusing him from going out to the yard at playtime, afraid that other kids will bump into him. And yet I'm paranoid that I'm fussing, paying too much attention to a child who might be just overreacting to a growing pain. Dr Finnegan examines Charlie, again. Finds nothing, again. The tiredness and 'pallor' she puts down to starting school and the fact that he hasn't been eating. Why he hasn't been eating she can't explain but talks about 'non-specific viral infections' that are common when one starts school. She recommends a tonic that I already have him on. She suggests an X-ray 'to be on the safe side', seeing as how he has had the pain, off and on, for two weeks now. She writes a note for St Gabriel's Hospital, then pulls out a roll of stickers sponsored by some pharmaceutical company. Charlie picks two. A dinosaur and a shark.

We are in luck. Charlie has the X-ray, enjoys the experience. We're ready to go. Just waiting for the result. Unofficially, there's no break. Officially, they're waiting for some specialist to have a closer look. He doesn't seem in too much of a hurry to appear, though. Charlie is getting tired and cranky. I'm getting edgy and thinking of asking if we really need to stay for the result. Then I see Simon Grace striding into the X-ray department, white coat swinging behind him. I duck back into the waiting room and turn my back to the door. *Phew!*

I try to interest Charlie in a toy made of coloured wooden counters that move over metal wires. He *was* interested — half an hour ago. Someone behind us calls out Charlie's name. *At last.* I turn. It's Simon. *Oh my God! How does he know we're here? Did he see Charlie's chart?* His eyes are scanning the room. He doesn't seem to know that he is calling my Charlie. I think about staying quiet, then dismiss the idea. *How immature would that be?* I put down the toy, get up, take Charlie's hand and walk towards him. When he sees us, he rechecks the chart, then looks at us again.

'Oh, it's you,' he says, paling. 'I'm sorry, I didn't realise. When I saw the name on the chart, I didn't make the connection . . .'

Hang on! What does he want us for? He's an oncologist. He must have the wrong chart. There must be a mistake. Charlie's just here for an X-ray.

'Jenny,' he says, gently. 'Would you like to come with me for a moment?' He looks down at Charlie and smiles. 'Hello, Charlie. How are you?'

'I'm sorry. I think there's been a mistake. Charlie's just here for an X-ray.'

'Yes, I have it here. They've just asked me to have a look at it.'

My turn to pale. 'Why?' almost doesn't come out.

'Let's talk somewhere quieter.'

Sweet Jesus! I follow him in silence, telling myself over and over. *It's a mistake. It has to be a mistake.* Charlie's ahead, holding Simon's hand, chatting about the X-ray. We reach an office. I follow him in. He asks me to sit. I don't feel like sitting. I feel like running. With my son. Out of here. But I sit, silently, with Charlie on my knees, my arms wrapped around him.

You've made a mistake. You've made a mistake.

'Jenny.' He drags a swivel chair out from behind the desk and moves it close to where Charlie and I are sitting. He smiles what he probably thinks is a reassuring smile. Well, he's wrong.

'I've been asked to have a look at Charlie's X-ray . . .'

'I think you've made a mistake, Simon. Charlie's X-ray is fine, they told me. They just wanted to get a specialist to have a quick look at it.'

'Me,' he explains.

'You're an oncologist.'

He looks uncomfortable. 'Yes, I am. But my involvement at this stage is just a precaution. There is no reason for alarm. There are one or two things in Charlie's X-ray that cause some concern. There could be any number of reasons for these. We are just being thorough.'

'What other specialists are involved?'

'Well, none. At the moment. But, in fairness, that doesn't mean anything. This is very much a step-by-step process. If I don't find anything, we'll take it from there. I would like to examine Charlie, now, if that's all right with you?'

'Charlie, Simon wants to have a little look at you. OK?'

'OK,' Charlie says cheerfully.

Simon walks over to an examination bench that is covered in disposable paper. He pats it. 'Do you think you could climb up here? Only really clever boys and monkeys can get up here.'

Charlie gets down from my lap, guarding his leg. 'I can get up there,' he says. He climbs the portable steps. 'See?'

'Hmm. You *are* smart,' Simon says.

'No, I'm a monkey. Ooh ooh,' Charlie replies, lifting his arms and pretending to scratch under them. He beats his chest. We laugh. But I don't mean it.

'So, how are you, Charlie?' asks Simon.

'Ooh ooh,' Charlie chirps.

Oh no.

'Can you be a boy again for a minute?' asks Simon.

'Can I be a doctor, like you?'

'You can. Would you like to examine me?' asks Simon, displaying an I'm-a-friendly-doc-who-loves-kids smile. 'This is a stethoscope. Do you want to listen to my heart?'

Charlie takes it. 'Nifty,' he says.

Simon laughs.

'Breathe in,' says Charlie, putting the stethoscope to Simon's chest, frowning and turning his eyes towards his left ear as though listening with them. There is something unnerving about the two of them being so close together.

'Again,' instructs Charlie.

Simon breathes in.

'Again.'

Simon inhales.

'Again.'

He obeys. Then says, 'Now, my turn.'

I examine him examining my son — throat, ears, eyes — the usual drill.

'I'm just checking for swollen lymph glands,' he explains to me when he starts to feel Charlie's neck.

Lymph glands, lymph glands. Why lymph glands? I'm trying to remember all the articles I've written, all the conferences I've attended. *Lymphoma?* I panic.

'They're fine.'

Thank God! I breathe out.

'Now I'm checking to see if his liver is swollen.'

Liver? Why liver?

'Fine.'

It's OK. Everything's going to be OK.

'Now I'm checking to see if I can feel Charlie's spleen.' He stops, shifts his position. Presses around a bit more. 'I can feel the tip ever so slightly.'

So? What does that mean? I'm afraid to ask.

'How has he been?'

I list the symptoms. They sound so familiar, having called them out so many times, to so many people, including myself. I feel like a suspect in a murder inquiry.

'How long has he been having these?'

'About two weeks. Though, he's been pale for longer.'

'I see.'

'I've been to the GP twice. She said Charlie's fine. The X-ray is only a precaution.'

'I see. I'd like to run a few blood tests, if that's all right with you.'

'What tests?' The journalist in me finally emerges. About time.

'A Full Blood Count to check for anaemia, to see why Charlie is so pale. And a test to check for inflammation, to see why his spleen might be swollen.'

Swollen? You didn't say 'swollen'. You said 'tip', you didn't say 'swollen'.

'We will know more when we have the results. I'll organise someone to take them now, if that's all right with you.'

I nod.

'I will need you to sign a consent form. It's just a formality to say you agree with tests being carried out.'

I nod again.

'Have you had a cup of tea?'

'We're fine, thanks.' *We'll be going home soon.*

'I'm thirsty,' Charlie insists.

I pull a carton of apple juice from my satchel.

Simon smiles, then gets up, looking a bit weary. 'I'll just sort out the paperwork,' he says.

8

A woman in blue arrives with news that she will be relieving my son of blood. She taps his arm, 'looking for a suitable vein', then rubs 'magic cream' onto two areas — the back of his hand and the area where his arm flexes. It's an anaesthetic she explains to me. Then she covers the cream with something like clingfilm. It will take forty-five minutes to work, apparently. That's when she'll be back for the real action.

I distract Charlie by taking him to look for the canteen. We stop a man to ask for directions. He has two children with him, one in pyjamas — he knows his way round.

'Go up that ramp, turn left and down the stairs,' he says.

'OK, thanks.'

I'm about to head that way when he says, rather loudly, 'I wouldn't touch the coffee, though.'

I laugh.

Charlie finishes his apple juice and doesn't want anything to eat. I risk the coffee and survive. We kill ten minutes, then get restless, so it's on to the hospital shop to buy colouring books, crayons and a toy Ernie that sings and wiggles its bum. Enough, I hope, to distract Charlie from Dracula.

She's there when we get back. Waiting. Like a bird of prey. She smiles. Charlie doesn't notice her, too busy checking to see what colour crayons he has. He doesn't want the pink.

'We'll just pop in here for a second, love,' she says cheerfully, heading for the room we were in earlier. I wonder is it the Bad Luck Room or even the Bad News Room. In any case, I don't like it. But I'm the adult. Agreeable. Co-operative. Malleable. I follow her. In five seconds flat, she has me in a chair with Charlie sitting crossways on my lap, just so. I wonder how many times she does this in an average day.

'Now, sweetheart,' she says, quickly applying a tourniquet to his arm. 'I just have to give your arm a little squeeze for a moment. You look at your mum, pet. I think she's got something she wants to show you.' She gives me a meaningful look.

'Oh, Charlie, look — Ernie sings,' I rush.

'I know,' he says, eyeing Dracula.

'Let's see what he says,' I try.

'You ain't nothing but a hound dog,' says Charlie. 'I know. Dara's got a singing Ernie. What are you doing?' he asks the Count just as she produces a needle.

'It won't hurt, love, because you've got the magic cream on.' She doesn't give him a chance to change his mind. In the needle goes. Charlie screams, 'It's sore, it's sore, take it out.'

'I just need to keep it in for a little bit longer, pet. Then it'll be all over.'

She lets my son's blood drip into three test tubes, each with a different coloured plastic top.

'Now, Charlie, I want you to meet Freddie,' she says, and to me: 'It's a cannula that stays in his vein in case he needs medicine intravenously.' She see-saws back to Charlie. 'We'll just put on his little green hat.'

'Take it out, take it out. I don't want it.'

'Charlie,' she says. 'You need Freddie. He's going to stay in your arm for a little while.'

'Dr Grace didn't mention this,' I say to her. 'He just said about the blood test. We're not staying.'

'It's probably just a precaution. We do it all the time if we're taking blood. It saves the child having to have another jab later if he needs intravenous medication.'

What intravenous medication?

'Don't want Freddie. Don't like Freddie. Take him out.' He is crying now, his little face contorted and red. I want to stick a needle in her arm, see how she likes it. I'll even let her have the magic cream. So she can see just how magic it *isn't*.

'Freddie is just a straw,' she says to Charlie. 'He's not a needle. I took the needle out, Charlie. Freddie is just a tiny little straw. He's all bendy. He doesn't hurt. I think he wants a little drink. Will we give him a drink?'

'No. Freddie's not thirsty. Leave Freddie alone.'

'Just a little tiny bit of 7Up. It won't hurt.'

'You said that before. And it *did* hurt.'

'Charlie,' I say. 'If you just let Freddie have a little drink, this nice lady will go away and maybe then we can play soldiers, OK?'

'But you didn't get the soldiers.'

'I will. We'll go back to the shop and get them.'

He looks down. Frowns.

'OOOOK,' he says at last.

It's over very quickly. Dracula starts to pack up her things, like a pro. Charlie climbs down off my lap and starts to poke at her box of tricks — it's like a plastic toolbox and I can see the attraction to a child. Loads of nooks and crannies and interesting, unfamiliar objects.

'Charlie, stop, love. Leave the lady's things alone.'

'Can we get the soldiers now?'

'In a sec.' I turn to the phlebotomist who is snapping her toolbox closed and lifting it up by the handle. 'How long will the results take?' I ask.

'There's a rush on these, so we should have them in a couple of hours.'

'Hours?'

Simon arrives. She smiles hello to him and bye to me. Then off she hurries to puncture someone else.

'The results will take hours,' I tell him. Stupidly. He, of all people, must know that.

'I'm afraid that's the quickest we can get them, Jenny.'

'Maybe we could go home and ring in for them, rather than waiting?'

'I'd prefer you to wait, if you don't mind.' He pauses, looks at me directly and says, slowly, clearly. 'There is a possibility that we might need to admit Charlie for further investigation.'

Oh God!

'Maybe there is someone who could come in and keep you company?'

Oh God! Oh God! Oh God!

'No. No, we're fine, thank you. We're fine.' I fold my arms.

He looks at Charlie, then back at me, his face full of meaning. 'It might be an idea.'

My stomach whooshes towards my chest. *It's cancer. It's cancer.*

'A family member, friend?'

Stop, stop, please! You're going too fast. This isn't happening. It can't be.

67

I look at Charlie, his face all innocent and light. He is banging the 'I've been brave' sticker Dracula gave him onto his chest. I feel like bursting into tears but know that it's me who must be brave now.

'I have a friend. Mary, I need to call Mary.'

'Good. Good. You can use the phone here. Maybe I could show Charlie his X-ray? As he's going to be a doctor.' He stoops down to my son. 'How about it? Would you like to see your X-ray, Charlie?'

'Yeah, cool, wow.' He rushes over to Simon and takes his hand. He gives a little excited jump. *My baby. Don't take my baby.*

'We're just going to the room opposite. We'll be back in three or four minutes. Give you a moment to talk.' He produces a smile he must turn on for all us eejits who don't know what's going on.

'See you in a minute, Mum,' says Charlie, his energy suddenly recharged just when I'm about to be told there's something wrong.

Charlie returns with an impressive vocabulary of X-ray banter. Simon has 'a few things to do' but promises to be back as soon as he has any news. We go for the soldiers, then wander round the hospital. I'm distracting myself as much as distracting Charlie. The corridors are busy. So many people. So many uniforms. I pretend I care who is who. Who wears the white tops and navy trousers? Nurses? If so, who wears the green tops and navy trousers? Physios? The phlebotomists are blue, that I know. Doctors are identifiable as much by their attitude of cosy superiority as by their customary white coats and stethoscopes. People in scrub gear remind me of *ER*.

The people keep coming. Children in pyjamas and slippers. Some in dressing gowns, others not. Parents, brothers, sisters dressed for the outside world, some looking displaced, confused, others sadly familiar with the place. Every now and then a really sick-looking child passes, wearing a hospital mask, or in a wheel-chair, or attached to a drip, or all three. You think the boy with the sling is lucky that all he has is a broken bone, then you think again — maybe there's more to it. Same with the girl with the swollen, angry eye. The one thing that strikes me with force is the lack of smiles, the worry.

The walls are the colour of strawberry cheesecake, decorated at regular intervals with cartoon murals — *Bugs Life, Bear in the Big Blue House, Never Ending Story* and quite possibly every Disney character ever created. We end up back at X-ray and decide to stay put. Charlie needs to use the toilet. We find a single one. As requested, I stand guard outside the unlocked door. That's when I see Mary, coming through the doors of X-ray, looking around for us.

I wave. She looks relieved to see me. I'm relieved to see her. We hug. Cool outdoors air clings to her like an aura. Fresh and crisp. I try to suck in its energy.

'There's something wrong, Mary,' I say, pulling back and look-ing at her. 'It's, it's . . . ' I can't say it. 'He's an oncologist . . . ' is the best I can do.

'Have they said anything definite?' asks the voice of reason.

'No, but why else would they ask me to bring someone in? It has to be . . .'

'Maybe they just want to talk to you without Charlie there.'

'They wouldn't need to do that if the news was good.'

'Just wait and see, Jenny. Whatever happens, I'm here. OK?'

'Hi, Mary,' chirps a little voice. 'What are you doing here?'

I switch on my happy face.

'I just popped in to say hi,' says Mary.

'Oh. Hi!'

'Hi, Charlie,' she bends down. 'How're you doing?'

'Great.'

'Guess what I brought with me?' She starts to rummage in her bag.

'Wow, cool. Dara's Gameboy. Can I've a go?'

'Of course you can. It's *Scooby Doo*.'

'Cool.'

'Let's go in here,' I suggest. We sit in the waiting room. And wait.

The moment I've been simultaneously waiting for and dreading arrives. Dr Grace, the man who messed up my life once, is here to do it again. He gets a run down on how to play *Scooby Doo and the Phantom Knight*, then tells Charlie that he wants a 'little chat' with me. Mary asks Charlie to show her how to play. At the door, I look back at Charlie. Head down, thumbs busy. I won't be missed.

9

He takes me to *that* room, offers me a chair, then sits himself.

'How are you?' he asks, leaning forward.

'Fine, thank you.'

'Did you get a cup of tea?'

'Yes, thanks.'

'Good. I'm sorry to have held you up, Jenny, but we have a preliminary result.'

Three things tell me it's not good. One: he's asked me to sit. Two: the gravity of his face. Three: the forced calm in his voice. I hold my breath. And wait.

'Charlie is anaemic.' *Anaemic — that's not so bad.* 'Have you any idea why that might be?' he asks.

I remember what Dr Finnegan said. 'He hasn't been eating?'

'Yes, it could be that. Though it's quite marked. Is there anything else you can think of?'

I try to come up with something. 'A person might be anaemic if they'd been bleeding, but Charlie hasn't. I don't know.'

'His White Cell Count is quite low, too.'

It's the way he says it.

'What are you trying to tell me, Simon? Please, just come out with it. Tell me what it is.'

'Jenny . . . There are a few things it could be. Charlie has anaemia, a low White Cell Count, combined with tiredness, pallor and loss of appetite.'

I think of Great, who had all those symptoms. *But it couldn't be. Not Charlie. Not again.*

'It's not leukaemia, Simon. Please tell me it's not leukaemia,' I whisper, afraid to look up. *Because I couldn't take it.*

It's very quiet.

I have to look up. I have to know.

He seems to make a point of looking straight into my eyes. 'I am considering a few things, Jenny. But, in fairness, leukaemia is one of them.'

'Oh God.' I bite the back of my hand. Hard.

'We need to do a bone marrow biopsy. That will give us a clearer picture . . . Do you know what a bone marrow biopsy is?'

'Yes. My grandmother died of leukaemia.' I feel heat at the back of my throat, my eyes beginning to smart.

He wheels his chair closer.

'We don't have a diagnosis yet, Jenny. I know this is a very worrying time for you, but try not to think the worst, not yet.'

How can you say that?

'Children are *very* sensitive to their parents. You mightn't realise it, but Charlie can read you better than anyone. You don't want him to pick up on your anxieties.'

I fill my lungs as though to give me strength. The ribs in my back expand and rise.

'With children, we do bone marrow biopsies under anaesthetic because they can be quite sore. But they are a very straightforward

72

procedure and over quickly. Charlie would need to be fasting for six hours, though, so he would need to be admitted overnight. I've checked with theatre, and they can fit us in tomorrow.'

Slow down. Slow down. Stop.

'I will need you to sign another consent form to say that you agree to his being admitted and to any tests that are needed,' he says, eyebrows raised.

I nod.

'I'd like to get Charlie up to the ward now and settle him in. He should have something to eat. It's been a long day. I need to confirm some things with the ward and get that consent form. That will give you time to arrange things.'

I sit, unable to move, the ground whipped from under me. I'm afraid to get down from the chair in case I fall.

He must have said something because he is looking at me as though waiting for an answer.

'Can I just sit here for a few minutes?'

'Yes, of course. Take all the time you need. Do you want me to stay?'

'No. Thank you. I'll be fine. I just need a few seconds before going back to Charlie.'

'Would you like me to get a nurse?'

'No. No, thanks.'

'I'll be back soon.' He puts his hand on my shoulder on the way out.

I don't like asking Mary to get the few things we need but I can't think of another option. Or anyone else to help. As it turns out, she offers before I can ask. Not only that, but she reminds me that we have a dog that needs to be fed and walked, remembers to ask for the key to the apartment, and thinks of getting Charlie's pillow so he'll sleep. She even knows to ask where things are. My brain has shut down, my thoughts telescoped into Charlie and *this*.

Mary goes, reminding me that she has her mobile if I think of anything else we need. Simon returns and walks us to the ward, carrying Ernie, the soldiers and colouring paraphernalia. I think it strange for a doctor to volunteer his arms in such a way but take him up on the offer — my hands are full, carrying a very tired little boy. We were offered a wheelchair but No Thank You. The man who tried to stop his daughter baby-sitting for us is being suspiciously kind. He knows something.

It looms ahead of us, at the end of a long, long corridor. 'St Anne's' says a big yellow placard. 'Haematology/Oncology/Bone Marrow Transplant' declares another. *Does everyone need to know?* There are so many signs I can't take them all in. 'Please Switch Off Mobile Phones Now.' 'Parents Only Allowed On Ward.' 'Please Keep Door Closed.' 'Door Locked after 7.30pm.' We all go quiet. Even Charlie.

We are about fifty yards away when one of the doors opens out. A lone girl emerges, quiet and slow. From her height, I reckon she must be in her early teens. Otherwise, she is ageless — hair gone, replaced by a vague coconut-type fuzz of frosted light brown. Her head is big in comparison with her body, which seems shrunken behind a pale pink dressing gown. Her ankles are thin. I think of Belsen, Auschwitz. She glides forward, head erect, nothing moving apart from her legs, which make their way slowly, silently, along the marmoleum floor. Her feet are on the ground, yet she seems to float. Like a ghost. The full force of what's happening to us hits me and I feel like throwing up. I turn away but realise that the girl might think I can't look at her. So I face her, smiling as if to say, 'Hello, you look perfectly normal and aren't scaring me to death.' She smiles back. She is only a child. How can she be so

74

calm, so serene, so confident? How can she not be panicking? She waves at Charlie.

'Why doesn't she have hair, Mum?' he asks at the top of his voice as she passes by. He says it innocently, happily, as if it's a choice she's made.

'I'll tell you later,' I whisper, which of course I won't.

'But I want to know now.'

'Later, Charlie.'

Simon holds the door open.

The place is cheerful. Too cheerful. Primary colours everywhere, bright posters with happy faces, natural light pouring in through skylights and large windows. Everything looks clean, fresh, modern. A woman in green is coming towards us, smiling.

I want to grab Charlie and run.

'You must be Jenny.' She smiles hello.

How much does she know? More than me?

'And you must be Charlie.' My son gets a bigger smile, a special smile reserved for small sick people. 'I've been waiting for you. My name is Anne. See.' She shows him a smiley badge pinned to the pocket of her uniform. 'How are you?'

Suddenly shy, Charlie hides his face in my chest.

She smiles at me.

'I'll leave you to settle in,' says Simon. 'I'll call in to see you before I leave. He ruffles Charlie's hair. All right, son?'

An innocent expression. But it makes me catch my breath.

'He is a wonderful doctor,' sighs Anne, as we watch his back disappear down the corridor and into a room marked Oncologist. 'He's in charge here, but you'd never know it. We're a team. I'm the sister, which officially means I'm the nurse in charge but, as I say, we're a team. If you need anything at all while you're here, please, just ask. And I'll introduce you to everybody else . . . '

'Thanks, Anne. But we should be gone tomorrow.'

'Yes, yes, of course. Maybe I'll show you Charlie's bed now? He looks tired. And must be hungry. You're just in time for tea, Charlie.' Her voice starts to sing. 'Do you like chips?'

He doesn't answer.

'He hasn't been eating much, but he might try a few chips,' I say, passing a large metal trolley with meals on it. The smell of hospital food reminds me of Great and I feel sick again.

We get to a room with five or six beds. Children and parents go about their business. I don't take in detail, apart from three things — a little bald boy scooting around in a yellow and orange toy car, a tube coming out of his nose; an empty cot; and a teenage boy sitting cross-legged on his bed, wearing a grey tracksuit with hooded top. The hood is up. I can guess why. His head is down. He is concentrating, I see, on a Gameboy. Though sitting very still, he is a mass of small movements. His head nods. My eyes follow a black wire coming from out of his hood to a yellow Discman on his bed. His jaw is chewing – gum, I guess. But it's his thumbs that are busiest, pumping aggressively at the little black console. The boy's bed is covered with cards, the mattress scattered with an enormous collection of CDs, computer games and music magazines. He looks up and nods hello.

I smile.

'That boy has a Gameboy, Mum. Can we go over?'

'No, Charlie,' I say, taking his hand and moving him on. He keeps looking backwards. We reach Charlie's bed. It looks bleak and empty by comparison. He whines.

'I want a bed like the boy with the Gameboy.'

'We won't be here long enough for that, Charlie.'

'Where's everyone's hair?' he asks, quieter this time.

Why did they have to put us on this ward? Couldn't they have put us somewhere else? It's just one night.

'Their hair has fallen out, Charlie, because of the medicine they're taking. But it will grow back,' explains Anne and I am grateful for her natural honesty. There is something strangely reassuring about it.

'Everyone looks sick, Mama.'

'They are sick, Charlie. That's why they're in hospital,' I say, trying to mirror Anne's honesty.

'But I'm not sick, sure I'm not?'

Anne answers for me. 'Charlie, the doctors need to check out why you haven't been feeling well.' She sits on the bed with us and explains in children's terms what a bone marrow biopsy is. Charlie has no difficulty in grasping the concept of taking a teeny tiny piece of bone so the doctors can have a look at it under a microscope. He asks are his bones like the ones Sausage eats. After about twenty minutes of chat — some of it strangely funny — Anne leaves us alone.

I take Charlie's runners off, ready to put them in the otherwise empty locker. I bang them together to make the lights flash. I make a wish.

10

Mary arrives, globe in one hand, my case in the other.

I have to laugh. 'Where did you dig that out?' Mine is a case for moving house rather than going on holiday, purchased when I was moving in with Great.

'It was either that or a bin bag,' she says with a smirk. 'I'm thinking of your image here.'

'Are we going on holidays?' asks Charlie.

She smiles at him. 'No, handsome. I've just got a few of your things in here.' She heaves it up on the bed, pops open the clasps and starts taking things out.

'You're like Mary Poppins,' he says.

'Practically perfect in every way?' she asks, smiling.

'No. The way you're pulling stuff out of the bag. Mary Poppins does that. Have you got a lamp in there, too?'

We laugh. Charlie kneels up beside the case, holding on to its edge, peering inside. 'What have you got?' he asks.

Pillow, PJs, Barney, slippers, towel, hair gel, toothbrush, even the cool J-Lo tracksuit I was intimidated into buying by the yoga babes. It's for sleeping in, she tells me.

'You're something else,' I say.

'How's Sausage?' asks Charlie, grabbing Barney and squeezing him to his chest.

'He's fine, Charlie. Dara, his dad and the boys are taking him for a walk on Killiney Hill. They had a fight about who'd feed him.'

'Who won?'

'Dara.'

'Yes!' He punches the air and says, 'Go, Dara.'

'Alfie got to hold his lead.'

'You don't need a lead on Killiney Hill, Mary,' says Charlie who's been given a mood boost by the sight of his favourite books, jigsaws and trucks.

'I'll let them know, Charlie,' she says. 'Come here. Have you got a hug for Mary?'

'I'm not a hug man.'

'Is that right?' She smiles a been-there-done-that smile, then hands me a packet.

'What's this?'

'Earplugs. You'll need them. I'll never forget the noise when Dara had his tonsils out. Drips bleeping, kids crying, other parents snoring. Anyway, with these little babies, you won't hear a thing.' She has put on the voice of M, from the James Bond movies. 'Now, go and get your mattress before all the good ones are gone.'

'What mattress?'

'A mattress for you to sleep on. Where did you think you were going to sleep?'

'Hadn't got that far.'

'Beside your son on the floor. Here, I'll get one for you. They leave them outside in the corridor usually. I'll get some blankets in the linen cupboard. They're a bit tight with them so I'll sneak as many as I can. You'd be surprised how cold it gets at night.'

'Mary, they don't strike me as being like that at all. They seem very nice so far.'

'You're lucky — there were a few cows looking after Dara.'

Charlie's head pops up. 'Were there cows looking after Dara when he was in hospital?'

'No, sweetie.' I ruffle his hair.

'Now, let's see.' Mary continues. 'Is there anything else you should know? Food. Yes. Well, you'll have to look after yourself on that front. Pop down to the canteen and collect something and bring it back to the ward. There's usually a sitting room where parents can eat. There's a kitchen too with a microwave, fridge and water dispenser. But some of the staff don't like you going in helping yourself. Others don't mind. Play it by ear.'

'Mary, we're only staying a night.'

'Oh yeah,' she says, laughing. 'Got a bit carried away. OK, look, I'd better go. I'll call in, in the morning. Are you sure you're all right? Nothing else I can do?'

'No. You've been great. Thanks. And you don't have to come in tomorrow. You've loads to do.'

'It's fine. The boys'll be at school. Free agent.'

'School! I'd better tell them.'

'Want me to?'

'God, Mary, that'd be great. I'm not supposed to use the mobile. It affects the machines or something.'

'I know, yeah, but everyone does. Anyway I'll tell Ms Ford.'

'Thanks.'

As she leaves, a nurse we haven't seen before walks into the ward and over to the boy in the tracksuit.

'Is that the pig?' asks Charlie.

'What?'

'The pig that was looking after Dara. Is that her?'

'Charlie, shhh. There were no animals looking after Dara. Just people, OK?'

'OK, Mum, but Mary said . . . .'

'Mary was joking. Joking. Now come on — let's get dressed for bed.'

He slides onto the floor and starts to take off his trousers. I watch in amazement.

'Good boy — you're dressing yourself! Wow!'

'Dara does.'

'Does he now?'

'Yeah.' He holds his pyjama bottoms up much too high, then tries to get his leg into them. I'm about to come to the rescue when he falls over.

'You OK?'

'Yeah. Dara does that all the time. He says you're supposed to.'

'I see. Here, I'll hold them — now you step in. Great. Now sit up here and we'll take off your top.'

He holds his arms up. I pull the jumper over his head.

'Ow. What was that?' he asks.

'Gosh. We must have given each other a little shock.'

'Why?'

'It's static electricity. It's probably because the air is so dry in here.'

I pat down his hair, which is still sticking straight up. His skin looks like it's never seen sunlight and his ribs stick out. I hurry to put on his comfy white cotton top with long sleeves. Then give him a hug.

The noise of four televisions competing with each other keeps Charlie awake till close to nine, when exhaustion finally takes over. I'm getting my own 'bed' ready, dragging the mattress into position, when Simon appears, so quietly I don't realise he's there for a moment.

'Oh, hi,' I say, leaning the mattress against the side of the bed and rubbing my hands together.

'Did he settle in all right?' he asks, looking down at Charlie.

'Once he got his toys and pillow.'

'And you? How are you?' He sits on the wooden arm of the standard-issue wipe-clean armchair beside Charlie's bed. I take it as a signal and lean my bum against the end of the bed.

'I'm fine.'

'It's not an easy time.'

'No.'

'You know, Jenny, family can be a great support at times like this.'

I say nothing.

'Do you have family?'

'We're not close.'

'Anyone outside your friend . . .?'

'Mary?' I think of Jack but Jack is my boss. I'm not going to ask him for help. 'Not really, no.'

'Neighbours?'

I think of Louis. 'No.'

'No one at work?' He looks at me. *Does he know? Has he remembered?*

'No.'

He looks down for a moment, hand holding his chin.

'Charlie and I, we can look after ourselves. We're fine.'

'Well, if you need it, you'll find a lot of support here.'

'I'm hoping we won't need it.'

He produces that understanding smile of his that, admittedly, does seem genuine.

'Jenny.' He loses the smile. 'We'll get a preliminary result while Charlie is in theatre tomorrow. Depending on what we find, I need your permission to insert a permanent cannula into a vein in Charlie's chest. It's a better way of giving medication than the Freddies in the peripheral veins which don't last and need to be replaced constantly. We can also take blood samples this way. It's much more convenient for the children.'

Every time he talks, he seems more and more certain of what he will find. If Charlie comes back with something in his chest, I will know.

'You're tired.' He stands. 'Try to get some rest. I'll bring a consent form in the morning and talk to Charlie about the Freddie.' He has one last look at him. 'He's a lovely little fellow,' he says.

'Yeah,' is my hoarse reply.

The mattress is a child's one — wafer thin and about the same dimensions. My feet overshoot it. I try pushing my rolled-up-blanket-for-a-pillow (Charlie wants both the hospital one and his own) to the uppermost part but it doesn't make much difference. I try sticking my bum out and pointing my legs forward to the opposite corner. A bit better. Temporarily. I turn over and adopt the foetal position. My direct line of vision is the underside of Charlie's bed. My eyes adjust in time to see a spider of tarantulan proportions crawling determinedly towards me. I spring up, impressively silent, and kick the mattress out of the way. I imagine it crawling into my ear or hair while asleep (if I ever do) and think about killing it. I wimp out. All I can do is stand watching it continue on its hairy way under the next bed towards a sleeping mother with an open mouth. Which is another problem. She snores. Loudly. The earplugs take the edge off but now that I've become familiar with the timing of the honks I'm waiting for them, expecting each one, like drips from a tap.

Three things stop me from lying back down — arachnophobia, snoring and stiffness. I stretch, then circle my shoulders, let my head fall forward and then backwards. A walk might help. I feel around for my glasses, check that Charlie is sleeping soundly, take out the earplugs (they're pushing against the walls of my ears), slide my feet into my slippers and pad out of the room and along the corridor. My head is muzzy, my eyelids heavy. From somewhere near the nurses' station comes the sound of inconsolable, unformed crying. It must be a very young baby. *Surely, you can't get cancer that early? But why else would it be on an oncology ward? And what are they doing to make it cry so?* I walk in the opposite direction and try to blank it from my mind. What I need to do is remember. Everything I've ever heard, read or written about leukaemia. I think about Great and how it affected her. But I can't do it. Not in a detached way. Not without getting upset. Too tired.

Leukaemia. Leukaemia. What about that woman from Dun Laoghaire I interviewed whose daughter had it? Elaine. How brave she was. How well she seemed to cope. It came on quickly — I remember that. Her daughter . . . what was her name again? God, I can't remember . . . was fine, then started getting infections one after the other. Charlie hasn't had that. But her blood count was like Charlie's — everything down. And she had Acute Lymphoblastic Leukaemia. She was doing very well on chemo. If she stayed in remission for five years, she'd have pretty much the all clear. I wonder how she's doing. Please God . . . .

I hear the sound of vomiting and rush back to the room. It's not Charlie. It's not anyone in this room. My boy is in a happy, restful sleep. I move a strand of hair back from his face. My little angel. I wander over to the window, pull back the blind with my finger and peep out at the clear night sky. The full moon looks like a poppadum. The stars wink at it — 'come on, don't hang there all night, taking everything so seriously; come play.'

I try to think of anything else it could possibly be — something with the same symptoms, something that needs a quick course of antibiotics and a little rest. I look over at my baby. Back to the sky. I ask whoever's up there why he should have to go through this. If he does. But in my heart I know he does. Why else would I be standing here in a cancer ward at three in the morning looking up at the stars?

11

A man stands in front of you, a shotgun pointed at your stomach. He squeezes the trigger. You get the full blast and reel back against the wall. Your insides are blown out. You cannot breathe. An animal wails. But it's not an animal — it's you. You slide down along the wall to the ground, wrapping your arms around your legs and pressing your face into your thighs, hands over the back of your head, eyes shut. You can't speak, react, move. Just crouch there like a fool.

That is what it is like to be told that your child has leukaemia. At least, that is what it's like for me.

I don't know what Simon is saying. And Mary might as well not be here. I ignore them and cling, like a spider at the edge of a drain, to the possibility that it's a mistake. *Preliminary results, he said — not final, not definite. Charlie has anaemia, nothing more. The other thing is a mistake. It has to be. What are the chances that the two people you love most in the world will get the same disease? Tiny. Minuscule. Impossible. It just couldn't happen.*

Why won't he shut up? Can't he see I'm not listening? Why don't they leave me alone?

He is only four. HE IS ONLY FOUR.

I'm supposed to be next, not Charlie — he has another eighty years. Let this be a mistake. Let him be OK. I'll do anything. Be a better mum. Whatever it takes.

I hear the words 'cure rate'. Eighty to eighty-five per cent. That's-really-good, Mary's face says, eyebrows up, head nodding. She looks stupid. She forgets that I've watched the person who has been my mother all my life being eaten away by this disease. I looked on the positive side then. It didn't work.

I won't go through this again. I won't. It's just not fair.

I should have known something was wrong. Charlie knew. He must have. He was worried. He didn't want to be away from me. The nightmares. He knew. Why didn't I notice sooner? What kind of mother am I?

There will be a cannula in his chest, now — my little man, lying unconscious, oblivious to the cancer cells attacking his bone marrow, suffocating the good cells. I want them to start treatment, now. Now, this minute. Don't wait another second. But what will I tell Charlie? I can't tell him he has leukaemia. He knows what that means.

'I can't tell him,' I say, my head jerking up and swinging in panic from Mary to Simon. 'I can't tell him he has *leukaemia*.'

Mary looks from me to Simon, eyes wide. But he is calm, unruffled.

'Would you find it easier if I told him, Jenny?'

'*No*.' I snap. 'He's *my* son. *My* responsibility. I will tell him. But I can't tell him he has leukaemia. His great-granny died of it. He was mad about her. He'd be terrified. He'd think he was going to die.' I find myself up from the chair now, standing with a hand on either side of my face.

Simon comes over to me, puts an arm loosely behind my back and leads me to a chair. He hands me a plastic cup of water. My hands are shaking so much, I'm afraid it will spill, so I reach forward and put it on his desk. I knock it over. Water spills out and spreads across his desk. I watch it, fascinated, hypnotised by it. Mary starts to mop it up with hankies. Her rapid movements bring me to attention. I look at Simon. 'I can't tell him,' I say.

'Jenny, I am very sorry about Charlie's great-grandmother. But, in fairness, childhood leukaemia has a significantly better prognosis than adult. You could almost consider them different diseases.'

Is he telling the truth? Please let him be telling the truth.

'In terms of explaining things to Charlie, in my experience, you can be honest with children without frightening them.' He pauses. 'And it is best to be as honest as you can. You would be surprised how sensitive they are to their parents. If you are worried, they will know, and they will worry too. If you're not open with Charlie, he'll hide his feelings from you so as not to upset you further. But he will worry.'

'But he's only four.'

'At that age, instinct is very strong. And you must remember that there is an especially strong bond between you and Charlie because it is just the two of you. You are the most important person in his world. He is highly sensitive to you. There is another issue. If you are not open with him, when he goes back to school — and he will, Jenny — other children will know that he has leukaemia. News travels. Being children, they will say it to him. He needs to be prepared for that.'

'But telling him he has leukaemia would be like telling him he's going to die. That's what he'd think.'

'In fairness, we could explain that his great-granny . . .'

'Great.'

'Sorry?'

'Great. We called her Great. You should know that in case you're ever talking to him about her.'

'Oh, yes, of course, thank you. We could explain that Great had a different type of leukaemia. And that the type of leukaemia that children get is much easier to fix. Then if he is confronted with it, he won't be afraid. He will have an answer for himself and for them. He pauses, then says, 'Would you like me to stay with you while you're telling him — just in case?'

'I don't know . . . Yes . . . maybe . . . I should tell him though. But what if I make a complete mess of it? Look at the state I'm in . . . Do we have to tell him now?'

'No.' Pause. 'Not until you're ready. But he will sense that something is wrong and he will worry, so we can't leave it too long. Maybe this evening, when he has recovered from the anaesthetic. I'll be around.'

His bleep goes off. He fishes it out of his pocket, squints at the number, picks up the phone and dials. 'Simon Grace . . . Thank you. We're on our way,' he says, looking directly at me. He replaces the receiver and smiles when he says, 'Everything went well. Charlie will be coming out of the recovery room in a few minutes. Let's go up to meet him.'

I stand up too quickly and my head spins. I reach forward to the desk to steady myself. I close my eyes in an effort to stop the spinning. I feel an arm around my back.

'Sit back down, for a second, Jenny,' he says. 'Catch your breath.'

'I'm fine. I'll be OK.' *I have to be there when Charlie opens his eyes*. But I've started crying. *Of all times . . . .*

'Sit for a moment. You got up too quickly. Wait for your blood pressure to adjust. Sit.'

I give in. *Only for a second.*

A hankie appears. I blow hard, shove it in my pocket then wipe each eye with the heel of a hand. I take a deep breath and hold it, pushing myself up using the arms of the chair.

'Let's go.'

Simon leads the way. He asks us to wait at the entrance to the theatre. He continues on and disappears. Mary takes hold of my hand and gives it a squeeze. I'm embarrassed because mine is soggy. She smiles. I notice for the first time that I'm not the only one who has been crying. Poor Mary — she's doing her best.

'Thanks, Mary,' I say. 'Sorry for being such a wimp.'

'You're not a wimp. You're great. I don't know what I'd do . . .' Her voice breaks and tears collect just above her lower lids. 'Oh, for God's sake,' she says crossly and then we laugh. 'It'll be OK,' she says, though we both know it won't.

The end of a trolley appears out from one of the doors. Two people in scrub gear arrive with the rest of it. *Is it Charlie?* The emergence of Simon answers my question. To hell with the rules. I walk towards my son. No one stops me.

As I get closer, I see that he is lying on his side, behind bars to stop him falling out. I'd forgotten how small they are at four, still babies. He looks so delicate, like a pale little Lladro. *Was he really that thin and weak-looking when he went in?*

He opens his eyes.

'Mama,' he cries and stretches out his arms to me through the bars.

I go up to him, a smile plastered on my face. 'It's OK, Charlie, I'm here.' I rub his cheek. The backs of my eyes burn. *Don't cry.*

'We're just going to transfer him to the ward now, Mrs Dempsey,' one of the people in scrubs says. I catch Mary's eye and throw mine to heaven. She gives me a be-patient-they're-only-doing-their-job look, which I ignore. So much for modern Ireland! *Mrs!* They start to move the trolley and I walk beside Charlie's head, holding his hand. It feels tiny in mine.

We reach the ward and Anne leads us to Charlie's bed which she has pumped up so that it is level with the trolley.

'Mama, I'm cold.'

'OK, sweetie. We'll sort you out now. The doctors are going to put you back in your own bed, OK?' I have to let go of his hand as they lift his light, limp body across. Some paper from the trolley comes with him. There is dried blood and orange staining on it. A small blanket covers Charlie's thin hospital gown. It wasn't designed with heat in mind. Charlie is shaking all over. His teeth are chattering. He moans when they land him gently on the bed.

I hurry to his locker and yank it open, grabbing the little quilt he had when he was a baby. One of his runners falls out and disappears under the bed. The light flashes as it bounces along the floor. I cover Charlie with the quilt, up to his neck. I cover that with the blankets on his bed. I brush back his hair and kiss his forehead. When I become aware of my surroundings again, Anne is taking Charlie's chart back from the theatre staff. They talk to her for a moment, then wheel away the trolley. Simon and Mary are talking quietly together. She is holding the runner. I take it from her, and try to be polite when I ask them both to leave. I want to be alone with Charlie for a while. Simon looks like he's about to say something but changes his mind. Mary hugs me goodbye and says she'll call in later. I tell her I'd prefer if she didn't. She looks hurt.

'I'm sorry, Mary. You've been really wonderful. But I just need to sort this out in my head. OK?'

She smiles. 'See you tomorrow,' she says.

We hug again. 'Thank you, Mary. Thank you.'

When they're gone, I pull the bedside chair back into position, dragging it level with Charlie's face. I sit on the arm to get closer to him. I say nothing, just rub his cheek with the back of my finger.

'I was scared, Mama. I couldn't find you,' he whines, weakly.

'I'm sorry, sweetheart. I'm here now.' I put my face right up to his, noses touching, staring into his eyes. We do that sometimes.

Little tears well up in his eyes. 'I thought I was in a spaceship.' *All those bright lights, equipment, uniforms.* 'I thought they were taking me away.'

'Well, you're here now, with me. See?' I rub his nose with mine.

'Want to go home.'

I sit up. 'Charlie, pet, you've had a test. You need to rest for a while, OK?'

'I'll rest at home. Come on, Mama. Let's go.'

He makes an attempt to get up but is groggy and falls back on the pillow.

'Mama,' he panics. 'What's this?' He touches the bandage on his chest.

'It's the new Freddie, sweetheart.'

'Don't want a Freddie. Don't like Freddies.' His face has gone from sad to mad.

'This one's different, Charlie. This one's cool. D'you want me to show you?'

'No. I don't want a Freddie. I want to go home.' He starts to cry. Turns his head away. Oh, that frown. I've always loved it. I want to reach out and flatten it with my finger.

'D'you remember what Simon was telling you? This is a *proper* Freddie,' I try to explain. 'The ones in your arm aren't the real thing. Just copy cats. This is a *real* Freddie.'

'Don't care. Don't want it.'

'You can even take blood tests from him and it doesn't hurt at all.'

Nothing.

'It's true. Ask any of the other kids.'

In an effort to distract him, I get up and pull back the curtain that separates us from the next bed. I smile at the mum. She is an overweight (which might explain the snoring) woman, in her thirties, I'd say, with a soft, gentle face and a short, dated hair cut. She is sitting beside her son's bed, holding a drink up to him.

'Ribena's your favourite, Seán,' she says, with an accent that sounds like it might be from the west. Seán, who I guess must be around five, doesn't look convinced. She sees me and smiles back, rolling her eyes. 'Come on, Seán,' she says, pointing the straw in the direction of his lips.

Not wanting to intrude, I walk back to Charlie and sit again. I look around at what will be our new home. It's busier than I've seen it. A young girl — couldn't be more than nineteen — walks slowly back into the ward, keeping pace with her little boy. He looks about two — an age when children normally tear around. Pale and frail like the rest of them, he is in no hurry. His mother is carrying a wash bag and towel. The teenage boy, whose name turns out to be Mark, is having a lesson from some kind of teacher. No privacy here. They are doing the history of Rome. A baby who was admitted during the night is being wheeled off somewhere in a hospital buggy. A nurse holds his file, his mum pushes the buggy and his father follows quietly, his face strained and tight.

We're not the only ones, then.

'I'm hot,' says Charlie.

'OK, sweetie. I pull off the blankets, leaving the baby quilt. 'How's that?'

'OK.'

'*Mark* has a Freddie, you know,' I say.

'Who's Mark?' he asks, grumpily.

'The big boy.'

'The boy with the Gameboy?'

'Yeah.'

He lets it sink in. '*Mark* has a Freddie?'

'Yes,' I say, having seen a nurse attach it to a drip at six in the morning. 'Maybe he'll show it to us later. Now, you have a little rest.'

Anne brings Charlie 7Up and toast. She sits with us for a while and I'm glad of her easy company.

12

Rain is coming down in shafts, like strands of uncooked spaghetti, slamming into concrete, merging into muddy puddles. It's day but it's dark, the fluorescent lights of the ward reminding me of school in wintertime. Mark's TV, tuned to Sky News, zooms in on a woman knee-deep in tea-coloured water. Reports of flooding have newscasters excited. 'More to come' warn the tickertape words that slow train across the bottom of the screen. The woman wades into her home, anxious to show the world the full extent of the damage — everything that couldn't be moved upstairs, ruined.

Swap, I think miserably, turning back to the window and the rain.

I am staring out, mind numb, hardly noticing, hardly caring, when Simon arrives at the bed. He has someone with him. A 'play therapist', apparently. Siobhán is her name. Her role, to 'use play to keep children's spirits up, to explain things and to distract them from difficult procedures'. *How many of those are we going to need?*

She has a Playstation, which makes her an instant hit with Charlie. And she does seem genuinely friendly and helpful. I'll like her, provisionally. They settle into a game. Then Simon needs 'a chat', expanding Siobhán's job description to include 'occupying mums while doctors break more bad news'. Despite my cynicism, I could do with the so-called chat. There is so much I need to know — what's going to happen? How soon can they start? What treatments are planned? What can I do? I worry that I won't take it all in. It's a problem I'm having.

I do all right. The bad news, I pretty much knew already. Charlie has Acute Lymphoblastic Leukaemia, the most common cancer in children, more common in boys. Cells called lymphoblasts are attacking his bone marrow, suffocating his blood cells, snuffing them out, making him prone to anaemia, infections and bleeding. There is good news. The cure rate is high. And more bad news. The drugs are strong. They will depress his immune system, making him even more prone to infections, anaemia and bleeding. Regular blood tests will keep tabs on the cell levels and they will intervene with transfusions or antibiotics to prevent 'events'. The medicine might make Charlie sick but anti-nausea treatments are 'very advanced' now and should prevent this from happening. His hair will fall out. Soon.

Treatment will begin once Charlie has had a blood transfusion. He will get a short, sharp blast of chemotherapy — their version of short, sharp being ten to fourteen days. They hope this will induce remission. If we are lucky and it does, Charlie will start an 'intensification phase' — intense chemo for months. He will be on oral therapy at home and will need to come back to hospital, once a week, for chemo and blood tests. Then it's on to 'maintenance therapy', which he can have at home. *One step at a time*, I think. *Remission. Just aim for remission. The rest can wait.*

Simon's approach is straightforward. This is what we have to do — let's do it. No pity, no condescension. And I am grateful for that. I tell myself I'm not afraid. Of the treatments. Of blood transfusions and their risks. Of coping alone, especially at home. Of the looks Charlie will get when his hair falls out. Of the fact that despite everything they do, every horrible treatment I let them inflict, my little boy might die anyway. Like his great-grandmother. Who was my real mother.

'Do all parents feel as useless?' I ask him.

He leans forward, puts his hand on mine and looks at me directly. 'Jenny, believe me, you will be anything but useless.' He lets go, sits back. 'I have worked on this ward for ten years and the one thing I've learnt is that parents, especially mothers, are amazing. *Amazing.*' He shakes his head, as though in wonder. 'The last thing you could call parents is useless. They have, without doubt,' (he nods) 'the most important role on the ward. *Seriously,*' he says when he sees the disbelief on my face. 'It is parents who make sure that medicine gets taken, that spirits are kept high, that boredom is kept at bay, that difficult tests go ahead smoothly. You couldn't pay parents for what they do. In fairness, nurses don't have the time to give the constant attention that parents give — the jumping up and down to get drinks, the constant monitoring of the child. Sure, just think of how lonely each child would be without their parents in hospital. It just wouldn't work. The whole system would break down. Jenny, while you are in here, expect to be overworked, but,' he says, shaking his head again, 'don't expect to be useless.'

Fine speech. He has convinced me. 'Sounds like I'll be busy,' I say, my spirits beginning to lift.

'You won't be alone, Jenny. You will have me; Anne; Siobhán; the other nurses; Pat, the psychologist; Mairead, the social worker;

Sheila, the nurse specialist . . .' He must see my what's-that face because he adds, 'She explains all about the disease, the tests, results . . . .'

'You seem to have everything,' I say. *Except a guarantee.*

We get back to Charlie. He and Siobhán are playing doctor. Barney is the patient, Charlie the doctor, complete with stethoscope.

'It's good practice for when I'm big,' he says. And I wonder how many times I have taken for granted simple statements like that. 'When I'm big' claps in the air now, a cheeky, thunderous presumption.

'Barney has a Freddie, Mum, see? I'm just going to give him a rejection.' He squirts air into a Freddie that has been bandaged to Barney's chest. He carries out the task with the efficiency of some-one who has been at this for a good ten minutes.

'How is Barney?' Simon asks Little Doc.

'Not great,' says Charlie, frowning, one doctor to another.

'Oh?'

'He's really tired. His tummy is always full and his leg is sore.'

'Like you,' says Simon, sitting on the bed beside him.

'Yeah. But Barney's sick.'

Simon looks at me, then at Charlie.

Oh my God. He's going to tell him. Wait. Not yet.

'Charlie, do you know the way your leg has been sore?'

'What?' he asks, disconnecting the syringe from the Freddie. 'That's it,' he says.

'Do you know the way your leg has been sore?' Simon repeats, patiently.

Charlie is too busy screwing Freddie's cap back on to listen.

I squat down in front of him, put my hand on the knee of his good leg. 'Charlie,' I say gently. 'Listen to Simon, love.'

He looks at Simon.

'You know the way your leg has been sore, Charlie?'

'Yeah.'

'And the way you've been tired a lot?'

'Yeah.'

Normally I'd tell Charlie to say 'yes' not 'yeah'.

'Well, there's a reason for that,' Simon continues.

Charlie looks at him.

'You are sick, Charlie . . . .'

'Am I?' He looks at me for confirmation.

I nod.

'I *knew* I was.'

'You have leukaemia,' Simon continues.

Full attention now. Big, big eyes. 'Like Great?' He looks at me in panic.

I shake my head. No, it says. No, definitely not.

Simon continues, 'You have a different kind of leukaemia from Great. A kind that children get.'

'Will I go to heaven too?'

Jesus! 'No, sweetheart,' I say, ignoring Simon. I don't care what I'm supposed to say or not say, I'm not going to have him thinking he's on the way out. I get up and sit on Charlie's other side, then lift him onto my lap so that he is facing Simon. His feet touch the doctor's legs. Simon cups them in his hands. 'Charlie,' he says. 'The leukaemia that Great had is not at all like what you have. The leukaemia you have is much easier to fix.'

Charlie looks up at me.

I nod yes, yes, absolutely.

Simon continues. 'What's happening is that in your body . . . Siobhán, do you have that book? Thanks. Here, I'll show you in this book . . . .' He hooches up closer to my son, lifting his little feet, settling them on his lap. 'Look, see these guys,' he says, pointing. 'They're goodies. They're called cells. Now, you need them in your body to stay healthy and full of energy. And see these guys — these are bad cells. And they have moved into your bones and are taking up all the space that the good guys need, squashing them. Now, what we need to do is get rid of the . . . .' The intonation of his voice goes up; he pauses, hoping that Charlie will finish.

'Bad guys,' says Charlie, as though it's a game.

'Exactly.'

'Will we shoot them?'

'Yes. But not with guns.'

'Oh,' my son says, disappointed.

'With medicine.'

'Oh,' even more deflated.

'We will give you medicine into your Freddie. And that will kill the bad guys.'

'Oh.' Nothing exciting about that.

'You and your mum are going to stay here for a few days with Siobhán and myself and Anne and the other kids. Have you met the other kids?'

He doesn't answer.

'Well, you will and it will be good because kids like to be friends with other kids, don't they?'

No answer.

'And after a while you can go home to your own friends.'

'When?' Charlie asks.

'Two weeks, maybe.'

'Is that before Christmas?'

'Long before Christmas,' the doctor reassures him.

'What about Sausage?'

Simon looks at me, his face a question.

'His dog . . . I presume they're not allowed?'

'Not in the hospital, no. But there won't be a problem when Charlie goes home, as long as . . . Sausage . . . is wormed.'

Simon spends a lot of time explaining to Charlie about leukaemia. He says that nothing we did or didn't do caused it. 'Being bold doesn't make you get leukaemia or not tidying your room, or anything like that. It just happens. And it happens to lots of kids, not just you.' He explains about the blood transfusion and chemotherapy. Charlie believes everything he is told, unquestioningly, the way he believes in Santa Claus. He assumes he will get better.

13

We are in the jungle with the armadillos and David Attenborough. I am sitting on my favourite armchair (I'm being sarcastic). Charlie is lying flat on his stomach, propped up on his elbows, knees bent, legs swinging. One armadillo climbs up on the other. *Oh, oh.*

'What's he doing, Mum?'

'Ah, must be giving him a piggyback. Actually, Charlie, it's time for bed, sweetheart.'

'Aw, can we just finish this programme? It's good. Will you give me a piggyback later? You haven't given me one in ages.'

'Ah, OK, maybe tomorrow.' And I try to think of something else to say to distract him from the screen. But it's OK — the armadillo's getting off. *That was quick.*

'. . . coitus complete, the armadillo . . .'

I let him watch it to the end, seeing as how I'm hooked anyway, then it really is time for bed. Not easy to convince Charlie, though, when the ward around him is buzzing with noise and activity. Visitors in and out. Voices raised. The shock of sudden laughter.

Televisions blaring. Nurses rattling around with drips and medicine trolleys. I start the bedtime routine: collecting his cuddly toys and putting them at the foot of his bed, slotting his crayons back into their increasingly tatty cardboard box, tidying away as many games as will fit into the second drawer of his wooden locker. I pull down the white, blackout blinds and turn off the TV. I do this every night so that he learns to associate it with settling down. I go about it quietly, determinedly, sending a signal without fuss. It does tend to work. Now, in the bottom part of his locker, a cupboard with two shelves, I find a change of pyjamas and his baby quilt. I look for his toothbrush and a fresh facecloth in the top drawer.

'Is this your book?' Charlie asks.

'Hmm?' I say, rummaging for toothpaste.

'I'm just drawing circles on the front.'

'OK,' I say, not looking up.

'These are shells.'

I'm curious and look to see what he's at. Happily drawing on the cover of . . . *Oh God!* . . . The *Children With Cancer* booklet that Siobhán left.

'I'm tracing this guy,' he says.

Fear grips me. It's like he's tempting fate, playing with cancer. I want to snatch it from him. But don't want to overreact. Frighten him.

'Good boy,' I manage. 'Now let's go wash your teeth and face.' I slowly slip it from his hand, then fling it to the end of the bed, afraid to touch it myself.

He sleeps. I eye the booklet, lying discarded. I pick it up, put it down. Sit looking at the cover. A family on a beach — Mum, Dad, two kids. Nice neat nuclear family. *Which one has cancer?* I pick the booklet up as though it is carcinogenic, hold it with the tips of my fingers. *Paper and ink — that's all it is*. I open it. *It's supposed to help. Read it.* I start, in a detached, this-has-nothing-to-do-with-me way. And some of it doesn't. Statements like 'two heads are better than one', 'work together' and 'share the burden' are designed for the family on the cover. There is a small section for people like me — single parents. The main message to us is 'try not to make your sick child the centre of your world'. I'm sure it makes sense. One problem though — my child was already the centre of my world before we even got here. Now, he is my entire world. I have shut down everything outside him. I called Jack, told him not to expect his health page. Not this week, not ever. He asked why. And I told him, though I had promised myself I wouldn't. But I owed him honesty. So that's what he got. His words didn't form sentences. Kept repeating 'little Charlie' and 'poor little fella'. Kept asking what he could do. I said, give the health page to someone else. But he didn't seem to grasp that I was quitting for good. Kept saying, 'Take as much time as you want.'

I snapped, 'It's not a cold, Jack.'

He went quiet.

I was sorry but all I could say was, 'Look, I've got to go.'

To the principal of Charlie's school I divulged, out of necessity, that Charlie was 'sick'. I even admitted that he was in hospital. But instead of leukaemia, I spoke about blood tests and investigations. She bombarded me with sympathy and questions, promised to get a mass said, reassured me that the children would make cards and visit when Charlie's up to it. I told her I'd let her know, then warned Mary not to give her any details.

They have started treatment, most of which is given through Freddie. Charlie 'tolerates it well' but *hates* the one medicine he has to swallow, and is very fussy about how he takes it. I have to give it to him. In a syringe. Millilitre by millilitre. Our system is as follows: Start with a crisp — not just any crisp, a Snax. This gives him a taste in his mouth. Then squirt in one millilitre, then a drink (7Up only acceptable, with ice and a straw, in his Mickey Mouse cup), followed immediately by another Snax. This is repeated until five millilitres are taken. The routine averages fifteen minutes and has to be followed with a sweet. Mint Toffo. They tell us not to spoil our children. This, I assume, breaks that rule. But at least he takes it and that, surely, is the point? Or so I tell myself, while wondering how quickly he'd down it for someone who wouldn't tolerate nonsense.

He is tired and rests without being asked to — a sure sign of a sick child. It may be the treatment or the disease or the lack of fresh air, exercise or appetite. It may be all of the above. But, overall, his form is good, thanks mainly to the fact that he has 'made friends with' his superhero, Mark. Together, usually sitting on Mark's bed, they battle alien invaders and enemy star ships. They fight each other on game boards too. Ludo and draughts have been taught to him by Mark, who has also been known to let him win, more often than occasionally.

'I've a brother who's four, you know,' says Mark, shaking the dice, one day.

'Do you?' Charlie looks up at him in wonder. He could have said 'blah, blah, blah' and it would still be amazing to Charlie.

'Yeah. His name is James.'

'Where is he?'

'At home.'

'Why doesn't he come to see you?'

'We don't live near the hospital, Charlie,' he says, counting to six and shaking the dice again.

'Where do you live?'

'Donegal.'

'Where?'

'It's a place that's very far away.'

'Where's your mum? Why isn't she here with you?'

'She has to mind my brothers but she comes to see me once a week.'

'Do you have a dad?'

'Yeah.'

'Does *he* come?'

'No,' says Mark, looking out the window.

'Is he too busy?'

'Yeah, that's it — too busy.'

'My dad is too busy, too. Dads work too hard, don't they?'

'Yeah.'

And maybe that's why Mark decides to adopt Charlie as his little protégé, spending time with him, teaching him games, playing with him, listening to him, explaining things, calming him down when he's worried about something. He misses his own brothers. Or is lonely. Or feels a bond because both of them have missing fathers. Or both are sick and in here. Or maybe he just likes Charlie. Whatever reason, it is a gift, giving Charlie something to focus on, something to get excited about, something to distract him from treatments, tests and the boredom of hospital.

After three days, I'm beginning to know my way around. The bendy straws and ice machine (both lifesavers) are in the kitchen, the ice machine 'kindly donated' by a boy and his family. I look at the plaque and wonder if he made it, survived. And whether Charlie and I will be donating something in the future. And if so, what?

I know the pattern to Charlie's medication, hospital meals,

doctors' rounds. I know the television schedules and how to put on a video. I know who wears what uniform. I know where X-ray is, the playroom, the nurses' station, and I know what time the play volunteers arrive. I know the nurses by name. I know all the children in our room and their parents. I've discovered that hospital food lives down to its reputation and have found ways round it — Mary, primarily, who brings an endless supply of healthy options. I keep thanking her and reassuring her that we'll be home in two weeks. I have become used to the expression, 'Don't worry about it.' She has even wormed the dog.

I know where the chapel is. And I've remembered how to pray.

I learn to bath Charlie without wetting his Freddie. I learn how to keep him entertained and upbeat (the Playstation when he's feeling down or bored; videos when he's tired; good old-fashioned stories when he needs attention or a cuddle; and playing with other kids when he's feeling energetic). I learn what upsets him and try to avoid these situations or distract him when they're happening.

I've developed habits like banging his runners together to make them light up every night before going to, well, mattress. I've taken to brushing his teeth with great precision because he is going to make it, and he'll need them. I run my hands through his hair rather than brush it — an attempt to delay the inevitable. I devour Cornflakes in the kitchen during the night, when hunger pangs finally remind me to eat. I forget to taste.

Máiréad, the social worker, and Mary keep trying to get me to take 'little breaks', but really I don't want them. I do give in, once, and go across the road to the shopping centre where I stock up on multivitamins and echinacea, which I hope they will let me give Charlie. Then I buy a bag of his favourite foods, follow up with Lego, colouring books and jigsaws. I wander into a computer shop but don't know where to start. The sales assistant could pass as a Gallagher brother and makes as much sense. I do manage to work out that a Gameboy Advance is 'the business'. So I get one.

'Eh, you'll need games too', he says in a 'wakey-wakey' tone. *Lilo and Stitch* and *Monsters, Inc.* are duly selected.

'And batteries,' he reminds me.

I'm cleaned out but at least I'm 'the best mum in the world'. I feed Charlie yoghurt while he plays on the Gameboy.

'Get me out of here, get me out of here. Quick, Mum — I'm going to get kilt.' He is shoving the Gameboy at me.

'Charlie, you know I don't know how to play.'

'Quick, Mum. Oh, my God, here they come.'

'Here, give it to me . . . Where does he have to go?'

'Through the door, quick, through the door.' Charlie's hopping up and down on the bed beside me.

'Sit down, sit down. Is this how you move him?'

'Yeah, yeah, quick or I'll get kilt. I've only one life left.'

'OK, there. Saved you.'

'Phew,' he says, taking it back.

If only saving lives *were* that easy.

14

I'm not superstitious. But . . . some people are bad luck. Simon Grace is bad luck. Once wasn't enough for him to collide with my life and send it into a spin. Twice even. He's going for a record. Sitting opposite me (always beware the sitting doctor), grim-faced, talking about the results of a blood test, about a chromosome called Philadelphia. Which Charlie has. And which changes everything, altering the treatment course, hammering his prognosis. He sits there and tells me that Charlie won't survive without a bone marrow transplant.

I don't understand. What? What is he talking about? What test? I didn't know he was doing a test. It's standard, he says. Maybe, but this is too much to take in. I need him to repeat everything. Say it all again. Try to understand. And then, when I do, I want to lash out. Physically. Verbally. Especially physically. *Why is he doing this to us? And why now? Did he know sooner? Is he trying to break it in stages as if I'm some kind of fragile flower?* It's like going through the diagnosis all over again. Only, it's not. It's worse. Because I had bent down, gathered my hopes and dreams back up off the floor and started again with the new hand I had been dealt. I had begun to get going again after everything had stopped so suddenly, so frighteningly. But, now. *Now*, I'm flattened.

They have to find a donor. *Where, though? And will they? How quickly? In time?* It is too much. *Too much.* I don't feel I can cope any more. They roll out the psychologist, then the social worker. But it's a waste of time trying to reassure a catatonic. I am numb, not listening, useless, stupid. They take over, arranging for someone to stay with Charlie and for Mary to take me home for a while. I don't want to leave him but don't want him seeing me like this either. It makes me want to scream. Mary is firm. And I find myself wishing I had a mother like her, a mother who'd care enough to get cross, a mother who'd be here for us, with us now, fussing over Charlie, insisting that we do rosters. Not painting on a plastic smiley face and walking out the door.

Charlie, glued to the hospital Playstation, hardly notices when I kiss him goodbye. 'Bye, Charlie,' I say, clearly, to make sure it is registering with him that I'm leaving, that he won't be looking for me as soon as the game is over.

'Bye, Mum,' he says, without taking his eyes off the screen.

The tears start as soon as I turn to go. This time, I don't try to stop them. This time, I don't care. Out in the fresh air, I squint in the glare of natural light and wrap my jacket around me. My head is fuzzy, heavy. Head down, eyes closed as much as I can without bumping into something, I walk with Mary to the car park. I could fall asleep walking. The hum of traffic and the movement of cars passing remind me that people are getting on with their lives — no worries, going to work, school, whatever. Carrying on. While we are stuck. Not moving. Left behind. We find Mary's car and I don't notice the journey home.

I don't want her to come in. And she seems to understand that I need to be alone. To think, to sleep. I let myself in. It's silent, still, cold. Sausage hasn't come to the door. I find him, nose to the window, staring out as though waiting for us to return. The first time he has ever acted as a watchdog. He turns to look at me, then away again in a sulk. I call him. He ignores me. I go over and sit beside him. 'I'm sorry, Sausage.' I rub his head and pull him to me. 'Charlie's sick,' I say and the tears come again. He looks up at me with sad chocolate eyes, then around the room as if to say, 'Where is he?' He whimpers. I lift him onto my lap and cuddle him. Feel his heart. Ka thunk. Ka thunk. I carry him over to the couch. He snuggles into me. I am forgiven.

I'm home. But it doesn't feel like home. Just a shell. Hollow, empty, the life gone out of it. Everything is as we left it, four days ago. Charlie's half-eaten melon slice on the worktop, his pyjamas in a heap on the floor, the 'proper shoes' he refuses to wear, clean and tidy on the shoe rack inside the door. Everything the same. But not. My body jerks involuntarily and I let loose a wail that has been building inside me for days. The dog jumps up and disappears. I wrap my arms across my stomach, fold forward, then rock. Another quieter wail, then unchecked crying, the crying of a Palestinian father on the evening news holding a blackened child's shoe in the air. Nobody to hear, now. No need to hide.

Sausage's wet nose nudges my hand.

'What will we do?' I wail into his head. He tilts it back and looks at me upside down. He's a dog. *Why are you asking a dog? What's a dog going to do? Oh, God. Why didn't I stay with Dave? What was I thinking? I wasn't. I was a fool to let him go. If he'd stayed, he'd be here now with his chest to lean in to, his arms to wrap around me, his shoulders to soak with tears. He'd hold me. And be strong. And I wouldn't have to be. For five minutes. Just for five minutes.*

I have to get up or I'll drown the dog. Already his hairs are sticking to my hands, coming off on them. I wash my hands first, then my face. The water is cold. I reach for the kitchen paper and knock over a framed photo of Charlie. It smacks off the worktop. A bad omen. I snatch it up. I hold it between wet hands and gaze at my little boy. He beams back at me. Sparkling, dancing eyes. Gleaming rows of white teeth. Tanned and freckled summer skin. His hair highlighted by the sun. The picture breathes life, health. And I'm off again. '*Stop*,' I say crossly and out loud. Sausage looks up from the tiled floor where he is sitting, leaning against my leg.

'*Right.*' I grab a black plastic bag and tear around, dumping stuff in — the melon peel, gone-off milk, bread, fruit, the contents of the pedal bin and the one in the bathroom. I leave it outside Louis's door with a quickly scribbled note. Louis, being Louis, will need instructions. Sausage, constantly at my heels, follows me back into the apartment. I turn on the heat and climb into my unmade bed. The bed I've taken for granted, the pillow and quilt suddenly soft, luxurious, heavenly. The dog, ever the opportunist, steals up and snuggles in beside me. I let him and fall asleep, my hand resting on his warm tummy.

When the alarm goes off, I drag myself out of a near coma. Eyes still closed, I feel my way to the shower. I turn it on full blast. Water pounds onto my scalp, massaging it. I let my head drop forward, directing the cascade onto the back of my neck. After a few minutes, I move the blast onto my shoulders. It hardly touches the tension that has built up there. I let my head fall back now. Something clicks inside, loosens. Water smashes against the tight elastic bands that have formed on my forehead. I circle my shoulders, turn my neck from side to side, bend down with straight legs to retrieve the soap. Stretching, loosening.

'You can only do your best,' I hear Great whisper, or is it just the sound of the shower? You can only do your best — the phrase she repeated time and again to a little girl who spent too much time trying to impress a mother who didn't notice. 'You can only do your best, Jen.'

I stay in the shower until it starts to go cold. Rub myself briskly with a towel as though it will help me to come back to life. Oddly, I want to wear something very specific — something soft, cosy, pale pink. I've nothing to fit that description so opt for an old baby-blue, baggy jumper and stretchy denim hipsters. They hang from my body and I tell myself to start eating again. I blast my hair with the dryer, now in a rush to get back. I promised Charlie I'd make it before dark. *Where is Mary?* I call her to say I'll take a taxi. She won't hear of it and arrives in minutes.

'Have you eaten?' she asks.

I don't answer, grab my satchel.

'We're going nowhere until you eat.' Firm.

'Mary, we have to go. I promised Charlie I'd be back before dark.'

'Have you eaten today?'

'No.'

'Right, I'm ringing the hospital to see if he's OK. If he is, then you can eat. It will take fifteen minutes.'

She makes the call.

'He's fine. Asleep,' she tells me.

'Are you sure?'

'Yes.'

'Was he OK? Did he have a good afternoon?'

'Great. Now, *sit*,' she orders.

Both Sausage and I obey.

She laughs at the dog. 'Good boy,' she says.

113

She marches over to the fridge, opens it and starts to check dates on what's left of the food. She pulls out cheese and a tomato, cutting the edges off the cheese. She checks the freezer and pulls out a frozen sliced pan.

'Have you a toasted-sandwich maker?'

'In the press beside the fridge.'

She yanks it out, gets busy. Puts on the kettle.

'No milk,' I say.

'Right, juice then. It's better anyway.' She pours OJ, leaves it on the counter, feeds the dog and puts out fresh water for him. I can't believe I had forgotten Sausage. Mary puts my breakfast, lunch and dinner in front of me. A glass of juice for each of us.

'Eat.'

I have no appetite but know not to argue. Silently, I bite into it. Tomato burns my tongue and I fan my mouth.

'Sorry,' she says.

'Doesn't matter.'

'How are you?'

'Fine.'

'Did you sleep?'

'Yeah.'

'You look a bit better.'

Silence.

'Jenny, I've been thinking. I've been thinking about this all afternoon. And I want to ask you something. And I hope you don't think I'm being nosy because I'm not. I'm just trying to help. OK?'

'OK.'

'Is Charlie's father alive?'

I look at her. 'Why?'

'Well, if he is, don't you think he should know?'

I shrug, look down, push back a cuticle.

'OK, look at it another way. If you are going to need donors, don't you think Charlie's father might be an option?'

My head is throbbing. I don't need this right now. I hold my head between my hands. 'It's not that easy. You don't understand. It's not as easy as going up to a person and saying, "Your son is in trouble."'

'Why not?'

'Because I don't know who he is,' I say, too loudly.

That's stopped her.

'I don't know who he is, OK?' I say more calmly.

'OK.'

'Look. It's not what you think. It's not like there are hundreds of possibilities out there — there aren't. Just two. I'm not a slag, if that's what you're thinking.' I am fighting so hard not to cry. So hard.

'Jenny, I'd never think that,' she says, reaching out for my hand and holding it. 'But if there are only two possibilities, couldn't you approach both?'

'No.'

'Why not?'

'Because one of them is in America getting on with his life and one of them is Charlie's doctor,' I say, finally giving in, admitting it. I don't look at her when I say, 'And he doesn't know that Charlie might be his.'

'His doctor? Who? Simon? Simon Grace? Dr Grace?'

'Yes.' I concentrate on the cheese oozing from the sandwich.

'I don't believe it.'

'Well, it's true,' I say, quietly.

'But what are the chances of that happening?'

'What?'

115

'That you would end up with him as a doctor?'

'I don't know, Mary,' I say with a sigh. 'He's the chief oncologist in Ireland's main cancer centre. Charlie has cancer.'

'And he doesn't know about Charlie?'

'No.'

The pressure in the silence builds. And builds. Until I have to tell her. I can't keep it all in any more. I just can't do everything on my own any more. I need to share with someone.

'Five years ago, I was engaged . . . .'

'To Simon?'

'No, Mary. Can you just listen?'

'Sorry.'

'I was engaged. To a guy called Dave. He's a journalist. We'd met through work and had been going out two years, engaged six months. Everything was planned, organised. We were happy. He was my best friend. I was sent on a work assignment. It was a big international medical conference in Brussels. Simon Grace was the only Irish speaker and I had to interview him. I arranged with the pharmaceutical company sponsoring the post-conference meal to sit next to him to do the interview. But he didn't show. I had to file the piece that night. I needed to talk to him. I rang his room. He answered but only because he thought it was his wife. He said he couldn't do the interview. I didn't ask why. I didn't care. All I could think about was my stupid deadline. I lied. Told him I'd lose my job. I was desperate. I wouldn't let it go. I was so ambitious. So *stupid*. He said he'd give me five minutes in his room . . . .'

One of Mary's eyebrows — the cynical one — springs up.

'It wasn't like that. He wasn't . . . .'

'I know, I'm sorry . . . go on.'

'As soon as I saw him, I knew something was wrong. He looked terrible. Red eyes, hair all over the place, so pale. He was

116

trying to put up a front, pretend everything was fine. He offered me a drink and poured one before I could even answer. His hand was shaking so much the bottle kept hitting the glass. I felt awkward. All I could do was pretend I didn't notice. I started the interview. We didn't get far. It was about cancer — well, it would be, he's an oncologist. About five questions in, he couldn't go on. That's when he told me his wife had been diagnosed with lung cancer, just before he'd left for the conference. He'd wanted to drop out. She'd insisted he didn't. He'd managed to hold everything together until he'd done his presentation. Then, back in his room, he broke down. And I walked in on that.'

And suddenly I'm in that room. Just me and him. I take the drink from his hand. Sit him down on the neat hotel bed, stay beside him, stay close. Listen as he talks. Hold him when he shakes. There is little hope, he says. The cancer is an aggressive one. She doesn't know how aggressive. She doesn't know what it will do to her. How quickly it will win. I don't know how to calm him. He is crying now. And I am desperate. Maybe if I wipe his tears, kiss them away like you do with a child. Tiny kisses. Salty kisses. It's working. He is stopping. But his mouth is on mine now and the kisses are no longer gentle and calm but hungry and searching. They rear up like waves on a stormy sea, engulfing us. And I know he's losing himself in them, forgetting. And I am relieved. It feels right. It feels like the right thing to do, to keep going, let the storm follow its course, like all storms do. Leaving us spent, washed up. And surrounded by the debris of his sudden embarrassment, guilt, shame. His distress. He springs off the bed as if it's on fire, drags his clothes on, almost tripping over when his leg gets caught in his trousers. He strides around the room, head down, running his hand through his hair, telling me, over and over, as I hurry to dress, that he loves his wife. He loves

Alison. He's saying he's sorry, but that doesn't hide the fact that he can't get me out of the room quickly enough. Which makes me angry, as if I am some sort of slut who deliberately set out to seduce him. It's so weird. Like a nightmare. Happening so suddenly, so fast that I find myself back in my own room wondering if it really happened.

'So many times, I've told myself I should have walked out of that room as soon as I saw him,' I continue. 'So many times.'

'Did you tell Dave?'

'No. Not at first. I thought about it. I thought about nothing else. But I didn't want to risk what we had. It had nothing to do with my life or our relationship or future. I didn't even know Simon Grace, apart from the fact that he was an oncologist who could give a good talk and had a sick wife. I didn't want to make more of it than it was . . . But I became pregnant. And I couldn't be sure . . . I had to tell Dave.'

'So he broke off the engagement?'

'No, Mary, he didn't. He was gutted. Really, really hurt. The way he looked at me. As if he couldn't believe what I'd done. We seemed so separate, suddenly. I knew then that what had happened *did* affect our relationship. Because it affected the way he looked at me. He took leave, went away for two weeks. And I thought it was over. But he came back, told me he'd forgiven me, and that he wanted us to pick things up and carry on, the way we were before, as if nothing had happened. I should have been happy, I *should* have been relieved. Everything back to normal. But it wasn't. I couldn't stop thinking, "What if the baby isn't Dave's?" I couldn't get it out of my head. I couldn't expect him to take it on. It wouldn't work. He'd always be wondering, thinking . . . So I ended it.'

'But what if he was the father?'

I shrug.

'*Jenny*. Couldn't you have done a paternity test?'

'Yes, of course I could. But think about it. We do the test. What then? If Dave's the father, I marry him; if not, forget it?'

'But you loved him, Jen.'

'Yes.'

'And he forgave you.'

'He said he did. But did he really, Mary?'

'I don't know, Jenny — he sounded like he did, or at least wanted to.'

'It's easy to pretend everything will be happy ever after. But it's not easy to make it that way. There would always be the uncertainty. It would start as a niggle, then grow to resentment. I didn't want to go there. I'd ruined it. It was never going to be the same.'

'How pregnant were you, then?'

'Ten weeks.'

'And you never thought of . . . ?'

'God, no, *never*.'

'So Dave just accepted that it was over? That was it.'

'No. He tried to convince me it didn't matter. But the more he tried, the more sure I became that it would be a mistake. In the end, he got tired of trying or tired of me. Probably both. I don't know. He left. A post came up in the States with a sister newspaper. He applied and got it.'

'But didn't you miss him? You were together for two years. You were going to get married.'

'Yes, I missed him. I missed him so much I almost went after him. But I got sense.'

'You got sense,' she repeats, incredulously.

'It's hard to explain, Mary. But I knew that if he came back, I'd just start feeling the same again. Like we were making a mistake.

119

What was the point in telling him I missed him if I wasn't going to go through with it? I'd messed him up enough.'

'So what happened with Simon?'

'Nothing. I never told him.'

'Why not?'

'Think about it. I wasn't sure the baby was his. We didn't know each other. His wife had cancer.'

'It must be awkward for you, now. I must be stupid. I never noticed any tension between you.'

'He doesn't remember me.'

'What? He ruined your life and he doesn't even have the decency to remember you?'

'He didn't ruin it.'

'OK, maybe he didn't but you spent a night together . . . .'

'More like a mad, crazy tussle that was over in minutes.'

'Still . . . .'

'Mary, it was five years ago. He was in a state — you should have seen him — he'd been drinking. I don't think he was even *seeing* clearly . . . .'

'Still, I . . . .'

'Look. He loved his wife — it's not something he'd want to remember. And there are other reasons, practical reasons — I've thought about it — he knew me as Jennifer Grey, the name I use for the paper, my hair is different now, I wear glasses, I'm a mother with a completely different attitude to life from the one I had then. I dress differently. I am actually a different person.'

'I've always meant to ask, why do you write under a false name?'

'To dissociate myself from my politician mother. I didn't want people linking us in any way. I wanted my views to be seen as impartial and my own. Grey was Great's surname. It was nice to be able to call myself after the person I saw as my real mother.'

'I see.'

'Of course another reason he hasn't recognised me is that he *is* a man.'

'Ah, you see, now you've convinced me,' she says, smiling. 'You should have started with that argument. *That* I understand.'

She has managed to wangle a half-smile out of me. We are silent, now. 'Actually,' I suddenly remember. 'He did think I looked familiar once but I talked him out of it.'

'So, you ended up bringing Charlie up on your own.'

'And sometimes, like now, I think I made the biggest mistake of my life. Charlie could have had a father, maybe not his real father, but a father . . . Do you know how much he'd *love* that?' I'm starting to get upset. 'Do you know how often he mentions his father? Especially since he started school. And what if Dave is Charlie's father and I've stopped them being together?'

'But maybe you could tell him now? Tell him what's happened. I'm sure he'd help.'

'I sent him away, Mary. How can I expect him to come running back as soon as we get into trouble?'

'Maybe you don't have a choice.'

'All this is happening so fast. I'm being backed into a corner, forced to face this. And I don't want to. I'm not ready, not yet. I'm going to lose it, go mad. I really feel I'm about to go mad.'

She takes both my hands in hers and looks at me. 'You won't, Jen. You are strong. Just look at how you have coped so far. You've been terrific. And you will be fine. Just one step at a time, OK?'

'That's the only way I can do it, Mary. I just have to try, myself, first. Maybe I will be a match and I won't have to tell anyone. Not Dave, not Simon. I just want to keep things as they are. Get through this. Get on with it.'

'And I'm here for you — you know that, don't you?' She squeezes my hands.

'Yes, Mary, I know. And thank you.'

We hug.

'Everything will work out,' she says. 'I know it will.'

'Yeah.'

'Anyway, come on — we'd better go.'

Sausage wants to come with us. He whimpers from the other side of the door as I lock it. I walk wearily down the corridor.

15

On our way back, my mobile rings. I panic that something is wrong with Charlie. But it's the school. Looking for an update. I keep it brief and vague. It rings again. Jack.

'Can I do anything?' he asks.

'I think I'm OK, Jack, thanks.'

'Are visitors allowed?'

'Only a small number.'

'Are you getting many?'

'Not really, no. I haven't told anyone outside you and a friend.'

'Oh,' he says, then is quiet for a second. 'Could I come in, d'you think?'

'Maybe in a day or two, Jack. Today isn't good.'

'D'you want me to come in at all?'

'No, yes, I mean, yes, of course — that would be fine, really.'

We pass a woman in a dark, wintry coat, hunched over an ancient, black penny-farthing bicycle, her flat, rubber-soled shoes and thick calves circling slowly as though she's going up a hill. The road is flat. She is old. Strapped onto the back carrier of her bicycle, as though it's a joke, is a white jumbo box of Special K. For a second, I think I'm imagining her. I blink but she doesn't turn into a skinny woman in red swimming togs.

He has asked me something.

'Sorry?'

'Is there anything I could bring in?'

'No. No, thanks, Jack.'

'Can I do anything?'

'No, I'm fine, honestly.'

'What about the Net? Do you want me to look anything up?'

'Gosh. Yes. How did you think of that? There is something. Could you do a Google search on the Philadelphia Chromosome?'

'The what?'

'The Philadelphia Chromosome. Philadelphia, as in the city. Chromosome as in genes.'

'Grand, yeah, OK.' He doesn't ask what it is though I know he hasn't a clue. 'When do you want it?'

'Always the deadline, Jack.' I smile.

'You know me.'

'There's no rush. Whenever. Or would that stress you out?' I can't believe I'm slagging him. What's wrong with me?

'I'll call in a day or two and bring it with me. Would that do?'

'That'd be great. I'm hanging up now, Jack — we're at the hospital.'

'Right then. You take care.'

Take care — now there's a new one for Jack.

I switch off the phone.

Charlie is still asleep. There is no one with him. Siobhán, playing with Seán at the next bed, excuses herself and comes over.

'I stayed with him until he fell asleep, Jenny. I decided to make myself useful' — she indicates Seán with a quick eye movement

— 'while keeping an eye on him.'

'Thanks, Siobhán.'

'How did it go?' she asks.

'Good, thanks . . . How was he?'

'Grand. He played on the Playstation for a while then wanted to lie down.'

'He wasn't sore or anything?'

'No, just tired.'

'And he got all his treatments?'

'Yes. They were IV and he slept through them.'

I bend over him and kiss his pale cheek. No tan, now, just a few stubborn freckles.

'Simon was around . . . .'

I look up, then straighten. 'Did he say anything?'

'He'll be in his office for a while if you want to talk.'

'I'll stay with Charlie if you like,' Mary offers.

'I'll head off,' says Siobhán. 'I'll just say goodbye to Seán. I'll see you tomorrow.'

'Thanks, Siobhán,' I say. 'Mary, you go. You've probably loads to do.'

'It can wait,' she says.

'But Phil. The kids. You're in here all the time.'

'I was with them all afternoon. And I'll head back when you've finished.'

'Are you sure you don't mind?'

'Sure. Now, go on.'

'Won't be long.'

'Take your time.'

I knock on his door and wait. Nothing. I am about to leave when it opens. He looks tired. *Too much time in here.*

'Jenny, hello. Come in, come in.'

125

'You sure you're not busy?'

'No, no. Not at all. Sit down.' He pulls out a chair. 'I wanted to talk to you.'

Oh God.

He waits until I've settled. It doesn't take long.

'That was a bit of a knock this morning.'

'Yes.'

'It's not the kind of news I like giving.'

'No.'

'And you seemed to be coping so well.'

I shrug. 'Yeah, well, there you go. Not your fault.' *What is he trying to do — start me off again?*

'How are you now?'

'Fine.'

'How did this afternoon go?'

'What, going home?'

'Yes.'

'Good.'

'Did you get some rest?'

'Yes.'

'Good, good. You need to keep your strength up.' He seems to realise that I've no intention of talking about how I am. He changes tack. 'We have some results back.'

My stomach lurches. *More results.*

'They're good, Jenny. Charlie is responding to treatment.'

'But I thought you said he wouldn't.'

'I'm sorry — I mustn't have explained myself properly. In the *long term*, the original treatment course will not be adequate. Charlie will need a bone marrow transplant. But the *current* treatment is to induce remission. And so far, that is going according to plan.'

I nod, afraid to say anything that will change our luck.

'Is there anything you would like to ask about the bone marrow transplant? We haven't discussed it.'

My mind is bursting with questions. And I'm sorry I haven't written them down. I know I'll forget something.

'How soon can we start looking for a donor?'

'Straightaway. But it might take a while to find one.'

'How long?'

'It varies. It could be months.'

'Does that give us enough time?'

'Yes, it should.'

Should?

'Do you think we *will* find a match?'

'I would be very hopeful. We have two ways of searching. Immediate family and through a register of donors.'

'Which is the most successful?'

'It depends, Jenny. The best matches are usually found among siblings. Charlie has no brothers or sisters?'

'No. Only me.'

'And his father?' he asks, his voice softening.

'Yes,' I say, avoiding eye contact. Everything has speeded up again. Taken off without me.

Silence.

'I'm sorry. It was insensitive to ask.'

'What about grandparents?' I ask, looking up.

'In fairness, it would be unlikely for them to be a good match. But, of course, we can try, if they are willing.'

Suddenly I wish I had a great big brood of children. A family of Waltons lining up with their sleeves rolled up. I remember reading about a high-powered business exec who had a baby with the sole purpose of finding a match for her ill daughter. The little girl died anyway.

God, what will I do?

'I'll get to work on the register, then?'

'Yes. Of course. And you can do whatever test you need to do to me — right now, if you like.'

'It's a simple blood test for tissue typing. We can set it up for the morning if that suits you.'

'I'm going nowhere . . . How long do the results take?'

'Two to three weeks.'

'And you'll let me know as soon as you get them?'

'Of course. I know how anxious you must be. But please, try not to get your hopes up too much. We rarely have success with the first person we try. This may take a while, Jenny. Maybe you would like to talk to Pat.'

The psychologist.

'Do you mind if I think about that?'

'No. Not at all. We are all here if you need us.'

I've taken in enough. I'm conscious of Mary waiting outside and start to make moves to go.

'Jenny?'

'Yes,' I say looking up from bending to get my bag.

'Would you mind if I told Debra? She thinks she's baby-sitting Thursday night.'

'Oh God, I'd forgotten. Debbie. The yoga. I'm sorry. Of course — tell her, please. Or maybe I should.'

'I'll talk to her tonight. She'll probably be a bit sensitive. Her mother . . . .'

'Yes, yes of course. Poor Deb . . . .'

'One more thing, Jenny? I don't think we need tell Charlie about the bone marrow transplant until closer to the time. Better to concentrate on getting through the initial chemotherapy and home. There are a lot of ups and downs associated with looking for a match. I think we can protect him from that.'

'Fine. Whatever you think.'

'And he is doing remarkably well. If he keeps responding like he is, I would hope to have him home in less than two weeks.'

'That's great.' *But frightening. Home. Alone. No support. No advice. No Simon. What if he gets an infection? What if he bleeds and bleeds and I can't stop it? What if . . .? Stop. They won't let him home till he's ready. But what if he is ready but then gets sick again?*

I look at him now and wonder what he's been saying. He smiles and stands. I follow suit. He walks from the other side of the desk and puts his hand on my shoulder. 'Things will get easier. This is the worst time.'

Charlie and I stay up late, sitting side by side on the bed, eating popcorn, watching *Stuart Little 2*, and pretending that everything is normal.

I watch him examine Charlie. *Is it unfair to keep him from knowing that he might be touching his own son, feeling his breath, listening to his bright chatter? No, because Charlie may not be his. And even if he is, Simon mightn't want to know about it. Just leave it, Jenny.* I watch him now and remember what Mary said about him being the first doctor she has seen who 'doesn't just dive in and poke around'. She is right. He does not rush, instead chats with Charlie, asking about his Gameboy, genuinely interested, not pretending to care. When he does get down to business, he is sensitive to the fact that Charlie knows the routine now and wants to lead the way, pulling up his top without being asked, coughing when the stethoscope rests on his chest, volunteering to stick out his tongue and say, 'aaah'. And because he is allowed the freedom to do this, it's a game, not a chore. They are like a two-man production company putting on a performance. And I know that Charlie trusts Simon. As do I. Why wouldn't I? He approaches everything with a quiet confidence that makes you feel as if all's being taken care of, nothing forgotten, overlooked.

He washes his hands now, using his elbow to dispense the pink medicated liquid soap from its container. Round and round his hands move over each other — good hands with thin, straight fingers and short, clean nails. He gives them three quick shakes, holds the paper roll with a wrist and yanks off a section with the other hand. You would know he was a doctor just by the way he washes his hands. He does it unconsciously, not taking his eyes off Charlie who continues to fill him in on his favourite Playstation characters, Crash Bash and Crash Bandicoot.

'They had nothing like that when I was a boy,' Simon says.

'When were you a boy?'

He smiles. 'A long time ago.'

'When the dinosaurs were?'

He laughs and looks at me, still smiling. 'Not quite that far back, Charlie.'

'When Jesus was born?'

'A bit later than that.'

'The same time as Mum?'

'Well, I don't know if it was *that* far back,' he jokes, winking at me.

'Yeah, she's *ancient*.'

Simon laughs.

'Thanks, Charlie,' I say, smiling.

'So,' says Simon. 'Do you still want to be a doctor, Charlie?'

'No.'

'Why not? I could do with a good helper around here.'

'I don't like hospitals, Simon. I'm going to be a hairdresser.'

'Now, there's an idea,' he says.

Simon pulls back the curtain. I catch sight of a man leaning awkwardly against the doorframe of the ward, arms folded, looking down at his shoes. A little pile of bags circles his feet. He stands like Jack. He is Jack. He waits for Simon to pass, nods to him, then slowly collects up the bags and walks our way, smiling self-consciously. I know I wasn't enthusiastic about his coming in, but now that he's here, I'm thrilled. A familiar face! I want to hug him, but don't want to embarrass him any more than he already is.

'I'm not staying,' he excuses himself.

'You'd better,' I say.

He seems to relax a little. 'Just brought you in a few bits and pieces,' he says, shoving them under the bed with his foot.

'Sit down. It's *great* to see you.' Upper arm pat. 'I know how you feel about hospitals.'

'Ah, they're all right . . . How's he doing?' he asks, looking at Charlie who has managed to switch on the *Pink Panther* with the remote. We really need to get out of here.

'So far, so good, Jack.'

'Good.'

'How're you doing, Charlie?' asks Jack.

'I can't hear,' he whines.

'Oh, sorry,' says Jack.

'Charlie, don't be rude. You know there are no words in the *Pink Panther*. Jack asked you a question.'

'What?'

'It doesn't matter, Jenny. Let the kid watch the telly.'

'Jack asked you how you are.'

'Fine.'

'Fine, *thanks*, Charlie,' I say.

He ignores me. I roll my eyes.

131

Jack lowers his voice. 'So, what's the story?'

'Well, he seems to be responding to treatment, for the moment. It's one step at a time.'

'I know.'

'Thanks for coming in, Jack. How are things?'

'Sure, grand . . . The page isn't the same though.'

'I hope you're not going to try to persuade me to start writing . . . .'

He looks horrified. 'Can't a man come in to see how you are without being taken up wrong?'

'Sorry.'

'I got you that stuff you wanted on the Philadelphia Chromosome.' He fishes an expandable A4 envelope out of one of the bags and lands it on the bed. 'I couldn't make head nor tail of it.'

'Thanks, Jack. It's all right. I'm used to reading medical jargon.' I pick it up. 'God, there's a lot.'

'I got everything, just in case.'

'Listen, thanks. I'll go over it later.' I put it in the locker so no one sees it. Don't want them thinking I'm checking up on them.

'Got you a few magazines and things,' he says, nodding at the bags.

'Thanks.'

'And a few bits and pieces for the lad. Does he like snakes?'

'He loves snakes. How did you know?'

'He's a boy, isn't he? I got a book on them. It's pretty good. How about spiders?'

'I thought you didn't know a thing about kids?' I say, eyebrows raised.

He looks chuffed.

'You'll have to read them to him though,' I say. 'I've arachnophobia.'

He chuckles. 'God, he really loves the old *Pink Panther*, doesn't he?'

'Takes after his mum.'

'Sure, isn't he lucky then?'

He stays for a half an hour then starts to get itchy. 'So how long will you be in?'

'Not sure — two weeks maybe, if all goes well.'

'Sure, I might call in again, so.'

'That'd be great, Jack. You know, it's great to see a friendly face.'

'Espec an old codger like me?'

'Especially an old codger like you,' I say, smiling.

I walk him to the door. I'd go to the hospital entrance only Charlie won't leave the *Pink Panther*, and I won't leave him. As we are saying goodbye, he surprises me with a hug. A real hug.

'Good luck, now,' he says and hurries off.

16

I sit beside a sleeping boy. The light is dim, the ward quiet. I squint my way through every page of Jack's print-out. Leukaemia. The Philadelphia Chromosome. Bone marrow transplant. I take in factual medical details, trying to stay equally factual myself. No cause, it says. *Not that they know of*, I think. There are case histories from websites, mostly American, set up by parents whose children had leukaemia. Their diaries, open for all to see, chronicle their hopes, battles and ultimate heartbreak as their journeys end in tragedy. Jack has obviously not screened the information or he would never have given me these. Tears blur my vision. I am crying, not for my boy, but for Ben and Shaun and Nadim, who didn't make it, despite their fierce will, despite their undying hope. I do not sleep tonight. I do not try, just sit in the chair beside the bed. I am not going to raise my hopes that a donor will solve our problems. It didn't for the children who moved so quietly from the Net to heaven.

I'm walking back from the toilet, half-asleep, when I see Simon walking onto the ward. He looks so full of energy, so full of life.

134

He stops when he reaches me.

'Are you all right?' he asks.

'Mm hmm. Just a bit tired.'

'Did you sleep?'

'Off and on.' *Just off.*

'Maybe you might doze later, when Charlie has a rest.'

'Yes, maybe.' I smile. I'm about to walk off when he hands me a small parcel wrapped in *Monsters, Inc.* paper.

'From Debra,' he explains.

'Aw, that's so sweet. She needn't have . . . .'

'Try stopping Debra when she wants to do something.' He smiles.

'But how did she organise a present so quickly?'

'It seems she had seen it in a shop already and had thought of Charlie. She had bought it as a surprise.'

'How did she take the news?'

'Very badly . . . But, in fairness, I had anticipated that.'

'Poor thing.'

'She really wants to see Charlie but the thought of going back into a hospital, especially under the circumstances . . . It's too much for her.'

'Of course. I understand. Tell her we *absolutely* understand and we'll see her when Charlie gets out.'

Simon nods. 'There's a note in there for you, too. She said to make sure you got it. There's something she wants to ask. And I need an answer before leaving this evening or my life won't be worth living.' He smiles again.

'Sounds mysterious.'

'Not really. But I'm sure she'd like to ask you herself. Anyway, I'll leave you to it. I'll be around later.'

'OK, thanks.'

He strides off down the corridor, like he strides everywhere —

always something else to do. He is relaxed and unhurried when talking with you, making you feel that Charlie is his only patient. Then he shoots off, reminding you that he's not. I walk back to the bed, smiling at Mark as I pass, and saying hello to a woman who, I guess, must be his mother, perched on the edge of her chair, looking weary and falsely optimistic. Like the rest of us. Her shy hello has a Donegal lilt.

Charlie is watching his *Monsters, Inc.* video. It's almost at his favourite bit. He doesn't notice when I sit back in the armchair and open my note from Debbie.

Dear Jenny,

I am so, so sorry about Charlie. I can't believe it. I just can't believe this could happen. It's so not fair. But he'll be OK, I know he will. He just has to be.

I want to mind Sausage, Jenny. I know you'll be polite and say no, but I really, really want to. I have to do something. I've thought about it and I've asked Dad. We both think it would be good. You've enough to worry about besides a dog. I would love so much to come in and hug Charlie but I just can't. So I'll hug Sausage instead. And he can cuddle up to me, because I know how much he must be missing his family.

I really hope you say yes.

Lots of love

Debbie

PS Will you read Charlie's card out to him, please?

Debbie doesn't need this. Bad enough being without a mum at fifteen. And Simon spends so much time in the hospital. I sigh and open Charlie's card.

Dear Charlie,

I hope you're feeling OK. It's not easy being in hospital but I know you are being very brave. I can feel it in my bones.

You are lucky to have your mum in there with you. Don't forget to give her plenty of hugs, especially when you are fed up or sore.

I would love to come and see you and it's hard to explain why I can't but I want you to know that I am thinking about you all the time — when I get up in the morning, when I'm eating my Coco Pops, when I'm going to school. I'm thinking about you all the time.

Would you like me to mind Sausage for you while you're in the hospital so he won't be lonely? If you'd like me to, nag your mum a bit, OK?

Here is a baby Sausage to keep you company until you come home. You decide what to call him — he's really cuddly, isn't he? That's the little beans inside him. I love his eyes. I think he looks like Sausage — do you? If you can't think of a name, how about Cocktail because he's like a cocktail sausage and his tail cocks up in the air. See what you think.

Lots and lots of love, and millions of hugs, but no kisses, 'cos I know you don't like them.

Debbie

PS I will come and see you the *minute* you come home.

Can I read this out to Charlie without blubbering?

'What's that, Mum? Is it a present for me?'

I look up.

'Yes, sweetie, it's from Deb. Let's turn off the telly.'

'OK. Can I have the present?'

I hand it to him and he rips at the wrapping. I switch off the television, glad of the relative silence.

'He's just like Sausage!' he exclaims.

'There's a card. Want me to read it?'

'Yeah!' he says, very excited.

I've almost made it to the end when he says, 'Are you crying, Mum?'

'No, sweetie.'

'You look like you're crying. Are you sad?'

'No, Charlie. I'm fine.'

'Do you have a pain in your leg?'

'No, I'm fine, really. I think I might have a sneeze coming on or something. Anyway, what do you think of Cocktail?'

'He's good,' he says matter-of-factly. 'Can Debbie mind Sausage? He's lonely all alone without us, Mum. And Debbie loves him. And he loves Debbie.'

'We'll see.'

'Aaaw, Mu-um.' He bangs his heel onto the bed.

'I'd need to talk to Simon, Charlie. It would be his decision, not mine. He owns Debbie's house. And he mightn't like a dog in it. Especially if he isn't used to dogs, and he isn't.'

'Can you ask him now?'

'Don't nag, Charlie. We'll see Simon later. I'll ask him then.'

'Aaaw.'

'If you keep that up, I won't ask him at all.'

Instant silence.

Charlie calls out a message to Debbie. I scribble it down in my jotter.

Hi Deb,

I hate hospital. The food is soggy. I want to come home. It's a good idea about Sausage. I think Mum will say yes. I have a friend. His name is Mark. He's big. Love, Charlie. Thanks for the present. I think Cocktail is a good name.

I tear the paper out, slip it into the envelope Charlie's card came in, write 'Debbie' and draw a smiley face. When Simon calls, I hand it over.

'I'm under instruction to ask about the dog,' he says, smiling.

'Simon, it's really kind of you to offer, but the last thing you need is a dog.' I see Charlie glaring at me. 'Mary's husband, Phil, is walking and feeding Sausage. He'll be grand, honestly.'

'In fairness, it wouldn't interfere with me at all. Debra has it all planned. The walking, feeding, brushing, whatever needs to be done. Actually, she really wants to do this . . . I think it would be good for her, Jenny, you know, to feel she is helping in some way. I'd encourage it.'

'But a dog in your house. It'd be like having a baby all over again.'

I know immediately I've said the wrong thing because his face has fallen.

'Maybe you're right,' I rush. 'Maybe it would be good for her . . . .'

'Yes, I think it would.'

'But if it isn't working out, Simon, you'll have to tell me, OK?'

'I will,' he says.

'*Yes*,' says Charlie victoriously.

I smile. 'This must be a first.'

'What?'

'Your doctor minding your dog.'

He laughs. 'Don't tell anyone or I'll have a house full of pets.'

'Like *Dr Doolittle*,' says Charlie.

'Now there's a frightening thought.'

'Are you really sure you don't mind?' One last check.

'I. Really. Don't. Mind.' He smiles.

Then he examines a very happy and co-operative Charlie. Everything is going so smoothly. I have finally learnt to relax with Simon, to have a normal conversation without stressing out. He is at the sink now, washing his hands, back to us. A student nurse, whom we haven't met before, arrives by the bed to take Charlie's temperature and blood pressure. She chats away happily for a while then does a double take on me.

'Aren't you Jennifer Grey? You write the health column in the *Irish Express*?'

I say nothing. Just go bright red and will her to keep her voice down.

No such luck.

'I read it every week. It's *brilliant*. I *loved* the one on piles,' she says at the top of her voice.

Sweet God! Make her go away.

I hear something drop on the floor behind me and realise it's too late. I turn slowly, almost afraid to. Simon is picking something up off the floor. He fumbles with it and shoves it quickly into his top pocket. He picks up Charlie's chart. Whatever colour he had has drained not just from his face, but from every visible patch of skin. Eyes fixed on the floor, he clears his throat, mumbles, 'Excuse me', and strides from the room, looking like his life depends on instant disappearance.

'Oh, I didn't see you there, Dr Grace,' she calls after him, loudly, the way she seems to say everything.

So that's it. He knows. I feel suddenly sick, suddenly guilty, strangely relieved.

We don't see him for three days. He sends his registrar, Dr Howard, instead. I catch sight of him, though, flying past the room, head down or dead ahead. Always in the distance, talking with Anne or Siobhán in the nurses' station, or showing other parents into his office. Not ignoring *them*, I see. I don't like Dr Howard, instantly suspicious of a woman who is on her feet all day but wears slingbacks. My problem is, genuinely, with her ratio of efficiency to caring — off balance, markedly light on the caring side. And, yes, if I had to choose between the two, I would pick efficiency. But I don't see why I have to. I didn't before. I want both. Charlie needs both.

Charlie doesn't like her either.

'Where's Simon?' he asks.

Exactly, I think.

By day three, I'm ready to crack. *This is ridiculous. Is he just going to ignore us? Well, he can't. I'm not going to let him. I'm not going to accept anything less than the best for Charlie. And this registrar/model is not the best. How could Simon let what happened five years ago interfere with his job? It's not as if he's a biscuit tester. It's kids' lives we're talking about.*

When Charlie is asleep, I corner Simon working late in his office.

'Simon.'

'Oh . . . Jenny . . . hello.' He stands up from his desk, looking like a sixteen-year-old caught with a dirty mag.

I march in. 'This can't go on.'

141

'Sorry?'

'You are avoiding us.'

He says nothing but has the decency to look awkward.

'And, you know, that would be fine if Charlie wasn't sick and you weren't his doctor.' I talk slowly now in an effort to control my anger. 'But he is sick, very sick, and you have a responsibility. I'm not going to let him be seen repeatedly by your registrar. I'm sorry. I won't have him fobbed off. He is entitled to see a consultant. And if you're not prepared to see him, I'd like to know now, so that I can take him elsewhere . . . .'

'Jenny,' he holds up both hands. 'Slow down.'

'I will not slow down. Charlie has leukaemia, not the common cold. I will not have his health put at risk just because you are feeling guilty about your past. The past is the past. I've put it behind me a long time ago . . . .'

We stand facing each other across his desk. Again he stops me mid-sentence.

'Jenny, I'm sorry. It does seem bad from where you're standing. But, in fairness, I wasn't deliberately avoiding you. I was . . . I was just trying to sort this out in my head. I hadn't come up with a solution. And, though it might not look like it, I have been working as hard as ever on Charlie's health — just not visibly, perhaps.'

'Yes, Simon, but we need visible. Charlie needs visible. I need visible.'

'Yes, I know. I'm sorry.'

'You're looking for a solution to handle this? Here's a solution. Forget about what happened. It was five years ago. It happened. It's over. Both of us have got on with our lives. Charlie is sick now. And he needs you. And, to tell you the truth, he misses you, Simon.'

'I'm sorry. It's not like me. At all. It's just that, well, in fairness, it was a bit of a shock. But, you're right, it was unprofessional . . . .'

'Look, I understand that what happened must have been hard to live with considering . . . your situation . . . and everything . . . .'

'Yes, well . . . .' He starts to fidget. 'Maybe we should go in to Charlie now . . . ' he suggests.

'He's asleep.'

For a moment, he is silent.

'Can we sit down?' he asks.

I sit.

He picks up a folder.

'I was going through Charlie's chart when you came in.'

I am silent. Maybe ever so slightly guilty.

'He is doing very well, Jenny. Better than expected. If he keeps responding like he is, I think he might be home in another week, maybe less.'

'Oh.'

'Have you spoken to Máiréad about how you might handle things?'

'I don't need a social worker, Simon. I am fine financially. I'll be able to look after Charlie full-time so he doesn't have to go back to school.'

'You don't want him to go to school?'

'It's not worth the risk.'

'Of infections?'

'Mainly. But I also don't think it would be good for him to be seen as different either.'

'I can see your point, Jenny, although, in fairness, I would like you to consider that there might be positive aspects to Charlie's returning to school. We won't discuss them now, but it is important to try to keep things as normal as possible for

Charlie, psychologically — for him to have his friends, lead a normal life. We'll talk about it again. How is his form?'

'Good, apart from worrying about where you are.'

He gives an 'I'm-sorry' look.

'Other than that, he's fine. He has made friends, especially with Mark, whom he adores.'

He smiles. I notice he doesn't talk about other patients. Which I appreciate — if I want to tell other parents what's wrong with Charlie, I will. In fact, I have. And they have told me about their children, making me realise that it could be worse. Charlie could have leukaemia *and* kidney failure or leukaemia *and* Down's Syndrome, or leukaemia *and* a broken home.

'I'll call in to Charlie first thing,' says Simon.

'Thanks.' I know I need to say more. 'Look, I'm sorry about earlier. It's just that I was, well, frustrated.'

'I don't blame you. And you were right to clear the air. I'm glad we spoke.' He stands. *That's it then.* We walk up the corridor together. He continues home. I go to Charlie.

17

Simon has become more attentive, appearing at Charlie's bedside two, sometimes three, times a day. I can't tell whether it is because of what happened or because Charlie's health is slipping. My little boy is paler, weaker, quieter. Dark circles, the colour of storm clouds, gather and build in intensity, not just under his eyes, but all round. Even his lids appear grey. Blond hairs attach themselves to clothes, pillowcase, lips. Mine and his. Sometimes, I look at him and see a frail old man rather than a four-year-old boy. I itch to get him home, feed him up and surround him with fresh air, fun and laughter. Debbie, Sausage, Dara. Operation Rosy Cheeks.

In here, I do what I can. I keep the window open until people complain of the cold. I teach him yoga, and laugh when he creates his own positions — gorilla, standing pencil and crocodile. I make up crazy games that get him off the bed — enemy capture and gung-ho ghouls. I ask Mary to bring in little messages from Dara, even if they are two lines and in her writing. When Debbie sends in notes, presents or pictures of Sausage, we reply instantly to keep them coming.

'I'd give you the world if I could,' I tell him one night I'm feeling mellow. We're lying side by side, doing nothing, just resting.

'Would this hospital be in it?' he asks, without looking at me.

'I think maybe they could keep the hospital.'

I've become a big promiser. Already, I've agreed to a party, a Playstation and a 'Walkman like Mark's'. I've also become a deliverer — four large cuddly toys (all from *Sesame Street*), every appropriate game or book in the hospital shop, and all the inappropriate ones too. All it takes is some kind of uncomfortable test, X-ray or scan, particularly when landed on us at the end of a long day. Simon was right — Charlie does know my buttons, which to push, when, and in what order to get what he wants. I let him. Hospital is an alien, scary place. He can behave out of character while he's here. I'll sort it out when we get home.

Despite being bombarded with chemicals, Charlie has had a growth spurt. From the waist down, he could be a clown. The gap between his wide-legged pyjama bottoms and giant cartoon slippers reveals an inch of pale, skinny ankle. The slippers are new, bought by Mary after his original ones had to be decontaminated and 'removed' when he sprayed them with radioactive pee. Special people in special uniforms with special equipment seemed to materialise, to take the slippers away and treat the floor. It was like a scene from *Monsters, Inc.* All I could think was, if a tiny bit of urine is such a danger to mankind, what about the amount of radioactive dye that must have been pumped into Charlie for the test. I joked about it, though. Because what else can you do?

In here, alone with Charlie, and seeing other grandparents coming and going, I find myself thinking about my mother. The sensible part of me feels I should tell her — she *is* family, she should at least *know*. But the stubborn part won't have it. She has never shown any interest in seeing him, meeting him. Yes, I know

I told her I couldn't take her any more, that I had had it, never wanted to see her again, never wanted her to *interfere* again. But that was five years ago. She needn't have taken me so literally. I *am* her only child. She could have made some kind of effort. She could have at least *tried* to find out about Charlie, how he was doing, how we were getting along. But she never did. Well, apart from that time at Great's funeral, but I wasn't myself then, wasn't ready. And she never tried after that. So, fine, let's leave it.

It's only eight, but Charlie is already asleep and I'm tired. I drag my wafer into position and cover it with a sheet. I pull the curtain around, take off my shoes and start to do a few gentle yoga stretches. This is something I've taken to doing every night. It relieves the stiffness that comes with sleeping on the floor, getting no exercise and constant worry. It works. I've stopped having to take painkillers for headaches that had become constant. I have more energy and am less tense. On my hands and knees now on my wafer, I'm in a position called 'cat'. I've just arched my back upward into a feline stretch. Now, I let my lower back dip, sticking my bum in the air. *Loosening up nicely*, I think.

A throat clears. 'Hello,' says a voice I recognise as Simon's.

Jesus!

I drop my bum to my heels, kneel up. My hair covers my face. I flick it back, throw him a smile and an awkward 'Hi!' I clamber to my feet, trying to maintain some sort of composure. All this in three seconds. *Why wasn't I doing that elegant, straight-back twist that brings out the best in everyone?*

'Yoga,' I explain.

'Is that what it was?' he asks, with a *definitely* cheeky smile. 'I'm on call this weekend, so I just thought I'd come by to see how everything is.'

'Fine . . . thanks.' I tuck my hair behind my ear.

He looks more relaxed, younger, dressed casually in a dark sweater, light shirt and chinos, reminding me that he has a life outside the hospital. *A life he'll be heading back to in a few minutes. Friday night. He's probably going out. With a few friends, maybe. Doctors, no doubt — they all stick together. A woman? No. Not Simon. Why not? He's a man. Who then? The gorgeous Dr Howard? Not his type. I wonder, though . . . Stop. Obsessing. About. The. Hospital. Staff. God, I need to get out of here.*

'Well, enjoy yourself,' I say to him.

'I'll try . . . Debra's taking me out to a movie.'

'Really?' I say, thinking it odd. Friday Night with Dad — not your typical teenage activity. 'That's nice.'

'I don't know. She seems to have developed some sort of notion that I'm a case for self-improvement.' He makes a God-help-me face.

'Really?' I smile.

'Yes. It's very odd. Normally, she has no interest in me. Suddenly, she's on some kind of mission. We've already been to see *The Hours* and she's got *Mrs Dalloway* out from the library for me to read.'

'Any good?'

'You don't think I *read* it?'

'She might ask you questions — make sure you have.'

'Oh God,' he groans. 'I hadn't thought of that.'

'So, what are you going to see tonight?'

'*Gangs of New York*. It's "historical".' He puts his fingers in quote marks and pulls a doubtful face.

'It *is* supposed to be good.'

'I'll probably sleep through it.'

Is there anything more attractive than a vulnerable man? I catch myself thinking, then warn myself that I'm spending too

148

much time in this hospital and need to get out before the furniture starts to look attractive.

I'm in the kitchen zapping Six Vegetable Soup for Charlie, one of the few things he'll eat. Mary brings in cartons, which we label and store in the fridge, along with other favourites — cranberry juice, Actimel, salami, olives, pickles, Cheesestrings and salty crackers. I spend a lot of time in here. For practical reasons, yes, but also to escape. There is nobody sick in here. And nobody trying to heal the sick. Just kitchen staff who arrive for their shift, listen to the radio, and serve up 'food' — simple uncomplicated people with simple, uncomplicated lives, or at least that's how it seems to me.

I am alone now, my only company the sun, filtering in through opaque windows, filling the room with ethereal energy. Coldplay are on the radio. 'Let's Go Back to the Start.' I loved that song. Until it took on new meaning. I can't listen to it like I used to any more, unaffected. I imagine people all over the country — teenagers, mums, businessmen, busy doing whatever it is they are doing, half-listening, oblivious to the words. It's about death. Separation. And rewinding the clock. I think of Charlie, of life without Charlie. I let my guard down, *just for a second*, and allow the tears to come.

I have my back turned to the door. I hear someone kick the bottom of it, then push it in. It's either a staff member or a parent who knows their way round, then. It's the quickest way to get in. I run the flat of my hands over my face to clear the tears, then blow my nose. Normally I'd turn and smile because in here you need smiles like air. But now, I just can't. I hear the person open and close a cupboard, then the fridge. They arrive quietly beside me, waiting to use the microwave. Charlie's soup was ready ages ago. I take it out. I can't ignore them any longer. I turn to offer that smile.

I know that face.

'Elaine?'

'Jennifer? Jennifer Grey. How are you? What are you doing here? Another interview?'

As soon as she says it, she seems to realise her mistake. If I were interviewing someone, what would I be doing in the kitchen using the microwave?

'My son is a patient.'

'Oh. I'm sorry.'

'Yeah, well, there you go. Nothing I can do about it, I suppose, except get on with it. How is . . . ?' Damn, I can't remember her daughter's name. Which is terrible considering I did an article about her . . . considering her situation. *Oh God, how could I forget? Jessica? Was it Jessica? I'm sure it was.* But I can't say it — what if it's wrong? '. . . your daughter?'

'Jessica?'

'Yes, yes, Jessica.' *Why didn't I risk it?* 'How is Jessica?'

Elaine's head falls. For a moment, she says nothing, then takes a deep breath and says in a sigh, 'She's not well, Jennifer.' She looks at me. It's a whisper when she says, 'She's had a relapse.'

'Oh, Elaine, I am so sorry.' My hand automatically touches her arm.

'I really thought we'd make it.' Her voice is beginning to rise. 'We did *everything*, fought it all the way. Took every dose, did every test, went to alternative healers, set up the support group, prayed . . . *God, how we prayed* . . . but you know all that . . . you did the interview.' Yes, I did the interview, and I admired this woman so much. So much fight in her, so much hope, so positive, facing the worst possibility in the world. How she could think of others in the same situation, setting up the support group, when she could have been so selfish about her energy? *And then I went on to the next interview and forgot all about her. How could I do that? How could I just move on, when she was stuck, in trouble?*

I look at her now, head down again, a tear hanging precariously from her chin. It falls into the dry Ready Brek she's holding, displacing tiny flakes. I take the cereal bowl from her and set it down on the counter. I put my arms around her. She sobs and shudders and I hold her.

'I never gave up hope. And where did it get me? I was so *naïve*. I even had Jessica believing she'd make it. Mind over matter, I thought. And now, *now*, the prognosis is . . . well, there is no prognosis, and she still thinks she's going to make it . . . Dr Grace says we have to talk to her . . . .'

She pulls back. I don't know what to say.

'But surely there is hope. It's just a relapse . . . '

'Just a relapse,' she laughs. '*Just* a relapse. It's the end, Jennifer, the end.'

Oh God. Oh God.

I hold her again and she gives in, let's her body go. Limp. There is nothing I can say. I should have known that. You'd think I, of all people, would have known that. There is nothing anybody can say. And nothing worse than some eejit with false hopes. We stay drowning each other until we both feel the pressure of our sick children waiting for us, expecting us to return. Somehow, we emerge from the kitchen, with perfectly heated Six Vegetable Soup and Ready Brek, each of us with the right bowl and the right stiff upper lip. Back to coping mode. How is she going to tell her daughter?

18

Mary wants me to take 'time out'. I've turned down her suggestion of a walk. Now she's talking about a bath.

'You wouldn't be trying to tell me something?'

'I might,' she says cheekily. 'Come on, I want you to try out these aromatherapy oils Phil gave me for my birthday.'

'When was your birthday?' I ask, shocked that I missed it.

'Last May.'

My turn to smile. 'And you haven't touched them?'

'Nope.'

'Poor Phil.'

'He's used to me,' she says, rummaging in her bag. She produces what looks like a pencil case, zips it open and pulls out a tiny brown bottle. 'Lavender — for relaxation, healing and harmony.'

'Why haven't you used them?' I ask suspiciously.

'Too busy.'

'I thought that's what they were for — busy people.'

'Busy people with time to soak in baths.'

'Now you're making me feel guilty. You're spending too much

time here, Mary — you really are. You must have a million things to do.'

'No, I don't. Now that Dara's started school, I'm practically a lady of leisure. Phil's even started nagging me to take up golf so we can play together when the kids grow up.' She throws her eyes to heaven. 'Already thinking of retirement.'

I imagine what it must be like to have that kind of easy, comfortable relationship. Behind the tut-tutting, she loves it — the security of having a man who loves her, thinks of her and plans their future together.

'I want to be here, Jen. What better excuse to sit on my bum, where I'm happiest? I've spent the last ten years running round in circles. Now that I've my mornings back, I'm going to take advantage of them. This break is long overdue. So, stop with the guilt and go and have a bath. Go on — you're coming between me and Catherine Zeta-Jones.' She lifts up a copy of *Hello* that Jack brought in.

'In fairness, I could do with a soak.' I say. 'I can't believe I just said that.'

'What?'

'"In fairness."'

'What's wrong with that?'

'Nothing,' I say, starting to get embarrassed.

'What? . . . *What?*'

'It's just something that Simon says. *All the time.*'

'Does he now?' she asks, looking at me, a glint in her eye. 'I can't say *I* noticed.' Eyebrows raised, smile starting to form.

'Oh, for God's sake, Mary. Don't be ridiculous.'

'What did I say?' she asks innocently, hands inverted.

'Nothing. Forget it. I need to get out of here, that's all. I'm so bored I'm beginning to notice the bad habits of the medical staff.'

153

'I wouldn't say *all* the medical staff.'

'Mary, it's you who needs to get out.'

She just laughs. 'I can't say I blame you though,' she continues, eyebrows up again.

'I'm going for my bath. I hope you'll have matured by the time I get back.'

She throws over the aromatherapy kit. 'Better take your time then.'

'Will you take that stupid look off your face?'

'Make me.'

'Don't think I'm not tempted.'

She laughs.

Charlie's turn to throw his eyes up. *Women*, he's probably thinking.

Steaming water roars into the bath. I squint at the labels on the bite-sized bottles of essential oils. *Hmm, Clary Sage, for euphoria. Could do with a bit of that.* I tip the bottle upside down. *Oh, my God!* I gag, breathe through my mouth, quickly screw the lid back on the bottle and bin it. *If this is euphoria, I'll take depression.* Risking third-degree burns, I yank at the stopper. Out swirls the water. Not quickly enough. I throw open the window and start to fan the air. An icy current rushes in and pokes at the steam. I search for the lavender oil. *Safe with that*, I think, and empty the bottle into the fresh water that's now rushing into the bath. I begin to relax, panic over.

I hold my nose and slide under the water, drowning out all noise. I try to empty my mind but Mary keeps intruding. *Honestly, for a grown women, a mother of four, she ought to know better. So what if I notice something Simon keeps saying? I'd want to be stupid not to. He says it all the time. I mean, all*

154

the time. Sometimes I want to laugh out loud because it's not even in context. But so what? It means nothing. Apart from the fact that I'm becoming institutionalised. Like a prisoner longing for mealtime to brighten her day, I look forward to seeing Simon. But there's a good reason for that. Reassurance. A reminder that we are in good hands. Yes, I breathe easier when he is around. But that has nothing to do with Simon the individual, everything to do with Simon the doctor. Yes, I feel a bit deflated when he goes. And, yes, I know it's pathetic. But it's just part of being cooped up in here, nothing to do, horizons contracted to a decimal point. I bet every mother in the place feels the same. He's probably got a whole fan club going on without knowing it.

I surface for breath. Go under a few more times, then, conscious that it's a communal bathroom, carry on with the job of cleaning. My head is covered in shampoo when I realise there is no shower attachment. I fiddle with the 'mixer', trying to find some sort of balance between ice-cold and scalding. Crouching forward on my knees, head under the mixer, I rub my hair rapidly until it squeaks. Forget conditioner.

I feel better. Relaxed, clean, fresh. Even positive. Could it be the Clary Sage after all? For the first time since we came in, I put on make-up. And dry my hair properly. I slip on a pretty pink top that Mary insists she's finished with. Then my jeans. You can make out the shape of my hipbones through them. I need to get home, de-stress. Eat.

Instead of 'you look great', I am greeted with 'Urgh, what's the smell?' — Charlie.

Mary's look says, 'The boy's got a point.'

'It's Clary Sage. It's supposed to make you happy. I thought it was gone. Don't you smell lavender?' I sit beside Charlie and pluck a hair off his shoulder.

155

'Frankly, no,' says Mary at the same time Charlie offers, 'Pe-ew.' He holds his nose and shifts up the bed.

'If you're not careful, I'll try some on you.'

'Urgh, no way.' He scrambles further up the bed, forgetting that he is attached to a drip.

'Charlie, stop,' I shout, visualising his Freddie being yanked out of his chest. He stops but not before the drip starts to bleep. Something's wrong. I rush to get a nurse. It turns out to be nothing serious. Doesn't stop me feeling a fool.

A week goes by. Mary keeps us nourished. Jack keeps us in clothes, arriving with two pairs of olive-green Action Man pyjamas. They bring out the colour of Charlie's eyes, which has to be an accident — Jack would never notice something as subtle as eye colour. The matching baseball cap, though, does strike me as pretty impressive forward planning — getting Charlie interested in caps before he has to wear them as camouflage. He decides to sport the back-to-front look, the way SuperMark does. It suits him.

The following day, Anne takes me aside and suggests we shave off Charlie's hair, get it over with, end the torture of finding it everywhere. She can organise a hairdresser to come to the ward. *Can I do it, go from child with hair to child with no hair just like that? Couldn't be any worse than what I'm looking at now. His scraggy head makes him look sicker. In any case, I could do with controlling something.*

The appointment is made. Just before the hairdresser arrives, Mark comes over to the bed and sits beside Charlie.

'I shaved off my hair, too,' he says.

'Did you really? Cool,' says Charlie. 'Did you shave it all by yourself?'

'Yeah. But I'm big. If I was four, I'd let the barber do it.'

'What's a barber?'

'Oh, like a hairdresser.'

'OK.'

'Do you like Winders?'

'Yeah.'

Mark reaches into the pocket of his tracksuit top, pulls out a Winder and hands it to Charlie.

'Thanks. D'you want half?'

''s OK. I just had one. Want me to stay while the hairdresser cuts your hair?'

'Yeah.'

'OK.'

And that's what's great about life. Just when you're about to give up on everything, someone comes along and restores your faith in humanity. Here is a boy at an age when his only worries should be girls, whether or not to shave, the odd spot and his voice breaking, landed in here with a terminal illness, broken family, absent father. Instead of doing the obvious and feeling sorry for himself, he is selflessly focusing energy on someone else. I look to my far left, then far right, then up, in an effort to disperse the tears that are flooding into my eyes. I wipe my nose with the back of my hand and try to collect myself. I smile at them, the two buddies, chatting away, oblivious to their age difference, surroundings or fate. United by illness.

The hairdresser, a pleasant cuddly woman in her fifties, arrives. I try to hide my upset, my embarrassment. I watch clumps of blond hair, like sheep's wool, drift onto his shoulders, lap, the floor. It breaks my heart. But I continue to smile. I sneak a lock for myself, wrap it in tissue, hide it away. Without his hair, Samson lost his strength. It makes sense, suddenly. I look at my new boy and try to adjust. How small his face seems compared to the size of his head. No longer does it dominate. Now it's only a third of a skin globe. *His eyes are the same though. Focus on his eyes, Jenny, his soul. Not his body. Which keeps changing. And will keep on changing. His eyebrows will go. His lashes. His face might swell. But he will still be Charlie, my Charlie, my boy. Smile, Jenny. Keep smiling.*

'Cool, Charlie,' I lie.

'Want to look in the mirror?' suggests Mark.

I look in panic at Anne. She nods go ahead.

'Yeah, OK,' says Charlie, happily. Game for anything as long as he is with Mark.

The hairdresser hands him a mirror.

He just sits and stares.

'Well?' asks Mark.

Charlie looks up at him. 'I'm like you now, amn't I?'

'Yeah.'

'That's OK then,' he nods.

'Would you like one of my Nike caps? I've two.'

'Cool. We'll be like twins.'

Mark smiles at him, lands his hand gently on top of Charlie's head and rubs it back and forward, making me feel it's OK, it can be touched, it won't break apart. And I think that Mark must be a great brother. And how he must miss his.

19

Every day, Charlie has his blood tested. And every day, we receive results. I wake, worrying, 'How are his bloods?' and think of little else until I find out. If I let it, my mood would follow the ups and downs. It did in the beginning, until I learnt a trick. I write the results into a record book they have given me, and, in doing so, try to detach. I trick myself into believing that once I record them, I can forget about them. Sometimes it works. Sometimes it doesn't. Depends on what else is going on. I get bad days when everything seems to be going against us.

It turns you into a bit of an expert, though, all this information. Which isn't necessarily a good thing. I know the levels of each blood cell, what's normal, how far from normal Charlie's have been and how he has progressed. Not steadily — that would have been too easy — but in waves and troughs, like everything else. Overall, they have been creeping up, though, and that's the main thing. I just have to force myself to believe that when there is a dip, it will turn again. It is easy to become obsessed. When your child has leukaemia, your constant fixation is how close or far away he is from remission — your dream, your utopia, your escape.

At the end of the second week, Simon arrives at Charlie's bedside with a beam on his face and a pep in his step. Highly unusual. Maybe Dr Howard finally threw herself at his feet, revealed she couldn't live without him, and asked to borrow his gold stethoscope. No. It's not that. It's better. Much better. The cancer cells have disappeared from Charlie's blood! A giant step.

'Oh, Simon,' I put my hand to my mouth, and start to cry. 'I can't believe it.'

He smiles.

'I can't believe it.' I hug him, squeeze him, let him go and jump up and down. Tiny little excited jumps. More rabbit than kangaroo.

'What, Mum?' asks Charlie.

'It's just good news, sweetie.' Hand briefly over mouth again. 'Simon has good news.'

'Am I better?'

I look at him. 'Yes, sweetheart, much better.'

'Can we go home now?'

I'm instantly sorry I didn't control myself.

Simon sits down beside him on the bed.

'Charlie,' he says. 'We are winning the fight against the bad cells. They have all gone from your blood now.'

'Good,' says Charlie, sensing the 'but'.

'We just have to do a test to see if they have gone from your bones too.'

'Oh.' Flat.

'Do you remember when we put you to sleep the last time for the bone test, the bone marrow biopsy?'

He nods.

'Well, we're going to do that again.'

Charlie looks at me, eyes wide. 'The space ships, Mama.'

'Sweetheart, that was just a dream,' I say, coming over to him and taking him on my lap. 'Like the nightmares you had before.' I rub his cheek with my finger. 'If we do this test, and if the bad cells are gone, that means we can go home. Doesn't it, Simon?'

'Yes. It does.' He smiles at Charlie. 'You will be in remission.'

'Remission,' I say. I hold my breath and pray.

This time it works. Charlie. Is. In. Remission. He has made it. The first step. What we've hoped for. Prayed for. Dreamed of. But now that we're here, my brain automatically fast-forwards to the next hurdle — the bone marrow transplant. *When can we do it? Am I a match? Any news of my blood test?* But I stop. Surely I can allow myself a sliver of happiness, a slice of relief, a segment of victory. Just for the rest of the day, I'm going to stop thinking ahead. Mary smuggles in a baby bottle of champagne. The night nurses pretend not to notice.

Simon, Anne, Siobhán, Máiréad and the rest of the team prepare us for discharge, what to expect, how to look after Freddie, how to take the medicines. They write everything down. They give me booklets. Phone numbers. A medi-alert bracelet. I know what to look out for — temperatures, bleeding, bruising, rashes. Anything unusual. I have the direct line to the ward and Simon's mobile. We will be in once a week for chemotherapy but I am to call or come in at any time, if I'm worried. If Charlie gets a temperature, we have to make it back in an hour. It's things like that that worry me.

I am afraid of having to cope alone. But hide it. I know that when I get home I *will* cope. Because that's what we do, in life, isn't it? Cope. We are thrown into situations and we get on with it. Because we have to. No choice. I just need to get home. Walk through the door and start again. Back to a normal atmosphere

161

where Charlie can have a healthier life — fresh air, organic food, exercise. He won't be the sick boy any more; he'll be the boy who is getting better. And we will cope.

I feel guilty looking around the ward at the other children and their parents, still waiting for that news. I want to sneak out. Not tell them. But they know. News travels. And they do seem delighted for us. As I would be for them. We are all fighting the same thing. And if one of us has a victory, it makes us all feel more hopeful. Another mum took her son home three days ago, and that's what I felt then. So I shouldn't feel guilty. But I do. Mark gives Charlie his favourite cap and his mobile-phone number. He tells him to text. Charlie's mouth falls open. Sending messages to a teenager. Wow!

Telling Elaine and Jessica is the worst. And I almost don't. I make a few false starts up the corridor, then find some great excuse to turn right, left or back. Then I do it, go in to the sweet-smelling room — the room that smells of death. Their energy is flagging. But they are so happy for us, so genuinely happy it makes me want to cry and shout and beg God for a miracle. They offer hugs and hope, and tell me to keep fighting. Then it's time to go. Like a deserter, I turn my back on them. We will talk on the phone every day. I will call. I promise. This time, I won't forget.

I want to get moving now, get out. Mary has taken home most of our things already. I have the remainder packed, ready for the off. We have to be officially discharged by Simon. He comes at last, all smiles and chat with Charlie, then writes a prescription that seems to go on forever. I watch his thin, confident, black scrawl and wonder how I'm going to get all that medicine into such a small person, every day. He signs his name. Whoosh! He writes with his left hand, I notice, like Charlie. This throws me. Everything becomes embarrassingly personal. Though of course it isn't. He's a doctor writing a prescription. That's all. He hands me his card and tells me to call any time, something he does with all his patients. But when he passes it to me, and our hands touch, I get flustered. *What is wrong with me?* I am actually blushing. *Jesus!*

He looks at me and smiles.

Which makes me worse.

'How are you getting home?' he asks.

'We've the car,' I say.

'Are you OK to drive?'

'Yes. Fine. I have to get the car home anyway.'

'I'll walk you out,' he says. And I wonder does everyone get this treatment or just me. *Am I special? Oh stop it. Grow up. You're not seventeen. You twit.*

On the way out he checks that we have everything, know everything, are ready for this. And I think *he cares.* Then tell myself he's only making sure we're all right. Just doing his job. Nothing more.

We are all set. In the car. Charlie strapped in. Stuff in the boot. Simon standing by the car waiting for us to take off. I turn the ignition. Nothing happens. *Oh God! That's all I need. Dead batteries.* There's no point trying again because it's flat. Totally flat. Not a sound, not a movement. But I try again, because what the hell else can I do? I close my eyes. *Come on, come on.* Nothing. Suddenly I'm furious with myself. *Why didn't I think of coming out to warm the engine once or twice? It's not exactly a top-of-the-range BMW.* Charlie starts to whine. The car is cold and damp. Already he's tired and fed up. He's not the only one. I sit here regretting that AA membership I never took up, regretting that I bought a cute rather than practical car, regretting pretty much everything that's ever gone wrong . . . On top of that, I'm mortified, Simon is coming up to the fogged-up window. *Shit*. I roll it down.

'Everything OK?'

'No,' I say, feeling like a six-year-old. 'It won't start.'

'Mmm, I thought that might happen,' he says. 'There's been a lot of rain.'

So that's why he walked us out, I think, feeling even more stupid. To think that I felt I was getting special treatment.

'You're not the first person it's happened to, if it makes you feel any better.'

'No,' I say, smiling. 'It doesn't.'

'Would you like a lift home?'

'No, no thanks. You're busy. Let me think . . . Jump leads. Do you have jump leads? It's the battery. It has to be.'

He disappears and returns in a Merc. His jump leads are bigger than the Mini — well, almost. Charlie is jigging in his car seat at the excitement of it all. Energy restored. Simon pulls up, his engine purring like a tiger. He reminds me what I have to do — basically, switch on the ignition when he tells me. I think I can do that.

It starts. *Thank God*.

'Thanks, Simon. Thanks a million. Sorry for taking up your time.'

'All in a day's work.' He smiles, looking delighted with himself. Must make a change to find a problem that's easy to solve.

'Thanks, Simon,' shouts Charlie from the back.

'We'd better go. Thanks again.'

'Good luck, then. Call if you've any worries.'

He waits, standing beside his car, until we reverse out and drive off. I check my rear-view mirror as we insert our parking ticket in the machine and wait for the barrier to go up. He is still there watching, making sure we're all right. I thank God I remembered

to pay. Couldn't face another episode of *How Stupid is Jenny?*
Talk about an eejit. Thank God, I'm leaving. My judgement had
obviously gone out the window. To think I thought he liked me.
God! What a moron!

We stop off at a pharmacy close to home. The hospital has given
us a supply of medicine to get us over the first day or two but I
want to get organised, get on top of this. Maybe it wasn't such a
good idea. We have to wait while they fill three paper bags full of
medicine containers. Máiréad, the social worker, has signed Charlie
up for a 'long-term illness' scheme where he gets free medicine. I
just have to fill out a form. When I see how much we would have
had to pay, I nearly drop. The pharmacist looks sympathetically at
Charlie. She offers him a lollipop from a glass jar. He takes ages to
choose one and I wonder if she is as tolerant with children who
have hair. She doesn't charge the fifteen cent marked on the jar. We
stop at a convenience store, for bread and milk.

We get home, exhausted, to a warm and tidy flat. A big
Welcome Home banner is strung along the mantelpiece, and there
are bunches of brightly coloured balloons everywhere. An unfamiliar vase stands on the coffee table, holding an enormous
bunch of white unopened lilies. In the kitchen, there is a Bart
Simpson cake with four candles on it. Charlie is running around,
laughing, asking if it's his birthday. The fridge has been emptied
and completely restocked with a mixture of essentials (milk,
butter, fresh bread), healthy food options (lettuce, cucumber,
peppers, baby tomatoes), quick meals (ham, salami, rashers,
sausages) and all of Charlie's favourites. Mary. An angel sent by
God. Or, the thought strikes me, an angel sent by Great? The
angel has left a note to say that she didn't arrange for people to
jump out from behind couches and shout 'surprise' because she
thought we might be tired. She will call later.

'Where's Sausage?' asks Charlie.

'Remember, I told you. Debbie and Simon will drop him back after dinner. We're going to have a little rest first. OK?'

'But I want him now.'

'Don't whine, Charlie. Sausage will be here later.'

'But . . . .'

'Charlie, just because you're sick doesn't mean you get everything you want when you want it, OK? We'll see Sausage when we wake up.' I say it nicely, firmly, but I have to say it. I've told myself that as soon as we got home, no nonsense. We're home. And it's not as easy as I'd thought.

I put the medicines up on top of the fridge-freezer, in an effort to 'keep them out of reach of children'. Hilarious considering the effort it takes to get them into him. There are about twelve bottles and containers of various shapes and sizes standing together, like the Manhattan skyline. I wonder will we ever get through them. I give Charlie his first dose and take his temperature, just to be sure. We head to bed. Neither of us wants to be alone so we climb in together. The warm glow of the lamp fills the room on this grey November day. We're home.

20

Such excitement! Charlie reunited with Sausage and Deb at the same time. Sausage jumps and slobbers all over him, causing me to panic about germs. I look at Simon, who lets me know everything's fine by shaking his head quickly, then nodding. Deb bends down. They both rush to her. She grabs them, one in each arm. Sausage barks and licks her face.

'Urgh. Get off,' she laughs, standing and lifting Charlie up with her. 'How are you?' She puts her face up to his.

'Fine.'

'I'm so glad you're home. I missed you. I've loads of news . . . .' She carries him to the couch.

'Would you like a coffee?' I ask Simon, who is hovering.

'Only if you're having one. It doesn't look as if I'll be going anywhere for a while.' He smiles.

'Do you want to sit down?' I nod to the counter that separates the kitchen from the sitting room.

He pulls up a stool, and I head for the kettle. It strikes me that I could offer to drop Debbie home later, so that he can go now, but I keep quiet. I could do with a bit of adult company.

'She's a great kid,' I say, catching him looking at them.

'Do you think?' he asks, looking doubtful.

'Just look at the way she is with Charlie.' I sit opposite him, while waiting for the kettle to boil.

'Yes, it *is* amazing how he seems to bring out the best in her.'

'She's a good kid in her own right, though. You can always tell.'

'She is.' He hesitates. 'Though she has her moments. Or, at least, she *was* having them. Since she started to mind the dog — well, no, it was before that — since she heard about Charlie . . . being ill, Debra really seems to have changed.'

'How so?'

'Well, she is so much easier to live with — calmer, more co-operative, less, less . . . explosive.'

I smile. *Poor man.*

'I don't know whether it was just being a teenager, or being a teenager without a mother, but she was beginning to get quite . . . difficult. And, in fairness, I don't think I was handling it very well. But, anyway, she seems to have forgotten that now. We are talking again, proper conversations. She asks my opinion on things, and actually listens. No, I have to say, we are getting on very well.' He looks equal parts relieved and bemused.

'Even though it means you get dragged along to the movies?' I smile.

'Actually, it wasn't bad. I quite enjoyed it. Bit of escapism.'

'You're lucky,' I say.

'Why?'

'Deb could be like I was when I was her age.'

He looks surprised. Then amused. Then interested. 'Oh, really?' He smiles.

I grimace. 'I was a bit of a handful.'

'Is that right?' His smile is getting bigger.

'You don't want to know.'

'Oh, but I do.'

'Right then, are you ready for this? I shaved off my hair.'

'All of it?'

'All of it.'

'Why?'

'It was the only thing my mother ever complimented me on.'

Look at those eyebrows. Up they go. Up, up, up. I'm enjoying his shock.

'She blew up, of course. Which only encouraged me. I started wearing Docs, black woolly tights with holes, stupid short skirts. Black, lots of black, buckets of eyeliner and white make up. You should have seen me.'

'You sound scary,' he says. And I can imagine him seeing me on the street and crossing the road.

'I was scary, to some people.' I'm serious now. 'Especially teachers. They came down hard. So I started mitching, avoiding homework, slipping grades. Mother lost it completely.'

'Why were you so keen to upset your mother?'

'I don't know. Rebellion? She wasn't into children. She had one — me — and left it at that. She had no time for me. I pretty much grew up with my gran, Great — I mentioned her.'

'Yes, yes, you did.'

'She's a politician, my mother . . . .'

He thinks for a second. 'Not Kathleen Dempsey, Minister for the Environment?'

I nod. His eyebrows pop up again but he says nothing.

'Your typical politician,' I continue. 'Belongs to her constituents. Always chasing the vote. Some eejit rings in the middle of the night with some stupid problem — a blocked toilet, whatever — and she'd practically go over there herself, roll up her sleeves and shove her own hand down the loo.'

'What about your father?'

'*She's* his world.'

'Where are they now, your parents?'

He must mean, where are they in relation to the hospital, in relation to Charlie being sick, because it's obvious from the media where they are — larger than life and living in Dublin. Coming to a television near you. Mother at least.

'We don't keep in touch.'

He picks up on my end-of-discussion tone. 'I'm sorry, I didn't mean to pry.'

'You weren't.' I get up to make the coffee. And come back with two mugs.

'Anyway,' I say. 'I think Deb is wonderful. And, don't worry — she won't start any of that attention-seeking behaviour I just frightened you with . . . .' I smile. '. . . because she has your attention. And that's the main thing. Take it from one who knows.'

'Well, at least we are getting on now.' He looks over his shoulder, lowers his voice. 'For a while there, I thought we'd never have a civil conversation again.' Quieter still. 'I think she thought I was a moron. She wouldn't talk to me, you know, was constantly snapping, slamming doors . . . .'

'I'd have thought that was standard teenage behaviour.'

'Maybe, but try living with it. I didn't know what I was doing wrong, didn't understand what was going on in her mind. And I knew if I asked, she wouldn't tell me. I had just gone out and bought a load of books on teenage behaviour.'

I smile. *Ah, God.*

'Anyway, in fairness, completely changed.'

'Maybe Charlie being sick has made her realise what she has. You.'

'Oh, I don't know about that,' he says, looking down into his coffee.

'Or maybe she appreciates your medical knowledge and the fact that you are Charlie's doctor.'

'You might be right there. That *is* how we started talking. Her asking me about leukaemia, about Charlie.'

'Glad we were of some assistance.' I smile.

'No, no. It wasn't like that . . . .' He looks mortified.

'I was joking.'

'Oh. I see. Sorry.'

'No, I'm sorry . . . It was a stupid thing to say.' And I can't believe myself.

We are both awkward now.

'So, have you worked out why you are being taken in hand, artistically?' I say, smiling. It's the first safe subject I can come up with.

'Well, no, but I'm going along with it. The main thing is that we're talking again, so I'll suffer a little sophistication. It's all in a good cause.'

We have a long, easy conversation until Simon notices that Charlie is tiring. He tells everyone it's time to go. Sausage looks from Debbie to Charlie and back again. Confused. He doesn't know which one to go with. In the end, he decides he's home. Luckily, or there would have been one deeply wounded boy. Charlie feeds him, while I rustle up supper. I pump my son with the vitamins I am allowed give him (everything except folic acid, which counteracts one of his drugs), then go through the stressful procedure of giving him his medicine. His temperature is fine.

Mary phones when Charlie's ready for bed. I report that all is well. When she hears that Simon has called over, she gets the wrong idea. As usual. I put her straight but she won't believe me. *What is it with her? Just because she has a great relationship, she thinks everyone needs one to be happy. Well, she's wrong. I'd be perfectly happy if only Charlie would get better.*

He wants me to lie down with him until he sleeps. I stay longer, gazing at his little face — so pale, so still. Too still. I rest the back of my hand on the pillow, near his mouth, to feel his breath. I rub his cheek to see if I can bring any colour back. It's no use. He is disappearing — first his complexion, then his hair, eyebrows, lashes. He is being rubbed out. And there is nothing I can do to stop it. Even his face is beginning to lose its familiar, sweet shape. The steroids, like they said.

I take his limp hand in my two, close my eyes and try to remember the way he was. Picture him, *before*. But his present image keeps intruding and I get frustrated, upset. I climb out of bed, walk quickly out of the room, take a breath and focus my mind on something else, someone else. Simon. There he is, so ready to pop into my thoughts. This time I don't stop him. I think about our conversation and how little you really know a person. You can have sex with them. See them everyday for two weeks. And still know nothing about them. In my mind, Simon has gone from unhappy widower and doctor, to struggling father, single parent, like myself. Worried about his daughter, how to do it right. Confident doctor, hesitant father. Trying to do his best, like the rest of us.

I like him.

But there is so much I want to know. His age — is he *much* older? Whether he has brothers or sisters and if any of them have children — they could be family to Charlie. Why he chose to be a doctor, and why a children's oncologist. How he got the thin, white scar just below his right cheekbone. What makes him

172

laugh. What makes him angry. I know what makes him sad. Why he never remarried. Did nobody live up to Alison? How often does he think of her? Every day, every hour? Is he still guilty about what happened? Do I ever pop into his mind? If so, in what context? Sometimes I think he likes me. But then, I figure, no more than any of the other parents. And sometimes (obviously, when I'm really tired), I feel that if things were different, I mean completely different, like the two of us stranded on a desert island, there might be something between us. And then I get cross and tell myself I'm being ridiculous. Childish. Desperate. I used always be able to tell if a man liked me. Somewhere along the line, I've lost that ability. This is all irrelevant, though, because Charlie is sick . . . But what if all this *is* because Charlie is sick. Maybe it's some sort of primal instinct driving me to find a mate to support us? *Rubbish*. It's obvious. I'm a very confused woman.

Mary gives Dara the day off school and we take the boys and Sausage to Brittas Bay, an endless white sandy beach in Wicklow, to let them gulp great breaths of fresh air. The sky is clear and blue but the water wild. It was a windy night. I hadn't realised how. *Can the wind do that to the sea, even after it has stopped?* Mary doesn't know. But it's beautiful. Waves pound, smash and roar to the shore, the smell of salt, invigorating. Cappuccino froth foams at the edge, as the angry sea sweeps forward onto the flat, wet, caramel sand. The boys, in their wellies, run ahead with sticks to join up horses' hooves. The beach is littered with things that have been washed off the decks of boats during the night. We pretend there has been a shipwreck. The boys are pirates. 'Har, Har, me mateys, step lively, or I'll 'ave yer guts for garters,' I threaten and am told to mind me manners or they'll make me walk the plank. They call Mary 'Polly' and tell her she wants a cracker.

I treasure every inch of sky, sand, sea, every pebble — smooth and round, in varying shades of wine, slate grey, luminous white. My favourites are grey with white stripes. Looking up, I follow the trail of a plane slicing through the sky. *I will appreciate everything from now on*, I tell someone — God, maybe. *So please give me back my life, my boy.* I watch Charlie draw in the sand. It's a Christmas tree made of three triangles. *Will we have found a donor by then?* We walk back towards the car. I look at the shadow of the two of us walking, hand in hand. We look normal. In shadows you don't notice pale faces or missing hair. Dara finds a bright green Frisbee. We don't know where it's been, who's had it. But what the hell? We let him keep it.

21

I've become a master strategist. To get Charlie to exercise, I resort to a variety of sneaky techniques. Firstly, I time it right — as soon as he gets up and after rests. Secondly, I trick him into it. One of my favourites is to stick my bum out and get him to slap it. I start out walking, a bit like a gorilla, then speed up, forcing him to run. We both end up laughing and out of breath. We dance to his *Lilo and Stitch* soundtrack, which consists mostly of Elvis tunes. Strangely, he moves like a little Elvis, though he's never seen the king. 'I'm a huk, a huk, a burning luv,' he sings, all husky, into a toy microphone Louis bought him, which unfortunately gives great 'amplification'. We walk to the shop to buy treats. 'Let's get you a treat,' he says, meaning, 'Let's get me a treat.' But if it gets him moving and out in the air, I won't argue. Then there's the 'we'd-better-bring-the-dog-for-a-walk' excuse. When Dara calls over, I organise games that require energy but not too much — treasure hunts, musical chairs, hide and seek. And maybe I'm a little too organised, too controlling but I'm not going to sit by and have Dara accuse him of being 'no fun any more'. My technique might be old-fashioned. But it works.

Getting Charlie to eat used to be a problem. Now it's the opposite. Steroids have given him the appetite of a rugby team (after a game). I have to watch his weight. They warn you about that. Just like they warn you his face might get puffy, which it has. Or that his moods might become erratic, making him giddy, hyper. Most of the time, he's too wiped out to be either.

I'm fussy about his drugs, making sure he gets every dose on time, the syrups syringed in, millilitre by millilitre, the tablets crushed and disguised in food. I also have to be very careful preparing his food and keeping him away from anyone sick. Charlie is fussy about hygiene. He has to be. Hand washing has been drummed into us. I have given him responsibility for the oral hygiene routine they want us to follow — washing his teeth four times a day, swishing round an antibacterial mouthwash and then swallowing an anti-fungal liquid. It's strange watching a child so small take an almost obsessive interest in caring for himself. But it's better than having to argue with him to do it, four times a day, every day.

A liaison nurse from the hospital calls to see how we are managing. She checks the way I clean and disinfect Freddie, and arranges for a public health nurse to call. I continue my Zero Spoiling campaign. 'Thank you, Mum,' I remind him whenever silence replaces manners. 'Thank you, Mum,' he repeats. I try not to give him everything he wants or jump to instant attention for minor requests. But the hardest thing is reminding other people, especially poor Deb who tries too hard — maybe to make up for not coming to the hospital.

They advise us not to get too involved with the other parents. All children are different, they say, with different conditions, tests, treatments and 'outcomes'. Another person's bad experience might not necessarily be yours and will only drag you down, worry you. It makes sense. Still, I ring Elaine every day. I can't help it. I feel a duty to her. We talk or, at least, I listen. And try to hide my shock. Everything is being handled with such practicality, such efficiency. Jessica has picked out a headstone, the songs she wants at her funeral. *How can she do that? Face death, straight on, eyes open. Could I, could Charlie, be that brave?* I am in awe, when I allow myself believe it.

If there is one good thing about what we are going through, it is this. I have learnt who my friends are. Real friends. Not the ones who call to say how sorry they are, and then never show up. No, not them. I'm talking about the ones who keep coming, helping, even when you think you don't need it, but you do. The ones who knuckle down, get their hands dirty. Like Elaine's sister. Always there. Always helping. Or Mark's granny. Same thing. For me, it's Mary who knows what we need before we do ourselves. But also Jack. We always got on, Jack and I, but he wouldn't have been the first person I'd have called in an emergency. He has been a surprise.

After his first visit, he became a regular. Arriving with newspaper cuttings and more Internet information. And the Action Man pyjamas for Charlie, of course. He bought me a pillow when he discovered I didn't have one. Oh, and a life supply of Lucozade which he reminded me 'replaces lost energy quickly'. He read Charlie his snake and spider books while I left the room 'for some fresh air'. Since we got home, he has been equally, if not more, attentive. He calls with take-aways from the best restaurants so I needn't worry about how the food is prepared; he baby-sits while I nip out for a walk or catch up on jobs; he e-mails constantly. And now, after arriving with and helping us polish off a take-out lasagne, he has just presented me with a voucher for a local beauty salon. This makes me laugh.

'How did you know about Jackie's?'

He smiles.

'And how did you know I loved Indian Head Massages?'

'That article you did about beauty salons?' He's fidgeting with the lapel of his jacket. *Is he embarrassed?*

'But that was ages ago.'

'Yeah, well, I looked it up. Do you want it or not?'

'I want it. I want it.' I start laughing again, then give him a hug. He really is such a gruff little cutie.

'Get off . . . I'll mind the lad if you like. Do it some evening, though, when I'm finished work.'

'Are you sure?'

'Yeah.'

'Will you be all right with him on your own?'

''Course I will. Aren't we two men? We can watch the snooker. I'll bring popcorn.'

'Or you could make some. I've got the stuff in the press . . . .'

'Don't push it.'

'How did you know he liked snooker?' Charlie *loves* snooker — stands two inches from the telly, fists clenched. When a ball is pocketed, he hops up and down.

'All men like snooker.'

'Right.' Everything is so simple with Jack. But he always seems to get it right.

'Jen?'

'Hmm?'

'I wanted to talk to you about something.'

'Sounds serious.'

'I hope you don't mind. And it's none of my business, I know, but have you thought of telling Dave?'

I look at him, and feel my stomach lurching forward and

upward, smashing against my ribs.

'I mean, don't you think he should know — as Charlie's father?'

My shoulders lift three inches. My neck stiffens. This is an issue I don't want to think about, let alone discuss.

'Jack, if I am a match, then we don't need to tell Dave. Let's wait and see.' My tone says *don't-go-there*.

But he does. 'I'm not talking about that, Jenny. I'm talking about just letting him know what's happening.'

'I don't want to disturb him.' *Or rock the boat. I just want to let it be. Everything has settled. I don't want to start it all up again.*

'Jen, I think he'd want to know.'

'How do you know what he'd want?' I snap.

'I don't want to argue. I'm just making a point. I think he should know. That's all. Charlie is his son.'

'I should have known you'd take Dave's side. Is that why you've been so good to us? You were just waiting for the right moment to put Dave's side forward. Your old pal.'

He looks hurt. 'I'm disappointed you'd think that.' He starts to get up.

'Sorry, Jack. I'm sorry. I shouldn't have said that. Sit down. Please. I didn't mean it. I don't know, I just get upset when people talk about my life as if they know best.'

'I'm not taking anyone's side, Jenny,' he says, sitting back down, but at the edge of the chair, ready to go if things take a turn for the worse.

'I know. I'm sorry. It's just that, well, sometimes, everything looks so easy from outside. And it's not — believe me, Jack — it's just not. OK?' I hear tiredness in my voice.

'OK. Look, I'm sorry, Jenny. I just wanted to say it and I've said it, now. You're right — it is none of my business.'

'I know you were only trying to help. But you don't know the full story, Jack — that's all I'm saying.'

He looks at me. Expecting it now.

'Thanks for the voucher, Jack. And thanks for calling.'

'OK,' he says, getting the message. He gives me a hug on the way out.

As I'm continually reminded, I have to look after myself to look after Charlie. I take up the yoga classes again. The first one is like a tonic. Physically, mentally. I lie on my back, focusing only on my breathing and the gentle stretches I'm doing. I feel the full benefit. Yawn after yawn, my eyes water. I relax deeper and deeper, the smell of incense calming, easing tension. I can't help feeling guilty, though. Charlie could really do with this. He is the sick one.

After class, I tell the instructor about what he has been through. She suggests I bring him to see her privately. She has an available slot tomorrow.

We go to her home, a small three-bed semi, in a pretty estate in Dalkey. There is a very good feeling about the place. She shows us to a back bedroom where she does her treatments. Charlie is a little giddy, probably nerves, but she calms him down by asking him to sit on a peculiar chair made of two flat planks — one to sit on, the other for his knees. She asks me what treatments he has had, takes out a tuning fork, hits it off a block and then slowly runs it around Charlie's body, 'clearing his aura', which she says has been damaged by radiation from tests and X-rays. Charlie doesn't like the sound and she stops.

She lies him on a plinth and chats to him while holding her hand over different areas of his body, a few minutes at a time. She is re-energising his chakras, she explains. Then they play together with large squares of silk. Red and orange, the colours of energy and happiness. This is the bit Charlie likes best. He sits on her lap, mesmerised.

'Do you know what a guardian angel is?' she asks him.

'Yeah, an angel in the garden.'

I can't believe I haven't told him about his guardian angel. What kind of mother am I?

'You have a guardian angel, Charlie.'

'Have I?'

She nods. 'Do you want to know what she does?'

'Is she a girl?' he asks, disgusted.

'Guardian angels usually are,' she says. 'But if you'd prefer a boy you can ask for one.'

'Ask who?'

'God.'

'Can I ask him now?'

'You can. Do you want to know what they do, first?'

'Yeah.'

'They mind you. They look after you.'

'Like Great.'

She looks at me. I explain in two words. His great-grandmother.

'Guardian angels give you whatever you want,' she says.

'No, they don't. Great doesn't.'

'Well, whatever's good for you. And they love you — I forgot the most important bit. They love you.'

'I'd like one, please.'

'Well, you have one now. And you can talk to him whenever you want. If you're sad or sore or need help, your guardian angel will be there for you. Isn't it nice to know you have someone there helping you out all the time?'

'Like my mum.'

I smile at him. *My angel.*

There was a time when I might have been cynical, dismissed this as a money-making racket. And maybe I am desperate, trying anything. But I do believe in it, maybe because I have to. What is true is that at the end of this half-hour session, Charlie has a beautiful pale pink glow in his cheeks, and an energy about him. He is leaving with something new — his guardian angel. And I'm taking all the help we can get.

I buy Charlie a wardrobe of red and orange clothes, including pyjamas and undies. There are other colours mixed in, usually blue or yellow, which isn't a bad thing, softening their intensity. I go a bit mad with towels, cushions and flowers. Wish I liked orange more. My mood is on the up. Maybe it's the colours. Maybe it's the fact that I'm doing something positive, taking action. In the pharmacy, we find a tiny guardian-angel brooch. It's silver with a little droplet of glass. Not bad value: a guardian angel for €3.50. We take it. I clip it to the corner of Charlie's pillow.

22

Then we have to go back. Chemotherapy.

The sight of the uniformed woman buffing the floor, and the mingled smell of floor polish and disinfectant bring it all back. Like a slap in the face. The sick, nervous feeling at the pit of my stomach returns. My shoulders stand to attention once more, ready for attack. My heart pounds. My breathing falters. Being here is a reminder that the ground under us could give way again at any minute, swallowing us up. We are not free. Charlie grabs my leg and I almost fall over. I bend down to him. His little worried face! I hug him, lift him, then carry him off, our cheeks together. He looks over my shoulder at the disappearing hospital entrance.

The whiny hospital voice and demanding, manners-free behaviour return. I keep reminding him (and myself) that we'll be out later. It helps that both Anne and Siobhán are here to make us feel at home. *At home!* There are no surprises with the treatment. Nothing we haven't seen before. Charlie looks for Mark and is told he has gone home. I explain why that's a good thing and that we should be happy for him. I tell him we will text Mark when we get home. Siobhán stays with Charlie while I go see Elaine and Jessica on my own. It is a matter of days.

Simon is in and out. It is almost time to go home when he tells me he wants to talk. He is not smiling. To his office, then.

I am not a match.

'Now, don't be disappointed,' he says.

Don't be disappointed!

'It would have been extremely unusual if the first person we tried matched. As you know,' — he says gently — 'the chances were very slight.'

But there.

'We have the register . . . .'

I nod. Squeeze my lips between my teeth. Pinch the inside of my hand. Look up and to the right.

'I know it's a disappointment . . . .'

I shrug, look out the window and sneak my finger up to plug the beginnings of a tear.

'Is there any other family member we could try? Charlie's father?'

'We're going to have to, aren't we?' I snap, as though it's his fault. I sigh. 'I'm sorry, Simon. It's been a long day. I'm sorry. I don't know . . . .'

'There's no rush, Jenny. You don't have to decide now. Take your time.'

'But there is a rush,' I say, verging on the hysterical. 'We need to find a donor. Charlie won't get better without one . . . .'

'Take a day or two to think over your options. In fairness, a day or two won't make a difference.'

I look down at my hands. They're in fists. I open them out. I think of Dave. The man I haven't seen in five years. The man I sent away. I can't just cry help and expect him to come galloping in on his white charger. *Why should he? He might not be Charlie's father. And if he's not, he owes us nothing. And he must think he's not. How else could he have left? He hates me. He has to. I ruined everything. His future. Our plans. Oh, how did I get myself into this stupid mess?*

'Can I ask you something?'

I look up.

'I know it's none of my business, but does Charlie's father know that he is sick?'

I almost laugh. *Assuming that Charlie's father is Dave, and not you.* 'No.'

'That might be a place to start.'

'Hmm,' I say, looking at my lap.

'People are full of surprises, you know. He might surprise you . . . And, technically, he has a right to know . . . .'

'You're right,' I bark. 'This is none of your business.'

'Of course.'

'Look, Simon. I'm sorry.' My hands are at my temples. 'I know I have to contact Charlie's father. I know. It's just that he has his own life. Everything has moved on. I don't want to be forced to go back. I have to do it, I know I do . . . .' I think for a second about the logistics of it. 'Would a person living in another country have to come home to do the test?'

'No — all they would have to do is a simple blood test. We could link up with the hospital in that country.'

'So it could be done without him coming back to Dublin?'

'Yes.'

We are home by tea-time. I try to get some soup into Charlie but all he feels like is sleep and for me to lie down with him. Into bed we climb. Charlie wants to talk to his guardian angel and Great. I'd like a word, too, only not as polite. We do it his way. And there is a degree of comfort in it. I suppose.

'Tell me a story of when you were a kid,' he says, sleepily.

'OK. Let me think. Ah . . . OK. I've got one.'

He props his head up on his elbow.

'Great took me on a boat once.' He's never too fussy — he'll take any old story from my childhood, which is just as well, because there isn't much to tell. 'She was wearing a bright yellow jacket and got covered in greenfly.'

'What's greenfly?' he asks.

'Little tiny flies that are green.'

'Oh. Do they sting?'

'No.'

'Why did they go after her?'

'She said it was her perfume. But I said it was because she looked like a daffodil.'

'Did she?' he asks, smiling, imagining.

'No, I was only teasing her. She really looked like a buttercup.'

He looks at me sideways to see if I'm serious. Then laughs. He is quiet for a second, then frowns. 'I don't like the smell in the hospital.' He flops down on the pillow.

I rub his cheek. 'Neither do I.'

'It makes me sick in my tummy. My tummy was sick today. I'm not going back again. 'K?'

'We'll see. Now close your eyes,' I say gently.

He gives in to the pull of sleep, going so deep it's scary. I lie here worrying about how to get him to hospital again, about how to ask Dave, about not finding a match. I force myself to stop and concentrate instead on remembering those positive affirmation things Pat, the psychologist, keeps talking about — 'Whatever happens, I can cope.' I don't believe myself. I try some 'positive visualisation', imagining Charlie's body recovering from today's onslaught. No joy. His latest blood tests are good, I remind myself, which relieves the worry for all of about eight seconds.

I get up. Drag on a warm jumper. Tidy up. Put on a wash. Iron things I don't usually iron. Pick up a heap of neglected post, and sit up at the counter with it. I decide to be methodical and get out the chequebook, envelopes, stamps. I take the letters as they appear. Bill, bill, a CD I've won in some competition I don't remember entering, an Air Mail envelope. An Air Mail envelope! I pick it up, look closer. Dave's handwriting. Dave's address in the corner. *It's not Christmas. It's not my birthday. What's up?* I run my thumb under the thin fold of paper. I pull out a card. An invitation. To a wedding. Dave and Fiona. *Who the hell is Fiona?*

I search for a note. Some clue. Nothing. Just the invite. I can't believe he sent it without an explanation. As if the card says it all. Which it does. 'I've found another woman. A woman who will actually marry me. A woman who loves me. A woman I love. Bye, bye, Jenny. I'm getting on with my life. Without you.'

I don't care, I tell myself. *I didn't want him. I don't want him now. So what if he's gone? So what if I am alone? So what if no one loves me? It's all my own fault. Who'd want me anyway, slumped here in a crappy jumper with shag-all make-up and a fuzzy head of hair? Bet she's beautiful. Fiona. He went all the way to America to find a Fiona. There are loads of them here. Loads of Fionas. We had our invitations made. Jenny and Dave cordially invite you . . . .*

I drop my head onto the table like a histrionic teenager and indulge in a good old feeling-sorry-for-myself bawl. Then, suddenly, I'm writing to him.

Dear Dave,

I'm sorry that it's taken five years to send you a proper letter. And I'm sorry that in this letter I have to ask for your help. But I do. Charlie was diagnosed with leukaemia three weeks ago. And it's not just any old leukaemia, it's a special kind that requires a bone marrow transplant. If he doesn't get it, he will die.

I thought I could handle this myself but I have had a blood test and am not a match. I'm sorry but I need your help, Dave. You don't have to do much, just a simple blood test which you can do there, in the States, through your own doctor. No need to come home. Charlie's doctor can co-ordinate with yours.

It's unlikely that you will be a match. But you understand that I have to ask, I have to check. I know you have a new life now and I'm glad you've found someone else. I am sorry to butt in again but Charlie is my life. I can't lose him.

If you say yes, and I pray you do, I'll find out exactly what you need to do.

I am glad you are happy. You mightn't think it, but that's what I've always wanted.

Jenny

I don't say I'm sorry I let him go, though that's how I feel. I don't say I miss him, but I do. I don't say I made the biggest mistake of my life but I did.

My head is full of decisions queuing up to be made. Do I contact my parents to see if they are a match or do I wait to hear from Dave? Do I send Charlie back to school for a 'normal' life and risk infection or keep him at home and risk smothering him? Do I tell Simon that he may be able to help, how and why? I hop from problem to problem without working out any solutions, until I drive myself crazy. In the end, I decide to tackle the easiest first. Parents. *Or is it the easiest?*

The chances that they might have the right tissue type are negligible, but there. I take a breath, try to detach from my feelings towards my mother, try to be logical and think. This takes two mugs of coffee. But the decision does come. And it's this: because the chances of their being any help are tiny, I'm going to wait to hear from Dave. I'll give him a week. If I hear nothing, I'll rethink.

They tell me at the hospital that it would be 'healthy' for Charlie to go back to school. But they've also given me a booklet that warns against him catching chicken pox or measles, which could kill him because his immune system is down. He has had chicken pox but not measles, and I was too afraid to give him the MMR. If I don't send him, he will miss months of school. But he is going to miss months anyway after the bone marrow transplant and will have to repeat the year as it is. He is only four. Many kids start at five. No, I'm not sending him. I want to build him up for the transplant, have him ready. Ensure that nothing can go wrong. If I smother him, I smother him. I'll get on to the Department of Education and Science to see if I qualify for Home Tuition. If I don't, I'll teach him myself, or ask Mary or Debbie to help. As for other faces, Dara can come over. And Jack. As long as their vaccinations are up to date.

As for Simon? That's the one decision that doesn't get made. Two out of three is progress. Seventy per cent progress. A 'B'. Or so I tell myself, before crawling in beside Charlie for the last few hours of darkness.

23

Charlie likes to swim but can't while he has a Freddie. So he's in the bath wearing his togs and swimming hat. It's the nearest we get. And he's happy enough to pretend.

'Do seals eat penguins?' he asks.

'No, fish.'

'Fish eat penguins?'

'No,' I say, laughing. 'Penguins eat fish, and seals eat fish.'

'And what do fish eat?'

'Fish. And other stuff.'

'Oh.'

There was a time when I wouldn't have had the patience for a conversation like this. But we're in no rush now. And I'm in Enjoy-the-Moment training. It's not so tricky once you slow down.

'D'you know what Great used to sing to me when I was a kid and she was giving me a bath?' I ask.

'Row, row, row your boat?'

'How did you know?'

'That's what she used to sing to me.'

'Of course she did. Silly me.'

'Why did she sing that?' he asks.

'Because she was a bit mad.'

'Yeah. I know.' He smiles.

'I like people who're a bit mad,' I say.

'You're a bit mad.'

'Thanks. So are you.'

'Ow'.

'What?'

'You hurt me.'

'What did I do?' I'm only washing his face with the softest of cloths.

'You hurt me on the forehead.'

'Where? Show me.'

'Don't *touch* it.'

'I won't. Let me see.'

'Ooow. I said don't touch.'

'There's nothing there, Charlie.'

'But it's sore.'

'OK, let's get out of the bath, dry you off and have another look.'

I can't find anything. *Should I call the hospital? And tell them what? Charlie has a sore forehead but there's nothing there?*

Two days later, I notice a small red patch with tiny blisters.

'Is your forehead sore, Charlie?'

'Nope,' he says, reaching for his Gameboy.

'Is it itchy?'

'No.'

'Were you scratching it or anything?'

'No.' As in, leave-me-alone.

'Weird.'

'What?'

'Nothing. It's probably nothing.'

I feel like an idiot ringing Simon. I mean, it's a few blisters. He's going to think I'm overreacting, call Pat in on the job again . . . But they did say to ring if I was worried and I'm — maybe not worried exactly, but suspicious.

He doesn't dismiss it.

'And it's nowhere else on the body?'

'No.'

'When did it appear?'

'This morning.'

'Is it sore?'

'No.'

'Was there any soreness before the rash appeared?'

'No. Actually, wait, yes. It was sore the other day but not in that exact spot. It was closer to his ear.'

'Jenny, I think you should bring him.'

'When?'

'Well, now, if it suits. It might be nothing but it's best to check.'

We are driving into dark, grey clouds. The sun in the rear-view mirror is blinding. It strikes me that we are leaving it behind. Stopped at lights, I stare blankly into the back of the space wagon in front. Two boys are fighting. Their heads have been closely shaved but strong stubble juts out of their healthy scalps. I can feel the energy coming from them and wish there were such a thing as an energy transplant. Hook up jump leads to their car and steal some of the energy for Charlie. They've too much anyway.

We arrive at the hospital in a downpour. The red neon 'full' sign in the car park glows. *Where can I park?* I drive down a nearby street, which is jammed with parked cars. I can't walk this far in the rain. I'd have to carry Charlie and he's getting so heavy from retained fluid. *To hell with it*. I drive up to A&E, park on double yellow lines and run in, carrying my son.

Simon shines his surgery lamp onto Charlie's forehead and moves in for a closer look.

'It's getting worse, Simon — even since this morning.'

'It's all on one side,' he mutters.

'Yes.'

'And he's had chicken pox,' he says, lightly fingering a pock-mark just over the place Charlie's eyebrow used to be.

'Yes.'

'It's not sore,' says Charlie, who has developed an expertise of knowing what doctors are going to ask before they do.

Simon smiles at him. Then looks at me seriously.

'It looks like shingles, Jenny.'

'But children don't get shingles.'

'It's not very common, but they can, especially if their immune systems are down.'

'Shingles is very painful, though, Simon. I did an article on it. And Charlie isn't sore.'

'Shingles in children isn't usually sore.'

'Oh.' Something else occurs to me. 'But he hasn't been in contact with anyone with chicken pox.'

'Jenny, shingles is a reactivation of the chicken pox virus already in the system. Charlie has developed shingles because his immune system is down, not because he has been in contact with chicken pox.'

'Oh.'

'It's shingles, Jenny. It's in the very early stages. We'll have to admit him and start intravenous anti-viral drugs.'

'Oh, no,' says Charlie, mirroring my thoughts. *Not again.*

'I'm sorry, Charlie. But it's the best thing for you. This time you'll have your very own room,' says Simon. To me, he explains that Charlie will need to be kept in isolation to prevent the shingles from spreading to other children.

'Maybe we could treat him at home? I could give the drugs into his Freddie. I already flush it twice a week with heparin and saline.'

'Jenny, Charlie is immuno-compromised. Any infection like shingles in the immuno-compromised is very serious. We need to admit him and start treatment straightaway. And, in fairness, I need to tell you that there is a risk of damage to his eye. Now,' he says, in a try-to-be-calm-now-that-I've-shocked-you voice, 'we've caught it early, and if we start the drugs immediately, there is a good chance that disease progression can be halted before it gets to his eye.'

'What's wrong with my eyes, Mama?'

'Nothing, Charlie. We just have to give you some medicine to stop the rash — that's all.'

'I don't want to stay here. I want to go home.'

'It's just for a little while. And I'll be with you. And Simon and Anne and Siobhán. And Mary will call in.'

'Will Debbie mind Sausage?' *God, here we go, all over again.*

A nurse we don't recognise brings us to the ward. She hands us over to another nurse we don't know. I ask where Anne is and am told she is on her day off. I reel off a few more names. This baby says she doesn't know who I am talking about. She is on loan from another ward for the day. Apparently there's a shortage of oncology nurses. Well, that's just great.

She shows us to a single room and tells us, without a hint of sympathy, that Charlie is allowed leave only to go to the toilet. I ask her which would he pass on — chicken pox or shingles. She doesn't know. I look around the room and wonder how I'll keep him entertained. A bed, locker, window with a brick view, and a TV, mounted high on the wall — presumably so it can't be stolen. No cartoon pictures, just 'no smoking' and 'no mobile phone' signs. No bright colours, just glossy yellow paint on a bumpy surface, giving the impression of lumpy custard. It has been scraped away in long lines in places — I imagine, by someone moving the bed. The old-fashioned radiator is the kind you see in convents. I imagine there was a crucifix here once. The only thing that is any way bright is the metal frame of the bed, which is red. It has the name of the ward painted on it. *Why? Do they think someone's going to run off with it?* Nothing unusual about the table trolley on wheels. *What's the surveillance camera for?*

From across the hall, in the kitchen, filter the echoing sounds of spoons in cups, a microwave door popping open, people talking. A woman passes by, her soft flat shoes squeaking on the marmoleum floor. She is talking to her little girl as though she's deaf, repeating everything in a singsong voice, five times at least. *Will the child grow up stupid?* I close the door, reading through a paper sign that has been stuck up on the window, ISOLATION (backwards). *At least we have a sink*, I notice, but it's a hospital sink, with a metal flap instead of taps and a roll of coarse blue paper towel hanging over it and a bin beside it with a sticker on the top: CLINICAL WASTE. *Oh for a bit of creative vandalism.*

Isolation describes it all right.

I look at my watch for the umpteenth time. It's almost an hour since we were put in here, and Charlie still hasn't received any anti-viral drugs. My legs are jigging, my fingers tapping. *If it's so dangerous, where are the bloody drugs?* I switch on my mobile and call Simon. He seems baffled that nothing has happened.

Minutes later, he strides past our room. A few more minutes and our friend the Nurse from Somewhere Else wheels in an electronic drip. She tells me it's the medicine Charlie needs and it will take about thirty minutes to go in. I relax a little.

Not so Charlie.

'Where are your sterile gloves?' he asks. 'You should have sterile gloves for this.'

She looks at him, her colour rising. Is it anger, humiliation or both?

'Have you done this before?' he asks.

'Yeah, I have, actually.'

He's watching — *examining* — her every movement. I am embarrassed. Firstly, that I didn't notice about the gloves. Secondly, that he's putting her under pressure. But he is right. The last thing we need is for his Freddie to get infected. I've seen it happen with other kids and it is serious. I watch the drops fall rapidly in their little capsule, imagining the drug whizzing through his veins, zapping the virus. At last.

She leaves.

'She didn't wash her hands,' he snorts.

Ten minutes later, Simon appears.

'How is everything?' he asks.

'That nurse didn't do it right. She didn't have the sterile gloves. Mum has to wear sterile gloves at home when she does my Freddie. She's very careful about it. That nurse isn't careful. That nurse should be careful.'

'You're right Charlie. I'll have a chat with her. She's not used to this ward.'

'She's not as good as Anne.'

'Anne will be back tomorrow.'

'Good,' says Charlie.

Good, I think.

'And she didn't wash her hands.'

'Oh, dear,' says Simon. He smiles at me and is gone again.

We have probably made an enemy. Well, maybe she'll do it right from now on, not just for Charlie but for the other children. And it's lives we're talking about here. Good man, Charlie! You might be getting precocious but at least you're keeping people like her on their toes.

I can't believe we're back in here again. Stuck. Trapped. I forgot to ask Simon how long we will be in for. I forgot to ask if Charlie can continue to have his chemotherapy while on the Acyclovir. I forgot to ask if it will delay the transplant. Am I or am I not a journalist? Should I not be a source of endless questions? What has happened to my head?

While I was busy feeling sorry for myself, Elaine was losing her daughter. Jessica died last night. The minute I woke, I knew something was wrong. Silence. Air, heavy with grief and defeat, seeped under the closed door of Charlie's room. The first person I saw was Anne, who came quietly. She brought me outside and across the corridor to the little room for parents, though Charlie was still asleep. I knew what she was going to say before she said it. Nurses aren't supposed to be attached to their patients, but how can you not let yourself hope that a child is going to get better, make it? How can you remain hard in the face of a mother's grief?

'And I thought I was the only one with problems,' I say to her now, squirming under the pressure of guilt.

'Everyone feels like that, Jenny. It's called survival.' She puts her hand on mine.

'Someone should have told me. Why didn't Simon tell me? Give me some sort of hint? I could have been with her for a while.'

'He must have had his reasons, Jenny. It's a very private time for a family.'

'Poor Elaine. Jessica's gone. *Gone*. Yesterday, she was there. She was dying but she was here. Elaine could talk to her. Jessica could feel her mother's touch. Now she's gone. Gone.'

'Elaine doesn't feel like that. It's a relief, Jenny.'

'*A relief?* To have lost her daughter?'

'Jessica is at peace now. No more pain, no more suffering. That's the way Elaine sees it.'

'Should I go to them? I don't know — what should I do?'

'Elaine and Jim sat with Jessica all night. They held her for hours after she'd gone. They are going to take her home now.' She must see the disbelief on my face. 'They want one last day together.' She smiles.

I'm staring at her.

'It helps.'

'I'd like her to know I'm thinking about her.'

'She knows.'

'So there's nothing I can do?'

'There will be, but not yet.'

What will I tell Charlie? is my next thought but I can't ask — how selfish would that be?

It's like she reads my mind. 'About Charlie,' she says.

'Yes.'

'Are you OK about telling him?'

'I don't know, Anne. Do you think I should tell him at all?'

'It's better that you do. He'll ask about Jessica when you stop mentioning her name and going to see her. Or he'll overhear you talking about her to someone else. He'll find out some way. And he needs to trust you, Jenny. So, yes, I would tell him.'

'How?'

'I would keep it very simple. I'd just say that Jessica got very, very ill . . . .'

'He knew that she was very sick.'

'Good, that will help prepare him. Well then, I would just say something like, "you know the way Jessica was very, very sick . . . ." Then I'd simply say, "Well, she didn't get better, Charlie." Then tell him that she died last night and is in heaven now.'

'He never got to know her, really. I was afraid, Anne. I used to go to see Jessica and Elaine on my own. To protect him.'

'I know. And that will make it easier for him. But he is still likely to be upset and possibly worried. I wouldn't talk about it too much with him but I would encourage him to express how he feels. Maybe, later, just ask him how he is. And take it from there. Pat might come round to have a chat.'

It's like the cancer has won a major battle in a war that is fought in here every day. A brave soldier has fallen. For once, I'm glad Charlie is in isolation because I don't want to face any of the other parents. I don't want to see fear in their eyes. I just want to stay in here, tucked away, staring at a TV screen and pretending to notice what the Pink Panther is doing.

24

Jessica's funeral. I race along the corridor, late. Charlie wanted to come at the last minute and had to be talked out of the idea. Poor little fellow. He wanted to say goodbye. I rush on, trying to remember where I parked. *The double yellow lines! Damn! Damn, damn, damn!* I stride outside and find the car, a white square on the window, a yellow triangle on the wheel. *Shit! Shit, shit, shit!* Twenty minutes to make it to the church. I look around for a solution. A bus stop. *Yeah, right. Dublin Bus.* Any taxis when you need them? No. I stand in panic, head swivelling. I can't be late. I'm taking out my mobile to phone for a taxi when I see Simon and Anne trooping towards the exit, coats on. *They must be going.*

Simon sees me.

'Are you all right, Jenny?' he asks, looking concerned.

Am I wearing the panic I feel?

'My car's clamped.'

'Oh, no,' says Anne. 'That's the pits. Are you going to the funeral?'

'I was.'

'Come with us,' she says.

'Would you *mind*?'

'As long as you don't object to fast driving,' says Simon. 'We've cut it a bit fine.'

Simon and Anne chat to each other up front while I look out the window in the back, like a child. Don't feel much like talking. The day is grey and bleak, standard issue for Irish funerals, almost as if it had been prearranged.

The church is heaving with people, many standing at the back and up the side aisles. A block of seats is taken up with school-girls in green uniforms. There are people in suits, women alone, and families. Lots of families. I expect to join the standers but Anne has other ideas, continuing up the centre aisle ahead of me, and I feel, out of loyalty, I have to follow. We are walking towards a little white coffin and I can't breathe. Head down, I follow her sturdy ankles. Finally, she stops. We excuse ourselves as we squeeze in front of three pairs of knees and find a tight spot in the pew. I'm convinced we must have lost Simon, but no, he crams in beside me. *Why didn't we stay at the back?*

All is quiet apart from compulsory throat-clearing and cough-ing. Someone is tuning a guitar. I keep my eyes focused on the altar, sorry that I'm sitting between Anne and Simon, who probably want to talk to each other. I sit quietly, waiting for it to start, for it to end, be over. So I can forget. And pretend. And not think. I check my bag for handkerchiefs. They're there — a thick bundle of real, fabric handkerchiefs, strong enough to withstand a tidal wave. Because I know what's going to happen. The coffin has already shot the first arrow at my heart. The coffin that holds little Jessica who, only a year ago, sat at their kitchen table with her twin sister, making their father a surprise birthday card, while Elaine brought me into another room to talk about living with cancer. I stop myself thinking about the child lying up there so still, surrounded by dark, and wood, and air, because if I don't, I just won't get through this.

It starts. And for a while, I hold it together. But then my ability to block things out starts to fail me. Suddenly I notice it — the utter, devastating sadness of it all. The paintings of horses on the altar, done by Jessica. Her black velvet riding hat and recently polished boots. The heart-shaped display of rosettes, little conquests that don't matter any more. The songs she picked for the ceremony — especially the one about there being no tears in heaven. The message Elaine reads from her daughter to the congregation, saying goodbye and thanking the nurses and doctors each by name, the people who donated blood, but most of all her mum, dad, family and friends. She has a special goodbye for her twin, Laura. Her parting words to us all are: 'Treasure each day. And give blood.'

Then the most disconcerting thing happens. Laura comes to the microphone. She is identical, or at least was, until the cancer and chemo took their toll on Jessica. How surreal, how *unfair* on Elaine.

'Jessica was my sister and my best friend. I don't know why she got sick but I wanted to get sick too. I tried so hard but I couldn't. I thought she'd get better. But she didn't. Even though I prayed and promised to be good. Mum says it was meant to be and that she's in heaven now and she's very happy and not a bit lonely. But I am lonely. I miss her so much . . . I don't want to go to school without her . . . .' Her voice breaks and she stops, her head drops and she shakes. A delicate little fist goes up to her eye. Elaine steps back up beside her daughter, puts an arm around her and leads her back to their seats. I hold my breath so I make no noise, I put my hand over my mouth, but sobs shake my body. Hands are going up to faces all around. Noses are being blown. Only the statues remain unmoved. Everyone united in grief. I fumble in my satchel for another handkerchief. They are all used and wet. Soaked. But I have nothing else. I am about to use a wet one when a clean, folded white one appears in front of me. I take it from Simon without looking at him. Anne puts her arm around me.

When the time comes, Simon and Anne go to the top of the church to pay their respects. I can't. I try to collect myself, regain control, think about something else. How naïve. As soon as Jessica's father puts his arms around his daughter's coffin and carries her out of the church as though there is no barrier between them, as though the coffin is not there, I feel actual pain in my heart. It is the last time he will ever carry his little girl.

Leaving, I see Elaine standing in the churchyard, surrounded by people, yet temporarily alone. People are hugging her children, her husband, but for a brief moment there is no one with her. Standing, staring straight ahead, in shock, missing her little girl, her baby. I forget everything and go to her. We just look at each other, say nothing and hug.

She pulls back, looks like she's going to say something, but nothing comes.

I try to smile but my lip wobbles and I'm off again. 'Look at me, I'm hopeless,' I begin, clearing tears with thumbs. 'I wanted to say something, do something . . . .'

'You came,' she says. And I feel someone beside us now, someone who wants to say how sorry they are. I smile one last smile, squeeze her arm and turn to go. I hurry away, head down, embarrassed by my tears and my inability to provide some comfort, however small. I feel a hand on my shoulder and look up.

'Oh, Simon,' is all I manage.

'Are you all right?' he asks, softly.

'Yeah.'

'Ready to go?'

'Mm hmm.' I sniffle. We walk towards the car park. 'Anne,' I say, turning around. 'We forgot Anne.'

'No, she's off duty. Gone shopping, then home.'

'I sometimes forget that you have lives outside the hospital.'

'Sometimes we forget ourselves,' he says, smiling.

Silence.

'That was tough,' he says.

I nod.

'Are you all right?'

'Yes,' I say, sighing.

'Ready to go back to the hospital?'

'No.' I laugh.

'Would you like a coffee first?' he asks, kindly.

'Don't you have to get back?'

'I could do with something myself. We're not immune, you know, doctors.' We are almost at his car. 'It's not easy,' he says. 'When we lose.'

'You did your best, Simon.'

He doesn't answer. We get to the car and he bleeps it open. I marvel at how silently such heavy doors close.

'So, coffee?' he asks.

'That would be nice.'

'Where?'

'Doesn't matter. Somewhere quiet.'

'I have to call home. I can make us one? Or would you prefer to go somewhere?'

'No, actually, that would be better. I'm a mess.'

'You're fine.'

'If you like red, puffy eyes and swollen faces. Then I'm fine.' I smile.

He leaves me in the sitting room while he makes the coffee. A mistake. By the time he gets back, I'm at it again. I hear him come in, and I look up. He puts down the two yellow mugs with smiley faces.

'I'm sorry,' I say, wiping my nose with the palm of my hand.

'For goodness sake,' he says gently. 'Don't worry about it.' He sits on the arm of the couch, then is up again. 'Hold on a minute.' He's back with a sheet of kitchen paper. I take it from him and blow.

'I'm sorry,' is all I seem to be able to say. That, and 'I don't know . . . .'

He sits beside me now, and puts an arm around me. 'Shhh. It's OK,' he says and takes my wet, sticky hands in his. 'Shhhh.' I'm sobbing now, the result of a crying overdose. I start to hiccup. Feel such a fool. He draws me into a hug. And, God, it feels safe. He smooths back my hair. And I need that. 'Shhh,' he says when I sob involuntarily. I sigh again. He pulls back, lifts my chin with his finger, looks into my eyes. 'It's OK, it will be OK.'

I don't know why but I lean forward, my mouth seeking his. Our lips touch. It's like flicking a switch. Everything becomes frantic. We kiss passionately, my face in his hands, his in mine, hungry for each other as if everything has been leading to this, building, destined to happen, and we are powerless to stop it. I tug at his shirt, too impatient for buttons, tiny, annoying, *stupid bloody buttons*. He yanks at mine causing one button to pop out and hit me in the eye. It makes me laugh and stops us. 'I'm sorry,' he says, mortified. He runs his thumb over my eye-lid, kisses it, then the side of my nose, then full on my mouth. He takes my upper lip between his, then my lower. Then lips, mouths separate us no longer, the boundary melts. He eases me back and I am eager for his weight. He cups the back of my head in his hand and

I am shocked and thrilled by the feeling of his tongue running, flat, from the base of my neck to my chin, a predator staking a claim. I open my eyes and find his staring into mine. He holds my gaze, then lightly kisses my mouth, neck, then he buries his face in the swell of my breasts. He groans. His hand slides up my leg and caresses me through my underwear. My turn to groan. Oh God! I arch my back, aching for him. Our eyes are locked when he enters me, locked when we move together like we were destined to, locked when I explode in waves and bite his fingers, and locked when he calls my name and tightens his grip on my hair. He shudders and I hold him tight. He lies very still now and I don't want to let go. Just stay like this forever. Not move. Not get up. Not carry on. He lifts his head now and we face each other, eyes only far enough apart to keep each other in focus. Pupils dilated. Staring. Bonded. When he takes his away, the spell will be broken. We will remember who we are and the reasons we cannot be together. I have a sick child. He is that child's doctor. I am his guilty past. And it will be over. So I hold his stare, until he looks away and takes himself away, the warmth of his body replaced by unheated November air. I pull my skirt back over my knees, turn on my side and cover myself with my shirt.

'I'm sorry,' he says, sitting on the edge of the couch, his head in his hands, making no attempt to get dressed. I want to run my hand along his back, kneel behind him and cling to him. But I don't.

'I shouldn't have let that happen,' he says.

I don't move, don't look at him, don't want to hear. Almost block my ears.

'Charlie is my patient. You are his mother. This is not right.'

'It is,' I say quietly but defiantly.

'No, Jennifer, it isn't.'

I shake my head.

'How would an outsider see it?'

I don't answer.

'They'd say I took advantage of a young mother trying to cope alone with the recent diagnosis of her son.'

'They'd be wrong.'

'It won't happen again.'

I say nothing. Give up. What's the point?

'I'm sorry,' he says again.

Me too.

He takes my hand in his. 'If things were different . . . .'

'Let's forget it, Simon,' I say, trying to sound calm, trying to sound as if I don't care, taking my hand back, sitting up. 'I need to go to Charlie now.' *Is that flat enough?* I sit up, turn my back to him, start to do up my shirt, crucial button missing. I stand and try to flatten out the creases in my skirt. Pointless.

'I'm sorry,' he says.

'Could you just drop me home, Simon?' I close my coat and try to hold myself together. 'I'll get a taxi to the hospital. Thanks.' I clutch my satchel to my chest, the way I used to carry my school bag on the short walk home. I'm ready. But I'm shaking, my whole body reacting, screaming, 'This happened . . . you didn't dream it . . . it happened, Jenny.'

'You don't need to take a taxi. I can wait while you get whatever you need.'

'Can we just go?'

'Of course. I'm sorry.'

'Yeah. I know.'

I shower and change, chin high. I tell myself to keep busy. *Action will get rid of the shakes.* I turf out the soggy handkerchiefs. *Fresh start.* I pack clothes for the hospital. *Begin again.* I get a new tube of toothpaste from the bathroom cabinet, catch my reflection in the mirror. *Weakling!* I get scissors. Cut off great chunks of hair. *Drink. I need a drink.*

They both stop what they're doing and stare.

'*What?*' I ask, crossly, impatiently.

'Your hair,' says Charlie.

'Are you all right?' asks Mary, standing slowly, coming towards me. She looks worried. *Damn!*

'Yes.' I turn my back on her, using the excuse of putting my coat away.

'Jenny? Did something happen?'

'No.'

'It's just that . . . I don't know . . . it's not just your hair . . . .'

'It's nothing. I was upset. I went home. I cut my hair — so what? It's just hair.' Coat sorted, I have to face them again.

Mary looks at me questioningly, but saying nothing. Not pushing it. She sits back down.

'Did they grave Jessica?' asks Charlie, kneeling up on the bed.

'Yes, sweetheart.' I run my hand along the side of his cheek. 'They buried Jessica.' I sigh, take off my shoes, sit up on the bed beside him. 'Can I rest on your pillows for a sec, Charlie?'

'OK.'

I lie back on the wall of pillows, close my eyes.

We are quiet for a second. I feel him on the bed, moving up towards me. His hand rests on my leg.

'Do souls have mouths, Mum?'

I hope Mary'll answer. She doesn't. I open my eyes, look at him, then at Mary. She's rummaging in her bag. *Forcing me to answer.*

'Do souls have mouths?' he repeats.

'I don't know, Charlie. I don't think so.' I close my eyes again.

'Why?'

'I don't think they eat in heaven,' I continue, eyes closed.

'What's heaven like?'

I am weary but open my eyes again. 'I don't know. Nice.'

Go on, says his face.

Oh, what the hell. 'I think it might be like a big garden where everyone's happy and the sun is shining.' The Irish approach to heaven — the weather's got to be good.

'Are the angels and the souls having a picnic?'

'That's a nice idea, Charlie. Yes, I think they probably are.'

'Well, they'll need mouths then.'

Mary smiles over at me.

'Do they have McDonald's in heaven?' he persists.

'No.'

'Why not?'

'Because it's run by humans not souls.'

'I bet souls could make chicken nuggets and chips just as good as human beans.'

'Maybe you're right.'

'Where is it, Mum?'

'What?'

'Heaven,' he says impatiently as if he's talking to an idiot. 'Is it on the top of the world?'

'It's in the sky somewhere, I think.'

'Is it in space?'

'Probably.'

'Is it beyond space?'

'You're right. That's where it is. Beyond space. Probably.'

'I think I might go someday.'

And that's what wakes me up. 'Not yet, Charlie. Not yet, love. Come here. Sit on my lap — I need a cuddle.'

'OK, Mum.' He sits up on me. 'But can I go tomorrow?'

'Wait a few years, Charlie, OK?'

'OK, Mum.'

Later, Pat, the psychologist, 'happens' by.

'How are things?' she asks too innocently. *Mary has said something. I know she has.*

'Fine,' I say, not in the mood to be analysed. Charlie is asleep. It's time for peace now, quiet. No more questions.

'It was a tough day,' she continues.

'Yes.'

'Terrible thing to bury a child.'

'Yes.'

'How are you feeling?'

'Fine.'

'I see you've cut your hair.'

'It's just hair — you don't have to analyse it.'

I expect her to react but she doesn't.

'Is there anything you'd like to talk about?'

Well, yes, actually, now that you ask. I fucked Dr Grace today. How's that? 'No.'

'Well, you know where I am if you need me.' She smiles. 'Try and get some sleep.'

Off she goes, making people's lives easier all over the world — or so she'd like to think.

I find myself in the chapel, looking for the answer to one question. *Why? That's all. Why? Why do children get sick? Why do they die? Why? Why bring them into the world in the first place if*

You're going to kill them off before they experience anything? What is the point? To make us stronger? I can be strong. You don't have to take my child. I can be good, be a better person. Don't take my boy. But there is nothing here, only echoes. And a register of deaths. A great tome, recording all the children who have died in this hospital. *What is that supposed to do? Remind us they are mortal? Or remind us that they lived?*

25

I can't forget. It's not that simple. I watch him wash his hands and remember how they felt on my skin. I look at the back of his neck where his hair curls into a V, and I want to twirl it around my finger. I look at his gentle face and want to take it in my hands and kiss his mouth. Start it off again, the spark. Sometimes, I see it in his eyes too. Or think I do. We might be discussing Charlie's blood count or shingles or how much he's been peeing during the day — business — when I catch him looking at me with such softness that it throws me and I can't remember what I was thinking or what he was saying. But then I look again, and it's gone, leaving me to wonder was I dreaming it, maybe just creating a distraction from the reality of blood counts, angry nervous rashes and the 'blasts' that might come back if we don't find a donor. Oh, we are doctor and parent of patient again — make no mistake. Professional, civil, even friendly, at times. It's just the eyes, every so often, the eyes. And if I'm dreaming, then I'm dreaming and I'll keep on dreaming until I get out of here, get home, away from him and his eyes, get on with my life. Forget.

Charlie turns a corner. The slow, steady creep of shingles appears to stop. Or is it just fooling us? Ready to strike with blindness as soon as we dare to relax, breathe. Maybe I should hope for that though, because what God would blind your son and then take him? But days pass and the rash starts to recede. And I thank that God and tell Him I'm sorry for doubting Him.

But another worry lunges in to take its place. I have not heard from Dave. It has been ten days. *How long does it take a letter to get to the US? I had the right address. I remembered to include our phone number. It's obvious. He doesn't want to do it. He's just going to ignore us. Pretend he never got my letter. Why should he get involved? I told him to go. I didn't keep in touch. He got on with his life. Why should he go backwards?* Still, I ask Mary to pick up my post and answering machine messages. My stress level creeps up like mercury in a thermometer. Panic. *Should I wait another day? Or should I approach my mother, ignore the hatred I feel towards her, get down, get dirty, seek her blood the way a politician seeks a vote? Or should I, after what we've just been through, approach Simon, tell him the truth, admit what I have been hiding from him all this time? Ask him to help. Oh God, I need to do something — time is ticking. I hate this cancer. It pushes me to the limit, on every front. Making me imagine life without my son, making me face things I don't want to, things I have successfully ignored for years, like my parents, and Charlie's father.*

I'm walking Charlie back from the toilet, pushing along his drip for him, looking down to make sure I don't knock its sprawling legs into his feet or move them in front of his slippers causing him to trip. Something, I don't know what — a feeling, a sudden

213

consciousness — makes me look up. I wasn't imagining it. Two people, one uniformed, are standing at the door to Charlie's room, talking, eyes on us. One of them is Anne, I see now. The other looks like Dave. But it couldn't be. Dave is in New York. I don't take my eyes off him until I get close enough to realise that it is Dave. It really is. An Americanised, denim-ised, loafer-ised, grey T-shirted version of Dave. His hair is longer, wavier. His body fitter. He spots me and smiles. The Dave I know, the face I know.

'Here they are,' announces Anne.

I have stopped. What is it about men? I cope perfectly without them but as soon as they turn up, I'm jelly.

'What is it, Mum?' asks Charlie, looking up at me.

I shake my head. 'Nothing, sweetheart.' It comes out as a whisper.

'Who is it?'

'A friend. It's just a friend.'

They walk to us, Dave leading the way. He is still smiling. Anne seems to read the situation because she says something cheery to Charlie, lifts him up and carries him to the room, pushing the drip with her other hand. Chat, chat, chat, she goes. He is not fooled, looks back. Suspicious.

I'm stuck. He comes to me.

'I can't believe you came,' I say, whipping away escapee tears.

'Of course I came.'

'I hadn't heard from you. I was about to give up.'

'Oh ye of little faith.' One of his sayings, which makes me laugh and cry at the same time.

He puts his arms around me and I feel tiny. He smells familiar, comforting.

'I'm sorry for not writing,' I say into his chest.

'I didn't exactly kill myself either.' His voice travels down.

'We should have stayed in touch.'

'I know.'

He pulls back, holding onto my arms so he can look at me. 'It's good to see you, Jenny.'

'You too.' I smile, half-afraid to look at him.

'You've changed so much. Your hair.' He touches it. 'It's beautiful.'

'It needs a cut,' I say, embarrassed by the recent hacking episode, still obvious, despite Mary's best efforts with a scissors.

'But it's so long.'

'It was a lot longer.' I smile.

'And the colour. Wow. I never liked those highlight things. And the glasses . . . I've always liked glasses on you. You are looking great.'

'Hardly,' I say, thinking of how exhausted I do look — how drained, how thin.

He lets me go. We stand awkwardly. I fold my arms. He stuffs his hands in his pockets.

'How is he?'

'He's OK, Dave.' We start to walk, very slowly, back to the room, heads down. The movement gives us purpose. 'He's in remission but we had to come back in because he has shingles.'

He stops, looks over at me. 'The rash on his face?'

'Yeah.'

'Poor kid.'

We start to walk again.

'It's not sore,' I say. 'And, hopefully, it seems to be clearing. We got it early.'

He stops again. Making me stop. 'You should have told me,' he says. It's a statement of fact. And, now that it's out, I know he's right.

215

'I know. I'm sorry.'

'Why didn't you?'

'I didn't want to bother you.'

'*Bother me?*' His chin juts out. 'He could be my son, Jenny,' he whispers. 'My only child. He has a *terminal* illness. This is something I should know.'

'I know. I know. I'm sorry. I wasn't thinking.'

'*I* wasn't thinking. Back then. Going off to the States, leaving you here, alone, pregnant with a baby that could have been mine.'

'I told you to go.'

'I shouldn't have listened. It's taken this to make me realise it. I shouldn't have just gone off and left you.' His thumb is at his temple and two of his fingers are rubbing back and forth over his forehead, like he always does when he's upset.

'You didn't just go off and leave, Dave. It was the right thing.'

'I had responsibilities. That little boy in there could be my son.' He sweeps out his arm dramatically. 'In there, dying, without a father.'

'Dave, Charlie is not dying.'

'If he doesn't get a transplant, he will.'

'He'll get the transplant. He has to. We can't think of any other option.' I look up, to spread the tears.

'I'm sorry.' He takes my hands in his. 'Of course he'll get the transplant.' He wipes away a tear. 'I'm sorry, Jen. I didn't mean to upset you. I was just disappointed you hadn't told me. That's all. OK? Let's forget about it now. Let's just get him better. OK?'

'OK.' But I'm still crying.

He hugs me and we stand together quietly for a moment. I close my eyes and rest my head against the side of his neck, glad of the support. Then I feel the pull to get back to Charlie and to let Anne back to work. I lift my head, open my eyes. Wham! My line of vision crashes into Simon's. He is standing outside the nurses' station, holding a chart, not looking at it, but at us. I flush. He drops his gaze instantly as though mine has burnt him, slots the chart into a filing trolley and disappears into the nurses' station.

'We'd better go in to Charlie,' I say to Dave.

'Who are you?' Charlie demands of Dave. What would normally be an impressive frown just manages to wrinkle the bottom of his now enormous forehead.

'*Charlie*,' I say. 'Be nice.'

Anne gives us an understanding smile. 'I'll leave you to it,' she says, getting up. 'See you later, Charlie.' She taps him on the shoulder.

'See ya, Anne. You might win me the next time. If you're lucky.'

She laughs.

When she has gone, Charlie glares at Dave. 'Did you make my Mama cry?'

'No, Charlie,' I rush. 'Dave didn't make me cry.' He looks at me. They both do. 'I just got a shock. I wasn't expecting to see Dave. Some people cry when they get a shock. But see, I'm not crying now.' I produce a grin. 'I'm glad Dave's here, very glad. He's my friend. And he's very nice.'

Charlie gives him a not-so-sure look.

'He's come all the way from America to see you. Remember the big yellow country on the globe?'

'The United States of America where Disneyland is?'

'Yes,' says Dave, smiling.

'Cool. Are you a yank?'

Dave laughs. 'Nah, but I know lots of them.'

'D'you know the Hulk?'

217

Real, genuine laughter now.

'No, but I'll keep an eye out for him for you, when I get back, OK?'

'Cool. Want to see my Gameboy? I'm really good at it. Especially when I'm playing with Anne. She's useless.'

Dave looks at me as if to say, 'He's gas', then sits on the bed beside Charlie. They get into the game. 'Ah, get me out of here. Yikes. Oh my God. Got him. Phew. It's OK, I've got another life.' When he glances up at me proudly, five minutes later, he looks like a dad. This is the way it could have been. I turn my back on them. 'The boys,' I might have called them or 'my boys'. I go to the sink and splash my face with cold water.

He stays for the rest of the day and I get a sense of how it must feel to have someone to share this with — not just the laughter, but the worry, the responsibility, especially the responsibility. They walk to the toilet together, Little Man and Big Man, allowing me a tiny break from endless routine. Big Man reads to Little Man, plays ludo with him, listens intently to him, allowing my head time to clear. Amazingly, Big Man becomes the only person Little Man will take medicine from outside of me. To be able to avoid that battle, just for once, is such an incredible relief. I feel my mood lift. Everything seems easier all of a sudden. Manageable. But, I remind myself, it's just for a day or two. *Don't get cosy. Don't get used to it.*

Dave proves an instant hit with Mary, who calls as usual but doesn't stay long, afraid of interrupting the happy family unit I can see she is imagining (judging by her furtive eyebrow raising). I walk her to the hospital entrance, prepared to set her straight.

As soon as we're safely off the ward, she turns to me, her hand grabbing my arm. 'He's goooorgeous, Jen. How did you ever let him get away?'

'*Mary*.'

'But he is. And he just dropped everything and hopped on the first plane?' eyebrows up again.

'He came because of Charlie.'

'Who seems to really like him,' she says, in a problem-solved manner.

'Now all we've got to do is walk into the sunset, is that it?' I ask, cynically.

'Don't see why not.'

'*Mary*. What's wrong with you? First Simon, now Dave. Why are you in such a hurry to pair me off?'

'I'm just saying he's cute. Nothing wrong with that.'

'He's engaged.'

'Maybe you'd better remind him. I saw the way he looked at you in there.'

'Now you're imagining things . . . Mary, please don't,' I say, seriously. 'I know how happy Phil and you are together but that doesn't mean everyone needs that kind of relationship to be happy. I don't. OK? Everyone's different. Dave and I have been through so much. It is over. I made sure of that. Please, don't joke about this. Please.'

'Sorry.'

'OK, but please, enough man talk. I'm confused enough.'

She looks at me suddenly but says nothing.

'I need to think of Charlie.'

Finally, Little Man sleeps. I make coffee, then sit with Dave in the relatives' room across from Charlie's. We keep the doors open, so I can hear him if he wakes. There is so much to talk about, so much to ask. I start with the practicalities.

'How did you find us?'

219

'You're in Ireland's main cancer centre for children. Not much of a challenge for a journalist.' He smiles.

'Where are you staying?'

'Somewhere near the hospital, probably.'

'Probably? You mean you haven't organised it?'

'It's not a priority.' He takes a sip of coffee.

'Stay at the apartment.'

'Nah.'

'Why not?'

'I don't know. You mightn't want me there.'

'Of course I do. I wouldn't want you anywhere else. You've come all this way for us. Stay.'

'Really? You sure you don't mind?'

'Dave, of course I don't mind'.

'All right then, if you're sure.'

'How long are you over for?'

'As long as it takes.'

'It only takes a few minutes, Dave. You could have done it in the States.'

'I'm not talking about the blood test. I came over to be with you for this and I'm staying as long as you need me to. Until everything's sorted.'

'What do you mean? Until we find a donor?'

'If that's what it takes, yes.'

'But that could take ages. What about Fiona? What about the job?'

'They'll wait. Fiona understands . . . .'

Does she? What has he told her?

'I'm owed some leave.'

'You don't have to stay, Dave. I mean, it's great to see you, really great, but if you do the test tomorrow, you can go. You can always come back if you turn out to be a match. Everything seems to be working out for you in the States. You don't want to mess it up.'

He sighs. 'Let me do the test, Jenny, wait for the result and take it from there, OK?'

'It will take at least two weeks.'

'Fine. Two weeks. That's fine. I'd factored in two weeks.'

'You sure?'

'Sure.'

'Thanks, Dave.'

'You're welcome.' He smiles.

'So tell me about Fiona.'

'Fiona?'

'Fiona.'

'She's nice.'

'*Nice*? The woman you're going to marry is *nice*.'

'Yes.'

'Is she American?'

'Yep.'

'Must be Irish-American with a name like Fiona.'

'Mm hmm.'

'Aa-nd?'

'And what? She's a nice Irish-American girl, called Fiona, and I'm going to marry her. OK?'

'OK.' No point asking where he met her, what age she is, what she looks like, then. 'How come you sent out the invites so early? The wedding isn't until the spring.'

'We just sent out the Irish ones now to allow people organise cheap flights if they wanted to.'

'Very organised.'

'That's Fiona. So what happens next with Charlie?'

'Well, once he gets over the shingles, I presume it's back home. In the meantime, we keep looking for a donor.'

'Who else have you tried?'

'No one.'

'What about *him*?'

'No.'

'Does he know?'

'No.'

'*Jenny*.'

'I will tell him . . . if I have to.'

'You mean if I'm not a match?'

It sounds so calculated — if Dave doesn't work out, I'll try the next sucker. But it's not like that. I'm just trying to keep everything the way it is — simple, uncomplicated, under control. Is that so bad?

Simon pops his head in. 'Just saying goodnight . . . Oh, I'm sorry, I didn't realise you still had company . . . .'

'No, no, it's fine.' Suddenly we're all standing.

'Eh, Dave, this is Charlie's doctor, Si . . . '

'Simon Grace,' he says, confidently, offering his hand.

'Sorry?' Dave's head juts forward.

'Simon Grace?' says Simon, taking back his untouched hand.

Dave shoots me a look. 'Is this some sort of joke?' he asks.

'Dave, calm down,' I say. 'We need to talk.'

He turns to Simon. '*The* Simon Grace? The famous oncologist who speaks at international conferences Simon Grace?' So much anger.

Simon checks the corridor behind him, steps into the room, closes the door. He squints, shakes his head and says, quietly, 'I'm sorry — do I know you?'

I can't believe this is happening.

'No, you don't know me. Why would *you* know *me*? I'm only the person whose life you ruined,' snaps Dave.

Simon looks at me as if to say, '*What is going on? Who is this person?*

'Dave, please,' I say. 'Please, leave it.'

'No. I won't leave it. Why should I leave it? I left it before and lost everything. I'm a fucking walkover, that's what's wrong with me. I'll tell you who I am, *Simon Grace*,' he almost spits. 'I am Dave O'Neill, Jenny's *ex*-fiancé. Our engagement ended five years ago. Not long after an incident in Brussels.'

'Dave, please,' I say. *Oh God.*

'*Someone* should get things out in the open, Jenny.'

Simon has done the calculations. 'I understand,' he says.

'You understand. That's big of you,' says Dave.

'Look, I am very sorry about what happened. I had no idea. But I don't think this is the time or place.'

Dave is quiet.

'I'm sorry to have disturbed you,' says Simon. 'I'll see you in the morning, Jenny.'

'Goodnight, Simon,' I say quietly.

I glare at Dave.

'Why didn't you tell me?' he demands before I can say anything.

'Dave, keep your voice down. I was about to tell you when he walked in.'

'I'd have been prepared — handled it better.'

'Is that an apology?'

'I don't know . . . But what do you expect? That guy pissed on my life.'

'Yeah, well, he didn't know that, did he?'

'So what? The end result is the same.'

'Look. He didn't know I was engaged. He knew nothing about

223

me. I don't think he even *saw* me properly.'

'He didn't give a shit, though, did he?'

'Dave. You know the story. It wasn't planned. It just happened. You know that . . . .' I sigh. 'At least you didn't tell him about Charlie.'

'He doesn't know?'

'That's what I was telling you.'

'I thought you were saying he didn't know that Charlie had leukaemia.'

'Well, he obviously knows that — he's his doctor.'

'Yeah, but I didn't know he was.'

'Well, you do now. Simon knows Charlie has leukaemia. But that's all he knows.'

'Why didn't you tell him?'

'What was the point? He had his own life. I had mine. Sure, I didn't even know him. Why would I want him involved? I thought you understood that?'

He looks down now. 'When you didn't want me, I thought it was because you wanted him.' It's a mumble.

'*Dave*. I told you. I explained.'

He looks guilty.

'You didn't believe me, did you?'

He says nothing. Won't look at me.

'You big eejit. So you were over in the States thinking I was with him?'

'No. Jack told me you were on your own.'

'What? You asked Jack?'

'No. I didn't, I didn't want to know. Jack spent a lot of time trying to convince me to come home. I think he saw us as the perfect couple.'

'Poor Jack. But didn't that tell you, the fact that I was alone?'

'Not really, no. I thought you might have wanted him but he, well, he didn't . . . .'

'Jesus! You've a busy mind.'

'You'll have to tell him now, though.'

'No. Not if you're a match, I won't.'

He looks at me now. 'I'm sorry. I shouldn't have gone off like that.'

'Dave, I'm going to be here long after you go back to the States. He is Charlie's doctor. Will you try to be civil to him while you're here? Please — things are tough enough.'

He shrugs, nods. 'I'll stay out of his way.'

'And if you happen to bump into him?'

'I'll apologise. If it makes it easier for you.'

'It would, Dave.'

'You OK?' He puts his hand on my shoulder.

'Yeah.'

'I'll go.'

'OK.'

We walk back to the room. He collects up his things. He's about to walk out without saying goodbye.

'Dave?'

'Yeah.'

'Thanks for coming.'

'Yeah.'

I know he's furious with himself.

'You'll need the key.' For once I'm the one doing the thinking.

26

Time for Dave's blood sample. Charlie talks him through it like a pro. Reassuring stuff like 'Yeah, that's the magic cream. It *kind of* works', 'Take a deep breath, now, yep, in it goes — are you OK, Dave?' and finally, 'That's it, all over now, good man.' Once he gets into the swing of educating Dave, he can't seem to stop. He gives him the lowdown on leukaemia, what's happening at bone level, how it affects the body, the drugs he has to take, in what order, how to turn off a drip, which nurses are the best. And which are 'hopeless'. Dave keeps throwing me can-you-believe-this-guy? looks. It's hard not to smile. He's like a bite-sized lecturer. All he needs is a pointer and a little less attitude.

'Oh, and it's nobody's fault,' he finally ends.

Once he's sure that Charlie has definitely finished, Dave announces that he has brought presents from the States. Charlie perks up again, like Sausage when I pick up his lead and he knows it means 'walk'. Dave's gifts emphasise how little he knows about children, which in itself is cute. A book of edible paper, so you can write secret notes and swallow the evidence. Good idea. Slight problem. Charlie can't write. Instead, he draws the sun. And eats it. Then proclaims to everyone who passes the room, 'I ate the sun.' Dave has also brought two sticks of candy with *Muppet Show* characters attached. *The Muppet Show* is still a bit over Charlie's head. It's *Sesame Street* he knows. Not Fossie Bear and Beaker.

I know them, though.

I pick up Beaker. '*Brilliant,*' I say, straightening his orange mop of hair. 'Did they have Dr Bunsen Honeydew as well?' I continue, ignoring Charlie's what's-she-on? face.

Dave smiles. 'No, they only had six different types. Kermit, Miss Piggy, Animal, Fossie, Beaker and . . . I can't remember the last one, but it definitely wasn't Dr Bunsen Honeydew.'

'Ah ha — so, I'm not the only Beaker fan then. Wow.' I do the little Beaker noises and make the scared Beaker face and mouth movements. 'Ah, God, look at his little lab coat.'

Charlie stares.

'I didn't know what he'd like,' says Dave. 'So I went for the kind of things you used to.'

'You remembered my love for Fossie and Beaker?'

'It's not the kind of thing you'd forget, Jen.'

So there — I mustn't have been all hot ambition back then. Must have had some good points. And here's the man who knew them.

'Thanks, Dave.'

'They're for me, Mum,' reminds Charlie.

'Oh, yeah. Sorry.'

'I can get you more,' says Dave.

'It's OK — I can play with these when Charlie's asleep. Can't I, guys?' I say to F and B. 'You know, I never noticed that Fossie had lavender eyelids. So cute. So fetching,' I say, cuddling the stick of candy to my cheek.

'You're mad,' they both say, then look at each other and laugh. They are good together. I was a fool.

Later, Charlie sleeps. That's when Dave bombards me with the real questions. Prognosis. Success rates for bone marrow transplants. The likelihood of finding a donor. The big questions. The worried-parent questions. The questions that allow you plot your chances on an imaginary graph. *Been there, Dave. Know what you're up to.*

Simon keeps his distance. Official. Very official. Hard to believe that he is the same man who is looking after our dog. Or that his daughter is our baby-sitter. Or that we have ever lost ourselves in each other. I feel let down, pushed aside. I know that it is partly to do with Dave's outburst, but to what extent, and whether or not he is just using it as an excuse to withdraw, I can't figure out. *But I don't care*, I tell myself. *I. Don't. Care.* He stops calling to say goodnight. *I don't care.* He channels as much as he can through Dr Howard. *I don't care.* He never says my name. *I. Don't. Care.*

He thinks I'm trouble.

Our days fall into a routine — Dave calling early, leaving late — Mary popping in to let us out for a blast of late November air, or even, one night, a drink. Charlie inches towards recovery. Anne and Siobhán are as warm and caring as ever but I appreciate them more now that Simon has distanced himself. It is a shock to be reminded once again how much love you need when you're isolated in a children's hospital.

And then it comes. News that Charlie can be discharged. He is out of danger and can continue his antiviral medication at home, in the form of creams, eye ointment and oral suspension. We're packed and ready to go in minutes. Dave rushes ahead with our things to collect his rent-a-car from the car park. He has organised for the mini to be declamped and has driven it home for me. Now he will be out front already waiting for us. No trying to remember where I parked, no lugging things for miles, no getting soaked, and no worries about the car starting. Just arrive like landed gentry at the pick-up point where our chauffeur takes care of the details, opening the doors for us with a flourish. The car is clean, tidy, fresh. It smells new. I should upgrade the mini to something safe, practical and without temperament. Sitting up front, I feel like a locum princess, waiting to be whisked off, not quite into the sunset, but at least away from the clouds for a while.

But a cloud does follow us, hovering overhead. Dave's test results. They won't be back for another week.

'I'll get a room,' he says, pulling up at traffic lights.

'No, you won't. There's plenty of space. Charlie sleeps with me now. You can have his bed — can't he, Charlie?'

'Ah, yeah, OK, if you want.'

'Thanks, Charlie.' To me, he says, 'It's OK. I'll get somewhere.'

'But I want you to have a sleepover,' whines Charlie. 'You're my friend.'

'Can't argue with that.' I smile.

'I don't want to get in the way, Jenny.'

'Dave, if you were getting in the way, I'd tell you. Seriously, I could do with the company. It's been great having you here. And you'll be gone soon enough. Please stay. We'd like it — wouldn't we, Charlie?'

'Yeah. And you can play *Scooby Doo and the Phantom Knight* with me. But if you don't practise, Dave, I'll keep winning, I'm warning ya.'

'With an offer like that . . . ' he says, smiling and pulling off from the lights. 'You sure?'

'Yes.'

'All right, then.' He smiles again. And I know he's happy.

We settle in. Aim for cosy. I turn on the heat and every lamp in the place, then settle Charlie on the couch with his pillow and quilt.

'Put on "mama, I feel my temperature rising",' he says, handing me his Discman. I find his favourite song, then he lies back and crosses his legs. He's like a woman on a beach in Juan Les Pins. He holds on to the headphones and nods enthusiastically, singing loudly and off key. Underneath it all, he's a softie. He might watch all the latest cool movies, but his favourites still are *101 Dalmations*, *Lady and the Tramp* and *Bambi*. And then there's Barney, who he won't leave out of his sight. It's so easy, when he's whiny and bossy, to forget that he hates all this — the tiredness, the endless hospital visits, the tests. If I had to go through it, how polite would I be?

I start to make dinner. Dave puts on some music and gets a fire going.

The doorbell.

'I'll get it,' he offers.

'No, sure, your hands are black,' I say, laughing. I move the pasta to a cold ring at the back and make my way to the door.

In bursts Sausage, skidding on the wooden floor. Like a scud missile, he homes in on Charlie.

'Debbie,' I say. 'Hi, come in. How are you?' I check the hallway behind her. Empty.

'Great, thanks. Dad told me Charlie was home. I thought he'd want to see Sausage.'

Dave, squatting at the fire, turns to say hello.

'Debbie, this is Dave . . . a friend.'

She flushes.

Dave produces a dazzler. 'Can't shake,' he says, holding up his hands.

'That's OK,' she says, shyly.

'Hiya, Deb,' shouts Charlie. 'Thanks for bringing Sausage. D'you want to stay for a sleepover? Dave's having a sleepover.'

She looks at me, shocked.

'Charlie,' I say quickly, in case there is any confusion. 'Where would Debbie sleep? Dave will be in your bed.'

'She could squeeze in.'

The poor girl. She is a deep shade of tomato.

'Not tonight, Charlie,' I say to him.

'Aw.'

I ask Deb to dinner. She says she can't stay. I've never seen her in such a hurry to leave.

I'd forgotten what good company Dave can be. Though Charlie and I are like an elderly couple, set in our ways, with our own little routines, idiosyncrasies, Dave slots in like an egg in a cup. Helping just enough, stepping back just enough, knowing when to make himself scarce. And knowing when to take over — bringing Charlie to the park so I can have some time alone, making the odd meal when I'm too tired, answering the phone. We settle into a routine of cosy domesticity. Of sorts. Fiona keeps ringing. I hear snippets of hushed conversation.

'I miss you too . . . There's no need, really, I'm grand . . . How are you? . . . Yeah? . . . That's great . . . He's a great kid, a real character . . . Yeah, well I offered to find a room but Jenny won't have it . . . Any day now . . . Yeah, OK, I'd better go. Take care . . . You too. Bye.'

He takes us out every day. The zoo, Sea Life, the movies, Natural History Museum, art galleries. The Phoenix Park.

'Do you see the squirrel?' he asks Charlie, pointing.

'Where?'

'Up there, on that branch.'

'Oh, yeah. I see it. It's laying an egg.'

He laughs but doesn't correct him.

Neither do I. I kind of like the idea of squirrels laying eggs. I look around. Inhale the fresh air. It's so peaceful here, surrounded by nature. Deer, metres away, lock antlers and push forward, backs arched. The females are disinterested, sitting, looking away, chewing. I like animals. They don't stare. They don't ask. Just mind their business. Pushing each other around.

'There's the ranger,' says Dave.

'Where? Where's the reindeer?'

Dave and I smile at each other.

'I need a wee,' says Charlie.

'Can you hold on?' I ask.

'No.'

'OK — well, just go in these bushes.'

'But people will see my bum.'

'No, they won't. I'll stand in front of you. Anyway, there's no one around.'

'OK. But don't look.'

'OK.'

Ah, God, his little bum!

'Why is there steam on the leaves?' he asks.

'Your pee is hot.'

'Oh, cool.'

'Is it supposed to be red?' asks Dave, trying not to sound panicked.

'It's OK. One of the drugs turns urine red.'

'Wow. Cool,' says Charlie, 'Christmas pee. Ho, ho, ho.'

'Charlie, it's still four weeks.'

'Can Santa fly on his own, Mum?'

All this attention! But it's more than attention. It's not having to do everything alone — the thinking, the worrying. It's a relief to share them, for a while. Dave is going back, I know, and I dread the day. I try to prepare Charlie for it. Try to prepare myself. *Enjoy him while he's here. Don't think ahead.* We don't talk about test results. We don't make plans. We don't discuss what-ifs. We even ignore our past and what went wrong.

Instead, we talk about Charlie. Dave wants every detail — Charlie as a baby, Charlie's first steps, first words, first laugh, favourite toys, favourite food, little accidents. If they have something in common, Dave notices. We go through photos. All the birthdays. Great keeps popping up. And it's wonderful to see her again, remember her, touch her face with my finger. Then she isn't in the photos any more. He asks what happened. Leukaemia, I explain. And he can't believe it.

'I didn't know,' he says.

'How could you have?'

'I'm sorry I wasn't there.'

'My own fault.'

We talk about Great for a while and laugh at funny stories, like the first time they met and she asked was he a virgin, and what his 'intentions' were regarding me. She was very liberal, Great, until it came to protecting her granddaughter. It's the first time since she died that I've spoken about her to anyone who knew her. It feels good to admit how much I miss her, how much I loved her.

Then the call comes.

Dave answers.

'It's him. Looking for you,' he says, his hand over the mouth-piece.

I take it. Dave stays put, eyes scanning my face.

Doesn't take Simon long to get to the point. 'I'm sorry, Jenny, but Dave O'Neill is not a match.'

I have to sit, catch my breath.

'I thought you'd want to know as soon as we found out.'

'Yes, thank you, Simon. That's fine — thank you for calling.' I hang up.

He knows. Just by looking at me. He knows.

'I didn't match, did I?' he says.

'No.'

He slams his fist down on the arm of the couch. 'Damn.' His jaw tightens, something twitches on his face but he says nothing. He grabs his coat and storms from the apartment. I stay where I am, letting my head drop into my hands. *Another hurdle. Another fall. When is our luck going to change? Is it?*

'Where's Dave?' asks Charlie, when his video is over.

'Gone for a walk,' I say.

'He didn't bring Sausage.'

'Oh, the silly billy,' I say. 'Why don't you give him his dinner to cheer him up?'

'OK.' He puts his hand into the sack of dog food and pulls out about ten fistfuls.

Then I feed Charlie and put him to bed. I stay up, lights out, curtains open, hugging my knees, staring at stars, waiting for him to come home. He doesn't. I go to bed. The red figures on the clock say 01:32. The date is the twenty-third of the eleventh month. Could it really be? The twenty-third of November? The date Dave and I started going out. If we were still together we'd probably be celebrating. Instead, here I am, lying beside my son, time ticking, options narrowing. If only I could stop it. Time. Or store it up, maybe. Save it, in a bottle, like the man says in that song. Keep it, ready to pour out as we need it. There would be no rush for a donor. There would be no *need* for a donor. If only. But life's not like that. We need a donor and we're running out of time. I badly wanted Dave to be a match. To save Charlie, of course. But also, I know now, to have him stay. He has no excuse to, now. He will go, leaving us, alone, again, back where we started.

He turns up next morning, pale and unshaven.

'Hi,' he says, awkwardly.

'Hello.' I smile. 'You OK?'

'Yeah.' He takes off his coat. 'Sorry about that, Jen.'

I give my head a forget-it shake. 'I'm making coffee. Want some?'

'Please.'

'Sit down.'

He yawns, takes a place at the counter, propping up his chin with his hands, then running his fingers through his hair.

I hand him a mug. He looks up.

'If it's any help, Dave, I know how you feel.'

'I thought it would work. I thought I could just come home and fix everything. Sort it out. Make it right again.'

I smile. 'The knight in shining armour,' I say, pulling out a stool for myself.

'Something like that.'

'The chances of you having the right tissue type were slim, Dave.'

'But there.'

'Funny.'

'What?'

'That's what I said when they told me I wasn't a match.'

He stares into his coffee.

'It's like you're useless, isn't it?' I say.

He turns to me. 'It doesn't mean I'm not the father, though, does it?'

I've thought about this.

'No, Dave. I'm his mother and I'm not a match.'

'Right.' He takes a sip. Then looks around. 'Where is he anyway?'

'Over at Dara's. We thought it would be good for him to have a change of scene. Get away from his mother for a while.' I smile. 'Prevent her from suffocating him.'

'I don't know how you keep going.'

I shrug. 'Don't have a choice.'

'So many ups and downs, though.'

'I know.' I look out the window.

'What do we do now?' he asks.

'Keep searching.'

'I rang Fiona last night.'

I look at him.

'She thinks I should come home.'

'. . . Maybe she's right.' Though it kills me to say it.

'Do you really think that?' he asks.

'Dave,' I put my hand on his. 'I'd love you to stay. Charlie would too. But Fiona is your fiancée. And it's obvious she misses you.'

'But what about you? What about Charlie? I have a responsibility . . . .'

'Dave, you took care of your responsibility. You did the test. You did your best. There really isn't anything else you can do.' *Outside of being here for us, like you have been, which has been so amazing I can't tell you.*

'He could be my son, Jenny.' His voice is breaking now. 'I can't just leave him. I'm not going to. Not yet. Not until we find a donor.'

'Dave, that could take weeks, months. You can't expect Fiona to wait that long. And they won't hold your job. It's America.'

'I'm not walking out on you, just because my blood isn't good enough.'

'But Fiona?'

'She can come over.'

'Dave, you really should go home.'

'I'm going to book Fiona and myself into a hotel for a week. It'll be a holiday.'

'Not much of a holiday.'

'I'm not changing my mind.'

Thank You, God.

He rings Fiona. She agrees to it. *Not much choice*, I think. *Poor girl.* She's going to organise it with her employer, a law firm, and come over as soon as she can.

In a very out-of-character move, Jack invites Dave and me to lunch. I assume it's because his old mate is back in town and he wants to make some sort of statement of support. Or, if what Dave says about his matchmaking efforts is true, maybe he hopes that there's a chance we'll get back together. God love him — it would take a lot more than a lunch. Anyway, surely he knows that Dave's engaged. *He must.* Well, whatever the reason, I'm not going to argue with a free lunch. Charlie is already going to Dara's, so there's nothing holding me back.

The place is not Jack's usual haunt. *Thank God!* Modern and bright with a Scandinavian feel to it, pale wood and stainless steel. Simple lines. Orange flowers add a splash of colour on each table. The salt and pepper cellars are chunky glass, as are the square slabs that support minimalist slices of butter. The waiters are young and attractive, dressed in trendy black. I feel light years away from hospital or home and wonder if maybe Charlie is right — maybe heaven and food are related. My mood soars. *Wine? Sure, why not? Ah, this is the life*, I'm thinking dreamily, *sitting, relaxing with pals — good food, a little vino . . . dessert, ah, go on then. What more could . . .?*

'I had a call from someone you know,' Jack says, suddenly serious, landing down his cup of black coffee. This is the part of a meal where business people get down to business. But we're not business people and there's no business.

'Who?' I say, still floaty, dreamy.

'Your mother.'

'*My mother?*' That's woken me up.

'Yes.'

'What did *she* want?'

'To know why your columns have stopped.'

'Nosy cow.'

'Slow down, Jen. She seemed worried about you. Wanted to make sure you were OK. She reads your column every week. She's very proud of you.'

'I'm sorry, Jack, but that's a load of bull. She's a politician. She has to read the papers.'

'I think you're being a bit hard on her . . . .'

'What did you tell her, Jack?'

'Nothing.'

'You must have told her something.'

'I told her you were taking a break.'

'Is that all?'

'I said I'd pass on her message to you.'

'Which is what, exactly?'

'That she's asking after you and hopes everything's all right.'

'So you've done it, now. Thanks.'

'You should tell her about Charlie,' says Dave, as if none of this is news to him.

'You knew about this?' I ask, turning on him.

'Yes, I did.'

'Hang on a minute.' I look from one to the other. 'You planned this lunch to tell me about my mother, didn't you?' I'm about to explode. *So there is business, after all. Silly me.*

'You're looking for a donor, aren't you?' It's Dave.

'You don't waste time,' I snap.

'How much time do we have?' he asks, looking at me directly.

'Thanks, Dave,' I say, sarcastically.

'Look, Jenny,' he continues. 'You don't get on with your mother. Not everyone does. So? It's not the end of the world. But Charlie needs a donor and she might be able to help. She is his grandmother. There is a possibility. And there's your father. That's two possible donors.'

'You've it all sorted.' Still indignant.

'I'm certainly trying,' he says in a tone that implies I'm not.

'Now, now, children,' says Jack. Quite bitchily, I think.

'You plotted this, didn't you? The two of you.'

'The three of us,' says Dave. 'The lunch was Mary's idea.'

'Mary?'

'Yes, Mary, your friend — your very good friend, who cares about you, about Charlie. And who knows how to pick a good restaurant,' says Dave.

Jack nods enthusiastically, until he gets to the bit about the restaurant.

And finally it becomes clear. The people I love are only trying to help.

'Sorry,' I say.

'So are you going to ring your poor mother?' asks Jack.

'No.'

'Why not?'

'I'm not going to beg.'

'I'm sure you won't have to,' says Dave.

'You don't know her.'

'I do,' says Dave. 'And you know what I think.'

Dave O'Neill actually likes my mother.

'Look, Jack. She rang you. It's up to you to ring her back. Tell her what's happened, give her my number and leave it up to her.'

'What if she doesn't call?'

'Then she doesn't. The chances she's a match are so minute, it's hardly worth trying anyway.'

'A chance is a chance,' says the ever-hopeful Dave.

'Let's just see what happens,' I say.

Inside? I hope she'll ring.

27

Here's Fiona: child-free singleton with time for self. Body familiar with the inside of a gym. Hair, on first-name terms with some funky New York stylist — short, blond, layer-free, cut in at the neck, pathetically perfect, glossy *and* frizz-free. Hands, manicured. Of course. Clothes (charcoal polo and black, flared woollen trousers that swish when she walks), what my mother would describe as having 'a cut' — clothes she'd have liked me to wear. Boots, high and black, *designed*. But forget all that — let's see some ID. This woman can't be more than twenty-two. Fiona would be easier to like if she had some flaw — cleft lip, hump, webbed foot. She's not exactly falling over herself to like me either, what with the You're-the-Woman-who-Wants-My-Man vibes. I don't want her man. But am I going to tell her?

NO.

And yet, in a way, I do appreciate that if the roles were reversed, I would be nervous, unsure, coming to his country, the hub of all his connections, memories, ties, the home of the woman he had planned to marry, the boy who might be his son. I would want him safely back in the States too. So I try to like her, and remind myself of what it must be like for her and how young she is. It makes me warmer than civil. But not much. There is just something about her.

Dave moves out. The apartment is quieter. No one now to lift our spirits, dilute the intensity of everything we're going through, distract us from ourselves, each other and 'it'. I take up the job of storytime again. *Where the Wild Things Are*. It's one that Dave bought and has become Charlie's favourite.

'You're not *reading* it properly,' he whines, taking his disappointment out on me.

I'm falling down in every way imaginable. I'm not doing the voices right. The faces I'm making aren't like Dave's. And worst of all, my pace is off. I try to improve. By the time we make it to the end, he's fed up. Turns on his side, away from me, to sleep.

'Pat my head like Dave,' he says.

'What do you mean?'

'When I go to sleep, Dave pats my head.'

Weird. 'Like this?'

'No-oh. Like this,' he holds my hand and moves it over his head, stroking.

I give it a go.

'You're not doing it right,' he whines.

'Sorry,' I say, realising how close to tears he is. He misses his friend.

'Your hands are too small,' he snaps.

I keep trying, slowly, carefully, until I fall into a pattern. His frown eases. His breathing becomes regular, calm. He sleeps, his eyes flickering from side to side behind their lids. I get such a strong protective urge, I could kill with the ferocity of it.

Dave calls every day, sometimes with Fiona, most times not. It doesn't work when she's here. Everyone is on edge. Even when she's not, the magic has gone, it's just not the same any more. He seems stressed, under pressure. As if he can't relax into it now. *She's* putting him under pressure to get back to her. I know it.

About five nights after her arrival, I'm about to go on the Web to do a search on bone marrow transplants. The doorbell rings. I get up, annoyed at being interrupted when I'm about to work. Because this is work. Getting Charlie better is my career now.

I open up.

Fiona stands there. Alone.

'Can I come in?' Not friendly.

'Sure,' I say, standing back to let her through.

In she marches. A woman on a mission.

'Would you like a coffee?'

'No, thanks. I've come to talk with you.'

I look at her. 'Do you want to sit down, take off your coat?'

She slips out of her elegant navy overcoat, folds it, then positions herself at the edge of the couch, back ramrod straight. This works wonders for my own posture, my body strangely prepared for attack.

'This has gone on too long. He has to come home now,' she says, looking directly at me.

I say nothing.

'You have to make him see reason.'

'I don't know what you mean.'

'There's no reason for him to stay. He can't help any more than he already has. He should leave now, with me.'

'Surely that's up to him to decide.'

'Are you kidding? Don't you see? You've got a hold on him,' she says, her voice rising. 'He will not see reason with you around.'

'Not true.' I shake my head. 'He's just trying to help.'

'He's not a match. He can't do any more.' She's wrapping the strap of her bag round and round her finger. If it's possible to garrotte a finger, she's doing it.

'Dave has been very supportive, Fiona. He has done a lot more than give blood. He has been a real help.'

'Yes, well, he can't stay here forever.'

'No one is asking him to.' She sees me examine her garrotting technique and quickly unwinds the strap. Her finger is white, bloodless, squished. She doesn't see it.

'You've got to tell him to go. Don't you see? He won't leave because he's guilty about the past, about leaving you before. He won't go if you don't tell him to. So you have to tell him.'

'Why?'

'Because he'll lose his job. He's getting too involved here.' She's wrapping her finger again. And unwrapping when she becomes conscious of what she's doing.

'But what if he *is* Charlie's father? He has a right to be here with him.' I make the obvious point.

'This is crazy. Can't you do a paternity test? Dave should know whether he is Charlie's father or not. We all should. It's gone on too long. What are you trying to achieve?'

'I'm not trying to achieve anything. I just want Charlie better — that's all I want.'

'Well, you don't need Dave then, do you? He's not a match. He can't help you.'

His just being here is a help. But I don't tell her that.

'Do the paternity test. And then let him go,' she says.

'Aren't you taking a gamble? What if Dave *is* Charlie's father?'

'Then we'll deal with it. But at least we'll know.'

After she's gone, I can't calm down. I stride, wall to wall, tempted to pound my fist through. I am so angry I could do something really mad. But I don't. I do the most sensible thing I could possibly do, ring the most sensible person I know. Mary. I rant for an hour. She doesn't say much but it's exactly what I need to hear. 'The cow' features strongly. 'Who does she think she is?' at least three times. 'Absolutely right,' about five. And best of all: 'Don't mind her,' said in such a comforting tone it reminds me of Great, talking to me when I was a child.

Later, much later, after walking miles (indoors), I go to bed. By now, I've semi-calmed. I think of Dave. *I'm not keeping him here. I didn't ask him to come and I haven't asked him to stay. Still. I haven't given him the information he needs to make the right decision for him. He's here because he might be Charlie's father. If he isn't, then it's unfair to let him hope. If he is, then let him have that fatherhood, the certainty of it. He wants to do the right thing. I owe him the freedom to do it. I will arrange a test. Once I know how. Once Dave agrees to it, which I expect he will. He has nothing to lose. But he has. Everything to lose. Charlie. Confirmation that he's not his father. I know how close they have become, though it's only been weeks. I know how much in awe of each other they are. How much time they have spent together and how happy they have made each other. And I know he wants to help. If he's not Charlie's father, what excuse does he have to stay? But maybe what Dave wants isn't what's best for him. Maybe he should go back to the States, pick up his life again and . . . marry . . . Fiona.*

28

Dave assures me that we don't need to do the test. But doesn't put up much of a fight. I suspect Little Miss Action has been working behind the scenes. I ring my GP. She can't do paternity tests but directs me to a private hospital nearby. I make an appointment for the three of us. Charlie wants to know where we're going, what we're doing and why. He doesn't get the truth, obviously.

They take swabs of saliva from the inside of our cheeks, to check for DNA. Normally, they'd take blood but Charlie has had a transfusion in the last three months and has other people's cells in his blood. I can't think about that.

I feel a surge of anger with myself when she takes the sample from Charlie. *We shouldn't be doing this now. Not with him sick. It shouldn't matter who his father is. I don't even want to know. But it matters to Dave. And he has given enough, been patient enough. So I say nothing, just open my mouth when it's my turn.*

Apparently the swabs have to go to a lab in the UK for genetic testing. The results will take six weeks. *Six weeks!* I can't wait that long. I'll have to approach Simon to see whether or not he is a match. If it was one week, even two, I could have held off, waited until I knew, then either gone to him with the certainty that he was the father, or not gone to him at all. Now, I will have to approach Simon, tell him he *might be* Charlie's father, and hope that he will do the test. Is *might* enough?

'*You've a mother!*' says Charlie. '*I* didn't know that.'

'Yes, Charlie, I have.'

'Where is she?'

'In Dublin.'

'Dublin? But we live in Dublin. Why don't we see her?'

'She's been kind of busy.'

'Like my dad,' he says moodily. 'Everyone's busy.'

'Well, she's not busy today. She wants to meet us.'

'*Great.* D'you think she'll bring treats?'

'I don't know, Charlie. Don't always think about what you can get.'

I should offer myself the same advice.

When we arranged to meet, I chose the venue and time. Half nine, at a playground that's not local, but not too far away. Reasons for choice: 1) It will be deserted. 2) It's designed for small children, so Charlie won't need much supervision. 3) It's not in the neighbourhood, so we shouldn't meet anyone we know.

I wrap him in his quilted coat, cap, scarf and mittens. Colour scheme orange and red, like a confused traffic light. She's already there, sitting on a light blue bench with chipped paint, huddled against the cold. Not marching around in her usual businesslike way. No entourage. Posture gone to hell. She hears Charlie's chatter and lifts her head. She smiles and stands. Charlie runs to her.

'Hi,' he says loudly. 'Are you my mum's mother?'

She bends down to him, takes his hands. 'Yes, Charlie, I am.' She smiles. 'And I'm *your* grandmother.'

He pulls his hands away. 'No, you're not. My granny's in heaven.'

She looks at me, horrified, as if I've told him she's dead.

'No, Charlie,' I say. 'You're thinking of Great.'

'Yeah.'

I try to explain. 'Great was *my* granny, your *great*-granny. That's why her name was Great. But this is *my* mother, *your* granny.'

He looks confused. 'I thought she was called Great because she was great.'

'That too, Charlie,' I say, smiling and giving him a hug.

He stands, hands in pockets, eyeing up his new grandmother.

'Hello, Jenny,' she says.

'Hello, Mother,' I say, coldly.

'What's wrong?' Charlie interrupts. 'Aren't you friends?'

'Charlie, look,' I say in a really excited voice. 'No one's on the slide. Quick, come on — you can have a go.'

'I want to talk to my granny.'

'I know. You can in a minute. But if you don't hurry up, other kids will come and you'll have to queue for everything.'

He hates queuing. 'OK,' he says. 'But I'll be back in a minute.'

I rub the dew off the slide with a hand towel.

'Why don't you like her?' he whispers.

'I do.'

'No, you don't.'

'Well, smarty-pants, you play away here for five minutes and let me see if I can make friends with her, OK?'

'OK.'

'Call me if you need me.' I hold his chin between my thumb and index finger and give it a little shake. He turns and climbs the toddlers' slide, both hands gripping the ladder, the way I taught him.

I go back to her. Unfortunately, I need her blood.

She's on the bench again. I sit beside her, say nothing.

'He's a lovely child, Jenny,' she says.

What would you know?

'Is he . . . all right?'

'He has leukaemia, Mother.'

'Yes, but how is he doing?'

'He is in remission . . . for the moment.'

'Thank God,' she says, letting out a breath. Then, 'Why didn't you tell us?'

'Didn't think you'd be interested.' I look away.

'We've had our differences, Jen. But we are still your parents. We still expect you to call us if you're in trouble.'

'And you'll come rushing to the rescue like you did when I told you I was pregnant.'

She sighs. 'Jenny, I am sorry about that. I reacted badly. I was just worried about you . . . .'

'About yourself,' I quip. 'And your image.'

'That's not true. That's not true at all.'

'It's all you're interested in. It's all you were ever interested in.'

'That's not fair, Jenny. I tried to get on with you but you always pushed me away.'

'*Wrong.*' I fold my arms. I'm not budging on this.

'Look, Jenny, I know I never understood you the way your grandmother did but I did try. And just because I never knew how to talk to you doesn't mean I didn't love you.'

'So where were you, then?'

'Jenny, a politician's life is a busy one. There are so many demands . . . .'

'Here we go.'

' . . . Whatever free time I had, I wanted to spend with you but you weren't interested. You were always with your grandmother. You preferred her, got on better with her.'

'And why do you think that was?'

'I don't know, Jenny. I did try.'

'Did you? Because it certainly didn't feel that way. I'll tell why I got on with Great. Because she was there. She cared. I didn't have to wait around until she had five minutes, squeezed in between clinics and the funeral of someone she'd never met. She was always there when I needed her. When I had a problem. She didn't just rush in and try to catch up by asking me deep and meaningful questions that just stressed me out. She was just there.'

'And I wasn't,' she says, her head hanging.

'You treated me like some sort of rag doll that you could pick up whenever it suited you. The only thing was, I wasn't a doll. I was a child who needed her mother. Anyway, it doesn't matter. I'm a big girl now. It just makes me so cross when you say I got on better with Great. Of course, I got on better with Great.'

'Mu-um.'

Charlie is coming over.

'Will you push me on the swing?' he asks slowly, watching us from under the peak of his cap.

'OK,' I say. *Anything to get away . . . This isn't going to work. I knew it was a mistake.*

I push the swing and pretend not to notice that she has got up and is walking slowly away from the bench, head down. She starts to rummage in her bag. Pulls out a hankie, dabs her eyes and blows her nose. *Oh, great — this is all I need. One of her stunts.* I pretend to be busy with Charlie. *Maybe she'll go.*

'Is Granny crying?'

'No.'

'She is.'

'No, Charlie. She's fine.'

She goes back to the bench and returns the hankie to her bag. She tilts her head back as though taking a deep breath.

'I want to get off,' says Charlie.

I stop the swing and hold it while he jumps off. He runs over to her. I follow, slowly.

'Granny, are you OK?'

'Yes, sweetheart. I'm fine, thank you,' she says, rubbing his cheek. 'How are you?'

'Fine. D'you want to see me go on the slide?'

'I'd love that.'

'OK.' He runs off. I'm about to follow, when she calls me. I walk over, avoid eye contact, sit down, fiddle with the car keys.

'Jenny,' she says. 'Look at me.'

She *has* been crying.

'I love you,' she says, her voice wobbly.

First time she has said that.

'I loved you from the first moment I held you.' *She's not like that. Politician first. Mother, last.*

'. . . something went wrong between us and I thought it was a phase, that it would just get better, that you would grow out of the *resentment* you had for me. But it never got better . . . Just worse and worse . . . .'

She's crying now, really crying. Tears flooding her cheeks, dropping off her chin, splashing onto her coat. This is not an act. *Unless she's a complete genius.* I've never seen her cry. I am mortified. I check to make sure no one's coming. She won't stop. *Jesus!* Charlie's coming over now.

251

'What's wrong, Granny?' he asks, rubbing her back, the way I do with him when he's upset. 'Are you OK?'

'Yes, sweetheart. I've got something in my eye.'

'Let me have a look . . . Tears,' he says. 'Yeah, I see them.'

She laughs, rubs his cheek again. 'You're a lovely little fella, aren't you?'

'Yes,' he says, proudly.

And she laughs again. 'Would you like to sit on my lap?'

'What'll you give me?'

And she's laughing again.

'A hug,' she says.

'Hugs are OK. But no kissing, right?' he warns.

'Right,' she says with a decisive nod. Up he goes.

Why can't I get on with her? Charlie doesn't seem to have a problem. Dave definitely doesn't. Is it me? It is weird, this sight — my mother and my son. Together. Happy. And the strangest thing happens. From nowhere, a memory flashes. We're at a park. She's young, pretty. Her dress is yellow. With flowers. I'm at the top of the slide and she's at the bottom, waiting for me, her arms out, smiling. And I trust her. I want to go to her. *Where did that come from? Did that really happen?*

'Are you any good on Gameboys?' he asks her.

'No, sweetheart, I don't think so, but maybe you could show me some day?'

Don't push it.

'Yeah, that'd be cool,' he says. 'D'you want to come to my house now? We've no plans.'

She laughs again. 'You're full of business, aren't you? Like your mum.' She looks at me, still smiling.

I blank her out.

She sighs.

'So, are you coming?'

'Not today, Charlie.'

'Don't tell me. You're busy,' he says, pulling a face.

She smiles at him, kisses his cheek and hugs him. Her face is so sad when she looks at me.

Stupidly, madly, crazily, I feel sorry for her.

'Will you come a different day?' he asks.

'I really hope so, Charlie,' she says, looking at me.

'Charlie, one last go on the slide and we have to go, OK?' I say.

'OK.'

Charlie climbs down and walks off. A little man's walk.

'I want to help, Jenny.'

'Why?'

'Please, Jenny . . . I am sorry about the past. I am sorry I didn't have enough time for you, I am sorry about how I reacted to the pregnancy. You don't know how much I regret that. We are two obstinate people . . . .'

'You want to help?' I ask coldly.

She nods.

'Charlie needs a bone marrow transplant. We have to find a donor. I'm not a match, Dave isn't . . . .'

'Dave? Is Dave home?' she asks, full of hope.

'For the moment,' I say flatly. 'He's engaged to some yank.'

'Oh.'

'She wants him back home in the States where she can keep an eye on him.'

'Oh, dear.'

'Did you see that, Granny?' shouts Charlie, proudly, from the bottom of the slide.

'Yes, wonderful, Charlie,' she says, clapping.

'Will you do a blood test? See if you have the right tissue type.'

253

'Yes, of course. I'll help in any way I can. And Father will do one too,' she says, starting to get excited.

'Do you want me to do it again?' shouts Charlie.

'Yes, love. I'd love to see it again,' she calls back.

'The chances of grandparents being a match are tiny.'

'When can we do it?'

'Whenever you want.'

'I'll talk to your father.' She seems happy now, optimistic. A new campaign. *Maybe she'll go now.*

'How are *you*, Jenny?'

'Fine.'

'Are you looking after yourself?'

'Yes, Mother.'

'Your father is well.'

'Great.' What can I say? 'He said to send his love.' *All this love, all of a sudden.* 'He would have liked to come but he thought one of us was enough.'

He was right.

'I'm sorry we haven't been in touch . . . But that's what you wanted, isn't it?'

'Yep.' I look away, hoping she'll take the hint and go.

'But maybe it wasn't such a good idea.'

I continue to ignore her.

'Because we've missed you. And we've missed seeing that very special little boy growing.' Her voice starts to break.

'Yeah, well, I'd better be going now. You have my number, so you can ring to arrange the blood test.'

'Yes, yes. Thank you, Jenny, for seeing me. Thank you for letting me meet Charlie . . . I hope you're very proud,' she says, looking at him coming back over to us. 'He's a wonderful boy.'

'He's all right.'

254

'No, Jenny. He's much better than that.'

I need a distraction. So I do something out of the ordinary. Bring Charlie to a car showroom. *Let's have a look at these Golfs.* I'm in the driver's seat, eyes closed, savouring the smell of new car, the steering wheel, sturdy in my hand. I'm not in a showroom any more but on a bumpy country lane, wind in my hair (it's turned into a convertible), long, silvery grass on either side, butterflies, wild flowers and swallows. Beside me is the happiest, most energetic little boy, his thick blond hair flapping in the breeze and his cheeks the rosiest in the world. *Whoa!* The radio blares suddenly, snapping me out of my dream. *Charlie!* My eyes spring open. I flick off the radio and turn to him, about to get cross.

Oh my God!

There's blood everywhere. All over his top, face, left hand. It oozes from his nostrils. He rubs it with the back of his hand, too busy to notice.

I don't want to panic him.

'Charlie, love, you're having a little nosebleed. It's OK. I had them all the time when I was a kid. I just have to pinch your nose — OK, sweetie? Breathe through your mouth, now.' I hold his nostrils together. The blood feels warm and sticky. With my free hand, I fumble around for a hankie.

He looks down at the blood, says nothing — so calm, it's scary.

'Now, lean forward a tiny bit. Good boy. Try not to swallow, OK?'

'DohK.'

We sit like this for about five minutes until Mr Teflon, the salesman, pokes his bird head through the open window to see if we have 'bitten'. Instantly less Teflon, he loses his insincere smile, becoming sincerely upset at the sight of all the blood decorating his brand new 'interior'.

'Can you get a cold, wet cloth, please?' I ask calmly. 'It will help stop the bleeding.'

'Can you get out of the car?'

'Not without bleeding all over it, no. Now, can you get the cloth, please? Thank you.'

I may look calm. I may sound calm. Inside I'm thinking: *His platelets must be low. That's why he's bleeding. If they're down, it's going to be hard to stop. And he can't afford to lose any blood or he'll become anaemic. Or more anaemic than he already is. I need to get him to hospital.*

Mr Teflon returns and I apply the cold cloth to Charlie's forehead.

'I'm tired, Mama,' he says.

'Can't you stop it?' says the pain.

'It's OK, Charlie. It's OK, sweetie. It will stop in a few minutes and then we'll go to the hospital.'

'The hawpital? Oh dno. Not again.'

29

I was right. His platelets are down. He needs a transfusion. *But how did they drop so fast? He's only had a test and his levels were fine. Please God, don't let him have relapsed.*

Anne reassures me that platelets can fall because of chemotherapy. I know this already. I am not reassured. They take blood to test for cancer cells. *We need this transplant. We need it soon.*

'I'm never going to get better,' moans Charlie, lying flaccid in the bed, watching a line of dark red run into his Freddie.

'Sweetheart, of course you're going to get better.'

'No, Mama, I'm not.'

'You will, Charlie, love, and we'll have a party and . . . .'

'Don't want a party, just want to get better. I'm tired, Mama. I'm really tired.' He starts to cry. I'm not far behind.

'I know, sweetie.' I stroke his head. 'I'm so proud of you, Charlie. Do you know that? You're such a brave boy.'

'I wish my dad was here.'

'I know.'

'Doesn't he know I'm sick?'

I don't answer, just continue to stroke. I kiss his temple.

'Where's Dave?'

'He's coming, love.'

'But he won't stay. He never stays any more. Just goes off with *her*.'

I kiss his forehead. 'I'm here.'

'Everyone goes away.'

'No, they don't.'

'Great did. My dad did. Simon and Dave were my friends and now they hardly ever come.'

'Dara and Debbie are your friends and they haven't gone anywhere.'

'But they never come see me in *here*.'

'You have Mary. What about Mary?'

'Mary's *Dara's* mum. I want someone for myself. I want my new granny. She'll come.'

'Your granny?'

'Yeah, she'll come. I know she will.'

This is all I need.

'Ring her, Mama, please.'

Damn!

'Please.'

'OK, Charlie. I'll ring her.'

I get up, knocking a bright red toy Elmo off the bed. 'I feel great,' it says.

She comes, of course, like the cavalry, only quicker. She fusses over him and asks to see his Gameboy. She pretends it's the most fascinating thing in the world, acts dumb and gets him to take her through it. Lots of 'ooohing' and 'aahing', lots of 'you're so clever's. I have to give her credit. He's not as down as he was. He even sits up, major progress. I take her aside and ask if she could try getting a drink into him. He won't do anything for me. And she's on an obvious roll. She adopts the unoriginal 'Bet you can't drink all this' tack. He's so busy trying to impress her that it works. She stays for hours — odd considering there's an election coming up. She hasn't time for this. But, for once, she doesn't rush off.

They pretty much ignore me. *Fine. As long as he's happy.* When she finally goes, Charlie makes her promise to come again. She looks at me. I nod. As long as she continues to work her magic, she can stay.

There are no cancer cells in the sample. My body relaxes again, like a balloon deflating. The blood transfusion goes in. We can go home. *I never told Simon.*

Everyone's giving blood. My parents, Mary, Jack. I wonder if there is any point. But they want to help so I let them. Who knows? Maybe my own mini-register of donors will be more successful than the official one. Wouldn't be hard. My biggest chance is Simon, I'm convinced. I have to tell him. Especially after today. No more frights.

Where do you arrange to meet someone to announce that he *might* be the father of your child, that you need him to try to save your child's life — oh, and that you're sorry you forgot to mention it before now?

There is no suitable place.

I call him on his mobile.

'Hello, Simon. It's Jenny.'

'Is everything all right?'

'Yes, thanks. I need to talk to you.' Ka-thump, ka-thump, ka-thump goes my heart. He can probably hear it.

'You've caught me at a good time — I'm in my office. Do you want to call on the landline?'

'No, Simon. I need to *talk* to you. In person.'

'Oh. Do you want to come into the hospital?'

'No. Could I meet you somewhere else? There's something I have to tell you.'

'Oh.' As in, *Christ!*

'When suits you?' I ask.

'Today?' As in, are-you-sure-you-want-to-do-it-today, what about tomorrow, or next week, or maybe never?

'Yes, today.'

'Ah, after work would be best . . . although I said to Debra I'd cook her . . . .'

'Debbie's coming over here, Simon. I invited her for dinner. I hope that's OK with you. I thought she'd checked.'

'I'm sorry, she did. I'd forgotten. I'm a bit under pressure. Well then, after work, if that suits you.'

'What time?' I ask.

'About seven?'

'Fine.'

'Where?'

'I don't know.' *Did I just say that?*

'Somewhere local?'

'Yes.'

'Like a bar?' he suggests.

'No. Not a bar. Maybe we could go for a walk.'

'In the dark?'

'Ah, no, you're right, ah, OK' — *quick, quick* — 'the Four Seasons?'

'Fine.'

'See you there, then?'

'The lobby?'

'The lobby.'

Jesus!

I've a cramp in my hand from holding the phone so tightly.

'Where are you going, Mum?' Charlie asks.

Three faces look at me questioningly — my son's, his baby-sitter's, the dog's.

'Just meeting a friend. Are you sure you don't mind baby-sitting for a while, Deb?'

'No problem. Sure, I was here anyway.'

'Thanks.'

'What friend? Mary?' You couldn't call him a quitter.

'Ah, no.'

'Jack?'

'No, Charlie. Someone else. OK, see you later, bye.'

'Who, Mum?'

I can't say Simon. But if I say I'm meeting someone else and Simon happens to mention to Debbie that he was meeting me . . . But he wouldn't when he knows why we're meeting. That's it — a meeting. 'It's just a meeting, Charlie.'

'For work?'

'Mm-hmm.'

'Are you going back to work?' he asks, surprised.

'No. But I'm meeting someone to tell them I'm not going back, OK? Look, I gotta go. Bye.' I kiss his head, wave to Deb.

Well, it's official — I made a total mess of that.

First to arrive, I find the quietest spot and hide by a large fern-type plant. I order a glass of freshly squeezed orange juice and wait, going over the conversation in my head. When he arrives, I nearly spill the juice.

'Sorry I'm late,' he rushes. 'I had to wait for some results.'

'It's fine,' I say, standing.

'Don't get up,' he says.

I sit back down.

He takes the antique chair at right angles to, but beside, the dainty couch I'm on, though it's probably not called a couch. He puts his satchel on the ground. *Weird. It's practically the same as mine. Same tan-coloured leather, same shape. How have I not noticed that before?*

'How is Charlie?' he asks.

'All right. A bit tired.' My mouth is dry but I'm afraid to go near the juice.

'Due in for his chemo tomorrow?'

'Yes and you're probably wondering why this couldn't wait till then but it has nothing to do with Charlie's illness. Well, it has, in a way. Look, I'm sorry, I need to tell you . . . ' I squint, 'Do you need a drink or something?'

He shakes his head. 'I'll wait for someone to come round.'

'Oh. OK.'

He looks at me, expecting me to continue.

'Yes. Hmm. Ah. This thing I have to tell you?'

He shifts in his seat.

'I probably should have told you a long time ago. And I don't *exactly* know how to, now, but I have to, you see, because of Charlie. I'm sorry.' I take a breath. 'It's about the bone marrow transplant.'

He looks relieved, as if happy to discuss something clinical, manageable, impersonal.

'Simon?'

'Yes.'

'You know the way, I wasn't a match, and Dave wasn't a match?'

'Yes, Jenny, but, in fairness, I wouldn't worry . . . .'

'I was hoping one of us would be, so I wouldn't have to tell you what I have to tell you now.'

There is no visible movement, yet suddenly he seems to be sitting one inch off the chair, bracing himself.

I close my eyes as I say, 'You might be Charlie's father, Simon.'

I open them. A lounge boy, dressed like a penguin, is standing beside the table.

'A Jack Daniels,' Simon chokes.

'Yes, sir,' he says, then looks at me. I shake my head. He walks off.

I've seen Simon go pale before. It was nothing compared to this.

'Are you OK?' I ask. *Do men faint?*

'Yes. I'm fine.'

I don't know what to do, so I go on. 'Charlie was born on January twenty-fifth . . .'

'I know.'

'You know?'

'I saw it on his chart, the first day he came to the hospital. Charlie was born the day my wife died.'

'*God*,' I say, eloquently. Then, 'I'm sorry.'

The whiskey arrives. The waiter leaves. Simon takes a generous mouthful. Then another.

'Charlie was born nine months after the conference in Brussels.'

'I see,' he says, taking another gulp.

'Did it ever cross your mind that Charlie might be yours?'

'No.'

'Not once?'

He shakes his head, puts down the drink, looks at me intently. 'You need to understand . . . What happened in Brussels was madness, *completely* out of character. Not me. At all. I hated myself

263

for it.' He shakes his head again. 'But I couldn't let it interfere with my life. My wife,' he pauses. 'Alison,' he says gently, 'was' — he stumbles over the word as if he's not used to talking of her in the past tense — 'everything to me. She and Debbie were my life. What happened was a mistake. I had to treat it like that. I erased it from my mind. Completely. It was the only way I could deal with it. Do you understand?'

I nod slightly. We are quiet now.

'It never occurred to me that it might have affected your life too, Jennifer. I didn't think. Didn't realise.'

'Doesn't matter.'

'It does matter. Of course it matters. It split up your relationship.'

'Yeah, well, I was a grown woman — my fault too.'

'Well, I am sorry.'

'Thanks.' I don't know what else to say.

'Can I ask you something?' he says.

'Yes.'

'That time I thought I recognised you, when you called to the house with Debra's photo album — why did you dismiss that? Why didn't you tell me who you were? You knew who I was, didn't you?'

'Yes, I knew.' I stop, wanting to get this right. 'I recognised you the first time I called to collect Debbie. I said nothing because I didn't want to embarrass you . . . or myself. There was no reason to drag up the past. It was easier just to carry on the way things were. Leave them be. I considered changing baby-sitters, so I wouldn't have to meet you regularly, in case some day you did remember. But Charlie loved Deb, and I couldn't find a replace-ment, and then when they discovered each of them was missing a parent, I couldn't separate them. I tried to get round it by ringing Deb on her mobile when I was coming to the house. It was working too, until Charlie got sick.'

'You know, I tried to stop Debra baby-sitting too?' he says, smiling now.

'Yes, I know.' He looks surprised. 'She told me. Did you think I was a bad influence or something?'

'*A bad influence?*'

'Single mother.'

'Oh no. That wasn't it at all. My goodness! It was her studies. In fairness, she'd just started Junior Cert. I didn't want her to take on too much. I just wanted her to know that money wasn't an issue.'

'Oh.'

'I would never think that. My God! I'm a single father. I know how hard it is. I have great respect for people who struggle with parenting alone, especially with sick children. Believe me.'

'Oh. Right.'

We are silent again.

'Jenny, you said I *might* be Charlie's father?'

'I was in a relationship with Dave.'

He thinks for a second. 'Didn't you ever want to find out?'

'Yes, but there wasn't any point. If you were Charlie's father, I wasn't exactly going to track you down and make demands. And neither was I going to put preconditions on marrying Dave. "Yes, I'll marry you if you're the father, but forget it if you're not."'

'Are you saying that Dave still wanted to marry you? I thought the relationship ended after Brussels.'

'It did. I ended it.'

'Why?'

'I don't know. I believed the baby would have come between us. That Dave would have resented it eventually. But I may have been wrong about that. I realise that now. Anyway, I'll know for sure in six weeks. Dave and I have finally done a paternity test.

We had swabs taken at the Blackrock Clinic two days ago. We'll have the results in six weeks.'

'Six weeks. I see.'

'I can't wait that long, Simon. I came here to ask if you could check to see if you are a match for Charlie. I know it's awkward, you working at the hospital, but surely there must be some way round it? To keep it confidential. Could you do it yourself, put a false name on the test tube — I don't know, *something?* There must be a way. I know the chances are slim, but you understand, I have to try.'

'Can you let me think about this?'

What's there to think about — a dying boy, a chance at life?

'OK,' I say.

'I'll go now, if that's all right. There's nothing else you want to say?'

'I'm sorry to land this on you.'

'Don't be. If Charlie is my child, then, in fairness, he is my responsibility as much as he is yours. And if that's the case, you've carried it alone for five years . . . . If only I hadn't been such a dumb fuck- . . . sorry. I don't usually use bad language. Well, you know what I mean.'

'Yes, I do. I've told myself the same thing often enough.'

He pays for the drinks, walks me to my car.

'Goodnight, Jenny. I'll see you tomorrow.'

'Goodnight, Simon.'

I've no doubt that Brutus is an honourable man. It's just that Brutus doesn't know whether or not he is the father, whether or not there is anything to honour. Maybe Brutus won't feel he has a responsibility to do anything unless it is proven genetically. Maybe Brutus will want to wait six weeks.

30

Charlie's fed up. Tired, weary and in no mood to make the trek back to our second home, only to be made worse by more chemo. I'm not exactly tripping over myself to get there either, having spent the night awake, worrying about Simon and what he'll say. Or won't say. Dave, who has promised to spend the day with us, is not in great form either, but won't talk about it. Fiona-related, no doubt. So here we are — a bunch of miseries, driving together towards hospital.

And here we are now — same bunch of miseries arriving at the ward, so familiar with the place that there is no uncertainty, no confusion, just routine. *Which is worse?* Charlie wants to watch a Barney video, which makes me realise just how down he is. Dave switches on the TV and flicks through the channels.

'Stop, stop. I saw Granny,' shouts Charlie, suddenly animated.

'Where?' asks Dave.

'Go back. I saw her, I saw her.'

He lands on a breakfast television news bulletin.

I look up.

There she is, outside the Dáil, dyed auburn hair being whisked about by an unkind wind. *So that's why I've always wanted mine to be any other colour.*

'But coming up to an election, Minister?' says the interviewer. 'The timing couldn't be worse.'

'I agree that the timing could be better, Fergal, and I would like to take this opportunity to apologise to the party and to the electorate, but I have compelling family reasons for retiring . . . .'

'With all due respect, Minister, family reasons are often quoted when people retire from politics. Are you sure your retirement hasn't anything to do with the recent fall in popularity of the party, reflected in the latest MRBI opinion poll?'

'Fergal, I think you should know me by now,' she says, as though they're best friends, which she has probably made sure they are. 'There's nothing that motivates me more than a challenge. That opinion poll *almost* made me stay.' The media-trained professional pauses for effect. Then says, 'I have devoted over thirty years of my life to politics. I have always put it first. Someone reminded me of that recently.' She stops again. 'Time with my family is long overdue.' Another pause. *Something good coming up, then.* 'Who knows how much time any of us has left?' She beams at him as if to say, '*That, young man, is that — no more questions.*'

He thanks her, tells her she will be sorely missed and wishes her all the best.

'What'd she say, Mum?' asks Charlie.

'Dave, would you turn it down for a sec, please?' I look at Charlie. 'She just said she's giving up work.'

'Is she?' as in *wow*. Then: 'I didn't know grannies worked.'

'Some do.'

'Why's she giving up work?'

'She wants to spend more time with her family or something.'

'Who's her family?'

'Well, us, I suppose.'

'That's great. She's going to spend more time with us. Cool.'

'I don't know, Charlie. Just see what happens, OK?'

Dave has become as animated as my son. Amazing the effect she has on people. 'What. About. That?' he says.

I raise my eyebrows. 'It's a ploy. She wants them to beg her to come back. In the meantime, she's the main news story.'

'You don't believe that?'

I don't, actually, but I'm not in a hurry to admit it. 'I don't know what she's up to.' I shrug as if I've other more important things to think about.

'Can't you accept that maybe she's sorry? Maybe she's trying to make it up to you.'

'What are you talking about?' asks Charlie.

'Nothing, Charlie, nothing.' I glare at Dave in the hope that he'll shut up.

It works, giving me a moment to decide what I feel. It is this: I'll believe it when I see it. And this: Don't count your chickens. And this: I still don't trust her.

Barney is goofing around on screen — Granny and chemo are temporarily forgotten. Dave's sombre mood returns. I'm relieved when he goes to 'stretch his legs'. Two minutes later, Simon appears and I can't help wondering if he has been waiting for Dave to leave. Then I forget about that when I think of what he must want.

'Hello, Jenny,' he says. 'Hi, Charlie.'

Charlie doesn't hear, concentrating, as he is, on the run-up to the climax of the movie, fists clenched and twisting, chin sticking out in excitement.

It's only Barney, son.

Simon smiles at me. 'If only we could all be as easily distracted.'

I smile too, silently wishing he'd just get to the point. Yes or no.

'I've thought about what you said last night, Jenny.'

And?

'I will do the test. Of course, I will do it.'

Thank God. 'It's not awkward for you?'

'No. I can organise it. Don't worry. I can do it discreetly. And I have to be discreet for Debra's sake, Jenny. I can't have her knowing. You understand. It would upset her too much to think that I . . . .' He stops. Looks at Charlie.

My God. Why hadn't I thought of that? Debbie. Of course. We really don't realise the implications of half the things we do.

'Of course. Thank you, Simon.'

'I'm sorry,' he says.

And I don't ask him why.

'Fiona's going back to the States,' says Dave when he returns, over an hour later. The video is over and Charlie has fallen asleep. I wasn't far off it myself. I look up now, from where I've been resting my head on my arms on Charlie's bed. He sits opposite.

'We had a bit of a tiff,' he says quietly.

'I'm sorry,' I say, straightening up.

'She thinks I'm spending too much time with you and Charlie.'

I think for a second, then ask, 'Do you?'

'No. Charlie is sick. This is where I need to be right now.'

'Dave, I think you should go. Really. We're fine. And the results from the paternity test won't be back for six weeks.'

'I know, but don't you need me around?'

'Not if you're going to be moping over Fiona.'

'I'm not moping over Fiona.'

'You should see your face.' I smile. 'Go on. Six weeks is a long time.'

'Did you talk to him?'

'Yes, he's going to do it.'

'Great.' He smiles, reaches across and takes my hand. 'But don't get your hopes up, Jen.'

'I'm not — at least I'm trying not to.'

'I'm staying.'

'What do you mean, you're staying?'

'I want to be here. So I'm staying.'

'What about work?'

'I'm going to do some stuff for Jack — a series of features on New York versus Dublin — taking different topics — property market, night life, singles scene, crime.'

I'm amazed. 'When did you organise that?'

'I had a chat with Jack on the mobile just now.'

'Nobody could accuse you of being a slow mover.'

'I can think of one.' He smiles.

I frown. 'Are you sure you're doing the right thing? She really wants you with her. If you stick your heels in, you might lose her, Dave. She's young . . . .'

'Jenny, marriage is for life. It's about give and take. I need to do this. Fiona needs to understand. It will be OK. It's just for a bit longer.'

'I don't know . . . .'

'I do.'

'Dave, you've everything set up over there. We're fine, here. Really. We can manage.'

'I'm staying.'

I sigh. 'On one condition, then.'

'What?'

'Promise me you'll go any time you need to, OK?'

'OK.'

The Manhattan skyline on top of the fridge slowly turns into the Dublin skyline as the medicine bottles steadily reduce in number. Weeks pass. It's almost Christmas. The season to be jolly. We've got a taller tree than usual, spent a fortune on decorations, Santa's being particularly generous this year. My mother and father are introducing Charlie to Scalextric. Mary has presented me with an agenda of Christmas shopping, crib visiting and carol singing that would floor an athlete — we'll have to organise a pared-down version. Jack is coming over on Christmas Day. He invited us to his, but it's better for us to stay here, so I switched the invitation around. Anyway, I owe him lunch! And it will be good to have company.

Dave has left for New York. He got an ultimatum, which he wasn't going to give in to, until I convinced him that there was no point in destroying his future for a few days. When the bad news started to arrive, I kept it from him — I knew he wouldn't go otherwise. My parents: not a match. Mary: not a match. Jack: not a match. Though the chances that they would be were minuscule, each potential donor was as devastated as the one before. Not true — my mother took it particularly badly. And for a brief second, I might have loved her for it but I controlled that. She has given up politics, though. And has been to see Charlie every day. High achiever that she is, her Gameboy skills are now exceptional, as is her ability to text and e-mail. She and her grandson send regular messages to Mark and Dave. She even seems to have developed a sense of humour.

I am getting quietly desperate now. Christmas week, and no news from Simon. The results *must* be back. I debate repeatedly about

272

whether or not to call. In the end, I do.

'Simon, hi. It's Jenny. Just calling to wish you Happy Christmas.'

'Happy Christmas, Jenny. How are you?'

'Fine.'

'How is Charlie?'

'Very excited. He needed something to look forward to, get excited about.'

'I can imagine.'

'Have you heard anything, Simon?'

Silence. Then: 'Jenny, I was going to wait until after Christmas to tell you.'

'So you know?'

'Yes.'

'It's no, isn't it?' I hold my breath.

'I'm afraid so, Jenny. I'm sorry.'

Slowly, quietly, I put the phone down, sink to the floor and ignore it when it rings. He was my last hope. *This is it. The end. Nowhere to go now. Nothing more I can do.* The phone keeps ringing. I hardly hear it. Just sit here, thinking, this can't be happening. *What have I done to deserve this? Couldn't someone just give me a break, for once? Why does it always have to be bad news, time after time after time? If you're going to take him, God, just take him — enough cat and mouse.* Don't want to get up. Don't want to do anything. This is it. I. Give. Up.

But you can't give up when you've a kid because they won't let you. There is a loud bang on the door. The kind of bang Charlie makes when he comes home after being out for the day. *They're back.*

'Hello,' chirps Mary. But stops when she gets a proper look at my face. 'Are you OK?' she asks.

'No.'

'Come on, boys. Let's see what's on telly.' She puts them sitting in front of it.

'Into the kitchen,' she orders me.

She makes coffee, strong stuff.

'Now, enough of this keeping-it-all-in nonsense. Tell me what's going on.'

'Simon isn't a match,' I wail.

'OK.' I think she was prepared for more of a drawing-out process. 'When did you hear?'

'This afternoon.'

She thinks. 'OK.' Thinks again. 'It's a knock back . . . but . . . let's think of our next step.'

'There is no next step. I've run out of people.'

'What about the register?'

'The register, ha!'

'Jenny. You're feeling down. I know. And I don't blame you. But I've been thinking about this, right? About what we'd do if no one we knew turned out to be a match. And I've come up with an idea.'

I don't bother answering. What's the point?

'Want to hear it?' she asks.

I shrug. *Whatever it is, it won't work.*

'You're a journalist, right? You can reach people. Thousands of people, through the paper. Start your own campaign.'

I look up.

'Ask people to help. Set up your own register.'

'Could I?'

'I don't know. But I don't see why not? Someone out there has to have the right tissue.'

I start to brighten now. 'Jack! Jack would help — I know he would.'

'You see, there you go — that's the attitude.'

274

'I could write an article about what we've been through. People would want to help. I know they would.'

'Definitely — they just need to know.'

'Mary, you're a saint.' I jump up and hug her. 'What would I do without you? I mean. Really. What would I do without you?'

She smiles. 'We will get there, Jenny. We will find a donor — it's just a matter of time. And maybe effort. But we will do it. You just have to have faith. That's all. You've been great, really strong. Now just keep going.'

'You're right.'

I have a mission now — something I can do, focus my energies on. I'm not giving up, not yet. Jack will help — I know he will.

The phone.

'D'you want me to get it?' she asks.

'No,' I say. 'I'll get it.'

''Atta girl.'

'Jenny? It's Simon.'

'I'm not talking to you any more,' I say.

Silence at the other end.

'All you do is ruin my life.'

More silence.

'When are you going to give me some good news?'

'I'm sorry, Jenny, I . . . .'

'I'm joking, Simon.'

Another pause. 'You have a point, though.'

'No. It's all right. I've recovered.'

'Are you sure? I was worried. I was going to call over.'

'I'm fine. I'm usually better at handling the "no"s. It's just that you were the last in a long line of hopefuls.'

'I know. Which was why I was going to wait till after Christmas.'

'I always prefer to know where I stand, Simon. It helps me think of other options.'

'We have the register.'

'Excuse me, Simon, but shag the register. I'm going one better. I'm going to start a campaign.'

'A campaign?'

'Yes, to get people to donate samples.'

'I see.'

'Would that be OK? Could we do something like that? If people want to give blood to be tested, could the hospital deal with it?'

'I don't know, Jenny. I would have to check. But, in fairness, it is extremely unlikely that any such recruits would prove to be a match for Charlie.'

'But could you check, Simon, please? Just check to see if we could do it.'

'I'll look into it.'

'Great, thanks.'

Pat calls to the house. 'Just passing,' she says and I don't believe her. In any case, I don't need her. I'm a woman with a purpose now. Just try and stop me.

31

We have a magical day, apart from the four a.m. start. I wake to find something hard being shoved under my nose. It turns out to be a remote-control car. A tiny hand grabs mine and drags me into the sitting room. Apparently Santa got it right. Good man, Santa! I switch on all the winky lights, turning the apartment into a fairyland. Later, we go to Mass, say hello to 'baby Jesus' who arrived in the crib during the night, then share the first half of the morning with Mary and family. The older boys get 'really cool stuff', which reminds Charlie of Mark. We text him Happy Christmas. He calls Charlie back. My son's face shines brighter than any decoration. All is well with his hero. While we're on a roll, we ring Dave, who, it turns out, had been trying to get us earlier. It's snowing in New York. He promises to build a snowman for Charlie.

It's back home at noon, for my parents. A Christmas miracle — we get on. Without effort. And something in my heart melts to see the way they fuss over Charlie. My father jigs him up and down on his knee and I remember when he did that with me. He calls him poppit and sweetpea, like he used to do with his own daughter. I had forgotten. He chases Charlie with his dentures, letting them clap loosely against each other in his mouth. Clack, clack, clack. Charlie runs away, screaming, like I used to do. And it feels like we're a family.

I hug them when they're leaving.

And mean it.

After three, Jack arrives, laden down, a second Santa. We open presents. Pull crackers. Slide on paper hats (Jack, silver; Charlie, yellow; me, purple). Gobble up turkey, Brussels sprouts, roast potatoes. Chat, laugh. Take photos. Sing 'Jingle Bells'. Smile at Charlie's alternative version. Before we make it to dessert, he falls asleep, sitting back in his chair. I carry him to bed, tuck him in and send silent thoughts to Great and Jessica. 'I haven't forgotten you. Happy Christmas.' I switch on his globe and swirl it around, watching the world go round. Making my way back to Jack, I think about the day we've just had, and smile. For one whole day, I managed to forget.

Jack and I are mellow now, me stretched out on the couch, him sitting low in an armchair, legs sprawled out like a teenager, looking as if he could slide off. I'm drinking Baileys. He, Guinness.

'I never gave you your present,' he says.

'Jack,' I say crossly. 'You brought wine, pudding, that disgusting electric tarantula, the snake that glows in the dark, the Jack Stone Lego set . . . .'

'OK. If you don't want it, I'll just put it back.'

I smile.

He hands me an envelope.

Vouchers, I think, feeling it.

I open it up. Vouchers all right. Airline vouchers.

'*Jack!*'

'Jenny.'

'Jack.'

'Jenny.'

'What are you up to?'

'Nothing.'

'You can't go spending that kind of money.'

'I didn't. The airline keeps sending me freebies. We're always plugging them.'

'But I can't go. Not with Charlie. He's still on chemo.'

'It's open. Go when it's all sorted. You'll need it.'

'Jack,' I say, beginning to get a little teary. 'Why are you so good to us?'

'Why wouldn't I be?'

'I don't know. It's just that you've been really great since Charlie got sick. I mean, *really* great.'

'I got a bit of a shock. That's all. It made me think. And sure, I'm not doing much.'

'Well, I appreciate the "not much" you *are* doing. You've been amazing. Especially for a guy.'

'What does that mean?'

'I don't know. Just that men usually run from these things . . . .'

'Is that right?' he says.

We sit quietly for a while.

Then: 'Jen?'

'Yeah,' I say, scratching at a stain on the couch.

Silence.

I look up.

He's sitting up properly now, slouch gone. He clears his throat. 'I have a child.'

'Sorry?'

'I have a son . . . His name is Alan . . . He's fifteen.'

What? I find myself sitting upright. I'm frowning. 'How come you haven't mentioned him before?'

'You're the first person I've told.'

I say nothing.

'I walked out on them.'

'Who?'

'Alan, his mother. Left as soon as I heard she was pregnant.' He looks at me as if to say, 'Don't hate me.'

'What happened?'

'I wasn't ready.'

'For what? Marriage?'

'For any of it. To be a father. To be tied to one person forever, no matter how great she was. I did an awful thing. I asked her how she knew it was mine. The oldest trick in the book.'

'Could it have been anyone else's?'

'No. That's the awful thing.'

'Did you love her?'

'I don't know. I might have told her I did. But we hadn't made any big plans. We were just plodding along, enjoying the craic.'

'Were you going out long?'

'Six months or so . . . She was a gorgeous girl, Jenny. She didn't deserve that. I should have stuck by her. I *should* have. But I didn't.'

'What did she do?'

'You should have seen her face. The way she looked at me. She'd never been with anyone else. She knew I knew that. The way she looked at me, Jen, as if she couldn't believe it was really me saying those words. She said as much. Then she got angry. Really angry. Told me she was a fool ever to have loved me, that she never wanted to see me again. And I admired her for that. I almost gave in. I wish I had. Anyway, she went ahead with the pregnancy. A friend of ours looked after her, was very good to her. When Alan was born, he married her. Never spoke to me again. Either of them.'

'Do you ever see Alan?'

'No . . . If he knows about me at all, he probably hates me.'

'You don't know that.'

'His mother hates me.'

'Do you know where they live?'

'Yes.'

'Would you like to get in touch?'

'I couldn't, Jenny.'

'But you'd like to?'

'Only if I thought it would do some good.'

'Do you?'

'I don't know. If he got to know me, grew to like me, maybe. If I could help him, in some way, to become a man. That's what I'd like. To be part of his life, have a role, even a small one. He's in Junior Cert, this year. D'you know what I'd love? To be able to help him with his exams — English maybe. They do media studies, don't they?'

I shrug.

'D'you know what else I'd love? To cheer him on at rugby. To say, "Come on, son."' His voice softens. 'I sometimes go to see him play, hide in the crowd. He's captain of the team, you know.' The pride in Jack's voice.

I smile.

'But it's been fifteen years. I can't just land myself on him and expect him to give a shit about what I want. I'd only mess things up.'

'But maybe he does know about you. Maybe he'd like to know you. Maybe he's wondering why you left. Maybe he blames himself. Maybe he's like Charlie — always wondering about his father. Wanting to see him.'

'Is Charlie like that?'

'All the time.'

'Even though he's only four?'

'Yes, Jack.'

'But Alan has another father, who has been there from the beginning. It's different.'

'Maybe. I don't know. Fifteen years. It sounds a lot but is it — I mean, in a whole lifetime? No. Not compared to all the years you *could* have together.'

He doesn't look convinced.

'Look at it another way, then. What if he gets leukaemia? What if he has it right now and doesn't know it? What if he only has two more years left? Don't look at me like that. It happens. I should know.' I land a finger on my chest. 'You might have only two years left to get to know Alan. Can you waste any time? You get one life, Jack. One. You made a mistake. Don't let your whole life become one. If you regret what you did, do something about it.'

'Jesus.' He is running the palms of his hands along his trouser legs.

'Maybe if you'd asked someone else, they'd have told you forget it, it's not worth the hassle. But my priorities have changed, Jack. They're very clear now. There's simply no point wasting time.'

'But it's not just about me. It's about the boy, and what he wants.'

'So find out what he wants. Quietly, behind the scenes, if you can.'

'I don't want to open a Pandora's Box.'

'Jack. Live life. While you have it. That's all I'm going to say. No, actually, it's not. I think you'd make a great father.'

282

'You do in your arse.' He laughs.

'I absolutely do. You always get it right with Charlie. You always know what he wants — you understand him.'

'That's because he's a lad.'

'Just as well you've a boy then,' I say, smiling. 'Now get up and pour me another Baileys.'

Jack's revelation has made me think. About the male point of view. The father. Something I've happily ignored for years. It has given me some idea of what Dave might be feeling, thinking, hoping. I'm glad we did that paternity test. And sorry we waited this long. I've always seen Charlie as mine. But Charlie has a father — a father who deserves a chance to know him, to get involved, offer something, be there. If he wants. If it is Dave, Charlie will benefit so much. If Simon, well, we carry on as normal. We don't lose anything.

I write my article about Charlie, about our battle with leukaemia. I keep it simple, pared down. No frills. And yet I know it will move people. Getting it down helps, giving structure to what has happened. I can look at it from outside now, detach. It helps me focus on what I need to do. The campaign. I save the article onto the computer. I'll edit it later. I ring Simon to see if he has heard back from hospital administration. He hasn't, so I still don't know whether or not the hospital will test samples donated by people as part of my campaign. My impatience must come across because he talks about 'proper channels', about dealing with administration as 'probably *the* most frustrating part' of his job and about negotiation. Oh, and about it taking time and that finding an ultimate match in this way is 'extremely unlikely'.

I wonder if I can bypass the hospital. At two in the morning, I think of it. The solution. There is a register already in existence, a system in place. Surely it must be possible to enrol more people to join it. It's so simple I wonder why I didn't think of it sooner. We could do that, surely? Increase the size of the register. Everyone wins. I leap out of bed, fish out my laptop, hook it up to the phone line. In minutes, I'm searching the website of Ireland's bone marrow support group for details on how to join the register. I find what I'm looking for, jot down the contact number, then open up the computer document containing my article, and insert it. I e-mail it to Jack and cross my fingers. If this works, people will read our story and join the register. Not everyone will join, of course, but even a few more donors will make a difference, if not to Charlie, then to someone else who is waiting, hoping. I head back to bed and have the best night's sleep I've had in ages.

32

The morning of 25 January is as bleak as they come. I'm putting up surprise balloons, Happy Birthday banners and streamers for Charlie, who is over at Dara's, when the call comes through. Simon. He wants to come over. Why? He won't say. He sounds upbeat. Which is odd. It's his wife's anniversary.

He is grinning when I open the door. I've never seen him grin before. He looks mad.

'We've found a match,' he announces before he even steps inside. When he does, it's to grab me in such a tight grip that it squeezes air from my lungs. Sausage goes berserk. Barking as if I'm being attacked.

'Down, Sausage, down.'

When he sees it's Simon, he relaxes, shuffles back to the fire, winding down his tail wags with each swing.

Simon lets me go.

I'm laughing. And crying. 'Oh, Simon.' I have a hand on either side of my nose. 'I'm sorry. I'm so happy, so relieved. I can't believe it . . . Are you sure?'

'Yes,' he says, smiling. 'We've done a tissue test as well as a blood test.'

'There has to be a catch.'

'No catch.'

'What kind of match is it?'

He smiles again. 'Not perfect but good enough.'

'From the register?' *Must be.*

'No, Jenny. I need to talk to you about that. Can we sit down?'

No more surprises. 'Of course, sorry. Come in.' I walk ahead of him into the sitting room, all the time thinking, *Who? If not from the register, who? Everyone was negative. Have I forgotten anyone who was tested and didn't get results?* I go through the list. *Mary? No. My parents? No. Jack? No. Dave? No. Me? No. Simon? No. Well, who, then? No one else was tested. Unless we got a false negative.*

'You're frowning,' he says, when I turn.

'Thinking.'

'Who it is?'

'Yes. Who is it, Simon?'

'Maybe we could sit down?'

'Yes, of course, sorry.'

I sit on the arm of the couch, he on an armchair.

'It's Debra.'

'*Debbie.* But how? She wasn't even tested.'

'*Actually.*' He pauses. 'She was. She told me over Christmas, she wanted to do it. On Christmas Day. We'd a long chat. She was missing her mother. She always does at Christmas. It's not a great time for us. She started asking really detailed questions about leukaemia, about Charlie, about his chances. I told her about the Philadelphia Chromosome and that Charlie needed a bone marrow transplant and that we weren't having much luck finding a donor.

286

I wasn't in great form myself because, well, in fairness, I'd just told you I wasn't a match and I felt pretty bad about it.' He sighs. 'Anyway, Debra wanted to be tested. She was adamant. She has always felt guilty that she couldn't help her mother in some way and was very down about not being able to visit Charlie in hospital. This was something she felt she could do. It was important to her. I was afraid she'd get her hopes up and was straight about her chances of being a match. They were actually tiny, Jenny. That's when she decided to do it anonymously. She didn't want you to get your hopes up either, especially after the disappointments you've had.'

'She is so grown up for fifteen.'

'She's a good kid,' he says, proudly.

'She's a *great* kid . . . Does she understand what she has to go through, though?'

'Yes and she'll have counselling.'

'Actually, what *does* she have to go through?'

'She will have an anaesthetic, then some of her bone marrow will be removed. It's important to get enough cells, so it is good that Debra is bigger than Charlie. She'll be out of hospital in twenty-four hours and will be sore for a day or two. The biggest challenge is usually psychological. But, in fairness, her expectations are realistic, and, as I say, there will be the counselling.'

'So, she should be OK.'

'I really don't think there will be a problem. As I say, I think it will be good for her.'

'It's amazing. I still can't believe it.'

'As for Charlie, it's a very simple procedure. The marrow is just injected into his Freddie — it finds its own way home to where Charlie's bone marrow was.'

'It will be completely gone?'

He nods. 'We have to kill it before the transplant, using radiation and chemotherapy. It'll take three or four days. Charlie will be very weak and vulnerable during this time, Jenny.'

'But it is our only hope, right?'

'Yes.'

'Well, then, we have to do it. And we have to tell Charlie.'

'Where is he?'

'At his friend's house.'

'Well, when the time is right, we can tell him. Together, if you like — the way we told him about his diagnosis.'

'Yes. But first I need to know more about what's going to happen.'

'I'll arrange a meeting with Stephanie. She is the transplant co-ordinator. She'll take you through everything, answer anything you need to know.'

'I can't believe it's actually going ahead. I have to ring Deb and thank her.'

'Actually, Jenny, she doesn't know yet. She's still at school. I've just found out. I'll tell her as soon as I see her.'

'I'll wait till later this evening then.'

'Fine. I think it will give her a boost.'

'Maybe she'll worry.'

'I doubt it. I've already told her what would be involved. Her main concern was being able to do something. Now she can. I'm sure it will help her in more ways than one. Especially today. She'll need good news today.'

'Poor Deb. I'm so grateful. So grateful . . . .'

'You can tell her that when you call. It will cheer her up.'

'Of course. When do you think the transplant could go ahead?'

'We'll have to queue. Then, when we have a slot, we'll take Charlie in for a week of chemo and radiation. He'll have to have the radiation at St Matthew's Hospital. So there will be a bit of to-ing and fro-ing. He'll need to be in isolation to protect him, Jenny, because his defences will be completely down.'

'You said before, he'd be in hospital for six weeks?'

'Yes. And no school for nine months. He'll be on a drug called Cyclosporin to prevent his body from rejecting the transplanted cells. Have you thought about what you'll do with Sausage?'

'God, no. I hadn't.'

'It might be best if you had him stay somewhere else for nine months.'

'Right. OK. I'll sort something out.'

'We could . . . .'

'You've done enough. Honestly. I'll work something out . . . So, this is it. What we've been waiting for.'

He smiles. 'Yes.' And I could kiss him. I could definitely kiss him. But where would that lead? Something pops into my head. But that's where I keep it. *Does Debbie being a match mean that Simon is Charlie's father? Or is it just a coincidence?* I can wait for the answer. It's almost six weeks since we did the test. Any day now . . . .

I ring everyone. Dave, first. Then Mary, my mother and Jack. With each phone call, it becomes more and more a reality. The euphoria is contagious. When they arrive for Charlie's party, the mood is celebratory. Everyone suddenly upbeat. Even Charlie notices.

'Everyone's so happy that it's my birthday,' he says.

I look around and notice the absence of children around him. Just Dara. But that will change. Everything will return to normal. It will take time, but once this transplant is over, we can work towards building a normal life.

I open the door. A smiling Debbie bursts in and throws herself at me, then jumps up and down.

I start laughing.

'I can't believe it,' she says, eventually letting go. 'It's *brill*, isn't it?'

'Deb, you've no idea how brill,' I say, hearing the relief in my own voice. 'Thank you *so* much. You've no idea how much this means to us.'

'Where is he?' she asks.

'In the sitting room with his birthday presents. But Deb . . . .' I say, stopping her from rushing ahead.

'Yes?'

'He doesn't know yet about needing a transplant. We didn't want to tell him until we found a donor.'

'Well, here I am,' she says, beaming.

'Yes, but I wonder should we wait for your dad to tell him. He's very good at talking to kids about these things, explaining honestly but in a way that they don't worry. I was glad he was there when we had to tell Charlie about having leukaemia.'

'Oh, OK,' she says, disappointed.

'It's just that Charlie will need to go through some intense treatment for a week before and we need to explain this. And we need to explain about having to wait a little while. But, you know, I bet when he hears it's your marrow he's getting, he'll be thrilled.'

She smiles again. 'Maybe I could be there when you tell him?'

'I think that's a very good idea,' I say with conviction, but then wonder how we might do that if Deb doesn't want to come to the hospital. I'm not exactly going to ask Simon over here to tell Charlie.

'You know?' says Deb. 'This is the best day of my life. I was so down going to school. It's my mum's anniversary,' she says, letting her head drop. Her voice becomes almost inaudible. 'I'm always a bit fed up this time of year because it reminds me how much I miss her. As soon as the Christmas decorations go up, I start . . . .' She pops her head back up, takes a breath. 'But today, Dad picked me up from school and told me the news. And suddenly it felt like a new day. As if maybe I can do something for somebody after all. It's the best thing that could have happened today, you know?'

This time I hug her.

'You're great, Deb. D'you know that? Just great. Your dad must be very proud . . . And your mum.'

She flushes.

'Come on — let's go in to see the birthday boy,' I say, taking her by the hand.

33

Our GP's surgery is like countless others — clean, neutral, just bigger than small, with desk, doctor and plinth. Dr Finnegan's desk is probably tidier than most but does support the obligatory prescription pads, handkerchiefs, stickers, clock and calendar, all sponsored by various pharmaceutical companies. Dave and I sit on one side (he insisted on coming back for the test results), Dr Finnegan on the other. She is by no means lounging but, compared to us, looks like she is. Our spines are as straight as — well, one of Charlie's standing pencils. We take up the front third of our chairs. My clammy hands are pinned between my knees. Dave has his tucked under his armpits. Just as well, considering the pace of his tapping foot.

She produces a professional smile now, reaching across the desk to hand me an envelope that I see has already been opened.

'The results come addressed to me,' she explains. 'Registered mail. I have to open it, Jenny. Some cases can be sensitive or difficult — that's why they like GPs or solicitors to give the news.'

I examine the front of the envelope. URGENT PATHOLOGY REPORT, and, right enough, addressed to Dr Finnegan.

'Would you like to read it in private?' she asks.

'Yes,' rushes Dave.

'That's fine,' she says, standing. She extends her hand and smiles. 'If you've any questions, or want to talk about it, Jenny, just give me a ring.'

Passing a bin on the street outside, I'm tempted to fling it in. Leave everything the way it is. Safe. Not knowing. I stuff it in my pocket. We reach the car and sit in. Look at each other.

Dave smiles. 'Ready?' he asks.

'No.' I laugh, nervously.

'Want me to open it?'

'No . . . I'll do it.'

I slide my hand into my pocket, feel the envelope, hold it for a moment. I take a breath, then pull it out, look at it, then at Dave, then back at it. I slip my fingers in and remove the folded yellow sheets of paper, then unfold them, heart pounding. I stare at the words, black and definite, let my breath escape, look at Dave. I flick to the second and third pages just to see if there is anything else. Legal jargon. I already know all I need to. I refold the document and, wordlessly, hand it to Dave. He doesn't hesitate. Opens it quickly. Then stops. Takes an audible breath. Says nothing, eyes fixed on the document. I will him to meet my eyes. He won't.

'Dave?'

He doesn't answer.

'Dave?'

'Yeah,' he says.

'What are you thinking?'

'You know what? I'm going to walk back,' he says, handing the document back to me, avoiding eye contact.

'But it's freezing. And it's at least two miles.'

'I just want to be on my own for a bit, OK?'

'OK. But you *are* coming back to the apartment, aren't you?'

'Yeah. Yeah. I'll see you later.'

I watch him go. Hands stuffed deep into the pockets of his navy reefer jacket, black-capped head down, shoulders forward against the cold. I look back down at the document I've ended up holding, and feel like tearing it into confetti. Now, too late, I understand what Jack meant about a Pandora's Box. We have disturbed everything. There is no going back. I know who Charlie's father is. And I am disappointed.

I turn on the engine to clear the condensation. I try to be positive, tell myself the news is good. I was right not to marry Dave, expect him to accept a son who wasn't his. But that's rubbish because I know that if we had stayed together, Dave would have been a father to Charlie, a real father — been a presence in his life, loved him as a son. Now, Charlie has nothing more than he has always had — an anonymous and absent dad. So Charlie loses.

And Dave loses. He wanted it. I know he did.

I'm not going to sit here, getting myself worked up. But I don't know where to go. I'm not ready to face Mary, who is minding Charlie. She'll want to know the result. And I'm not ready to tell her. I start the car and just drive. I don't know where I'm going. Until I find myself parked outside my old home.

My mother opens the heavy door of the period house.

'Oh, Jenny. It's you. How *wonderful*. This is a surprise. How are you? Where's the little man?' She sticks her head out as though trying to find his hiding place.

'He's at Mary's.'

'Oh. Well, come in, love,' she says, and I know she's wondering what brought me here, especially without Charlie, the only reason we have been seeing each other again. 'Your father has just popped to the shops to get a few chops for dinner. He won't be long.'

'You've him well trained.'

She looks at me quickly as if trying to tell if I'm being sarcastic. She says nothing, though.

I follow her through the hall. It hasn't changed. Same pale blue used-to-be-plush carpet, same wallpaper (the type you get in country homes — beige with pale pink rustic scenes), same matching curtains. Same smell. Not one you could pin to something specific, just the smell of home.

She waves a hand as she walks. 'Ignore the décor,' she says. 'My next project is to give the place a good going over.'

'It's nice as it is,' I say, suddenly not wanting it changed.

Another sarcasm check from her.

Am I really that bad?

She offers me a coffee.

'Let's have it in the conservatory,' she suggests. 'You go on ahead. I'll be in in a sec. No sugar, lots of milk, or have you changed?'

'Nope, same as ever.' I continue on into the conservatory, don't feel like sitting, so wander around checking the names on the plants, filling her little red can with the long spout and starting to water. It's automatic. I used to do this when I was left to potter around on my own in the house as a child. It was the one thing I liked. She noticed, appreciated it, I remember. Of course, I stopped as soon as the poor-little-rich-girl routine kicked in. Every action designed to annoy. Nothing to please.

I trip over something, stumble and grab the arm of a wicker chair. I look down. The culprit is a heap of books, stacked up beside the chair. I bend to sort them back into a pile. That's when I notice what they are. Books on leukaemia, living with cancer, communicating with people who have cancer, medical encyclopaedias. I pick one up, flick through it. She has underlined and made notes beside chunks of text. I remember her doing this to newspapers on the rare occasion I was allowed into her office. I hear her coming now and look up.

'I see you've found my light reading,' she says, carrying in the coffee on a tray as if this isn't her house at all — as if she's a servant and the lady of the house will be here in a moment.

'You've been busy,' I say, putting it back.

'You know me — have to keep on top of things.'

'Any good?'

'They've answered a lot of my questions.'

It hadn't struck me that she'd have questions, but of course she must have had. She must have gone through the same uncertainty I did, but with no one to talk to, no one to ask.

'You should have asked,' I say.

'I didn't want to get in the way, love. And anyway, the books are fine. Funnily enough, I like the psychology ones, though I'd never any time for that kind of thing in my *former life*. You know, I never thought I'd survive without politics but I have to say I'm learning more than I've learnt in a long time.'

'Charlie helps.'

'*I know*. Texting, Internet, e-mail. Sure, without him, I wouldn't have been able to get some of the trickier titles at all. I've even ordered some games. Your father and I play chess on the laptop now. He wouldn't admit it but he likes the hints the computer gives him.' She chuckles as if fond of the old man. Which, I have to admit, she always was.

'Dave isn't Charlie's father,' I blurt. Don't ask why. She looks at me, expressionless, wordless, controlling her reaction. I keep going. 'I know how you feel about Dave but he's not Charlie's father.' She hasn't exploded yet. 'I know you never wanted us to split. I know you thought I was a fool but there was a reason. Now you know it.'

'Jenny . . . what I think of Dave is not important. I was wrong to interfere. I know that now. Your life is your life. All I saw was the surface of it. I didn't know you then, though I thought I did. I didn't understand your point of view, your reasons. I just thought you were throwing everything good away, like you did when you were a teenager. But I was wrong, Jenny . . . We are different, you and I. And I am very proud of you, the way you've brought Charlie up on your own. You're stronger than I'd have been. And he is a wonderful child, a special child. Thank you for allowing us to see so much of him.'

'He loves you,' I say simply. Because it's true.

'And we love him.' She reaches for a hankie.

'It's all right,' I say but keep my distance.

'I know, I know, I'm sorry — just a silly old woman.'

'You're not old. Or silly,' I quickly add, in case she thinks I'm making a point.

'No, I could be worse, I suppose,' she says, trying to smile.

'Look, I'm sorry for keeping Charlie from you. I just didn't think it would be good for him.' I see her face and add, 'Obviously, I was wrong. You have helped him and you were there when he needed you.'

'Thank you, Jenny. I'm glad we had this chat.'

It's not over, is it?

'Do you want to know who Charlie's father is?'

'Only if you want to tell me,' she says.

I tell her about Brussels, about Simon. She doesn't judge, doesn't advise, just listens. I ask her what I should do.

'It's up to you, Jenny. I've interfered too much. If there's one thing I've learnt, it's that I *don't* know what's best for you. You do.'

Isn't that what I've wanted? No interference? It's not what I want now.

297

'But if you were me, what would you do?'

'I don't know, Jenny. What do you want?'

'What do you mean?'

'What do you want from Dave? What do you want from Simon?'

'I don't know. Nothing.'

She throws me a be-honest-now look.

'I don't know. I just want Dave to be happy. I don't expect anything from him now. He'll go back to the States. There's no reason to stay.'

'And Simon?'

'I don't know. Well, actually I know what I *would* like. But I also know it's impossible.'

'What?'

'I would like him to be a presence in Charlie's life. To be a father to him. Charlie would love to know his dad. He likes Simon. And it's important for boys to have a father figure. But that will never happen. Even if I tell Simon he is Charlie's father, that's where it will end. He can't be a father to Charlie, not publicly. He has a daughter. Who would work things out, add things up. And realise he was unfaithful to her mother. Her dead mother. Even though it wasn't like that. How could she possibly understand? She's fifteen.'

'You can't control other people's actions. Maybe all you can do is give them the truth and see how they handle it . . . At least Dave knows. That's good.'

'It means he will go.'

'If he wants to go, you have to let him.'

'I know.'

'And if Simon wants nothing to do with Charlie, there's nothing you can do about that either. But you can tell him. And you've nothing to lose in doing so — he already knows there is a chance he might be the father. You'd just be clearing the uncertainty.'

'I know.' I sigh. 'Poor Dave, though.'

'Maybe not. Maybe Dave is better off in the States.'

'How can you say that? You love Dave.'

'Yes, but it's not about whether or not I like Dave, is it? It's about what you both want to do.'

'You've a pretty clear head — I'll say that for you.'

'God, I'd want to have. The bullshit I've had to put up with for thirty years. How did I ever get into politics?'

'You loved it.'

'You know, I never stopped to think about that. I just got caught up in it.'

'You talk like it's addictive.'

'That's exactly what it is. Anyway, I'm glad I'm out now. You've done me a favour. And Jenny, I am sorry. For everything.'

'I know.'

'Friends?'

'Friends.'

'Hug?'

'Yeah.'

She is all right. Maybe it was me, or a personality clash. I don't know, but I'm glad it's over.

34

I drive by the apartment on my way to Mary's. The light is on in the sitting room. Dave. It would be easy to keep driving. Not face him. Pretend there was no test, no result. But I need to know. I need to know what he's thinking. Feeling. Planning. We won't be able to talk when Charlie's home. Up I go. Wanting to get there, but not.

'Hi,' he says, from the couch.

'Hi.' I throw my coat on a chair.

'Where were you?' he asks.

'My mother's.'

He looks surprised but lets it go.

'Are you OK?' I ask him.

'Yeah.'

'Well?'

'Well, what?'

'I want to know how you feel about it, Dave,' I say, sitting down beside him.

'I thought you knew how I felt. I thought you knew what I wanted.'

'But did you want it? Really, Dave? Think about it. Sickness, uncertainty, maybe . . . worse? Who would want that? Your life will be so much simpler, happier. Head back to the States and get on with it. No guilt. No strings.'

'Maybe I wanted strings.'

'But those kinds of strings? Not knowing if Charlie is going to be OK. Living with cancer . . . .'

'You think I can just walk away now?'

'I'm not saying that, Dave. I'm just saying — oh I don't know what I'm saying — forget it.'

'We shouldn't have done that stupid test,' he says.

'But I did it for you.'

'And I did it for you.'

'Oh God!' I groan. *Stupid, bloody Fiona.*

'I didn't want to know,' he says. 'I just wanted to help. Be there for you. I told you, five years ago, I didn't want to know. I was committed to you. This had nothing to do with it . . . .'

'But it must have mattered, subconsciously . . . .'

He slaps his hand down on the couch. 'It didn't. I would have been a father to Charlie, loved him. I told you that. And I know now, it would have been easy. He's a great kid. I knew he would be. He's yours.'

I sigh. 'I'm sorry, I didn't know how confident you were about how you felt. I'm sorry. I'm a fool.' I look down at my hands. *Don't put anything in them, they'll only go and fuck it up.*

'Maybe we could get it back?'

'What do you mean?'

'Marry me, Jenny.'

'*What?*'

'Marry me.'

'Why?'

301

'I want us to be a family.'

'What about Fiona?'

He sighs. 'Fiona,' he says. 'Fiona. I've seen a different side to Fiona. You know, it's so easy when everything's light and it's all socialising and parties and fun. But I've seen her with you. And I've seen her with Charlie. She has no warmth. No understanding of what you're going through. She sees everything from her own point of view.'

'She's young.' *Why am I standing up for Fiona?*

'Maybe.'

'Dave.' I put my hand on his.

'That's a "no".'

'No, it's not a "no", but it's not a "yes". I have so much to think about now. So much to do. With the transplant.'

'I see.'

'Dave, I'm being honest. It's not a "no". It's just I can't think about anything else, right now. I can't make a decision like that with the transplant hanging over us . . . And I don't expect you to wait around either. You've done enough of that.'

'But you will think about it?' he asks.

'Yes. Of course, I will. But I want you to think about it too. Take time to. Away from us. You're reacting to the news. It's still a shock, a disappointment. But maybe, in time, you'll realise it's for the best. Maybe you don't need this in your life.'

'Maybe I do.'

'I don't want you to wait around, Dave. Go back to New York. Think about what you'd be taking on . . . .'

'I know what I'd be taking on.'

'But I can't promise you anything. Not now, Dave. I need to sort this out.'

'I know. I understand. And I'd like to help.'

'I know. But I really think you need to be away from us for a while. Think clearly about everything.'

'I have to go back to talk to Fiona . . . I have to end it . . . and in a week or two, I'll come back — that's if she doesn't murder me . . . Will you call me when the transplant is going ahead? I'll be over on the first plane.'

'You don't have to do that, Dave.'

'I want to.'

'Are you sure?'

'Jenny, I want to be with you, care for you, for Charlie. It's what I want. So don't feel guilty about it. It's what I want to do. OK?'

'I don't deserve you, Dave,' I say, hugging him.

He offers to come with me to collect Charlie. But I really need to talk to Mary. I tell him to relax, take it easy. He offers to make dinner.

We're holed up in the kitchen, out of kiddie earshot. Doors closed. Children occupied in various rooms around the house.

'It's not Dave,' I tell her.

She puts down her coffee. Says nothing for a second, then: 'Show's how little I know.'

'You thought it was Dave?'

'Well, I just figured, the other thing was once off — you were in a relationship with Dave; the odds . . . .'

'You make us sound like horses.'

'Sorry. You know what I mean . . . Who did *you* think it was?'

'I didn't want to think. I'd hoped it was Dave. But there you go.'

'Why Dave?'

'He's just been so supportive, Mary. He would have been a father to Charlie. I know he would have. He'd have announced it openly, proudly, to everyone, including Charlie. Can you imagine

303

what that would have meant to him? Having a father, at last. Especially now — these could be his last months . . . .'

'Don't talk like that. Maybe Simon could . . . .'

'*Mary*. Even if Simon wanted to get involved, which I doubt, he couldn't.' I explain about Debbie.

'I hadn't thought of that.'

'Maybe it doesn't matter,' I say.

'What do you mean?'

'He's asked me to marry him.'

'*Simon?*' Shock-horror-read-all-about-it.

'*No*. Dave. How did you even *think* of Simon?'

'I've seen the way he looks at you.'

'You say that about everybody.'

'No, I don't.'

'Yes, you actually do.'

'We're getting away from the point,' she says. 'When did this happen?'

'Just now.'

'Oh my God. *And?*'

'I said I'd have to think about it.'

'What's there to think about?'

'For starters, do I love him?'

'He's gorgeous, helpful, loves Charlie, has been so good to you . . . .'

'He has been great, Mary. And I'd love for that support, that security, that sharing of all this, just to keep on. But I have to ask myself do I love him. Honestly. Dave the person, not Dave the friend, carer? And if I do, would I need to ask? And anyway, how can I even think about this now? And . . . .'

'You're over-analysing. He asked you to marry him — simple. Forget the rest.'

'He *is* engaged.'

'Oh, yeah. What about Fiona?' She produces a silly-me laugh.

'He said he'll end it.'

'He seems to mean business all right.'

'Don't you think he's just reacting to the news, to the disappointment?'

'Maybe, but if I were a man, I know which of you I'd pick. No contest. Dave knows you, Jenny. Maybe this is just forcing him to see sense.'

'Or maybe it's a reaction.'

'You'll know soon enough, when he breaks it off with Fiona.'

'*If.*'

'What's he going to do — ring her? E-mail?'

'He's not like that. He's going over to see her.'

'Is that wise?'

'It's fair. Anyway, I told him to take some time to think about it.'

'In the States?'

I nod.

'Are you mad?'

'No. If he comes back in a week or two and still feels the same, I'll know he means it.'

'You're too cynical, that's what's wrong with you. He's a good man. He wants to marry you.'

'Mary, if you'd been through what I've been through, you'd be cynical too.'

'So, are you going to tell Simon that he is Charlie's father?'

'I don't know.'

'You should.'

'Why? If I'm supposed to rush off and marry Dave, why tell Simon?'

'He knows you've done the test, doesn't he?'

'Yes.'

'Well, he'll want to know.'

'Maybe he won't. Did you ever think of that? Maybe he won't want to know at all. And does it really matter when it's not going to make a difference anyway?'

'I don't know, Jen. You always seem to make things difficult for yourself.'

'No, I don't,' I snap. 'The man has made it clear that he wants nothing to do with me. And that's fine. *Fine.* I'm not giving him any opportunity to think that I want his involvement in any way.'

'When?'

'When what?'

'When did he say he doesn't want anything to do with you?'

Oops. *Oh, shag it! Might as well tell her now.*

'After Jessica's funeral.'

'Yes, *yes*, I *knew* something'd happened.' She's practically hopping.

So I tell her. She'd only drag it out of me anyway.

'I *knew* it. I *knew* it. Why didn't you tell me?'

'Mary, I wanted to forget it. And if I told you, you'd never let me.'

'So he *does* like you. I knew it.'

'Sweet, Jesus, Mary, will you *stop*?'

'OK, OK, but he wouldn't have made love to you if he didn't like you.'

'Oh. Yes. He would. He did before. When he didn't even know me.'

'That was different — his wife . . . .'

'No it wasn't. He was upset both times . . . .'

'He said, "If things were different . . . ."'

'But things aren't different. And anyway, it's so easy to say stuff like that — it's a typical wimpy cop-out used by people all the time.'

She sighs. 'Well, I think you should tell him. And I don't think you should send Dave off to the States. Really, sometimes I believe you don't want a man at all.'

'I don't. I would like a father for Charlie. And it looks like that's not going to happen.'

'Not if you can help it,' she says.

'You see, this is why I don't tell you things. You take them up the wrong way, give crappy advice and then make me feel like a complete eejit.'

'I'm only telling you what I think. And my advice is not crappy. And you're not a *complete* eejit. Just a bit of a one.' She laughs. 'Now, come here and give me a hug.'

'I *will* kill you some day — you *do* realise this?'

'Impossible.'

'Why impossible?'

'You love me too much.'

'Actually, I do. You've been the best friend I could hope for, Mary,' I say, starting to get teary. 'You've been so good to us.'

'You know what you need?'

'What?'

'A holiday. As soon as Charlie recovers from the bone marrow transplant, we're going somewhere. I don't know where yet but I've a few months to plan. Dolphins, I'm thinking, dolphins.'

'Jack's given me some vouchers.'

'Great. Nothing stopping us then.'

Another chemo day. Dave stays with us for most of it but has to go to catch his flight.

'But why do you have to go?' whines Charlie.

'I have to talk to Fiona.'

'Can't you ring her?'

'Well, I have to tell her something sad and I should really be there when I tell her.'

'What?'

'You're very nosy,' says Dave, pressing Charlie's nose with a finger.

'No, I'm not. What sad thing are you going to tell her?'

Dave looks at me to see if it's OK to talk about relationship break-ups.

I shrug, *you might as well*.

'I have to tell her that I don't want to be her boyfriend any more.'

'*Yes!*' He punches the air with a fist.

'*Charlie*,' I say.

Dave laughs. 'Don't you like Fiona?' he asks.

'No.' Charlie replies.

'Why not?'

'She doesn't smile.'

'You know, Charlie, you might be right about that,' says Dave.

'When are you coming back?'

'Very soon.'

'When soon?'

'Maybe next week.'

'OK. Dave?'

'Yes, Charlie?'

'Will you be looking for a new girlfriend now?'

'I don't know. I might take a rest for a while.' He smiles at me.

'Well, when you're finished the rest, I know someone *really* nice. And guess what?'

'What?' Dave smiles.

'You know her already. And you like her too. And she's pretty and she's a good cook and she's great if you're sick.' He frowns. 'She doesn't smile as much any more, but she still smiles much more than Fiona,' he adds hopefully.

'She sounds lovely, all right,' says Dave. 'Are you sure you don't want her for yourself?'

'Daw. I'm too small for girlfriends. Anyway, I've a dog.'

'When I come back, you can tell me a bit more about her. I might be ready for a girlfriend by that stage.'

'OK. And she might get her hair cut properly by that stage.' My son sneaks a look at me.

I raise an eyebrow at him.

I walk Dave to the door. I am already starting to feel an emptiness and he hasn't even gone. I'm sick of being on my own. Enough of having to be the constant coper. I need a rest. Feeling-sorry-for-myself tears collect. We hug and I don't want to let go. We stay like that for a long time. Until I see Simon swinging through the doors. Before I can look away, our eyes meet. He turns suddenly to say something to Dr Howard. She laughs.

'Good luck with Fiona,' I say.

'Thanks. I hate letting her down. She's so focused on the wedding.'

'Then don't say anything for a while. Go home, wait a few days and see how you feel. Then decide.' *What am I saying? Mary's right — I am a complete eejit. What do I owe Fiona?*

'I'm going to do it, Jen.'

'Just see how you feel. You owe us nothing, Dave.'

'It's not about owing. I'll text you when I get there.'

'Or phone.'

'You'll be in bed.' He holds both my hands in his. 'I will be back.'

'I know.'

'And if you get news on the transplant date, call me.'

'I will, Dave. Thanks.'

I watch him go until his back disappears around a corner.

309

I return to the room and my life. He has left me with so much to think about. But I'm not going to allow myself to do that. What he has said is just a reaction. He is trying to hold onto something that has been lost. Give him time, away from it all. He'll change his mind. For now, I'm going to wait. And not think. Until he comes home. See how he feels then. I do love Dave. But how much and in what way? When this is over, maybe I can think about that. In the meantime, it's good to know he's got the thumbs up from the junior matchmaker.

'Dave's gone,' says Charlie to Simon.

'Has he?' asks Simon, rolling up Charlie's top.

'Yeah. Back to America,' says Charlie, helping hold up the top.

'Oh,' says Simon.

'But he won't be long. He's just going to tell Fiona that he doesn't want to be her boyfriend any more.'

'I see,' says Simon, putting the stethoscope into his ears.

'Then he's coming back.'

'Charlie,' I say. 'Simon can't hear you — he's got the thing in his ears.'

He stays quiet for a moment but keeps looking at Simon, gagging to continue the news bulletin.

What is he thinking? That the results are back? That Dave is the father, not him? Why else would he be breaking off his relationship and coming home? Is he relieved? His professional face is on. I can't tell.

'That's a great heart you've got there, Charlie,' he says finally.

'You say that every time.'

'Well, it's true every time.'

'Can I tell you a secret?' Charlie asks him.

'I don't mind, if your mum doesn't.'

'Charlie, secrets aren't nice.'

'Just one, Mum.'

'All right — go on then.'

The thing about Charlie's whispering method is that it's not perfected. I hear everything. Unfortunately.

'Dave needs a new girlfriend. I think Mum would be good. What do you think?'

Simon's reply — 'I suppose that would really be up to your mum, wouldn't it?' — is directed not at Charlie, but at me. He looks straight at me while he says it, seriously, as though trying to tell me something, as though daring me to decide between him and Dave. *Which is ridiculous. He is not interested in me — he has made that clear. He turned himself off like a tap after the last 'mistake'. So what is he doing? What is he saying? Does he even know what he wants? Or is he just one of those men who wants something only if he thinks someone else wants it?* Not for the first time, with this man, I've no idea what is going on.

'I'll have a chat with her,' whispers Charlie.

'OK, Charlie,' he says, patting him gently on the shoulder and heading for the sink.

We have to stay overnight because Charlie needs a blood transfusion and the day ward is closing. We are transferred to the oncology unit, where there is a single room free. Someone is being admitted tomorrow, but we will be well gone by the time they arrive. I'm sitting in semi-darkness with Charlie asleep beside me. It is strangely peaceful. And for once, I have time to think. To work out what Simon wants, what Dave wants, and what I'd want, if they knew what they wanted. Obviously, it's a complete waste of time.

'Jenny?'

I jump.

'Sorry, did I frighten you?' he whispers.

'No, I just wasn't expecting anyone. I was miles away. Is everything OK?'

'Yes, fine. I just wanted to ask you something. Do you mind if I sit down?'

I am suddenly nervous. *Now what?*

'I was just wondering,' he says, without waiting for a reply. 'Did you get the results of the paternity test?'

Oh God! My stomach rears up like a startled horse.

'It's just that I've been thinking a lot about it since you told me about the possibility that, well, you know, Charlie could be my son . . . I would like to know, Jenny.'

'Simon, I have the results but I'm not sure that telling you would be a good idea . . . I think it was a mistake doing the test. It's upset things. Maybe it's best to leave everything the way it was . . . .'

'He is my son, isn't he?'

'Simon, I really don't think . . . .'

'He is. Otherwise you would have denied it already. He has to be. He was born the day Alison died.'

'That was a coincidence.'

'I don't believe that. I've been given something instead . . . Haven't I?'

If I didn't know before, I know now. He still hasn't got over his wife. 'Simon, I'm not sure that . . . '

'He is my son.' He says with a certainty that is scary.

I nod, suddenly weary.

'Thank you. That's all I wanted. Just to know. That's all.'

We are both silent. In the end, nerves get to me. 'Any idea where we go from here?' I regret it instantly.

'We get him better,' he says with firm certainty.

35

Morning. Simon comes to discharge us. He sits beside Charlie and chats as if he has all the time in the world. I notice it instantly. The difference. The softness in his voice. The tenderness in his eyes. The way he slides Charlie onto his lap. The way he tilts his head to listen. Simon has always been gentle, caring. This is different. This is a father with his son. It shocks me. I'm not ready for it. Charlie is *my* son. He has always been mine. No one else involved. Just me. I make the decisions. *I* decide. This is wrong. I'm not ready for this.

'OK, time to go,' I say, standing.

Simon looks up. He seems to understand. Lifts Charlie onto the floor.

'Well, Charles, I'll see you soon.'

'OK, Simon. See you soon.'

I feel suddenly guilty. *What do I want?*

For the next two days, we stay home, Charlie recovering from the chemo, me painting the kitchen, cleaning out the presses, keeping busy, trying not to think. About Simon and what he wants, expects. About Dave, who hasn't called. On the third day, Mary calls over with Dara, just back from Cork, where they were visiting her mother. The best friends busy themselves trying to save Scooby Doo from the Faceless Rider. Heads together, kneeling, one frantically button pushes while the other encourages from the sidelines, 'Get him, get him, yeah, yeah, you got him.' Two little pairs of red ears. We watch from the kitchen over coffee.

I can't do chit-chat. Too much on my mind.

'He knows,' I blurt out, unable to keep a lid on it any longer.

'Who knows what?' she asks, her Cork accent returning after the visit.

'Simon knows about Charlie.'

'How?'

'He asked.'

Her eyes say, *did-he-now?*

'When we were in having the chemo.'

'What did he say?'

'It was weird, Mary. He just seemed convinced that Charlie was his and he wanted me to confirm it.'

'How was he so sure?'

'Charlie was born the day his wife died.'

'Jesus!' She puts down her cup. 'That's spooky.'

'No, it's not. It's just a weird coincidence.'

'No, actually, Jenny, it is spooky.' She's nodding quickly.

'He seemed to think that he's been given something in place of his wife . . . He obviously misses her so much, he's prepared to believe that kind of nonsense.'

'Maybe he's right. Who knows?'

'*Mary.*'

'Well, we don't. Strange things happen — that's all I'll say.'

314

And I think of Great and the smell of roses, and my inheritance arriving on her birthday. I say nothing.

'So what did he say when you told him?'

'Just that he knew it.'

'Did he make any commitment?'

'What do you think? Of course not. Just some cop-out about getting Charlie better.'

'Always the cynic. Of course, he wants to get him better. Surely that is the priority . . . And nothing else?'

'Only that he was all over him like a rash the next day.'

'Aw, Jenny, that's sweet. He's obviously delighted.'

'I didn't like it.'

'What?'

'The way he was with him. Too familiar. Charlie is my son. He can't just waltz in and behave like a father. Especially when he's never going to admit it.'

'Jenny. You've done it all by yourself for so long. Of course it's going to feel strange. But think of Charlie, Jen. Think of how good it will be for Charlie.'

'What — a bit of attention? Simon will never admit to anything. Not openly. Even if he is around more, it won't be as a father.'

'Simon is a good man, Jenny. He's not going to piss you around.'

'He's already pissed me around.'

'Come on, Jen. That was two consenting adults and bad timing.'

'It'll never be good timing. He's still in love with his wife.'

'Things change. Give it time.'

'It doesn't matter. I don't want anything from him. The last man who offered me something is back in the States four days and hasn't even called.'

'No.'

315

'*Yes*.'

'I *told* you,' she says, pointing at me.

'I know, I know.' I rest my forehead on my hand.

'Ah, don't panic. Maybe he's waiting until he has everything sorted, made the break from Fiona.'

'How long does he need?'

'Don't rush him. You told him to take time. Now let him.'

'I know, but . . . .'

'He's mad about you, Jenny. He knows what he's doing. He's not going to rush back to Little Miss Snooty.'

'It's not about that. I just want him to call. Let me know he's OK, that's all.'

'I don't know, Jen. Two men on the horizon. I'm beginning to think my life is boring,' she jokes.

'No men on the horizon. Just two confused men, confusing me.'

'Could be worse.'

'Could it?'

'At least they both care for Charlie.'

'True.'

'Well, just concentrate on that. You said yourself you can't concentrate on anything until the transplant is over.'

'You're right. As usual.' I sip my coffee. It's cold. 'Want another?' I offer, lifting her mug.

'Yes, please. I need all the caffeine I can get. You'll never guess what happened!' Cork accent back again when it was just beginning to disappear.

'What?'

'Remember we took the boys ice-skating at Smithfield two weeks ago?'

'Yeah.' I had imagined the happy family scene when she told me they were going.

'And you know Phil fell?'

'No, I didn't.'

'Well, he did. Anyway, turns out he broke his elbow.'

'*Oh no*. When did you find out?'

'Today, when I got back.'

'Only today?'

'He had an X-ray as soon as I left for Cork. *I know*. I kept telling him, "Ah, you'll be grand — it still works, doesn't it?" If it were any of the boys, I'd have had them X-rayed, straightaway. You know, he'd never even have got it looked at, only for a guy in the office. After two weeks of listening to Phil moaning, he told him to shut up and get an X-ray. He'll never let me live it down, you know.'

'So is he in a cast?' I ask, wondering what she is doing over here, instead of being back home pampering the patient.

'No. It's too late to do anything now. They'd have put it in a sling two weeks ago. But there's nothing they can do now.'

'Oh, no.'

'I'm mortified.'

'Mary, I'm glad.'

'Why?' She looks confused.

'You're human after all,' I say, smiling. 'I was beginning to think you were a saint.'

'Damn, I've let you down. Another fan bites the dust.'

I land her fresh coffee down.

'Anyway, do you need any shopping? I'm going,' she says.

'It's going to be a bit harder than that.'

'Than what?'

'To get back up on the pedestal. A little bit of shopping, I don't know . . . .'

'Oh God, the pressure . . . .'

317

'Oh, all right then. But you're getting off lightly.'

'Ah, thanks, Jenny, you don't know how much this *means* to me.'

And we're laughing.

When Mary's gone, I think about ringing Dave. That's as far as I get. I decide not to push him. Let him call when he's ready. I turn my attention to my boy, whom I've neglected with all my busy-trying-not-to-think activities. Don't get me wrong — he has got all his medicine, all the things he needs, just not that extra bit of attention that means more than anything. We settle down, cuddle up with Sausage and read *Where the Wild Things Are*. I can do it right, now. And I know he's enjoying the togetherness. I'm just saying 'The End', when the doorbell rings. *Perfect timing, who-ever you are.*

'Debbie! What a nice surprise,' I say, genuinely thrilled to see her, as is Sausage, who has dashed out to her, barking excitedly and making pathetic but cute little jumps where all four of his legs lift together off the ground. There is another surprise. Debbie is not alone. Her father is standing, a little awkwardly, to her right.

'Hello, Jenny,' he says. 'I hope you don't mind. I was dropping Debbie off and thought I'd just pop up to see how Charlie is doing.'

Debbie shrugs and pulls an *I-couldn't-stop-him* face.

'Hi, guys! Come in,' shouts my son from the couch. You'd think he owned the place!

'Hello, son.' Simon smiles and walks straight over to him as if there is nothing else in the room.

Does he realise what he has said?

He sits in the exact place I've has been. I'm beginning to get edgy.

318

'What are you reading?' he asks, looking uncharacteristically young. Relaxed. Happy even. If only Charlie knew he was sitting beside his dad.

'*Where the Wild Things Are*. Dave bought it for me.'

He might as well have slapped him on the face. There's that vulnerable expression I'm such a sucker for.

'It's very good. D'you want to read it?'

'Maybe we could do some Lego,' suggests Simon, spotting a Lego mountain on the coffee table.

'Yeah, OK. But watch me first. I know what I'm doing.'

'Right-y-hoh.'

Debbie looks at me as if to say, 'What's going on?'

I feel the need to cover for him. 'I think your dad's just trying to get Charlie to feel comfortable with him, build a relationship, you know, so he's not so worried when it's time for the transplant,' I whisper.

'You haven't told him yet?'

'No.'

'Maybe we could tell him now?' she suggests. 'Since we're all here.'

'Oh, right . . . yes. Let's just let them play for a while and then I'll get your dad's attention.'

'OK.'

'How are you, Deb? Nervous?'

'No. But . . . I . . . like, so want it to work, you know?'

'I know. It will.' And just as I say it, I know it's a mistake. I shouldn't get her hopes up. Charlie has been given only a sixty per cent chance with this. If it doesn't work out, she will blame herself. Donors *always* do.

'I so want it to, Jenny. Charlie's like my little brother. You know, after the transplant, we'll have the same DNA? Brothers

319

and sisters don't even get that close. We'll be blood brother and sister.'

If only she knew. 'Have you spoken to the counsellor?'

'Yeah.'

'So you know it doesn't always work, Deb? Because I don't want you to be disappointed if it doesn't.'

'It will work,' she says. Adamant. She looks over at Charlie, her jaw firm.

'You *are* like a sister to Charlie.'

She smiles a beautiful smile. And I hug her.

'You're a very special girl, Deb. You are very special to Charlie and to me.'

Deb joins the construction site while I get busy making refreshments for the builders. Then we all take a break. Charlie is first back on the job. I manage to get Simon's attention. He is all for telling Charlie now, especially with Debbie here.

'Charlie?' he says.

'I'm doing a great job, amn't I?'

'Great, Charlie, very creative,' he says, smiling. 'Charlie, we'd just like to have a chat with you about your leukaemia.'

'But I'm in the middle of this tower.'

'OK. Do you want to finish that and then we can talk?'

''K.'

Once the Leaning Tower of Charlie is complete, we all sit down on the couch. Debbie with Charlie on her lap. Simon and I on either side. I hope he doesn't feel too crowded. But no, he seems quite comfy where he is.

'Charlie, you know what leukaemia does to the bone marrow?' Simon says.

'Yeah, the bad cells kill the good cells.'

'That's right. And you know the medicine is to kill the bad cells?'

320

'Yeah.'

'Well, we need to do something else, to help the medicine.'

'What?'

'Well, we want to give you brand-new bone marrow.'

'Can you do that?'

'Yes, we can.' Everyone's smiling.

'Well, why didn't you do it before so I wouldn't need all that medicine?'

'Good question,' says the proud father. 'Well, two reasons. Firstly, we had to get rid of the bad cells. Secondly, we had to find the right bone marrow.'

'Where did you find it? In a shop?'

'No,' laughs Simon. 'You'll never guess.' He looks at Debbie, smiling.

'Debbie found it?' asks Charlie.

'I have it in my body, Charlie. It's my bone marrow and I'm going to share it with you. Isn't that great?'

'How?'

'I'm going to have, like, a bone marrow biopsy thingy so they can get it from me. And then they'll just give it to you into your Freddie.'

'Don't you need yours?'

'I'm only giving you a bit. I'll have *loads* left.'

'It's not nice, Deb. They make you go to sleep and you dream about spaceships.'

'It's OK, Charlie. I like spaceships. And I love going to sleep. And it won't hurt. I'll be fine. And you know what? Afterwards, we're going to have the same bone marrow. If you rob a bank, they could blame me.'

'Cool. When can we do it?'

Debbie looks at Simon.

'In a few weeks, Charlie, but first you have to come into the hospital for a few days and have lots of medicine and things like X-rays.'

'Oh no, I don't want to.'

'I'll come in and see you every day,' says Deb.

We all look at her.

'I'm going to have to go in anyway. Might as well get used to it.'

'Will you be able to stay with me?'

'For a good while, but not all day and not at night. OK?'

'OK.'

'And I'll be there too, Charlie,' I say.

'Me too,' says Simon.

'OOOOK,' says Charlie. As if he has a choice.

And then it happens. Much quicker than I had anticipated in the end. We are given a date for Charlie's transplant. Ten days from now.

I should be thrilled.

I am terrified.

This is it. Our only hope. Our last chance. What if it doesn't work? What then? Where do we go?

In three days, Charlie will be admitted and his body bombared, his bone marrow destroyed along with a host of innocent bystander cells. It's like waiting for a time bomb to explode inside my baby. *Where is Dave? Why hasn't he called? He said to ring when I had the date. I have a date. And I need him now. But maybe he can't decide. Maybe he is back with Fiona and doesn't want to tell me. But maybe something has happened. Maybe he's not well or has had an accident.*

I ring. *Let him do the talking.*

'Dave?'

'Jenny?'

'Everything OK?' *Keep it light.*

'I'm sorry, Jen. I should have called . . . It's just that, it's more . . . complicated than I'd thought.'

I am silent.

'Fiona didn't take it very well.'

I say nothing.

'I'm worried about her, Jen. I'm worried she might do something, you know, stupid.'

Oh for God's sake!

'It's just something she said. She's . . .' — he lowers his voice — '. . . vulnerable.'

Try manipulative.

'She depends on me more than I'd realised.'

I'm tempted to laugh.

'You're not saying much.'

'I'm listening. Go on.'

He clears his throat. 'I think maybe I need to stick around here for a bit, just till I get everything sorted. Fiona's upset. I can't leave her. It would be too risky. It would be a mistake. I'd never forgive myself if anything happened.'

'Fine.' My voice is flat.

'How is Charlie?'

'Fine.'

'I'm sorry I haven't rung, Jen. It's just that I got a bit of a fright when Fiona started, you know . . . .'

'Threatening to pop herself?'

'I don't think that's very sensitive.'

'So, you're staying there, then?'

'For the moment. You don't mind?'

'Why would I mind?'

'You're strong, Jen. You're a coper.'

And you're a walkover.

'You don't need me,' he says.

'You're right. I don't.'

'Don't be like that.'

'Like what?'

'Snappy.'

'I'm not being snappy, Dave. I'm being honest. I've brought Charlie up on my own. Without anyone. You're right. I am a coper. And you don't owe us anything. It's fine.'

'Jenny, it's not about owing — you know that.'

'Whatever.'

'Are you OK?'

'Yep. Bye.'

'Don't go.'

I hang up. He calls back.

'I'll ring you,' he says.

'Don't bother,' I reply and hang up again.

He rings again. 'I'll come over soon.'

'Dave, Leave it. You've made your choice. That's fine. So let's just leave it. OK?'

'I haven't made any choice. It's just that . . . .'

'I know. She needs you.' I say it sarcastically.

'Just for the moment, Jen.'

'OK, listen, I've got to go. I'll talk to you, OK?' I put the phone down, again. Otherwise, it could go on forever. I know I could be more understanding. But he did offer to marry me. He seems to have forgotten that pretty quickly. You can't just go around proposing to people left, right and centre and then not even ring them. I know I didn't say yes. I know I wasn't sure how I felt. Well, I know how I feel now — furious. *Can't he see what she's doing? He's so gullible. All you've got to do with Dave is tell him you need him and hey presto, he'll climb every mountain. That's why he came dashing over to Ireland. That's why he's staying in America. SuperDave. Without him, the world wouldn't spin. He doesn't love me. He just wants someone to need him. Well, I don't need him. I don't need anybody. I should never have let myself forget that. From now on, I won't.*

36

It's time to go in. Home for the next six weeks will be a prison cell. Isolation in a room with specially filtered air. No visitors apart from Deb. And even she has to wear special clothing so that she doesn't bring germs into the room. I keep in touch by phone with Mary, Jack and my parents. I don't know what to do about Elaine, not wanting to remind her that *my* child is still alive. I write, telling her I'm thinking of her and that she should call me to talk, any time. I say where I am and, briefly, what's happening.

In here, I have Anne, Siobhán and Simon. There are others, of course, helpful and caring in their own way, but these three people are my rocks, my lifelines, people I'd trust with my life, people I do trust with Charlie's. Unfortunately, most of the time, they are on the other side of the door; mostly it is just Charlie and me.

And so, the countdown has begun. Fasten your seat belts, prepare for blast off. We will be in orbit for six weeks.

Charlie is five. But he knows this is serious.

'Mum?' he says.

'Yes, sweetie.'

'Would you be sad if I died?'

I look at him, shocked. 'Of course, I would. I'd be so, *so* sad.'

'Why?'

'Because I love you very much.'

'Do you?'

'Of course I do, you big eejit,' I say, trying to laugh it off.

He smiles. 'Would you cry?'

'I think I'd be too sad to cry.'

'Would you whine?'

'I'd probably scream.'

'Really loudly?'

'You'd hear me in Timbuktu.'

'Where . . . what's Timbuktu?'

'A place in Africa.'

'A dump?'

'I don't know what it's like. I think it might be like a desert.'

'Oh. And you'd hear me in . . . in . . . in . . . that place, if I was there and you were in Ireland?'

'Yeah.'

'Wow.'

'But Charlie.'

'Yeah?'

'You're not going to die.'

'I know, Mum.'

'Good. Now go to sleep, monkey.'

'Ooh, ooh.'

He has the chemo. He has the radiation. Bam. Bam. Bam. He becomes so weak, he can't get out of bed. He is floppy. Lifeless. At night, he sleeps like a corpse. And for most of the day. I am so scared. Simon is around constantly. Perhaps this is normal for such a sick child. Perhaps he is more attentive than he would usually be. How would I know?

He is more gentle when examining Charlie now. He holds his hand and strokes the back of it when he talks to him. He explains, with great care, what's going to happen, making sure Charlie understands. He talks about the future, not a future with him, of course — just a future of normality, school, football, hair. A future. The future. Something to focus on. Aim for. *Strive* for.

There are messages from Dave, Mary says. I don't want to know about Dave. Fiona needs him. Well, let Fiona have him and his so-called strength. Bullshit! I tell Mary to delete them.

The day comes finally. I am strong. Or so I tell myself. I am beside Charlie all the time, holding his hand, pretending to myself that Simon is here as his father. That he has both parents with him now. Supporting him. Which he has. It's just that we're not together, not a family. But I don't see why I shouldn't have my own little fantasy, my own way of coping with this.

I have to wear a mask because I have finally developed a cold. It hides my face at a time when Charlie needs familiarity so badly. My breath hot behind it, I feel I'm suffocating. I could panic. But won't. Charlie and I watch in silence as the transplant co-ordinator holds up a packet of Debbie's marrow — dark red, smaller and lighter than a blood transfusion, but otherwise similar. She draws it up in a giant syringe. I think of Deb and pray she's all right. The transplant co-ordinator, dressed in scrubs, smiles as she approaches Charlie with the syringe. I see him swallow. I smile encouragement but he can't see it. She attaches the syringe to Charlie's Freddie.

'Now, Charlie,' she says. 'This might feel a little cold, pet.'

His eyes widen.

I squeeze his hand. I hold his eyes with mine. Force myself not to blink.

'You're the best boy,' I tell him over and over.

And he is. For the past few months he has put up with so much, and for the last week, pure torture. And now it's all over. At last. Now, all we can do is wait. And hope. And pray that it works.

37

After two weeks of waiting and worrying, Charlie's blood cells start to creep back up, which means that the bone marrow has kicked into action. Thank God. A test for the Philadelphia Chromosome is negative, which means that the transplant has been a success so far. They are 'very hopeful'. Charlie is plagued with mouth ulcers, nausea, vomiting and diarrhoea. It's as if his digestive system has packed in. He has to be fed through Freddie. But, slowly, he begins to regain some of his strength. Debbie, allowed home the day after the transplant, is incredibly pale. I worry that she is at an age when she needs all the bone marrow she has. But she is on a high and allowed to call to see him every day. She jokes about the protective clothing she has to wear. And keeps our spirits up.

Another week passes and Charlie's white cell count is high enough for them to stop isolation. The doors are opened. We can walk in or out. Yipee! We concentrate on building him up. He starts to chatter again, making me realise how quiet he had become. Week five, and I'm marvelling at the resilience of children. We go home tomorrow.

But I am not the same. Isolation did something. It made me think. Realise. Open my eyes. I see now how close Charlie has become to his father. And I see — finally admit, maybe — how much I love his father. It is not reciprocated. I know that. But I don't care. I brighten when I see him, when he walks into the room. And flatten when he leaves. Can't help it. Think of him when he's not here. Don't want to help it. Wonder what he is doing, whether or not I ever make it into his thoughts, what his thoughts are, what his dreams are, if he allows himself to dream. My heart softens to see them together, father and son. I notice things I haven't before — tiny mannerisms that he and Charlie share. The way they scratch behind their left ear, when nervous, the way they breathe through their mouths when concentrating, the way they smile a little higher on the left than the right. Ever so slightly. No one would notice. Only me.

Simon is oblivious to me. Focused only on Charlie. And that has to be enough. I would be lying if I said I wouldn't like there to be more. The idea of a cosy family unit, like Mary's, is not unfamiliar territory in my mind. Simon, Jenny, Debbie, Charlie, Sausage. I have pictured it. Played around with it. And dismissed it. This is life. Dreams don't come true. The first time Simon and I met, he turned my world upside down and disappeared. The second time, he didn't disappear, because he couldn't, but I'm sure he would have if he had had the choice. That is the way it is between us. Wham! Poof! When Charlie is discharged, it will be poof again.

I don't want anyone else. So, I'll stick with nobody. It could be worse. I could have married Dave. Which would have been a mistake. Because I know now what was missing. Something I feel for Simon. Passion, not just physical, though that's there, but an enthusiasm for everything about him — what he says, does, doesn't say, looks like, everything. His hands, eyes, scar, mouth, with its crooked smile. His little V. His confidence. His awkwardness. His way. I wonder if I knew, deep down, five years ago, what was missing from my relationship with Dave, but never admitted it to myself. I wonder did something lead me to Simon back then, just in time. Maybe Simon didn't ruin my life after all. Maybe he saved it.

I have also had time to think about Dave. To cool down. To realise that the only thing I could hold against him, if I wanted to, was his being too nice a guy. Fiona may have been bluffing about suicide. But what if she wasn't? Could he afford to take that risk? And it wasn't as if he took back his proposal to me. He was just trying to cope with one loose cannon when another went off in his face — me. I shouldn't have exploded. All I succeeded in doing was making sure he dropped all the balls in the delicate juggling act he was trying to perform — the juggling act of trying to keep us all happy. Nothing like a bit of time, a lot of time, in almost-solitary confinement to make a person see the obvious. To remember everything he did for us, coming over, putting his life on hold, being there for us. I wrote to him last night. Apologised. Thanked. Explained. Told him about Charlie and the transplant. Told him that we leave the hospital tomorrow, prognosis good. Better than good. I wished him well with Fiona and meant it.

Once we leave the hospital tomorrow, we will have no excuse to see Simon. And he will have no excuse to see his son. It will be over and I will go back to writing my columns at night and minding Charlie full-time during the day. It is all arranged. Jack has been great as usual, setting me back up with my health column. It was the least he could do, he said, holding me single-handedly responsible for giving him the push to 'get up off his ass and do something' about his son. Jack approached Alan's mother. After her initial shock, taking some time to think, and talking with her son, she said she wouldn't stand in Jack's way. So they met. Alan and Jack. It wasn't the great reunion that dreams are made of, but it wasn't a disaster either. And they are meeting again. For Jack, it is more than he had ever hoped. One positive outcome from Charlie's illness.

There have been a few. My parents are part of our lives now, something I never particularly wanted, but should have. I don't know what happened back then — loneliness, resentment, rebellion, misunderstanding . . . I don't dwell on it. Point is, it took leukaemia to force me to face my mother. I'm not too proud of that. But I'm looking forward now. We've got to know each other. And I see things I never did before. A sharpness, a wicked sense of humour. But also a warmth. She is great with Charlie. And she is going to teach him. The Department of Education never agreed to home tuition. Charlie is too young, they said. My mother bounded to the rescue like an enthusiastic puppy. I had forgotten that she used to teach before becoming a politician. Even if I had wanted to, I couldn't have stopped her. And the weird thing is, I see so much of Great in her now — the same enthusiasm for life, the same honesty, the same sense of fun — things I didn't notice when her energy was focused elsewhere. She is also going to mind Sausage for the next nine months. She keeps saying how her life has started over. She has got a second chance at it. And claims to be feeling 'light years younger'.

I hold the leukaemia responsible for something else — the friendship I have with Mary. Yes, we would have been friends without it, but nowhere near as solid as we are. How else would I have known how far she'd go for us? That kind of friendship is something special. Something to treasure. And I do. I'm waiting for the day I can pay her back.

The leukaemia has helped Debbie too. By donating her marrow, she has done something positive. She has helped beat cancer, the disease that took her mother. It has given her strength, hope. And a blood brother. It was the leukaemia that started her talking with her father again, listening to him, communicating with him, respecting him. They have a relationship now — a good one. I know how proud he is of her.

Charlie's illness *has* been a nightmare. If I had a choice, no, I wouldn't go through it again. But, in fairness (oops!) it has made me face issues I have avoided for years. Issues that I have compartmentalised in my mind, like slotting pieces of paper into bottles and letting them drift out to sea, in the hope that I would forget them. Who Charlie's father is; the fact that my mother and I had no relationship; the fact that family, friends and health are everything. What we have been through has changed me. I am calmer. More sorted. It's not one day at a time — it's one step at a time, one breath at a time. If Simon wants to see Charlie, great. If he doesn't, yes, I will be gutted, but we will cope.

Elaine rang me as soon as she got my letter. She was going through a particularly difficult time, needed someone to talk to. Everyone else was shying away, afraid. All she wanted to do was talk about Jessica. Just talk, and talk and talk. Keep her alive by talking. And I listened. I wanted to. And in a strange way, it helped me too. Over the past six weeks we've helped each other through our separate but similar crises. She is a powerful woman. I am going to help her with a charity she is setting up for families who lose children to cancer.

The article I wrote about Charlie went ahead, even though we found a donor. The register grew as a result, and I hope that somebody, somewhere, has benefited. When I have built up my strength again, I will join it myself.

Debbie pops her head into the room. 'Hello,' she says cheerfully.

'Debbie,' says Charlie. 'I'm going home tomorrow!'

'I know. Isn't it great, blood brother?' she says, sitting him up on her lap.

'Yes, blood sister.'

Simon walks in.

'Hi, Dad,' says Deb.

'Hello, Debbie. What are you doing here?'

'Just called in to celebrate Charlie's last day in hospital.'

'Does that mean you can let Jenny out for a little walk?'

I look at him.

'Sure,' she says. 'I was going to offer anyway.'

'Are you sure, Deb? I don't mind, really. We'll be going home tomorrow.'

'No, no, honestly. I was going to offer.'

'Go on, Mum,' says Charlie, who wants his blood sister all to himself.

'OK, seeing as how you're all dying to get rid of me,' I say, smiling.

I get up, grab my bag. I might get a paper, see what's going on in the real world. Simon walks out with me. I expect him to say goodbye and head to the nurses' station. But he doesn't. He stays beside me, all the way out of the ward. We are both silent. I expect him to turn off at any minute. At the hospital entrance, I say, 'Goodbye, then.'

'Sorry,' he says. 'Do you want to walk alone?'

'Oh. Sorry, I didn't realise. You're coming?'

He looks awkward now. 'If that's all right?'

'Yes, of course. I didn't realise. Sorry.'

'Right then.'

We fall into step. Both silent. Then both talk together.

'So, you must be happy to be going home?' His comment.

Mine: 'You must be happy to see the back of us.'

Then together again.

He: 'No, of course not.'

While I say, 'Yes, dying to get out.'

Then both: 'Oh.'

Then silent again.

I decide to keep quiet.

Eventually he says, 'So Charlie won't be my patient.'

I panic. 'Why? Will someone else be looking after him in the clinic?' *We're not out of the woods yet. He can't shake us off that quickly. What if something goes wrong?*

'No, no, sorry. I will be seeing Charlie in clinics. I just mean he won't be an in-patient.'

'Oh, right, yes.' *What's wrong with him? He had me worried there.*

'So,' he says again. 'How is Dave?'

'Dave?'

'Yes, Dave.'

'Fine, getting married.'

'You're getting married?' His head swivels towards me.

'*No.* He's marrying his American girlfriend. Fiona.'

'Oh,' he says, sounding — what — relieved? 'I thought Charlie said that he was ending that.'

'That was the plan.'

'Because I thought that you were back together?'

'No.'

He stands back to let a woman with a buggy get by. I wait for him.

He clears his throat. 'Jenny?'

He is silent again. I look at him.

'Yes,' I say eventually, thinking he's forgotten what he was going to say.

'Had you given any thought to how I might see Charlie now?'

'Simon, it's up to you. Of course, I'd love you to see him as much as possible. And I know he'd love to see you. But I'm not sure how you could do that. Wouldn't Debbie wonder why you were always calling round? She'd probably think you were going out with me or something.' I laugh now, embarrassed by my stupidity in saying something like that.

'Would you?'

'What?' *Jesus, sometimes I've no idea what he means.*

'Go out with me?'

It is the weirdest thing, hearing a forty-something-year-old man saying 'go out with me'. I laugh automatically. Then see his face. *Oh God! He thinks I'm laughing at him.* 'I'm sorry, Simon. I wasn't laughing at . . . Sorry, I don't know why I laughed. I got a bit of a shock.'

'I knew I shouldn't have asked. I should have just taken it step by step. I'm not very good at this. I'm too straight. Say what I mean.'

'Simon. Of course you should have asked. If you want to go out with me. But please, don't feel you need to ask me out just so you can see Charlie. We can work something out. You could see him sometime during the day. I don't know. When Debbie isn't around.'

Hurt face again. This is not going well.

'Jenny. You misunderstand me. I asked you because I want to. Nothing to do with Charlie. I should have just asked you to dinner or something. But . . . .'

'You want to take me to dinner?'

'We could start with dinner.'

'You really are asking me out?'

'If it doesn't suit . . . .'

'But you said . . . .'

'What?'

'You said that the timing wasn't right.'

'It wasn't.'

'But what about your wife?' I see his face. All I seem to be able to do is hurt him. 'I'm sorry, Simon. But is there room in your life for someone else? We've done this. Been together and it's always been a disaster . . . .' *Why am I talking myself out of this?*

'Jenny.' He stops walking, turns to me, takes my hands in his. His wedding ring has gone. 'This isn't easy for me. I'm not going to pretend it is. But I would like to give it a try. Couldn't we do that? Give it a try? If you're interested . . . you might not be interested.' He stands awkwardly, looking as if he doesn't know what to do with my hands now that he has them in his. I help him out. I take them back. I can't admit it. I want to, but I can't. I would be leaving myself open to getting thrown aside again, ditched because he's feeling guilty, or has changed his mind, or who knows what reason?

More throat-clearing, now. He looks down, then suddenly up. 'It's just that I think I might love you. No, I do, actually. I think you are marvellous. I admire you so much. The way you've brought Charlie up on your own. It's not easy. I know that. The way you have handled all this. The way you've coped.'

Here we go again. A coper. But this time it's an advantage. Men! 'Simon, admire is different from love.'

'I know, I know. What do you want me to say? I'm passionate about you?'

'That would do it.'

'But I thought you knew that. Why else would I have got carried

338

away like I did, not once but twice? I am absolutely, *absolutely* passionate about you . . . .'

And I want to laugh again. *What's wrong with me?*

'. . . I can't help it. I've tried.' He brushes my hair aside with a tenderness that doesn't surprise me, he kisses me with a gentleness that doesn't surprise me, but then hunger and passion take over again, reminding me of the first time, the second time — and I wonder how I could have doubted how he felt. He looks at me now and I know I'm about to give in. *That face. I love that face.*

'I told myself you were too young. I told myself it wouldn't be fair on Alison. On Debra. I told myself Charlie was my patient. I told myself you weren't interested. That was the easiest to believe. Especially when I saw you with . . . Dave . . . in the corridor, the way he held you. Debra had told me he was staying with you. And then Charlie said he was going to end his relationship and come home. But then I couldn't let you go. I knew you were leaving tomorrow and I couldn't let you go. I had to say something. Tell you how I felt. When you're not there, I miss you.'

'Me too.'

'You too? Seriously? You're not *joking* again?'

'No.'

The side of a mountain when a cloud's shadow clears away — that's what his face is like now.

'Oh, Jenny!' He smiles. 'Can I pinch you?'

'No,' I laugh. 'But I'll pinch you if you like.'

He brushes my hair back again, then holds my hands again. 'I didn't think I had a hope. I just wanted to tell you how I felt. I thought if I was lucky, I might get a *chance* to convince you that you were making a mistake — that it was we who should be together. But really, in fairness, I thought you were gone.'

'I'm going nowhere,' I say, 'in fairness.' And lean forward to kiss him.

He takes me in his arms, in full view of the hospital. I panic that someone might see us, sack him. I pull back. 'Is this OK, in front of the hospital?'

'Probably not, definitely not.' He laughs and kisses me. 'You're gorgeous,' he says.

'No, you're gorgeous.'

'No, you are.'

And we laugh.

'So where are you taking me to dinner?' I ask. And I smile and take his hand in mine.

Epilogue

'Come on, Mum,' Katie shouts, racing up the path ahead of me, the pink soles of her runners flashing as each foot kicks back in the air. She makes it to the door. Jumps to reach the bell. Misses. Tries again. And again.

'Katie, I have the key, love,' I say.

'Oh,' she says. 'Yeah.'

I open the door. In she runs. Almost into Charlie who is standing holding the handlebars of his bicycle, about to head out. Sausage is jumping up on him, wagging his tail.

'Excuse me, Mum,' he says.

'Only if you give me a kiss.' I'm teasing.

'Urgh, Mum. I'm in a hurry.'

'Not even today?'

'I'll give you one later, OK? Gotta go.'

'Helmet, Charlie,' I say, stepping out of his way.

He mutters something I can't hear, leans the bike against the wall, grabs the helmet from a hook under the stairs and is off. 'See you later.'

'Where are you going?'

'Dara's.'

'Back by dinner, OK?'

'OK.'

'And remember, we're going out. I need you back by half-five.'

'OK.'

'And Charlie?'

'Yes?' Impatient.

'Don't go too fast. Sausage is getting old — you'll give him a heart attack.'

'OK.'

I drop the box of groceries on the kitchen table.

'Hi, Deb. Didn't expect you home.'

'Lecture cancelled,' she says, without looking up. 'That guy never turns up. They should fire him.'

'O'Malley?'

'Yeah.'

'Hmm.'

'Can I've my ice cweam now? Can I've my ice cweam?' comes from the little curly head.

'You can have some in the restaurant.'

'Aw.'

'Where's your dad?' I ask Deb.

'Upstairs.'

'Down in a sec,' I say, going to look for him.

'I'm hungwy.'

'Deb, get her a mandarin, would you, love?'

She reaches for the fruit bowl, without taking her eyes off her textbook, feels around for a mandarin, peels it, also without looking. 'Here, Squirt,' she says, handing it to Katie.

'Tanks, Deb. Whatchadoing?'

'Reading about hearts.'

'Can I see?'

'OK, but don't get juice on the book,' she says, lifting Katie up on her lap. 'Now, you know your heart? Well, this is a picture . . . .' Their chatter becomes inaudible as I head up the stairs. It's friendly, though, because they adore each other.

He's not in the bedroom.

'Hello?'

'Hello,' comes a voice.

'A bit more specific?'

'Attic.'

'What are you up to?'

'Getting Charlie's surprise.'

'D'you need a hand?' I call up to him.

'Mm hmm. Can you grab it?' A brown cardboard box appears through the hole in the ceiling, followed by my husband's arms and head. 'Hello!' He grins.

'Hello, yourself.'

'Got it?'

'Got it.'

'Great,' he says.

I lower it carefully to the ground. He hoists himself down onto the stepladder.

'Will it take long to put together?'

'Don't know yet — let's have a look.'

We rip off the cardboard.

'Actually, all you do is screw on these legs.'

I watch him assemble the snooker table. It's the real thing, just in miniature — proper wooden frame with green covering, proper pockets, proper cues, proper balls. Even has the little blue chalks.

I pick up a ball. It's heavy and cold, and I roll it around in my hand. 'He'll love it.'

'Do you want a go?' he asks. 'A trial run?'

'OK, but give me a few free tries — I'm useless at snooker.'

He stops and looks at me. Says quietly, 'Can you believe it's five years?'

I slip into his arms and look into his eyes. 'No, Dr Grace, I can't. Five years. And we're finally out of the woods.' There will be yearly tests for the rest of Charlie's life — I realise that — but this is the big hurdle, and we've jumped it. We hold each other. I rest my head on his chest.

The restaurant is Italian. Relaxed, casual and friendly, with genuine flamboyant Italian waiters and the best pizzas in Ireland. Suits all ages. Which is just as well, because that's what we are — all ages. Simon/Dad, forty-five; me/Mum, thirty-two; Deb, twenty; Charlie, ten; and Katie, three. And that's not counting Mary's lot or Jack. Or, indeed, my parents, who haven't arrived yet. In fact, when you think about it, we have a representative here from every decade up to seventy. Which is fitting, as this is a celebration of life. We have reached a day that, five years ago, I was afraid to dream we ever would. But here it is.

I smile across at Mary. She winks back, while fixing a bib on the little girl she and Phil always wanted but were too practical to plan. Amy had to spring herself on them. And, you know, they have managed fine in the same house. Bunk beds were a great invention. And Amy is an angel. No, really, she is actually an angel sent from heaven to thank Mary for all she did for us. A present from Great. At least, that's what I think at times like this, when I've every reason to feel soppy.

Jack is here with his new woman friend — someone we know,

as it happens. Anne. Yes, they met at the hospital. But it took fate to intervene, putting them together in the same evening class — psychology. Jack, not an evening-class man at all, was trying to pick up a few tricks on fathering, seeing as how he now sees Alan, twice a week, for golf — another something Jack would never have tried on his own. '*Golf*, Jack,' I tease him, regularly. 'Next thing I know, you'll have a double-barrel name and be moving to the southside.'

Dave and Fiona couldn't make it. Fiona can't travel in the last month of pregnancy. But they're here in spirit. The summer after Charlie's transplant, they came to visit and have made it an annual ritual. Fiona is a calmer person. Now that she has her man and is setting down roots of her own. I'm glad we kept the link going. It's true that Fiona and I will never be bosom buddies, nor will Simon and Dave. The important thing is that the bond between Charlie and Dave, which started in the hospital, has remained strong, firm and special.

Debbie hasn't brought her latest boyfriend, though we did invite Gareth. 'We're only going out, like, six months, Jenny. It's not like we're *married* or anything.' Debbie's studies come first. She's as serious as her father about curing the world. And you'll never guess who is in her class at college. Mark — Charlie's super-hero — also doing medicine, also determined to be a healer. And what better doctor than one who knows what it's like to be at the other end?

I turn to Charlie, who is sitting on my right.

'So where's my kissy kissy?' I pucker my lips exaggeratedly.

'Aw, Mum, cut it out. Stop messing in front of everyone.'

'I'll get you before the night is out,' I threaten.

He gives in to a smile. He is becoming more like Simon every day. I admire his thick, now dark, hair and have to stop myself from reaching out to touch it. He'd only slap me off. He's very precious about it, always gelling it some way or another, always conscious of it, like something that was taken away and given back. Which, of course, it was. To look at him, you'd never tell he had leukaemia. The only way you might guess is his attitude. So philosophical for one so young, so accepting, not worried about the small stuff. He understands things that other kids his age wouldn't even notice — like why people leave flowers at the place where they lost their loved ones. Charlie knows that this is the last place they were alive, and the flowers are to say, 'We haven't forgotten you.' He told me that once when we were driving along happily. It made me stop short, remember how close we got. There is a special bond between Charlie and Debbie that I don't think anything will ever be able to change. She saved his life. He needed her but she needed him too in a way. A part of her will always live in him, literally. It's not something you forget. I am so proud of them both. And grateful to have them here.

Katie wriggles up onto my lap. Our little girl. Who wasn't in my happy family dream five years ago. But here she is now. A born survivor, always finding her way to the top of any queue, never going hungry, never being left behind. I sometimes wonder if it's a genetic thing. The last mix of genes had some fault in it that gave Charlie leukaemia (I'm sure of it); this time, the genes weren't going to make a mistake. She is so plucky she makes me laugh, and her strength is, frankly, a relief. She, too, has her father's dark hair. It's already almost black. But she has her mother's kink — a full head of cheeky curls. Her eyes are bright blue sparkly discs, innocent but strangely knowing. Deb and Charlie take her in their stride, very casual with her, never fussing over her because she's not the kind of kid who needs or wants a fuss. Yet I know if she was ever in trouble, they would kill for her.

We are a family now, but it didn't happen overnight. It wasn't easy. Initially. Simon and I were in a rush. We didn't just want to meet for dinner and go our separate ways. We wanted to be together. Go home together. Share our lives, ourselves, with each other. We didn't want to wait. We had both faced death and knew that there is only so much time we are all given and we have to make the most of it while we have it. We didn't want to waste a second. But we had to tell the children. We had to be honest with them before we made any commitment, even before we started seeing each other properly. So we decided. No hiding from what happened. If we wanted this to work, we had to do it right, from the beginning. We had to deal with things. Face them.

But how do you tell a fifteen-year-old that her father — let's face it — had sex, with another woman — me — when her mother had just been diagnosed with cancer? With difficulty, that's how. The deliberation! The preparation! The nerves! But it had to be done. What gave us the final push was that I got a 'fright' of my own. A breast lump that turned out to be innocent. (That took some convincing.) But it frightened us enough to push us over the line.

How to tell her, though — that was the problem. I felt that if we did it as a couple, it would be harder on her — as if, I don't know, we were teaming up against her or something? I was also afraid it would embarrass her, put her in a position where she couldn't scream and shout, be honest. So Simon had to do it on his own, which nearly killed him. There were things that helped Debbie to accept it. We were being honest with her, not trying to hide what we felt or be together without telling her. What had happened in Brussels was an accident and there had been no contact after that. When I did bump into Simon, I had tried to avoid seeing him and would have cancelled the baby-sitting if she and

Charlie hadn't got on so well. But the main thing that helped Deb to accept what happened was that she already saw us as a potential family. Charlie was her blood brother and she had already instigated a plan to try to get Simon and me together, the Make-My-Dad-More-Marketable plan, involving movie trips and recommended reading. Which is also why she was so uncomfortable seeing Dave 'sleep over'. We had all been through so much with Charlie, together, and the enormity of that seemed to lessen the importance of other things. And, finally, she came to me and we talked about it, honestly and openly. There was no escaping the fact that I had had sex with her father when her mother was sick. And that was a major shock. Something that had to be got over, slowly and carefully. Sensitively.

And I have tried to be sensitive with Deb. I know that, for a while, she resented the fact that Charlie got his father but she still couldn't have her mum. Tempted though I was, I never tried to replace her mother because I know she wouldn't have wanted that. It would have been impossible anyway. Instead, I've told her I will always be here for her, to listen, to do things together. I told her we could both try to catch up on all the shopping we'd missed out on by having absent mothers. She liked that idea. So that's what we did. Went shopping, to the movies, had 'girly time'. Now that she's with Gareth, she doesn't need as much any more. But we spend time together, whenever she feels like it. And we get on. I've always said it: 'she's a great kid.' Sorry — adult.

As for Charlie, when he heard he had a father, well — 'Wow.' And that his father was the same father as Debbie's: 'Double wow.' And that it was Simon. And that he knew him all along. And liked him. And that he was going to be around, available, there. His face looked like it did that time we were watching the firework display on Killiney Hill. He did want to know why we

348

hadn't told him before, and that was a bit awkward. How much can you say to a five-year-old? But we worked something out.

We managed (with difficulty) to hold on for six months before getting married, to give the children time to adjust. When we did get married, it was a low-key affair, conscious as we were of Deb, not wanting it to look as if I was taking over the place of her mother. But it was a very special day, and we were surrounded by the people we love. Charlie was best man (so cute!) Debbie, bridesmaid (so pretty!) My father got very nervous about giving me away, and was delighted that the wedding speeches had a strict time limit of two minutes. My mother was tremendously happy. I couldn't help thinking that she finally got her wish of having a doctor in the family. It's hard just to get rid of a lifetime of cynicism towards a person, but actually, except for the odd moment, I seem to have managed it. And she is great. What she missed out on as a mother, she is more than making up for now, both with me and with her grandchildren. She adores Katie, but will always have a special place in her heart for Charlie who brought us back together as a family. Her life is so full now, it is hard to imagine her the way she was. In fact, when politicians call to her house to canvass, she runs them.

And then, there's my husband — the man about whom I used to wonder what he liked, what made him happy, angry, how he got the scar on his cheek. I will tell you. He likes Bruce Springsteen (*and I still manage to love him?*), *The Sopranos*, looking out at rain from somewhere cosy, club sandwiches, and the way I have a freckle on each of my erogenous zones (his discovery, not mine). He also likes yoga, which he took up, saying that anything that allows him see me with my bum in the air has got to be worth doing. What makes him happy? Family, making me laugh, sex (he's a man, isn't he?) and his patients recovering. What makes him angry? The only thing that makes him angry is when he loses a patient. And that anger makes up for all the times he doesn't get angry at the small things. He got the scar on his cheek when he tried shaving at the age of four with his father's razor — his first hospital experience. He comes from a family of four. (Charlie got six instant cousins.) I was wrong about his age. He was a few years younger than he looked. But, actually, he looks younger now than he did then. The worried, tense pull has left his face. His smile-per-day rate has shot up and he actually has a pretty wicked sense of humour. A new side to Simon Grace has emerged, or maybe it was always there behind the sadness. A fun side. He has learned to laugh again. Not taking everything so seriously. You would say he was happy, if you weren't, like us, aware of the next corner and what might be around it. Then again, when you've made it around one corner and survived, maybe it gives you something special — a will to treasure the simpler moments.

He looks across at me, now, and smiles, his face saying, 'Look what we have.' And I want to leap over the table and kiss him. Yes. We are lucky.

Note from the author

I wish a great deal of luck to anyone trying to cope with the worry of a sick child. For information on becoming a blood or bone marrow donor in Ireland visit www.ibts.ie or call Bone Marrow Support on 1800 200 700.

Also
by
DENISE DEEGAN

'Fresh, funny and astute — a highly readable debut'
Claire Boylan

Kim Waters seems to have it all: her own PR agency, a loving, wealthy husband and two perfect children. In their charming suburban Dublin home, everything seems picture perfect.

But then Kim announces she's fed up with plugging Flush toilet cleaner and writing snazzy press releases for boring products: she wants to write 'the great novel'. So, she throws in her job and settles down to a life of cosy domesticity: writing a wonderful novel that everyone will want to publish, and trying to keep the kids away from the television.

However, the dream rapidly turns sour: the novel is a tired cliché, life as a domestic supergoddess is not all it's cracked up to be, and then she discovers her husband is having an affair...

As the perfect life Kim has built for herself starts to fall apart, a revelation comes that will make her doubt everything she had taken for granted in her life...